WHAT PEOPLE ARE SAYING ABOUT
SUSAN MAY WARREN

"I'm proud of Susie; my friend gets better with every book."
DEE HENDERSON, author of *The Marriage Wish*

"Susan May Warren is an extremely gifted storyteller, always keeping her readers in suspense to the end. . . . Susan's books are guaranteed to entertain, thrill, and inspire. Without question, they fall in the Can't-Put-Down category!"
D.M., Amazon.com reader

"This author needs to write more books! I love her style."
C.T., Amazon.com reader

"Susan Warren is a writer to watch! . . . Susan's characters are so real you can almost hear them breathe."
Amazon.com reader

Escape
to
Morning

TEAM

HOPE

Susan May Warren

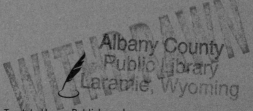

Tyndale House Publishers, Inc.
WHEATON, ILLINOIS

Visit Tyndale's exciting Web site at www.tyndale.com

TYNDALE is a registered trademark of Tyndale House Publishers, Inc.

Tyndale's quill logo is a trademark of Tyndale House Publishers, Inc.

Escape to Morning

Designed by Cathy Bergstrom

Edited by Lorie Popp

Scripture quotations are taken from the *Holy Bible*, New Living Translation, copyright © 1996, 2004. Used by permission of Tyndale House Publishers, Inc., Wheaton, Illinois 60189. All rights reserved.

Scripture quotations are taken from the *Holy Bible*, King James Version.

This novel is a work of fiction. Names, characters, places, and incidents are either the product of the author's imagination or are used fictitiously. Any resemblance to actual events, locales, organizations, or persons, living or dead, is entirely coincidental and beyond the intent of either the author or publisher.

Library of Congress Cataloging-in-Publication Data

Warren, Susan, date.
  Escape to morning / Susan May Warren.
    p. cm. — (Team hope ; 2)
  ISBN-13: 978-1-4143-0087-0 (sc)
  ISBN-10: 1-4143-0087-5 (sc)
    1. Missing children—Fiction. 2. Search and rescue operations—Fiction. 3. Government investigators—Fiction.
4. Terrorism—Prevention—Fiction. I. Title.
  PS3623.A865E83 2005
  813'.6—dc22   2005008029

Printed in the United States of America

11 10 09 08 07 06 05
 7   6   5   4   3   2   1

FOR YOUR GLORY, LORD

Acknowledgments

God is my portion and sustainer. And as usual, as I wrote *Escape to Morning*, He gave me talented people to encourage this project. My deepest gratitude goes to:

My Pinkie Promise Pals (You know who you are.)—I am so deeply grateful for your iron-on-iron friendships that keep me accountable, humble, and encourage me to walk deeper. You're all such gifts in my life.

The Twinklings—Jane, Michele, and Sharron. How I thank the Lord for giving me friends who are like-minded, passionate about God, and who make me feel like I'm not alone! God again answered my prayers when He gave me our group, and I can't wait to see what He's going to do.

Anne Goldsmith—Thank you for knowing how to help me take *Escape* deeper and for believing in Team Hope. You're truly gifted in what you do. Thank you.

Lorie Popp—For your gentle touch, your insights, and for catching all those errors I just want to cringe at. Your talents are a great blessing to me.

Curt and MaryAnn Lund—For enduring the Warren Family Canoe Trip with us and for your "Pots." Your support and encouragement are huge to me.

Dannette Lund—For letting me name a character after you and then chop off half that name to Dani and loving me anyway.

David Warren—Thank you for letting me read aloud to you and laughing in all the right places.

Sarah Warren—You delight my heart with your smile. Thank you for liking Dani and Will and for your constant encouragement. My heart swells every time you say, "My mom rocks!"

Peter Warren—For your happy dance. No wonder all the girls like you.

Noah Warren—For learning how to make your own peanut-butter-and-jelly sandwiches. I don't care what they say—you're much better than Ollie Herdman.

Andrew Warren—You're a daily reminder that God loves me. Thank you for walking this life with me.

*The faithful love of the L*ORD *never ends! His mercies never cease. Great is his faithfulness; his mercies begin afresh each morning. I say to myself, "The L*ORD *is my inheritance; therefore, I will hope in him!"*

LAMENTATIONS 3:22-24

Prologue

Dearest Bonnie,

If you are receiving this letter, then you know that I'm already worshiping at the throne of Jesus. And that's how I want you to think of me. Finally with my Savior. I know this is hard to accept, sweetheart, but we talked about it so many times and I need you to be strong. For the girls. Because of the hope we have that we'll be together again.

I want you to move back to Cotter. It's a good town, and the Strong family will look out for you. I know it is what you really want also. You've been a wonderful wife, and I know life with me, a soldier, hasn't been easy—the moves, the absences, raising our daughters as if you were single. A man couldn't ask for a better wife. Or a better friend. Because, Bon, you are my best friend. Ever since seventh grade.

I pray you find someone to keep you safe and cherish you as I have. You deserve it. And know that you gave me the happiest years of my life. From the moment I bumped into you in English class and scattered your books onto the floor (yes, that was on purpose, I now admit), I was lost in your smile. Being your husband made doing my job worth it.

I've asked Will to watch out for you. Mostly because I know he'll need some task to hang on to. He doesn't have our faith, and he'll be lost. He's so close to salvation; I just know that one of these days he's going to be swept into the arms of Jesus. And when that happens, he'll need a friend, someone who can support him. God has been good to give me a buddy like Will. If it weren't for him, I wouldn't have made it out of Iraq. Remember that when he shows up at your door, smelling like tequila or the back forty. Underneath that swagger and wild smile is a good man who has the potential to be used by God.

The days away from you are getting harder. Or maybe it's because the tension here feels as thick as a South Dakota windstorm. People in camp are on edge—rumors of attacks and fears about the future weigh conversations. I feel it and even though we're here to maintain peace, I sense trouble. Or maybe this is just my natural reaction after 9/11. It seems the whole world is anxious . . . waiting. Holding their breath for the next attack. Even here, among the nations who fight for peace, there is fear. Mistrust. I sometimes wonder if the terrorists planned it this way—for us to suspect each other and weaken us from within while they plot to destroy us from without.

I look back to my childhood and know I was blessed. Will our children feel the same? Will they know endless, carefree summer nights, cozy winters in a sleigh? I don't know. I do know that whatever the world looks like on the outside, our faith in God is the only thing we can depend on. Only He knows a person's— even a leader's—heart. Only He can heal our world. I have depended on my faith . . . and because of that, you can trust I am happy. Safe. Because, Bonnie, God is my portion.

I pray He is also yours, sweetheart. Please tell the girls I love them.

Your best friend and husband—always,
Lew

Chapter 1

TODAY, MORE THAN any other, reporter Will Masterson prayed that his lies would save lives. Starting with his partner's, Homeland Security Agent Simon Rouss, aka Hafiz Tarkan.

Please, God, be on my side today. Will raced on foot down the two-lane, rutted, forest-service road, cursing his stupidity as well as a few new souvenir bruises. He smelled rain in the air as the wind shivered the trees with a late-season breeze. His nose felt thick and caked with clots. He should have known his sympathetic commentaries in the *Moose Bend Journal* toward the recent immigrants flooding over the Canadian border would draw blood with the locals. Blood that would hopefully protect Simon while he embedded deeper into the terrorist cell in the hills.

Because Will knew the men who'd hijacked him and hauled him into the forest to beat the tar out of him over his recent op-ed piece weren't actually disgruntled rednecks but rather international terrorists.

The lie that had just saved Will Masterson's hide, the lie perpetuated by the boys toting 30.06s and wearing work boots, was the only thing keeping Simon from being brutally murdered. Which would only be the first in a hundred—maybe a thousand—murders by the Hayata terrorist cell hiding in the northern Minnesota woods.

If only Will hadn't been ambushed by the double-edged sword called failure sitting in his PO box. A letter from Bonnie. He'd opened it, and the words knifed him through the chest: *Bonnie Strong and Paul Moore invite you to a celebration of life and love in our Lord Jesus Christ.*

He should have dropped the invitation to his floorboard and crushed it under his foot. Instead, he'd let the memories, the grief, the failure rush over him and blind him to the three men lying in wait like a nest of rattlers. He should have done better by Lew's wife, protected her, made sure she was safe. Who was this Paul?

A year of undercover work, of slinking around this hick town, praying for a way to destroy the Hayata cell, and it all had to come to a head the same day his mistakes rose from the past to haunt him.

Sorry, Lew.

"Tell Bonnie and the girls I love them." Lew's words, hovering in the back of Will's mind could still turn his throat raw after three years. If Simon bought it, Will would be sending yet another letter home to a wife and loved ones.

Soldiers had no business getting married.

Will's breath felt like a razor inside his lungs. A branch clipped him, and blood pooled inside his mouth. Ruts and stone bit into his cowboy boots as he ran, and sweat lined his spine. The sky mirrored his despair in the pallor of gray, the clouds heavy with tears. How long had he been unconscious after they'd thrown him off the four-wheeler?

Better question—how much did they guess about his alliance with Simon? Obviously, the good ol' boys who snatched him as he'd sat in his truck, waiting for his contact, knew Will's habits. *Simon's* habits. They'd found them, despite the fact that he and Simon had picked the backwoods gravel pit for its remoteness. *But please,* please *let them believe my lies* . . . which would mean maybe Simon's cover hadn't been blown.

Maybe there wouldn't be another unnamed star embedded in the wall of honor at Langley . . . like Lew's.

Thunder rolled overhead when Will burst from the road onto the gravel pit. Yes, thank you, the thugs/terrorists/angry readers hadn't damaged his wheels. Probably, however, they thought his 1984 Chevy wasn't worth their time.

What they didn't know was that reporter Will Masterson didn't just spend his time penning controversial editorials and writing the crime beat for the local weekly. Under the hood of this baby, he had a 350 Hemi with a high-lift cam and a four-barrel Edelbrock Thunder carb.

They didn't call him Wild Will for nothing. Okay, he'd earned that nickname for different reasons, during a different life. But sometimes the moniker still meant something. Like now as he hopped in and slammed all three hundred and fifty horses to the floor, spitting gravel behind him as he raced to the Howlin' Wolf.

Plan B.

Please, Simon, be there. Or, if he'd been forced to make a fast exit, let him have taped his latest intel under Will's favorite table.

After a year of undercover work, he and Simon had one chance—one click in time—to get it right. One opportunity to avenge the thousands of victims who died at the hands of terrorists around the globe. Victims like Lew.

Please, Simon, be there.

✦ ✦ ✦

The late-afternoon drizzle seemed a fitting backdrop to the painful truth that Search and Rescue (SAR) canine handler

3

Dannette Lundeen had to voice to the crowd of damp search-and-rescue personnel combing Lookout Mountain near the fields behind the High Pines Rest Center.

June Hanson—dementia patient, age eighty-six, grandmother of seven, great-grandmother of fourteen, and recent escapee from the nursing home—would probably be returned to her family in a body bag.

Please, Lord, don't let her die alone. Dannette crouched beside Missy, her German shepherd/golden retriever mix, and scratched the dog's floppy ear. Missy's respirations came one on top of another, her stacked breathing a natural alert for the smell of something near or already dead. Trained in search and rescue, Missy and Dannette had recovered more than their share of casualties, and Dannette read the diminishing potential for success in her animal's demeanor.

Twilight threaded gray fingers around the trees, through the brambled forest, and around shaggy pines and spindly poplars. A crisp breeze, dredged up from the still-soggy earth, whistled against Dannette's hood. She felt chapped, hungry, and worn birch-bark thin. And, with night encroaching, hope had dwindled with the sunshine to a meager shadow.

From her backpack she drew out a water bottle, set down a collapsible bowl, and filled it. Missy lapped greedily.

Fifty feet away, she heard the echo of Kelly's call to her dog, Kirby. The younger SAR shepherd, out on his first real trial, probably hadn't yet picked up the scent cone or Kelly would be radioing Dannette for advice.

The overpowering smell of death scared most dogs. Then again, it didn't exactly warm Dannette's insides with a happy feeling.

Dannette stood and let Missy finish her water. Maybe Missy was wrong. She wasn't Super Dog, although Dannette had to admit that following Missy's instincts often led them to hideouts unthinkable even to the most keen SAR personnel. And Missy was an air-scent dog, which meant she followed the smells left by the scraping of skin on rocks, trees, and bushes. Sadly, Missy's abilities decreased as the day worsened.

If only it hadn't taken the nursing-home staff an hour after June turned up missing at morning breakfast to call the sheriff's office, then two more hours and the urging of the mayor—June's desperate son—to finally call Kelly, their local, nearly certified K-9 handler. Not only had a late-morning shower diffused the scent cone left by Mrs. Hanson by then, but the variable winds and temperatures had scattered the scent and confused Missy. They'd walked the perimeter in a hasty search for two more hours before Missy caught the scent and alerted them to Mrs. Hanson's trail.

Dannette found that, as usual, the dementia patient didn't stick to the deer trails or clearings. Mrs. Hanson had pushed through honeysuckle and raspberry bushes, climbed over downed birches, crossed a stream, and ascended a hill that should have put her in traction. Even dementia patients who struggled to move in ordinary circumstances proved they still had gumption when some errant impulse revved up their synapses. But Mrs. Hanson had lived a stout life, had run a farm until her husband's death a few years ago, and would probably still be milking her Jersey if her mind hadn't betrayed her. The woman could easily be a mile from here or sitting atop Lookout Mountain.

Or injured.

Or—if Dannette read her dog correctly—dead.

Missy sat on her haunches and licked her lips. Water dripped off her jowls.

Dannette picked up the empty bowl and shoved it back into her backpack. "Okay, ready?"

Missy tilted her head.

"I know, sweetheart. But if it makes you feel any better, I'm glad you're here. You handle death so much better than Sherlock. He'd have his hackles up and be cowering under that white pine." She stepped away from Missy, changed her tone. "Find."

They'd been working on a free search all afternoon, after Missy's first alert. With Kelly and Kirby twenty-five feet to the west, Dannette let Missy run twenty-five feet or more ahead, quartering the wind for scent debris. Dannette checked her GPS with her map, pinpointed her position, and radioed the incident commander.

"10-4, Search One," replied Sheriff Fadden.

Dannette pictured the guy as she'd last seen him, wearing a black, lined Windbreaker, his stomach rebelling against the snaps, using a bullhorn to direct traffic at the nursing home. Just what June Hanson's loved ones needed as they watched the chaos.

To add to their pain, Dannette had seen two news reporters from the local rags already lurking, smelling blood. The leeches.

"Just heard from Search Two," Fadden continued. "Kirby alerted to scent and Kelly is tracking north toward Lookout Cliff."

He had a flattened Midwestern accent, although nothing else about him could be labeled flat. Including his ego. One month of working with or around him with the local SAR crew told her that she'd have better luck trying to reason with a bull moose. Dannette had no doubt that if Fadden could get away with it, he'd drop-kick her and her SAR dog back to her home state.

Sadly, he needed her, and they both knew it. On hand to help Kelly and her K-9 Kirby pass their SAR K-9 certification,

Dannette and Missy were the only K-9 unit within two states with the teaching hours and credits to certify the team. Said certification would qualify the sheriff's department for a healthy government grant for rural SAR, an end goal that Fadden never failed to keep in the forefront of Dannette's purpose here in Moose Bend, Minnesota. Unfortunately, in his mind that goal didn't warrant tapping his force for live-victim-search training or scooping from the currently dwindling county SAR fund for K-9 training scents and devices.

The Fadden types in the world didn't put stock in the successes of the canine SAR community and, in fact, stirred up false hopes with their unrealistic, all-or-nothing attitudes. One failure and the entire SAR K-9 reputation suffered; one success and they were heralded as heroes.

It left little room for the long, dark, soggy afternoons that defined SAR K-9 work. If she and Kelly failed to locate Mrs. Hanson, Dannette knew Sheriff Fadden would push what buttons he could to shut down her K-9 training course and send her back to Iowa with a bill for expenses.

Which meant that more people, like Mrs. Hanson and four-year-old Ashley Lundeen, would perish, alone and afraid.

This is not about Ashley. Dannette's thoughts recoiled against the familiar stampede of memories, and she shook herself back to the search at hand.

"10-4," Dannette said as she checked her topo map with her flashlight and noted Kelly's sector and direction. She frowned, checked again. "Search One to Search Two, please confirm location."

Kelly's voice came over the line, young and just breathless enough to indicate she was following Kirby at a fast clip. "Crossing Devil's Creek, about one hundred yards from Lookout Cliff."

"10-4," Dannette acknowledged, her heart thumping. If Kirby had *also* alerted, perhaps Mrs. Hanson still lived and had simply holed up in a location that emitted a putrid odor, a cave with guano or even the remains of a dead animal. Dannette folded up the map, her heart lightening.

She plowed into the fractured, darkening shadows of the forest, watching Missy work the scent. The dog stopped, circled, her nose high, then turned and looked at Dannette. Dannette used her clicker to urge the dog forward. The hand-held device gave instant encouragement without having to rely on verbal cues.

The rain drizzled down into her jacket, and she shivered; she was hungry, cold, tired. But she refused to think of the hot shower waiting. Not until she found Mrs. Hanson.

No one deserved to die alone. Without family.

The thought roughened her throat as she steadied herself on a skinny poplar and climbed over a downed, softened birch.

Without family. No, Dannette had a family—her dogs, Sherlock and Missy. Probably the only real family she'd ever had, except perhaps for Jim Micah and the other members of Team Hope. Yeah, they felt like family. At least as far as she'd let them inside her heart.

It simply wasn't wise to let people that close. Because getting close also meant allowing them a glimpse of the nightmares she still hadn't shaken.

This is not about Ashley. Dannette told herself that twice more as she watched Missy run back to her, the hair on her neck bristled. Her breathing turned rapid as she sat, a passive alert to the target scent.

"Good dog," Dannette said. "Refind."

The dog bounded off, far enough ahead to keep the scent but not so far that Dannette couldn't see her in the growing darkness. *Please, Lord, have her on the trail of something real and alive.* She could still hear little Robby, June's grandson, pleading in the back of her mind.

Please find her, moaned another voice, one buried in her heart.

She pushed through a netting of branches and flinched for only a second when one backhanded her. The smells of decay and loam stirred up from the ground, and foraging animals clung to the night air. Darkness drifted like fine particles through the forest, so gradual as to nearly not recognize its accumulation. A cool breeze carried the echo of barking, a faint tugging on Dannette's ears as she pushed aside tree limbs and stomped through bramble. Hopefully Kirby and Kelly weren't far behind.

Missy waited at the base of a large rooted trio of birches. She looked at Dannette, her ears pricked forward. Dannette put a hand on her back. "Find."

Dannette fought to keep Missy in the beam of her flashlight. They'd have to quit soon, and that thought made her want to weep.

Please, Lord, let us find Mrs. Hanson. Alive.

Missy barked, an active alert that she'd uncovered something. Dannette marked a tree with a reflector, then trudged through the brush after the dog. Missy stood, outlined in a hover of pine.

"Search Two to Search One." Kelly's voice broke over the radio.

Dannette keyed her radio while she tried to get a fix on her canine. "Search One here." The deepening darkness turned the forest into a black-and-white, B-version horror flick, complete with escaping birds and the rustle of ominous wind.

Dannette aimed her flashlight on the ground in front of her. She froze.

Missy stood over a form, a body for sure, dressed in dark pants and a blue Windbreaker, crumpled in the fetal position, its back to her.

Mrs. Hanson?

Her heart banging against her ribs, Dannette held her breath and approached. Missy danced around the form, animated, her breaths fast.

Dannette's chest clogged, and a tiny, panicked voice inside told her to turn and *run*. Dark memories lurked on the fringes of this moment to snare her and suck her down, to drown her.

Dannette held back a gasp and reached for her dog.

The form wore a black bag over its head. The smell of death didn't permeate the air, but the fine hairs prickled on Dannette's neck as she inched away. "Good dog," she whispered.

Static proceeded Kelly's voice, punctuating the moment and frazzling Dannette's tightly strung nerves. "I found her! Mrs. Hanson is alive!"

Dannette's knees gave out, a weakness borne from part relief, part horror. And maybe a little from the ringing in her ears.

Whom exactly had *she* found?

Chapter 2

WILL PULLED INTO the Howlin' Wolf, and his chest tightened.

No Simon. At least his silver birch half-ton Chevy Silverado wasn't in the lot. Maybe that was good news. Like he'd already been here and gone.

Will shoved his truck into park, dug an old rag out of the glove box, and cleaned the blood from his nose, his mouth. It wasn't uncommon for a bloke to stroll into the Wolf looking like he'd had a run-in with a truck, but the fewer questions the better.

He blew out a breath, put on his game face, and hiked into the bar/burger joint. *Please, Simon, be here.*

The old log-cabin-turned-eatery and Friday night hangout had barely crept into the twentieth century with electricity and indoor plumbing. To expect anything but a raucous jukebox and the smells of beer and grease embedded in the walls would court disappointment. The dingy, dimly lit restaurant proved, however, a perfect clandestine rendezvous spot and plan B checkpoint.

Will beelined to his table near the back—the one with a good view of the door—and sat with his back to the wall, trying not to immediately dive under the table where Simon sometimes pasted the USB pendant with his latest communication.

Willie Nelson crooned from the jukebox, competing with the sounds of sizzling burgers from beyond the double saloon-style doors. Just over Will's head hung a mounted walleye, glassy eyes open in near panic.

Will wondered if he wore the same opened-eyed, *please, no!* expression as he slid his hand under the table and discovered . . . nothing.

A waitress sauntered over, her hair pulled eye-stretchingly tight into a wispy, mousy brown bun. Joanie was already pushing forty, and it made her look about ten years older than that. Not that he cared, but sometimes he wondered if there wasn't a story behind the eyebrow piercing, the missing teeth, and the haunted look in her muddy brown eyes.

Then again, everyone had a story, didn't they?

"Hey there, ace," Joanie said. "The regular?"

"Yeah." He glanced around the room, kept his voice casual. "My friend been in?"

She put two rolls of napkin-wrapped silverware on the table. "The one with the tattoo and beard?"

Will nodded. He certainly didn't mean Sally Appleton from border control. While she had a tattoo, she could hardly be confused with a six-foot-three former linebacker from upstate New York. Still, he supposed Joanie might confuse Sally as his friend, although he'd taken great pains to keep her at a healthy distance while he wheedled information from her.

Not that Sally didn't try to turn their informant-recipient relationship into something PG-13. Last week's working lunch still left a gritty taste in his mouth. Well, *he'd* considered it working. She'd somehow decided that their biweekly get-together merited her wearing a hot pink, spandex T-shirt and low-rise jeans that showed off a—*ouch*—belly-button ring. He could barely look in her general direction the entire meal.

Whereas she had given him a thorough scrutiny, one that had obvious meanings attached. He'd ignored it, just like he had such suggestions for the past three-plus years. He knew where temptation led and ended up. And the residual hollow and used feelings.

Will wondered if he didn't really know what it meant to have a friend of the female persuasion.

Then again, any friendship would require someone getting inside the layers to the real Will Masterson. There was a reason he worked so well under an alias. He'd been operating under one guise or another for most of his life—sheriff's son, trouble-maker, Green Beret, and now Homeland hero. He supposed out of them all, the last was the one that gave his life the most resonance. Still, his current profession left little time, ability, or inclination to let the real Will out of hiding. Perhaps women like Sally were all he could hope for.

Oh, he hoped not.

"Your friend hasn't been in," Joanie answered.

Will glanced at the door, then checked his watch.

Maybe Simon was simply late. He'd arrived late a couple of times—once, sporting a black eye, which didn't seed any feelings of calm in Will now. Simon had the rough part of this assignment, and Will knew it.

The uneasy feeling in his gut tightened into a writhe.

Two truckers eased in, followed by the night's chill. One hitched up his jeans as he cased the joint. The other chewed on a ratty toothpick. Their gazes ran over Will before they took stools along the bar.

Will dismissed them and pulled out his cell phone. No signal. Not that he expected any up here in the hills, but a miracle might have been nice.

No, the miracle would be if Simon showed up.

Joanie reappeared with his shake, set it on a napkin, and handed him a straw. "You're the only guy I know who walks into a place that sells fifteen different microbrews and orders an Oreo shake."

Will shrugged and gave Joanie a cryptic smile. "Thanks." He checked his watch again, frustration piling against him. He dipped his straw in the ice cream and stirred as Joanie walked away.

Outside, trucks flew by on their way to Canada and beyond. They splashed grimy spring puddles into the blackened lot. It might be mid-May, but northern Minnesota had just begun to creep out of winter hibernation. Chill still laced the nighttime air, and occasionally Will awoke to frost glazing his windows. It reminded him of South Dakota in October.

Trying to act nonchalant, he took a sip of his shake, letting the sweet chill fill the crannies of his stomach. *Simon, where are you?* Of all the meetings they'd had over the past year, this one weighted their future. Simon knew the stakes and the ticking clock. They had less than a week to round up the package and save the world from another Hayata attack.

If they didn't, more folded flags would be sent home in place of soldiers like Lew, thanks to the handiwork of a phantom terrorist organization that had the frustrating ability to slip through the CIA's fingers like Jell-O.

Perhaps if Hayata hadn't left their fingerprints—in the form of planning, equipment, and execution of the major terrorist attacks—from Irian Jaya to the Philippines to Spain and the Middle East over the past three years, Will wouldn't be so jumpy about Simon's absence.

Or his panic might have to do with his own up-close-and-painful encounter with Hayata's actions.

He considered driving up to the farm and nosing around.

He could say he was writing an article about . . . about—he scanned through his compiled information—predator activity?

That was an understatement. He chuckled ruefully and finished off his shake.

Joanie returned to the table. "I guess your pal isn't coming."

Will handed over a wad of ones. "Dunno." He shrugged on his jacket, aiming for casual, feeling bloated and sick.

"Thanks," Joanie said and tucked the cash into her apron. "See you next week?"

"Yeah, sure," Will mumbled. Actually, no. If everything went as planned, he hoped to be long gone by next week. Long gone and mission accomplished.

In fact, by next week, he hoped he'd no longer have to dodge the ghost of Lew Strong.

Will banged out of the restaurant, stood in the fresh air, letting the wind lick his hair. Now cut short, it still felt odd not to have to tie it back, like he had during his stint as a longhair in special ops. The afternoon rain had emptied the clouds and the sky twinkled, a million reminders that almighty God watched. Will swallowed the lump clogging his throat and trudged to his pickup.

He sat in the cab, sorting his options. Now what? Panic nearly drowned the sound of reason. Maybe he *had* been roughed up by a gang of north woods patriots so this wasn't about Hayata and a terror agenda.

Yeah, right. And he was just a hometown reporter, keeping tabs on the local police beat. He tested a tender spot on his side and knew that he'd find a boot-shaped bruise there tomorrow.

Thankfully, he'd gotten in a couple good licks himself before they'd beaned him with the butt of a rifle and he'd seen stars.

Obviously, those licks hadn't been enough to keep them from intercepting Simon, however. If he'd ever been here.

Shoving the truck into drive, Will skidded out of the lot toward Moose Bend, some thirty miles east. The rain slicked the roads, turning the pavement shiny. His heartbeat thundered in his chest, fury filling his throat. Please, please don't let his instincts be correct. Not today. Not with months of surveillance and sacrifice behind them. Not with the prize nearly in their hands.

Will headed straight for his cabin, located on the outskirts of town. The moonlight pooled on the hood of his truck as he pulled into the rutted drive. Sitting in the darkness, he stared at the waves pounding the Lake Superior shore and tried to escape the clutch of despair.

When he exited the truck, the breeze slicked his hair back from his face and curled under his leather jacket. He walked to the edge of the grass line and took out his cell phone. It beeped on, catching a meager reception. Figures that the terrorists would be hiding out in one of the few pockets of the world that didn't have cell towers. The closest decent reception was across the lake in Michigan.

The display indicated a text message. Will's pulse quickened as he recognized the sender's address. Simon's. So maybe he wasn't dead. Maybe he was back at the farm, getting his hands on the package right now. The one that General Nazar had promised to send with details of his defection.

Simon might be smuggling it out at this very moment.

Will read the message in the dim light. *Amina.* What did *that* mean? He scowled, scrolled down. Nothing.

Will tapped the cell phone against his forehead, frustrated.

From the truck, he heard the static of the police scanner, then the click and buzzing that proceeded a transmission. "Base to county. We have a 10-48 at Lookout Mountain base. Male, approximately thirty-five years of age. 10-35, ASAP."

10-48. Dead body. Will felt nearly light-headed as he stalked to the truck, turned up the volume, and listened to dispatch confirm the call-out of the medical examiner.

Closing his eyes, he leaned against the truck, tasting bile.

In the pit of his stomach he knew. The dead body was Simon Rouss, aka Hafiz Tarkan.

How he hated it when the bad guys won.

✦ ✦ ✦

Dannette sat on the back bumper of the truck and ran her hands through Missy's damp fur. She'd removed Missy's trailing harness and the shabrack—the orange SAR rescue vest that identified her as one of the good guys. "Tired?"

Missy laid her head in Dannette's lap, blinking.

"Yeah, me too."

No—correction. She felt light-years beyond tired. Try exhausted. Dead on her feet. Annihilated. She'd given up any realistic dreams of dropping onto her warm motel bed in the near future. With the activity buzzing around the incident command base, she'd be lucky if she could climb in next to Missy in her kennel in the back of her pickup and catch a five-minute snooze.

She rose, deciding it might be better to walk off the exhaustion than surrender to it. Missy heeled beside her on her lead. Six Suburbans and three pickups were parked in the field beyond the High Pines Rest Center. The ground had been chewed to mud, and headlights pushed the night back to the folds of the poplar and pine forest. Still, darkness crept into the pockets between the vehicles.

Kelly and Kirby held court in one area, the paramedic-in-training triumphant at her canine's success. *As well she should be,* Dannette thought. They'd all spent more time out in the bush the last few weeks than humans should. Dannette had dragged dummies and human scent through miles of woods, testing Kirby and Kelly to read each other and plot a search, to think like a victim. Finding Mrs. Hanson felt like the prize after a muscle-burning marathon.

Dannette didn't want to think about the scene that might have played out if they hadn't found the elderly woman. Or if the corpse Dannette had found had been Mrs. Hanson instead of some hunter . . . or kidnap victim or whatever. She hadn't examined the murder site—just made sure no one tampered with it before forensics hiked in.

Which felt like it took a couple of centuries.

The county ambulance honked, then moved slowly through the maze of vehicles. A bossy and confused Mrs. Hanson was inside strapped to a gurney. Dannette had gotten a good enough glimpse to confirm that finding her had been an act of God. Mrs. Hanson suffered from slight exposure, disorientation, and a sprained ankle, but she had plenty of kick left in her. Even with a blanket over her shoulders and her family trying to hush her. It was quite possible she would have kept trucking through the forest, her mind on a top-secret quest, until she hit Canada.

Sheriff Fadden seemed in worse shape than Mrs. Hanson. Mayor Tom Hanson had him in a verbal half nelson, wondering why it had taken the county two precious hours to call in the local, albeit temporary, SAR K-9 unit.

Dannette was sure that she or most likely Kelly would pay for the pasty look on Fadden's face the next time the SAR K-9 team asked for funding. Unless, of course, she could get the mayor on her team . . .

"Missy!" Dannette turned to see Robby Hanson as his

arms locked around Missy's neck. Good-natured and kind, Missy stood still while the eight-year-old buried his face into her fur. "Thanks for finding my grammy."

"Thanks, Dannette." Julie Hanson, Tom's wife, strode up. The blonde looked gaunt and as exhausted as Dannette felt. Her short hair had frizzed into a curly Annie bob, and her dissolved mascara streaked down her face. But she smiled as she touched Dannette's arm. "You saved my mother-in-law, and we're grateful."

"Actually Kelly found her, but I'm thanking the Lord with you for His providence." Dannette shot a glance at the departing ambulance. "Will she be okay?"

Julie nodded. "Well, as okay as an eighty-six-year-old Alzheimer's patient can be. She's so spry; it kills us to see her mind destroy her like this." She rubbed her arms. "Poor Tom. He doesn't handle his mother's disease well. It's so frustrating, not to mention heartbreaking."

Dannette nodded, knowing all too well how it felt to stand on the sidelines and watch a loved one suffer. "I'm keeping you all in my prayers."

Julie gave her a one-armed hug. "C'mon, Robby, time to head home."

Robby gave Missy one last hug, then allowed his mother to lead him to their SUV, where Julie's sister and her boys waited. Dannette watched as the sisters embraced. The emotional support of the Hanson family tugged at a soft place in Dannette, and she turned away lest memories swamp her. At moments like this, fatigue had the ability to play her like a marionette. In all likelihood she'd end tonight sitting by the window, staring at the stars, unable to face sleep.

Which would do marvels not only for her appearance but for her ability to file a decent incident report tomorrow. No wonder she felt—as well as looked—hollowed out these days, dangerously near snapping.

Maybe her SAR pal Jim Micah had been right when he suggested she take a break and head down to Kentucky instead of going canoeing with her NYC friend Sarah over Memorial Day weekend. Although Dannette had missed his and Lacey's engagement party in the fall, she'd come to enjoy the occasional e-mail from Lacey Galloway Montgomery, soon-to-be-Micah. The ex-spy/NSA computer whiz had a frankness about life that Dannette appreciated, and Lacey radiated her salvation in a way that felt both dangerous and intriguing. Although Dannette had been a Christian since childhood and had a solid relation-ship with God as her friend and companion, seeing redemption in Lacey's eyes made Dannette wonder why she had never wept for joy at the cross, never clung to God like Lacey did with every breath.

Perhaps Dannette had just never needed Him that much. Which was a good thing, right? She hadn't lived a prodigal's life, hadn't walked the alleyways of darkness and sin. So maybe she'd never really understand the showering of grace Lacey felt.

Lacey and her little girl, Emily, had embraced life on their Kentucky farm—a far cry from running from a paid assassin and trying to clear Lacey's name. It seemed both had begun to shake off the horrors of Emily's kidnapping, the event that had finally set them free. Even Lacey's fiancé, Jim Micah, seemed free of the demons that had tormented him. He'd surrendered his twenty-year career as a Green Beret without so much as a flinch. In his last e-mail he'd hinted at wanting to start up some sort of official Team Hope SAR organization.

However, as Dannette mulled over the idea of heading south ASAP, the thought of seeing Lacey again face-to-face made her tremble. She'd shared in Lacey's terror during the dark hours when Lacey thought her daughter might be dead and, well, seeing it firsthand stirred up too many memories.

"Ms. Lundeen?" Sheriff Fadden motioned her over with a wave.

Here to serve, she thought as she led her dog over to the Fadden-Hanson klatch. She pasted on a smile.

Tom wore a grim look. "We've done a tentative ID on the corpse, and we think the guy you found is from the community in Silver Creek, about thirty miles from here. Coroner guessed he hasn't been dead long—probably only a few hours before you found him."

Dannette couldn't help the shiver that went through her. Did that mean that if Missy had found Mrs. Hanson's scent sooner, Dannette might have witnessed a murder?

She let her thoughts stop there and focused on Fadden's words.

"They're a quiet bunch, religious even. But this guy has a tattoo on his hand. Maybe that will open up some leads." He snorted. "Good thing your dog can't tell the difference between an old lady and a dead guy."

"That's my mother you're referring to," Tom said in a low, cold voice.

Fadden's face twitched.

"Missy is trained to follow human scent. Not to give me a full description of the type of scent. I'd say that this case shows exactly what an asset an SAR K-9 unit can be to a police force. Definitely worth the extension of funds to train. Don't worry; Kelly and Kirby will pass their certification. Especially after today." She decided to blame the sharpness of her tone on her fatigue.

Tom held up his hand, shot her a warning look. "Have you already given your report to Fadden's deputies?"

Dannette nodded. "A couple times." She rubbed Missy's ears as the dog sat at her side.

"I can't tell you how grateful Julie and I are for your help today, Dannette. You and Kelly saved my mother's life. Thank you." Tom's gray eyes held warmth to match his tone.

Dannette smiled. "That's what we train for."

Fadden shook his head at the undercurrent in her words.

Well, could she help it that her life was about SAR canine training? She said, "We can thank God for His intervention."

Tom nodded. "What do you say, Fadden? Send this lady home?"

Fadden looked exhausted, bags of fatigue under his eyes. He sighed and rubbed his eyes with a beefy hand. "Yeah, sure. Somebody should get some sleep tonight."

Dannette allowed herself a sliver of sympathy. Fadden would probably spend much of the night processing Dead Guy from the Woods after his brow-wringing from the mayor. Still, a little appreciation from his direction might salve her frayed nerves. She gave him a small smile.

He turned away. "Wouldn't want to overwork you or anything."

Overwork? She'd like to remind him who sat in his warm Suburban downing coffee while she tromped through the waterlogged forest for hours. So much for appreciation.

"See you in church Sunday, Tom." Dannette led Missy away before her tongue could turn the moment into something dark and ugly. She usually had a handle on her emotions, but creeps like Fadden infuriated her. They didn't get it that she put her life on the line so others might live and only saw their budget dollars being scraped away for doggy treats. Right now she should remember wisdom, duct-tape her mouth shut, and hide out in the nearest java shop with a cup of chai and a biscotto. Or maybe a sweet roll. She wondered if Nancy's Nook was still open.

She let Missy off her lead as they exited the ring of vehicles and made her way across the dark field toward the parking lot. Missy ran, finally free from the obedient confines of work. Dannette wished she had a ball to throw.

Headlights turned into the parking lot, scraped across her lonely pickup. Dannette's heart lurched, and she started jogging. "Missy!"

The truck kept on past her parked vehicle and headed into the field.

Dannette stifled a scream as she saw Missy's form pass through the lights. "Missy!"

The dog froze, looked at her. During the snapshot in time all Dannette saw was Missy's sweet brown eyes, asking for directions.

Come.

The word clogged in her throat as she watched the truck plow toward Missy.

Chapter 3

AMINA. THE WORD throbbed in her brain like Morse code as Fadima Nazar walked through the causeway into the Winnipeg International Airport. Canada. *Amina.*

The instructions her father had given her felt like a gnarled tangle in her head. She tugged her backpack over her shoulder and fisted it, finding some courage in the press of the crowd around her. Fadima held her chin up, eyes roaming over her fellow passengers. Would Hafiz meet her here? or at the compound?

She felt naked in her Western attire. Her arms and legs hadn't seen light in about ten years, and at the moment, it didn't feel nearly as freeing as she had supposed it might. An American teenager. That description was enough to earn a spittle of disgust where she came from.

Amina. It meant "truth." Her father had written the word on the inside of her arm—high, where no one but she could see it—just in case. But she was hardly going to forget the one word that would set them all free.

Then again, maybe she needed the word imprinted on her arm to help her believe that she could actually pull off this charade. That she could be the person her father counted on her to be to save his life and many more.

While she didn't know the exact details of Hayata's next move, her father did and had told her enough to make her feel the weight of humanity on her shoulders. And only she knew how to find her father.

Fadima probably felt the same fear and disgust her mother had. But did she also possess her mother's courage?

No crowd greeted the British Airways passengers at the gate, another sign of Canada's crackdown on terrorism. Still, Canada was the highway into America, and people like her father and his cohorts counted on its more liberal immigration policies.

It was now, if ever, that she should bolt. Run to the bathroom, cut her dark hair, and blend into the crowd. She'd be free. Just like her father hoped and dreamed.

But if she didn't meet her new family, her father would be dead before sunset. Along with Kutsi, her brother. No, for them she would walk like a sheep into the wolf's lair and wait for her shepherd.

She moved down the causeway and into the clean, well-lit terminal. Her gaze darted across the crowd waiting for the disembarking passengers beyond the security checkpoint. She plunked her backpack down on the scanner and walked through, holding her breath.

No buzz. Not that she carried anything of suspicion, but right now anything out of the ordinary might send her out of her skin and make her courage flee across the ocean to the relative safety of her *sotnya*, the Hayata cell she called home in a village in central Kazakhstan.

Seventeen years old felt way too young to hold the fate of thousands of lives in her hands.

She retrieved her backpack and exited the line, standing for a moment in confusion. A sea of people streamed by her, no one paying any attention to the dark-featured girl in the low-cut jeans, running shoes, and Gap T-shirt. She hardly recognized herself for that matter. Makeup. Her hair long and loose. She even wore a dab of perfume. Westerners weren't noticed, her father had said, at least in Western countries. It was her everyday garb that would solicit attention.

But she'd left that world. Hopefully, forever.

She stiffened when she spied her contacts coming toward her, like jackals closing in on their prey. She sucked in a breath. *"Be brave, my Amina."*

"Fadima Nazar?" asked the taller of the two.

Fadima looked up into his dark eyes and pasted on a smile. "Yes," she said in her native tongue. "Ataman Erkan Nazar sends his greetings."

The other, a blond-haired white man with more cruelty than years on his pierced face, smiled. "Welcome to the promised land."

"Missy!"

The dog startled, jumped.

Dannette screamed.

The truck threw mud as the driver slammed the brakes. It shuttered to a stop.

Dannette froze. Missy? She advanced, her legs shaking, her eyes glazed with heat. "Missy?" she choked.

The dog barreled out of the darkness and jumped into her arms. Dannette landed hard on her backside and held on, her heart jumping out of her throat and landing somewhere in the dark forest beyond. "Missy."

"Are you okay?" A voice emerged from the dark void of

near disasters and held enough concern to keep her from launching at him, claws out. Instead, Dannette closed her eyes and tightened her hold on her dog, burying her face in Missy's smelly, wet fur.

"Miss?"

She felt a hand on her arm, large and strong against her rubber muscles. Then she blew out a breath and looked at him.

He *did* look sorry. She read it in his furrowed dark eyebrows, the grim slash of his mouth under his dark goatee, even the worry pulsing from his way-too-brown eyes. The fury she felt dissipated from her muscles, leaving only relief. "I'm okay. And so is Missy."

He supported her arm as she rose.

Dannette was a tall person, able to look most men in the eye, but this near killer stood a nose above her, and in his rumpled leather jacket, faded jeans, and cowboy boots, he emanated a quiet, unobtrusive power. Maybe it was the way he held himself, feet planted and his head slightly angled. She felt his gaze run over her, and it wasn't at all invasive. "I didn't see her. It's a good thing you yelled," he said without defense, with sincerity.

Still, Dannette felt another swell of anger forming in her chest, the residue that follows a soul-deep scare. She bit it back. "Well, I suppose I shouldn't have let her off her lead. It's just that it's been a long day." She ran her arm across her forehead.

He glanced at the party of lights and conversations beyond the darkness. "You a part of that over there?"

Dannette sighed, shoved her hands into her pockets, and glanced at the chaos. "Yeah. Missy's an SAR dog, and we spent all day in the woods."

When she looked back, she was startled to see his gaze on her, searching her face. His tiny frown spoke more concern than she could deal with at the moment. "Did you find the dead body?"

She quirked an eyebrow. "Uh . . . well, yeah. How did you know about that?"

"I've got a scanner in my truck."

Oh, a cop. No wonder he radiated this you're-okay-now-ma'am aura. Funny, with him standing a foot away from her, she sorta felt that way. Okay, now. All he needed was a badge and maybe a beat-up Stetson to complete his old-West-hero guise. "Well, I gave my statement to the deputies. I'm sure you can get the lowdown from Sheriff Fadden."

One side of his mouth drew up in a smirk. "Yeah, I'll bet." He squinted again at the lights behind her. "Hey, have you eaten?"

Eaten? She had begun to move away from him and now froze. He gave her a full-powered white smile, and suddenly she knew fatigue had already taken possession of her brain. She let herself wrap around the idea of making a friend, decompressing from the carnage of the day with a person who might nod and listen with his eyes, his smile.

She was reading way, way too much into this near hit-and-run. *Down, girl.*

"No," she heard herself answer, her mouth obviously out on its own tonight. And then it smiled, giving her the look of a teenage girl besotted with the quarterback. Oh, brother. She should turn and run and not look back.

"They make a great bowl of chili down at Nancy's Nook. How about you let me apologize for nearly running over . . . Misty?" he said, shoving his hands into his jeans pockets.

"Missy," she corrected. But his attempt to get her dog's name right had Dannette nearly to yes.

"Missy." He whistled. Missy, the traitor and all-knowing

judge of good character, bounded over. He held out his hand, let her sniff it. A few moments later she was on her back, in complete, embarrassing surrender, wiggling as he rubbed her stomach. "She's a sweet thing."

So much for holding out in an attempt to be coy. Besides, he was a cop. And Nancy did serve great chili.

✦ ✦ ✦

Will had redefined his definition of *pretty* over the years, and while this lady didn't have the exotic look of the women he'd met overseas, she had a simple, honest prettiness. Tall, with hazel eyes ringed with wariness, and short rain-wetted, breeze-dried hair, she sat and leaned on her hand and twirled her fork into her napkin, exuding a certain authenticity that made her intriguing. The fact that she hadn't tried to wipe the dirt from her high cheekbones before she joined him in the café said that she felt comfortable with who she was—what you see is what you get.

Too bad he couldn't say the same thing.

"Do you know what you want?" he asked.

She said nothing and shook her head, looking exhausted.

Maybe this wasn't such a hot idea. But he was out for answers or at least the clues locked somewhere in that tousled blonde head. And he would wheedle them out before the night was over.

He'd been right to follow his instincts and head up to the SAR site. After the dispatch on the radio, he'd weighed his options for all of 3.02 seconds, then floored it to the incident site to confirm that it was Simon/aka Hafiz they were zipping into a body bag.

Thirty minutes later, he'd pulled into the parking lot and

nearly mowed over the lady's dog—something that had scared him more than he wanted to admit. Or it might have been the way the lady dropped down in the dirt and hung on to the animal, her heart in her contorted face. He'd felt a little unnerved and slightly raw when he walked out onto the field, considering the possibilities. He didn't want to be the guy who destroyed something so well loved.

Already done that, thank you.

It felt like sheer divine providence that he would meet the person who had found Simon. He'd prefer to do an end run around Fadden—he hadn't exactly earned any warm fuzzy responses from the local law since he started nosing around town.

He had followed her into town, to Nancy's Nook, which was thankfully still open. He'd watched as she watered and fed her dog; then he helped dry off the animal and tuck Missy into the berth in her truck. She seemed single-minded in her care of the animal . . . something that struck a soft place in his chest. Or perhaps it was the affinity he had for responsible people. The army had taught him that.

Nancy had taken the main floor of an old bungalow and refurbished it into a bakery and café. Her limited menu was scrawled on a chalkboard on the wall opposite the door. In a display case sat a lonely brownie that might find a home in his stomach later tonight.

They were the only patrons in the restaurant—Nancy had informed them that she was closing shop within the hour. Will had wrangled the last remaining bowl of chili for the woman and a Reuben sandwich for himself out of her. And a basket of onion rings.

Will heard the floor creak in the kitchen behind the two-way swinging door, and a slight chill whistled in from under the log front door. He walked over to the far end of the room where, in a stone fireplace, a meager blaze sputtered, gasping for life. He moved the ash-covered logs around with a poker, added another log. He replaced the poker and grabbed a napkin from another table and wiped his hands.

The woman said nothing, still cocooned in fatigue—or thought?—as she twirled her fork.

"So, I never did get your name," Will said, returning to the table and squelching the urge to take the fork out of her hand. Tension laced the gesture, and he felt the errant and weird urge to help her unwind. He'd been on the dark end of body recovery a few times and knew that only time erased those images, if at all.

She leaned back, put the fork on the table, readjusted the table setting. "Dannette. Lundeen."

"Dannette. That's pretty. Do you go by Dani, because you know, you seem like a Dani. Are you new in town?"

She opened her mouth a bit, as if trying to form a response. Then, "No, I . . . ah . . . well, I'm kind of visiting."

Oh? He raised one eyebrow. Good. That made it easier to pass himself off as a nice guy from down the street. "My name is Will Masterson."

"Nice to meet you, Will," Dani said, then grinned. "Sorta."

"At least you're honest," he said. "Where are you from?" He leaned back, stretching his legs. A faux lantern affixed to the wall shed a pool of orange light over the wooden table.

"Iowa. And you? No, let me guess." She wore the slightest etching of a smile. "Home on the range?"

He chuckled. "Bull's-eye. Actually I'm from South Dakota."

"Land of the free," Dani said.

"And home of the brave," he finished. She giggled, and it sounded sweet. "Actually, I haven't lived there for a while. But

I still call it home. Cotter, South Dakota. Population 7,000 if you count the cattle."

A bigger smile, and it found places inside he'd thought cold and dead. Whoa, boy. This dinner date was about information, not extracurricular activities. Not only did Dani not look the type, but he hadn't been the type either for quite a while now, if he remembered correctly. Even if he'd had opportunity to find a few warm and willing friends in Moose Bend, he had given over that side of his life to Jesus to forgive and start anew. But he wasn't exactly sure how to go about being friends with a woman without an . . . agenda. Maybe it felt like this. Friendly banter. Dinner out. Sharing easy secrets.

Perhaps it was even supposed to feel . . . soothing. Like a balm on raw and wounded places.

Although he'd died to Wild Will, he still had to make sure the old Will didn't sneak up and lasso the one that wanted to be God's man. "So Dani Lundeen from Iowa, what brings you to Moose Bend, Minnesota?"

"I run an SAR K-9 training program in Iowa. I came up about a month ago to prepare one of the locals for her final SAR K-9 certification exam. She's the one who found Mrs. Hanson." A blush touched her cheeks.

He smiled, aware that it made her look . . . innocent. He liked innocent. "You look like you need a vacation."

She crossed her arms over her chest. "Actually, I'm waiting for my friend Sarah. She's meeting me for an early season canoe trip into the Boundary Waters Canoe Area Wilderness (BWCAW)."

"Two women alone in the woods? Aren't you afraid of bears?" He meant it as a joke, and wow, she even giggled. He hadn't expected to enjoy it quite so much.

"We're pretty capable, thanks. Besides, our friend Andee is going with us."

He frowned.

She laughed. "Andee is a girl. She works SAR in Alaska and is a helicopter pilot as well as a mountain climber. Sarah's a paramedic in New York City. We haven't seen each other since last October, and we have this tradition." She picked up the fork again. "The three of us take a vacation before Andee heads into the bush for the summer. It's our version of girls' night out."

"Sounds dangerous." He hadn't meant to say it quite as softly as it came out, and it sounded . . . worried. Oh no. He smiled, hoping she didn't notice.

"Naw. We're all SAR trained and spend lots of time on our own. We cave and kayak and hike—"

"What happened to shopping? I thought that was a girl's favorite pastime."

She actually glared at him. Well, sorta. He could hardly call it a glare when she smirked at the end. "We shop. For dehydrated food, proper footwear, the latest in Gore-Tex rainwear and climbing equipment."

He laughed, wondering why that felt so easy. Someone like Lew's ever-present ghost should slap him upside the head. What happened to coaxing information from her about the dead person she'd found—who was probably his partner? He winced at his own callousness and felt profoundly grateful when Nancy came out with a bowl of chili, a sandwich, and a basket of seasoned onion rings.

"Anything else?" Nancy, a backwoods type of gal herself, with no hint of makeup on her fifty-something face, had her blonde hair tied back in a long braid and wore moccasins under her prairie skirt.

"How about the brownie there in the case?" Will nodded toward the goodie. Maybe he'd split it with Dani.

He pulled the sandwich closer, noticed that Dani had scooted up to the table, and had her hands folded. "Are you . . . um, going to pray?"

She smiled, and it looked honest and vulnerable. "Yes, do you mind?"

Did he mind? He almost felt like singing, although he couldn't put a finger on why. "Nope," he managed.

Dani offered a short, sweet prayer and had dug into her chili long before he recovered. He knew two things. His instincts about her had been correct; she wouldn't go for any sort of late-night shenanigans. And he was the biggest jerk on the planet for wanting to charm her only for her information, especially when she seemed to be moving past that grisly moment.

He ate in silence, subdued by his scumball stench.

"You okay, cowboy?" Dani peered at him over her cup of chai.

"Yeah," he said, and then, despite his regrets, he added, "I was just thinking about that poor chum out there in the woods. The guy you found."

Yes, he *was* a class-A jerk, because his segue worked.

She put down her cup, and a shadow crossed her face. "Yeah. It was pretty awful. I've seen dead bodies before, but this one . . . well, when they took the bag off his head, he'd been beaten pretty badly. They tentatively identified him by a tattoo on his hand—they think he was from a cult somewhere north of here."

Will felt ill. He put down his sandwich. Swallowed hard. Yep. Simon had a tattoo—had gotten it when he joined Hayata as a sign of allegiance.

"You okay? Maybe I shouldn't be talking about this over dinner." She gave a burst of self-deprecating laughter. "Listen to me. I shouldn't be talking about it at all. But I guess since you're a cop, I'm okay, right?"

A cop? He managed not to let his mouth gape open, but he didn't need to broadcast his surprise.

Nancy did it for him. She put the brownie on the table, looked at the two of them, and snorted. "Cop? Hardly. Will is our local newshound. He writes the police beat for the *Moose Bend Journal*."

Dani looked like she'd been slapped. "A reporter?" she said on a whisper-thin voice. She gave him a look that made him want to crawl under the table.

Then she got up and simply walked out. The door banged shut behind her.

Will narrowed his eyes, flinching as if he'd been shot. A fitting sort of epitaph to his desire to find a friend in Dannette—Dani—Lundeen from Iowa.

Chapter 4

COULD SHE BE any more stupid, gullible, and act any more desperate? Dannette screeched her pickup to a halt in front of the Lighthouse Motel. She leaned her head against the steering wheel, hearing again the waitress's words. *A newshound.*

Figures.

She had an uncanny ability to attract people who wanted to dig around in her life and find the dark holes.

And she'd let him call her Dani. Yuck. It suited her? She must not have been fully lucid when she let him chop off half her name. She was so *not* a Dani. Cute. Sweet. Swooning at the feet of the nearest good-looking guy who had a nice smile and a charming swagger.

Swallowing her desire to turn around and floor it south, she climbed out of the truck and went around the back to free Missy. The two-story motel, equipped with rent-by-the-month rooms facing Lake Superior, was a sorry excuse for a lighthouse, but at least the landlord allowed dogs. Then again, Dannette felt like a sorry excuse for an SAR searcher. She'd broken a cardinal rule of SAR work: Don't talk to the press. At least not until the police gave clearance.

She didn't want to see Fadden's face in the morning . . .

maybe she should pack up and head home to Iowa, just like he'd suggested.

Only what would Sarah say when she arrived in Moose Bend and found nothing but the skid tracks from Dannette's quick exit? Dannette knew she'd been doing her hermit routine for the past six months, and Sarah had been more than pointed in her assertion that they were getting together before Andee's trip north. Dannette had little doubt Sarah would track her down to Iowa or Kentucky and finally wheedle out the conversation that had been simmering since they'd been involved in the kidnapping and recovery of Lacey Montgomery's daughter, Emily.

It isn't about Ashley. She'd told herself that for three days while they fought to save Emily's life. The entire episode hit way too close to Dannette's heart, and both her friends knew it. Hence the space. And the impending showdown with Sarah.

Besides, after today's near tragedy with Mrs. Hanson, it was clear that Moose Bend needed Kelly and Kirby's certification as soon as they could arrange the test, and Dannette had to stick around to administer it.

Dannette climbed the steps to her room and opened the door. The room smelled starchy and fresh, and sleep beckoned from the made-up bed. Off-season in Moose Bend had its benefits, and the first was the low monthly rate of this prime lakeside getaway. And it helped that Kelly's mother owned the place.

Dannette unlaced her muddy boots and toed them off, then shut the door and locked it behind her. Missy went straight for her cushion and curled up, closing her eyes before Dannette shut the bathroom door. She started the shower and got in before it had even reached full heat.

Ten minutes later, she lay warm and only slightly damp in her old Tasmanian Devil nightshirt and wool socks, channel surfing from her double bed. Hunger still gnawed at the outside reaches of her stomach, but she ignored it. Better hungry than in stomach-curdling company.

Obviously she hadn't totally run Cowpoke Masterson out of her head. And if she was honest, he wasn't completely disgusting. Not with his deceptively sweet smile. The way he helped her rub down Missy and settle her in the pickup had charmed his way too far into the soft spaces of her heart. She could hear the cowboy in his words, a soft Western twang that spoke of broad skies, lazy days, slow laughter, and sardonic humor.

But he'd all but lied to her.

Tricked her.

So he'd never actually admitted to being a cop . . . he hadn't jumped to correct her, had he?

She scrolled through the television channels without really seeing, her chest burning. *Jerk.* Just when she was starting to enjoy his company. Or rather *wanted* to enjoy his company. She hadn't had a real, I'm-interested smile from someone of the opposite gender for so long she'd forgotten what it felt like.

No, it hadn't been a real smile. *Reality, Dannette.* Her throat thickened. A reporter. She should have seen the ink on his fingers, recognized the predatory look on his face, alerted to the sound of sniffing as he leaned on the table and stared at her with those pretty, deceitful brown eyes.

She'd had her share of run-ins with reporters, thank you, and had no desire to get close to anyone who dug out secrets and splattered them across the front page of her hometown rag. Or wherever.

She blamed exhaustion for not seeing through his charm. No man with that much natural rough-edged charisma would ever give her so much as a two-second glance. His type, the ones with ego and eyes that could make a girl forget her name, weren't attracted to the plain Jane, unruly hair Dannette types.

They wanted makeup. Beauty. An easy smile that didn't look too long at the interior. They wanted a *Dani*. Her defenses should have pricked the moment he made that shopping jab. She should have smelled the suaveness radiating off him.

He saw her only as the inside track to a hot story.

She sighed as despair deflated her anger. She shouldn't blame Will. Maybe God was simply intervening. The Almighty knew her history with men. The two that preceded Reporter Will had been SAR types who lived for adventure and put adrenaline before romance. Sorta like she did. A gal with a career traipsing around the world risking her neck to rescue others had no business cultivating or even wishing for strong arms and a willing ear to come home to.

Any such hero would need to know her backstory, and frankly, she wasn't giving that up. Not without a crowbar to her heart.

She flicked to a rerun of a detective show and soon grew bored, her mind returning rebelliously to Will Masterson. She sunk into her pillow; her eyes grew gritty.

"I'm sorry. I didn't mean to hurt you." He was leaning against his truck, hands in his leather jacket, a grin denting the dark goatee. "I didn't know you were so sensitive about report-ers."

Dannette whistled to her dog, but Missy seemed strangely absent. That fact niggled in the back of her brain, but she ignored it. The sky had turned a sickly green. "We should get inside."

He didn't seem to hear her. His liquid eyes—dark and magnetic—reached out to her. "Why did you run away from me?"

She opened her mouth, and suddenly Will Masterson

morphed into a small blonde woman, slightly built, lines around her mouth. Her gentle hazel eyes held on to Dannette with a power that seemed otherworldly. A tear hung on her lash. "Why did you run away?" she said softly. Behind her, the sky darkened, a flicker of light, then thunder, low and rippling under Dannette's skin.

"I dunno," Dannette whispered, but the words stuck like paste in her mouth.

The woman crouched. Opened her arms. Smiled.

The ground rippled, cracked. Dannette watched in horror as it opened a gully between herself and the woman. Still, the woman stayed in her crouched position, unaffected by the storm that now whipped her green housedress and apron around her waist, her hair over her face. "Dannette?" she said, cocking her head.

"Mommy!" Was that her voice?

Dannette startled awake. The woman vanished, and the final scenes of the detective show slashed into her mind. Her heart pounded, and she summoned deep breaths.

Just a dream.

Dannette looked at Missy. In the wan, eerie light, she saw the dog's head raised, her eyes tender as she stared at her mistress. "C'mere," Dannette said softly and heard emotion in her plea.

Missy trotted over and hesitated before she jumped on the bed and joined Dannette.

Dannette turned off the television and scooted down. She rubbed her hand through Missy's fur and tousled her ear, comforted by Missy's warmth, her sweet eyes on her.

"I dunno," she repeated, then closed her eyes and tried to push the memories back to the dark corners where they belonged.

✦ ✦ ✦

Fadima sat between the two men, squashed in the front of the
pickup, like a prisoner. She hadn't been this close to a man
ever, even her brother, and it felt invasive, even through her
spring jacket. Their odor—a mixture of sweat, cigarette smoke,
and greasy food—rose and filled the cab, curdling the airplane
food that sat like a boulder in her stomach. She clutched her
backpack on her lap and tried to remember her father's words.

"You are the bride of Bakym."

Bride. That word meant so many things in her culture.
How ironic that for the first time it would also mean freedom.
She had been prepared for the tradition of arranged marriage
and the fact that her father had pledged her years ago to the
local Hayata leader, Bakym. She'd even managed to resign
herself to the knowledge that Bakym saw her only as an alliance, a means of securing for himself a higher position in the
larger Hayata organization. *Hayata* meant life, but only since
her mother had been killed had Fadima realized that her father
had plans to give her and her brother real life outside the
Hayata ring of power. Plans that, should Hayata discover them,
would lead straight to their executions.

Bride. Thankfully, any such ceremony wouldn't take place
until her father joined them, which of course, would hopefully
never happen. Until then she would assume her alternate
purpose as a courier.

Hayata dealt in surreptitious money and weapons transpor-
tation as well as identity theft, money laundering, and other
forms of fraud. Although started by a group of disenfranchised
Cossacks searching for unity, their leadership had refocused in
the last few years as suppliers, the brokers of information,
weaponry, and supplies. She would spend the next two months

polishing her English and learning how to pass herself off as a tourist—or better, as an American teenager. Then Hayata would put her to work, sending her to Detroit and perhaps the South, where she'd travel the coast in an RV with her supposed father and act as a decoy for their illegal activities.

Illegal activities that included the loss of American lives.

Unless she escaped and completed her real mission. *Amina*. She had held the flimsiest of hopes that one of these two men might be the contact who would not only stop Hayata's plans but remove her from their clutches so she could start a new life. Her disappointment sharpened with each mile. Night blacked out the landscape, save for the beam of head- lights furrowing out the highway. Jet lag washed over her in waves, but she refused to sleep, to let her head bob onto either man's shoulder. "How much longer?" she asked in her native tongue.

"English," the driver snapped. He had pale skin, light brown hair, eyes that seemed both brown and gold.

She stared at him, wondering at his involvement in Hayata. She'd seen Asians in their *sotnya* a few times, but even they had dark hair, dark almond-shaped eyes. This man seemed so white—she'd never seen anyone with skin so pale. And he had three earrings and a stud in his nose. She'd never seen a man with an earring, let alone face piercings. He'd shed his leather jacket and wore a black T-shirt with metallic letters printed on the front. A barbed-wire tattoo on his upper arm peeked from his shirtsleeve.

"We speak English in America, and you will too," he snarled without looking at her.

She nodded. Hopefully her years of English wouldn't become a tangled mess in her drying mouth. "Yes, sir."

On the other side of her was a man from her own country,

with darker skin, darker hair, and wary eyes. He sighed and leaned against the window. "We'll be there soon. Remember, when we cross the border, you're my sister. We live as Americans. Keep your mouth shut."

Fadima nodded again, unable to speak past the lump of fear forming in her throat. America.

Amina.

Will sat on a boulder overlooking Lake Superior, his cell phone to his ear. He listened to it ring, gave a verbal code, and waited while he was connected to Jeff Anderson, his handler.

"What's up, Will?" Jeff had a calm voice, all business, but without the edge that Will had become accustomed to in the Green Berets. At first he'd wondered if it made Jeff soft, but in the end he decided it made him likable. Lew had also had a calm voice. It had kept the rest of his team sane in a chaotic world.

Will needed sanity tonight. "Simon is dead. Hayata must have made him."

Jeff stayed momentarily silent, then sighed. "Sorry to hear that. Are you okay?"

Translation: Were you made? Or will you end up facedown in the woods before the week's end? "I don't know. I was ambushed before our meet, as if they wanted me out of the way. But maybe they thought he was passing information to the local paper, not to the CIA." Will braced his elbow on his knee, feeling anew the bruises he'd accumulated. Even worse was the mangy-cur feeling of shame over the way he'd treated Dani. "I want to head up to the farm, take a look-see."

"No. We know Hayata's up to something, and the feeling

around here is that they'll make a move . . . soon. Sit tight. Keep things business as usual. Go to work tomorrow. Put your ear to the ground. Talk to that girl—Sally—and find out who's been across the border lately. We'll wait until we hear from our other Hayata-embedded operatives."

Will said nothing, afraid that anger might lace his tone. Sit tight? Yeah, right. Perhaps, if he was real lucky, Hayata would make his death quick and painless instead of the boot beating he'd gotten the first time around.

"Simon hinted that they were planning something. He sent me a text message before he died," Will said. "One word— *amina.*"

"*Amina.* What is that?"

"It sounds like an Arabic word. Or maybe Turkish. I think I remember that from when I was stationed at Incirlik. Except what does it have to do with Simon?"

He could picture Jeff rubbing his temples, where his wispy brown hair was starting to recede. "I'll get analysis on it."

"Thanks, Jeff." Will clicked off and closed the cell phone, fighting the residue of frustration.

Lake Superior waves threw themselves onshore, the tail end of fury after today's rainstorm. Lights from Moose Bend twinkled against the pane of night, and the redolence of spring ladened the air. Will breathed deeply, suddenly missing the smell of prairie grass, the low of cattle as they roamed wide fields. How many times had he sprawled under the sky with Lew, hands behind their heads, dreaming of their futures? Lew's always included Bonnie, and Will had painfully endured many soliloquies of love and longing from his best friend.

Lew had things that Will envied. *Still* envied. Honesty. A relationship with a woman that went beyond expectations. Bonnie had believed in Lew, had let him free to serve his country, knowing that Lew's heart stayed at home. Bonnie's love had given Lew a strength that Will couldn't understand. Or maybe that strength came from something more.

Will put his hand to his chest, as if pushing away the burn inside. Memories of Lew always seemed to stir up longings and attune Will to the vacancies in his own life. He knew he'd made choices that left him empty, with regret pinging in his heart. But he'd given his life over to God a few years back, and somehow he thought that would change everything. That God might smile on him like He had smiled on Lew Strong.

Obviously God's smile on his life was too much to ask for a guy like him. At least, Will never felt like he deserved that smile. He wasn't a man like Lew and never would be.

He considered that his inability to latch on to a real relationship might be in his genes. Will Masterson hadn't exactly had a firm foundation in the area of family and commitment. Buck Masterson's idea of family night was taking Will out to the nearest field, shooting back a bottle of whiskey, and instructing his son on the finer points of target practice. Sloppy drunk, the man could hit a prairie dog at a full run from one hundred yards.

He had even better aim when it came to finding his son with his fists.

Will exhaled, blinking away the past, the rush of pain. No, he hadn't learned to love from his father. Rose Masterson, however, had lived on love. She loved music, nature, the earth, and every man in town freely. Will learned to ignore the jabs and instead focus on the truth. His mother had loved him, and when she decided to come home, she made cookies, drew pictures, and showed him what a hug felt like. As a child he blamed his father for his mother's absences. As a teenager, he had a taste of love and betrayal, and for the first time he saw Buck with sympathy.

The Green Berets taught Will that he was responsible for his own behavior, regardless of the circumstances.

God had helped him forgive the past. Still, scars ran deep and the thought of cracking open his heart for anyone to take a good peek had kept him moving, dodging, never speculating on a second date.

Until tonight. Something about the way Dani Lundeen had teased him—no agendas, no coy innuendos, just pure friendship felt . . . exhilarating. Sweet. Like freshwater over parched soil. For a moment he let himself wonder what it would be like to rub all that dirt off her cheek with his thumb, to see the smile in her eyes when he kissed her.

Okay, at any time, common sense could start waving flags and wake him up. Sanity, which had obviously decided to take a vacation, would say, let her go. Keep your distance. He had no business cultivating anything with Dani or any other woman that he couldn't follow through on. And that follow-through would be done God's way. Which meant no visions of kissing, no thoughts of running his hands through her unruly hair.

Only why had Dani fled as if he might be an ax murderer instead of the local scribe? Then again, he wasn't the local scribe. Not only that, but he'd lied to her, not once but twice: first by letting her think he might be a cop and second by maintaining his cover. One that freaked her out more, perhaps, than if he'd told her the truth. Which, of course, he couldn't do and keep his real job in national security.

The hard facts only made him feel as if he'd bathed in a fine layer of sand. Gritty. In his eyes, mouth, under his fingernails. Grinding against his heart.

He sighed, suddenly painfully aware that if he spent any time with Dani Lundeen, those mysterious hazel eyes would tug at all his vulnerabilities. He might be saved and sanctified, but he was 100 percent male and had experiences lurking in his heart that grappled with his desires to be God's man. Even if he wasn't quite sure what that looked like, he knew it wouldn't resemble anything like his old SOP. He'd do well to put Miss Dannette I-Hate-Reporters Lundeen out of his mind and focus on finding the package he'd been sent to Moose Bend to unearth.

Amina.

Will wiped his hands on his pants, pocketed his cell phone, and headed toward the house. Despite the way his mission rubbed his conscience raw, he had to complete it. Jeff's words rang in his head: *Sit tight.* Oh yeah, sure. And what? Wait for Hayata to learn his habits, maybe pick him off with a Russian-made Dragunov sniper rifle while he was exiting the Java Moose, holding his early morning latte? Hardly. There was a reason they'd hired him out of Special Forces.

He rushed inside the cabin and pulled a duffel bag out of the closet.

If Hayata had a package waiting, it was time for the postman to pay a visit.

Chapter 5

FADIMA'S GROOM WAS six foot two with midnight black eyes, two silver teeth, and a smile that looked more jackal than human. Bakym circled Fadima like she might be prey, his eyes roaming over her as he listened to the report from her two captors.

Fadima clutched her backpack to her chest. A buzz, produced by twenty hours with little sleep, simmered beneath her skin, and she blinked, trying to get a fix on her surroundings in the dim moonlight. They'd driven through the Canadian border control without so much as a raised eyebrow, something she attributed to both her American looks and her driver's suddenly smooth smile and accentless speech.

Beyond the border, America turned shaggy and menacing, the forest looming dark and shadows jutting across the highway as they drove in silence. She wasn't sure what she'd expected. Perhaps bright lights, a McDonald's, or even a grocery store. She had spent many sleepless nights conjuring up what it would feel like to live free, without having Hayata count her steps or hover as she visited the market. For her own good, they'd said. She was practically royalty.

A royal sheep intended for slaughter.

They'd finally cut off a road twenty kilometers or so south

of the border and driven through the woods on a rutted dirt road until they emerged by a weedy yard ringing a small unlit house. Fadima hadn't needed prodding to get out of the vehicle—she nearly gulped in the fresh air, despite her dread. Maybe here her protector, Hafiz, would find her. The air, scented with an unfamiliar crispness, lifted her hair and buoyed her spirit as she trekked to the house. The door squealed when she entered, raising gooseflesh, as if in warning tendered by watchful spirits.

Inside the house, the smells of cigarette smoke, grease, and mold obliterated the hope churned up by the breeze. The floor squeaked as a man appeared from what looked like a hallway. He stood in the middle of the room, flanked by two fraying, broken sofas, and gestured for her to approach.

Fadima collected the last fragments of courage and obeyed, recognizing Bakym from the photograph her father had showed her. Only this Bakym didn't smile, and he emanated the odors of sweat and vodka that made her blood curdle. She stood, then, her heart thudding through her chest, as Bakym surveyed his newest operator, his bride-to-be, the daughter of General Erkan Nazar.

"Welcome to Camp Azmi," said Bakym finally, but his tone hinted at disgust. "I will inform your father that you have arrived." He had a tight, low voice, and he stopped before her, his feet planted, his hands clasped behind him. He wore black jeans and a gray sweatshirt that did nothing to hide the outline of his arms, his chest. She'd heard of his physical exploits, namely his ability at hand-to-hand combat against the Russians, and knew that he could snap her neck without blinking. In the pale moonlight, his dark eyes sorted out her vulnerabilities, and her throat dried up.

Bakym smiled, glanced at his cohorts. "We have two

rules." He held up his fingers, as if she might need a visual reminder. "Number one, I am the *Kaya*. You do as I say. You may be a princess in Tazar, but here you will obey me as your king. Especially after we are married." He chuckled then, and it felt like a dagger to her chest. "Number two, if you forget rule number one, you will be executed."

She opened her mouth but caught the outtake of breath before it left her lips. She nodded.

Bakym reached out and cupped her face in his hand. It was cold and large, and she closed her mouth and tried not to flinch.

"I have waited for you, princess," he said, and there was nothing soft about his voice. He moved his hand around to the back of her neck, tightened his grip. He took a step closer, forced her eyes to his.

Amina. She spoke the word in her head as he stared down at her, ice in his gaze.

"Your father made a wise choice for you." Then he kissed her hard, with anger and power in his touch.

She stiffened, closed her eyes. *For you, Father.*

Bakym stepped back, released her, wiped his mouth.

Her lips throbbed, bruised from his touch. Bile pooled in the back of her throat.

He looked at the two men standing in the shadows. "Hafiz is dead. We caught him today sending a message to someone on a cell phone." Bakym raised one dark eyebrow, glanced at Fadima. "Odd, don't you think, that the very day our little present arrives, we'd find a traitor in our midst?" He ran the backs of his fingers over her cheek. She tried not to shudder as she read meaning in his eyes.

"Don't disappoint me, Fadima," he said softly. "We have much to accomplish for Hayata, and you're just in time for your first lesson." He leaned close, his breath on her face. "Come with me, my new bride."

Fadima felt a hand on her arm, felt her legs move, but her brain had frozen on *"Hafiz is dead."*

Dead. Fear welled in her throat, tasting acrid, and she fought tears. *Amina.* Only her protector was dead. So much for truth, for freedom. She gulped in quick, calming breaths, then blinked back tears as Bakym yanked her down the hall, opened the door to a room.

Her heart stopped, a heavy stone in her chest when he shoved her inside and followed her, closing the door behind him with a soft click.

But her father had said—

Fadima nearly crumpled in relief as two women sat up, eyes on the newest member of their group.

Bakym pointed to a mat next to the wall. A blanket lay bunched on the top. Fadima climbed onto it and watched as Bakym walked over to one of the women, grabbed her by the arm, and forced her to her feet. Dark hair tumbled down over her face, but it couldn't hide the fear in her eyes. She whimpered as Bakym pushed her out of the room.

The other woman said nothing as she turned back to the wall. But Fadima heard quiet sobs punctuate the darkness.

What kind of nightmare had she entered? *Father, I can't do this.* Fadima pulled the blanket up over her, her head on her backpack, her eyes to the wall. She missed the smell of the campfire, of lamb's meat cooking, the arid breeze on her face, even the barks of the village dogs as they roamed the night streets. She missed the sound of Emine's breathing on the other side of the room. Emine had been her nanny, her mother, after Saiba had left . . . or rather, been executed, as Fadima had discovered later.

Most of all, she missed her father. His gentle smiles, the way he enfolded her in his massive arms. He said he trusted these Americans, these people whom, outwardly, he pledged to destroy. He told her to trust his plan, but what had her father been thinking to send her here to this . . . this . . . She couldn't think of a word to describe Bakym, the cruelty in his eyes, the taste of pain he left on her mouth.

She knew just what kind of horrific lesson he had planned for America. But for her . . . ?

Father, I can't do this.

She feigned sleep, but her mind told her that she had only one option.

Run.

Readily will I display the intestinal fortitude to fight on to the Ranger objective and complete the mission, though I be the lone survivor.

The Ranger creed, the one he'd memorized before becoming a Green Beret, thundered through Will's brain as he lay in the forest, peering through his night-vision goggles at the Hayata compound. Lone survivor. That never felt more painfully accurate than it did tonight, with the moon slicing through the canopy overhead, the rush of wind under his black BDUs, the feeling of greasepaint filling his pores. The trees creaked, and he used the sound to rustle forward. He'd seen a guard dressed in a pair of green fatigues and a wool hat patrolling some thirty yards ahead of him and knew the sentry would swing by for another pass soon.

With Simon packed into the cooler in the local ME's office, Will had no choice but to devise a way to recover the package himself. He hoped to gather enough intel to formulate a plan, return in twenty-four hours, and snatch whatever package their Hayata insider had planned to pass to Simon/Hafiz. Will knew the package included intel regarding a certain high-ranking general in the Hayata hierarchy, but Homeland Security often operated under a need-to-know basis. They hadn't included Will in that category.

Yet.

But if he recovered the package, he might be privy to the larger plan, move into a position of influence. Maybe he'd eventually be a point man who took down the organization that stole his friend Lew Strong from his family three years ago. The organization that obliterated the lives of thousands of patriots and notched another victory for the bad guys.

Maybe he'd even help turn this war on domestic terrorism into a victory.

The Hayata compound had quieted over the last hour. Will had watched from his perch on a knoll overlooking the yard as a late-model pickup pulled up and three Hayata members emerged. Two men and a woman. No, a girl, and she'd been afraid, evident by her faltering steps as she followed the men into the house.

Another recruit? Hayata operated under the mistaken belief that Homeland Security was blind to their devices, but their practice of importing teenagers and using them to smuggle goods across the country hadn't escaped Homeland Security's scrutiny. Two years ago, Will had helped HS apprehend an Hayata cell that profited from transporting cigarettes from North Carolina to Detroit, where they sold them at a higher rate and pocketed the change. The operation netted the terrorist cell millions before HS operatives had trailed their ring of teenagers and shut it down.

Besides money laundering, Hayata ran a number of lucrative businesses in the flesh-for-sale category and imported Middle Eastern opium and ephedra with a brazenness that felt like flaunting. Will had no doubt this new recruit would be masquerading as an American teenager, complete with dyed hair, earrings, and tattoos while still secretly tethered to her Hayata keepers. The thought made his stomach clench.

Will stilled, his breathing shallow as the sentry passed. Even camouflaged with his smeared-on war paint and brush cover attached to his back, a wrong breath could annihilate his mission and everything he and Simon had worked for over the past year.

The sentry stopped, stared into the woods, as if reading Will's thoughts.

Will quelled the insane urge to jump the guard who held an AK-47. Will's brain felt too tired to figure out where Hayata had obtained Russian hardware. How they'd smuggled them into the country was an easier puzzle to solve—the border between Minnesota and Canada often seemed no more than a fuzzy line drawn on a map. Between miles of border lakes and thick pine forests, Hayata could practically drive a battalion of tanks through, and the border guards, despite their efforts, would be hard-pressed to corral them. Hence the need for men like Will to watchdog the pockets where Hayata set up shop.

The sentry stood so close scanning the forest that Will could have drawn a detailed caricature of his thin beard, dark eyes, and scar down his cheek. Will tightened his grip on his Beretta M9 pistol and prayed for invisibility. He may have had a few iffy moments, including his lie-by-omission to Dannette, but he had to believe that God was on his side.

Wanted to believe it. Despite his mistakes, his failures.

In fact, Will hoped the Almighty might, in fact, give him

another chance to make amends with Dani. The look of betrayal on the K-9 handler's face embedded itself in Will's brain, and he couldn't deny the pinch in his chest that felt like regret. Something about her—her smile or the way she let him in under her defenses to see her fatigue or even the nickname Cowboy on her lips—had churned up a desire that felt foreign, even impossible.

Friendship.

Except it hadn't ended well. He had as much chance to make friends with Dani Lundeen as he did with a Turkish blunt-nosed viper.

The guard gave one last look, then continued slowly along the perimeter.

Will released his full breath in a long, unheard stream. He needed to get closer if he hoped to sketch the layout of the compound in his mind. From this position, he outlined two buildings—a house and a garage, obviously not used for cars. Probably weapons. Or communications. Behind the garage, a twelve-foot satellite dish aimed for the Southern Hemisphere.

The sentry finished his stroll around the perimeter and sat on the steps. Will watched as he lit a cigarette, the faint ash glowing green in Will's night-vision goggles.

The wind rustled the branches, the quiet of the forest settling over Will, filling his pores. He had always enjoyed surveillance. The quiet of aloneness, the focus of analyzing details, of formulating hypotheses, the insight that came when watching the enemy on their private, safe turf. People became comfortable in the known, in their own territory. They dropped their defenses, allowed the enemy to penetrate, learn, possess. He'd seen too many blindsided because they thought the perimeter was safe. Maybe that's what made Will a good soldier—he had learned, via the life lessons of his father's fists, never to let his guard down, never to let a soul past the defenses that kept him sharp.

He'd feared the comfort of being known by someone and had instead substituted it with the pleasure of knowing.

No wonder he'd ended up alone—and empty. He wasn't a fool. He knew that Lew had a love with Bonnie that came only from letting a woman inside a man's heart and letting her love all the blemishes and scars.

But he wasn't that type of guy. And now, especially since he'd given his life to God, hoping to do things God's way, he had little hope that he'd ever find a woman like Bonnie. Not in the scarce time he had between missions.

Guys like him lived for the moment, hoping to snatch a morsel of that true love. Only morsels weren't in God's plan.

Which meant, neither was any hope of true love.

Will swallowed a sudden lump of regret. If he'd done it God's way from the beginning, he might have a woman like Bonnie right now, giving him a reason to be out in the woods, wet and a little cold, spying on the bad guys in the wee hours of the morning.

He'd have a reason to want to stay alive. To come home in one piece. And a reason to leave in the first place.

The guard stood, snuffed out his cigarette, began his perimeter round. Will tracked him past the garage and toward the end of the driveway.

Movement in the far corner of his lens caught Will's attention. He focused on a form climbing out of a window. He sharpened the focus and recognized the young lady who'd arrived earlier.

What was she doing?

He found himself holding his breath as she reached the

ground and hiked a backpack over her shoulder, then shot off toward the woods on the far side of the yard.

One of the Hayata operatives is escaping.

That thought pierced his brain, ignited his heartbeat. He should help her. Maybe she knew where the package was, could help him infiltrate the compound.

He scanned back to the guard and nearly choked on his frustration. The sentry was twenty yards away and closing fast.

Will searched for the escapee. He found her crouched against the garage, and as she turned to search for the guard, he caught a glimpse of her face—heart-shaped, young, with wide eyes and more than a touch of fear. But it was the hard-edged determination in her expression that buzzed under his skin. He frowned.

The thump of boots arrested his attention. He lowered the glasses, ducked his head. Lightened his breath.

The guard sauntered past him, his arm resting on his AK-47 like a sling.

Will couldn't help but smile. He put the glasses back to his eyes, scanned the compound.

The girl was gone.

Dannette slammed the door to her pickup, making sure the window was cracked open for air. Missy pushed her nose to the window, leaving a wet mark.

"Stay," Dannette said. "I'll be right back."

The fragrance of a new day rubbed off the lingering fatigue as Dannette crossed the parking lot and entered the Java Moose. The smell of coffee extended welcoming fingers and dug out the hunger in Dannette's stomach.

"Good morning," said David, the coffee shop's owner. He stood behind the counter, a flannel shirt with its sleeves rolled up to his elbows, revealing lumberjack arms. His wide smile had been one of Dannette's first welcomes in Moose Bend and had become a fixture in her day.

"Good morning, Dave," she said. "I'll take a chai—"

"With skim milk." David smirked. "You know we have other drinks. Even *coffee*."

Dannette shrugged but let the tease bathe the still-wounded areas of her heart. Friends. Although she hadn't known David long, at least he was authentic. He made coffee or chai and didn't pretend to be anything but what he was— Mocha Man.

Unlike someone else she knew . . . or didn't know, come to think of it.

She paid David, took the chai over to a corner, and picked up the local *Moose Bend Journal*. The front-page article of the weekly covered the latest road improvements and rules for the fishing season. She had no doubt that this week's issue would be a blow-by-blow account of the search for June Hanson, complete with pictures and astute analysis of the K-9 handler with the big mouth. She wanted to set the paper down in disgust, but a sudden urge to confirm Nancy's words about Will's profession—or maybe the errant hope that Nancy had been mistaken—made her thumb through the ten-page paper.

Her heart fell slightly when she found Will Masterson covering the police beat on the third page.

She folded the paper, turned, and stared out into the sunshine. Java Moose looked out over an inlet of Lake Superior. Morning light gilded the ripples of the water, and a slight breeze tousled wispy clouds in an otherwise clear sky.

She knew it would be a glorious day when she'd caught the

rose-and-gold sunrise around 5 a.m. Restless, she'd risen early, taken Missy out for a stroll, then returned, showered, and listened to the morning news report before facing the events of last night. She spent the morning at her laptop, rehashing the search, outlining in detail the reactions of her K-9 and decisions she had made. More than a few times her reports had been used to fortify SAR operational defense or occasionally as evidence in a homicide case. She never enjoyed testifying, and writing a thorough report whittled down that possibility.

She sipped her chai, letting it fortify her for her next stop—the sheriff's department. She hoped to print her report, file it, and escape without a verbal tar and feathering from Fadden.

And without seeing Will.

She heard the shop bell jangle and turned to look at the patron.

Speak of the devil. Her heart actually jammed in her throat for a full ten seconds as she watched Will Masterson stride across the floor. He looked particularly rumpled this morning. Although dressed respectably in blue jeans and a brown corduroy shirt under his leather jacket, he had the strung-out look of a guy going on no sleep. Lines around his eyes, a take-no-prisoners step to his demeanor. If she didn't know better, she'd recognize her friend Jim Micah in his bearing. A soldier.

Except Will Masterson was no soldier. Unless she counted the assault on her heart, one that left her feeling more wounded than it should have.

While he was ordering at the counter, she rushed out of the coffee shop before he could stop her and inflict round two.

The sheriff's office was located at the top of the hill, overlooking Moose Bend. *The king overseeing his kingdom,* Dannette thought as she parked near the door.

The office hummed with activity. Dannette strode through the lobby, nodded to the receptionist, who buzzed her into the back. She didn't slow as she passed Fadden's office but felt a gust of relief when she noted it was empty.

Or that could mean Fadden was prowling the building, looking for prey.

She cut into the office workroom and pulled out her laptop from her backpack. Connecting the laser printer to her USB port, she found the printer in her settings and sent it to print.

She dug her cell phone out of her pocket as she waited and speed-dialed Sarah's number.

The phone rang over to voice mail. "Sarah, it's Dannette. Just wondering when you're planning on getting here. I know we're not due to leave until Friday, but—" she swallowed— "anytime is good for me. Kelly's mom has a few unused rooms, and I'll book you one or you can stay with me." She sighed. "Okay, looking forward to seeing you."

She clicked off, feeling slightly hollow. She had hoped that Sarah would already be here. She'd missed the paramedic's honest friendship over the past six months. If Dannette was honest with herself, she'd label the feeling loneliness. She missed the comradery of her friends—Sarah, Andee, and two former Green Berets, Jim Micah and Conner Young—who shared her love of the outdoors and her drive to care for her fellow man. Although she felt comfortable hovering on the fringes of conversation, simply being with people who cared whether she answered the telephone and knew when to pray for her soothed the losses in her life. Thankfully, she had Missy and Sherlock to fill some of the raw places.

Dannette tapped the telephone against her leg as she watched the report print out. She speed-dialed the next number.

Andee picked up after two rings. "Dannette! How are you?"

"Good. Just came in from a search last night. We were successful, and I think Kelly's dog is ready for certification."

"That's great. Lacey and I were just talking about you, wondering how the training was going. By the way, you're only using Missy, right? Where did you board Sherlock?"

Dannette could picture Andee on the other end, her short curly black hair captured in a bandanna, flight suit bagging over her petite body. Although a sky jockey, Andee's first love was mountaineering, a skill she practiced with excellence in Alaska during the summer months.

Andee had roomed with Dannette for a year at the University of Iowa. Although Andee had eventually transferred schools, their friendship—constructed on a foundation of outdoor sports and a desire to walk with Christ—had only strengthened over time. Despite Andee's challenging upbringing, she had a quiet faith that ministered to the dark places in Dannette's heart. It was because of Andee and her commitment to her dreams and faith in God's plans that Dannette had scraped up the courage to begin work as an SAR K-9 handler. Also because of Andee, Dannette had met Sarah and then the rest of the SAR team that Sarah had dubbed Team Hope.

"Yeah, it's just me and Missy for this trip. Sherlock is staying with my father," Dannette replied, thinking of her bloodhound. "He likes my dad's kids and doesn't get much playtime with me when I'm training with Missy." She pulled page one of her report out of the printer, noticed a typo, and grimaced. "Hey, have you heard from Sarah?"

"Isn't she up there yet?"

"No. I called her cell phone."

Andee laughed. "She's got it on voice mail, doesn't she?"

Dannette frowned as she tucked the phone into her shoulder. "Yeah, why?"

"She was just here—"

"Where are you?"

"Well, at the moment, I'm driving out of Lacey's driveway, but Sarah and I spent the weekend working on Lacey's wedding preparations. And Hank sorta . . . hung out with Conner and Micah."

Dannette chose to ignore the stab in her heart at being left out of their lives again. "Hank still has a thing for her?"

Six months ago, while Team Hope had been searching for Lacey's lost daughter in the forests of Missouri, Park Ranger Hank Billings had caught Sarah in a tender moment, and for some reason it had ignited his interest. Dannette had to admit that there was something endearing about the six-foot-something good old boy from the hills with a twang in his voice and warm brown eyes. And the fact that he'd broken a few rules helping them locate not only the lost child but then Jim Micah, had won him a place of friendship in their tightly knit clan.

"Hank gave her yellow roses and a CD of hymns."

Dannette smiled. "Sarah needs to loosen up, let the guy in a little."

Andee stayed silent as Dannette's words hung between them. Trusting a guy after what Sarah had endured six years ago . . . well, Hank had a lot of territory to make up for.

"When did she take off?" Dannette asked, neatly changing the subject.

"Yesterday, early. I'd expect her anytime."

"Thanks, Andee. You'll be up by Friday?" Dannette pulled out page two and stapled the pages together.

"For sure. I wouldn't miss it. Be safe."

Dannette heard the smile in Andee's voice, and it ministered to that lonely place inside her. She clicked off, tucked the phone in her pocket, packed up the laptop, and headed toward the lobby. She stopped in Fadden's office and dropped the report on his desk, again relieved that he wasn't holding court.

She was entering the lobby when an elderly couple breezed into the office. Dressed in jeans, white tennis shoes, and down jackets, they looked like RVers—retirees who spent their spry years tooling around the country in a thirty-foot home on wheels. She glanced out the plate-glass window and spied their rig in the corner of the parking lot.

"We want to report a . . . lost child."

Dannette's ears pricked up and she halted by the door. Those two words strung together in a sentence still had the power to stop her cold in her tracks.

The woman leaned on the counter, trying to attract the receptionist's attention. "Please, I think there is a girl lost in the forest."

The receptionist/dispatcher looked up from her desk. Mary wore the brown uniform of the local law-enforcement crew, and it did nothing to soften her pushing-fifty curves. "Do you wish to file a report?"

The man stepped up behind his wife. "We want you to do something about it."

"Can I help you?" The words flew out of Dannette's mouth nearly of their own accord.

The couple turned toward Dannette.

The woman's appearance tugged at a soft place in Dannette. Pudgy, wrinkled face, white hair, gentle worried eyes. "We were in the rest area about twenty miles north of here and saw a girl, maybe fifteen, sitting at a picnic table. She seemed . . . lost. We just wanted to ask where her parents were, but when we made to approach her, she backed away from us.

She had a backpack, but she wasn't dressed for hiking. She wore tennis shoes and jeans and a light jacket and looked dirty, like she'd spent the night in the forest. We offered her breakfast, and for a second we thought she was going to accept. Then a truck pulled up, and she ran. We called to her, but she kept running, as if someone was chasing her." Her voice quavered. "I think she was afraid of someone."

The man clamped his hand on his wife's shoulder. "Two men got out of the pickup, and when they came down to the picnic area, they asked if we'd seen a young girl." His face reddened, and his Adam's apple bobbed in his throat. "We lied."

His wife touched his hand, glanced up at Dannette. "Will you go look for her? I think she must be in trouble."

Dannette felt herself nodding even as she saw Fadden in her peripheral vision. *Oh, super timing.*

He marched up to the group, wearing a forced smile. "Can I ask you two to fill out a report?" he said to the couple. "Miss Lundeen, a word?"

Dannette followed him, anger boiling in her chest. A quick look at the rest area didn't mean a full call-out, manpower that costs hours. Just she and Missy, sniffing out some clues. "What?"

Fadden shook his head. "If she was a runaway, her parents would have called."

"Unless they don't want our help. Doesn't that sound in the least bit fishy to you?"

Fadden glanced at the couple, gave them a wide smile, nodded. "Don't get my department involved in something we're not prepared to follow through on."

"A missing child?" Dannette couldn't help her tone. "Or do you have to be related to the mayor to get any help around here?"

Fadden narrowed his eyes, then sighed and strode away, leaving Dannette frowning after him.

"Don't mind him, honey," Mary said to Dannette. "He's . . . well, there're forces at work here you don't know anything about. It has nothing to do with you." She handed the form to the elderly couple. "Please fill this out."

Mary pulled Dannette toward her desk, lowered her voice. "The thing is, Moose Bend had an incident about seven years back. Three lost hikers. Kids, really, out for the weekend in early spring. Storm came in, and their parents got worried. After three days, the state sent in dogs. Got everyone worked up. Filled 'em with hope."

Dannette's chest tightened. How many times had she heard the same story? She could finish it for her but waited for Mary's next words.

"The dogs couldn't find them, and a month later a hiker came across their bodies. Hypothermia." She looked at the elderly couple in the reception area. "The sheriff's nephew was one of those lost. There's still hurt there. Some in the community don't think we should be spending time on dogs when we need equipment and more manpower instead."

Dannette looked away from her. Mary had just voiced the reason why K-9 search and rescue was still mostly a volunteer activity with little monetary compensation.

Well, Dannette worked for other compensation.

"We all appreciate your hard work," Mary continued. "Especially that you helped find Mrs. Hanson. But Fadden's right. We don't have the funds to outfit or tend a K-9 unit. And we especially don't have funds to go traipsing after the flimsy report of a couple of vacationers. This girl probably had a fight with her boyfriend. Kids hang out at the rest area all the time—sometimes overnight."

She gave Dannette a steady look. "If Fadden thought there was any truth to it, he'd send a cruiser out. I promise. He's a good man, caught between two forces."

Dannette let those words hang between them for a moment. Obviously, despite Mary's tell-all posture, she was one of those who didn't support Dannette's K-9 work. Dannette shot a look at Fadden's closed door. "Did he get any sleep last night?"

Mary gave a hint of a smile. "A couple hours. His wife brought him breakfast."

"Listen, I'm going to go out and do a hasty search. See what I can dig up."

Mary shrugged. "It's your hide. But if Fadden finds out, we didn't have this conversation. And, just between you and me, I don't feel good about this. They don't know for sure that group up in Silver Creek killed that fella. And I'm not feeding into any rumors, but there could be someone out there living in the woods, warped and very dangerous. It's happened before, and I'd hate to have you stumble into trouble. Or get hurt."

"I'll be careful."

"You'd better be. Because after we rescue you, Fadden will personally pack your bags and make sure you're safely on the other side of the border. It won't be pretty."

Dannette nodded, not liking the visual picture Mary's words conjured up.

Mary's expression softened. "Make sure you get yourself a slice of banana bread on your way out."

Dannette headed out to her truck. She had too many nightmares not to follow the cry of a lost child, regardless of what it cost her.

Chapter 6

WILL'S REPORTER/AGENT instincts ignited as he sat in the sheriff's office parking lot and watched Miss Dannette I-Hate-Reporters Lundeen stride to her pickup.

He'd hate to get between her and her next mission. She wore the look of a special-ops soldier—her eyes hard, even angry, as she slammed her door and peeled out of the lot. Still, mad and determined was a whole lot better than wounded and gun-shy. He'd relived the betrayed expression on her face one too many times while he scouted through the forest after the runaway Hayata operative. A search that had not only been fruitless but had nearly gotten him caught—twice.

By the time dawn fractured the night sky, he'd headed home, frustrated. He'd taken a hot shower, wiped off the war paint, and grabbed three hours of shut-eye before Jeff Anderson, his handler, called him from HQ.

He had the phone to his ear before he even knew he was awake. "Hello?"

"We unraveled Simon's message," came Jeff's calm voice. "It's a code word."

"A password?" Will's voice had betrayed his lack of sleep.

"No, an identifier. We think the package General Nazar is

sending is . . . his daughter. Sources listed her on a flight from Kazakhstan to Canada two days ago. She might be in America by now."

Will had winced, feeling punched right in the center of his gut. Nazar's *daughter*. "Amina is the name by which she was supposed to identify herself to Simon," he guessed.

"Right," Jeff said. "It goes without saying that if Simon was compromised, you and she may have been also. If we don't find her—and soon—they will kill her. Maybe they already have."

Will sat up, rubbed his eyes with a finger and thumb. The sunlight streamed through the milky curtains onto the wooden planked floor of his cabin. "No, I think she's alive. Or was as of last night."

"What are you talking about?"

Will swallowed, pretty sure that any way he phrased his next words they would incriminate him. "I went up for a sneak and peek around the property. I saw a young girl steal out of the compound."

Jeff was silent.

Will cringed. *Yes, I disobeyed orders.* But he hadn't spent the last year pecking out words on his computer and hanging around the local police station to let Homeland Security's best shot at destroying the Hayata cells and thwarting another devastating attack on American soil sift through his fingers.

"Then I'm not sure if this is good or bad news. General Nazar said that he wasn't leaving until the package was safe. Which means, I guess, until his daughter is in custody and hidden out of Hayata's reach. He said that the package would inform us how to contact him."

General Nazar. The big dog in the Hayata fortress. A big dog with juicy secrets. And his daughter was running for her life in the wilds of northern Minnesota. She held the key not only to her father's defection but thereby to the list of terrorist clients stationed around the world.

A list the U.S. and a few other in-the-loop countries needed their hands on. Rumors had popped the Homeland alert status to yellow, and if HS didn't wrestle out precious confirmation fast . . . well, Will wasn't about to dig through rubble again, dreading to find more familiar faces.

"Will," Jeff said quietly, "Nazar also told us that he knows the date and place of Hayata's next attack, but his offer has an expiration date."

Why? Because either Nazar or *America* wouldn't be around if they didn't get him in time? Will's chest tightened, feeling the possibilities. "I'll find her, sir."

"You do that. And stay in touch. We're sending another agent up your way, so we'll need you to check in every twelve hours or so."

"Roger that." Will had clicked off the line, wide awake, regrets souring his thoughts. He jumped in the shower again, not quite sure where to start hunting, and after a quick stop at the Java Moose, headed straight to the sheriff's office.

It couldn't be mere coincidence that the one person who might find a lost child in a million-acre woods just walked out of the building.

He shot a glance heavenward and started his truck, pulling out after Dani, far enough behind to be dismissed but close enough to keep her in his sights.

She headed up Highway 66 toward the Canadian border, driving the speed limit like a good little search-and-rescue citizen. Cutting north into a rest area, she drove back a quarter mile to a wilderness nook with outdoor biffies and picnic tables.

He stopped just outside the area, watching her but careful

to keep his distance so Missy wouldn't pick up his scent. The last thing he needed was Dani spotting him and thinking he might be after a hot lead. Or worse, a stalker. He wondered if she carried a tranquilizer gun in that supply box in her pickup bed.

She pulled on her jacket and added an orange vest with a white cross that identified her as rescue personnel. Opening Missy's box, she freed the dog, who trotted around, stretching. Will couldn't help but appreciate the way Dani watered her partner before she dressed Missy in her own orange vest and her trailing harness. He imagined her voice, soft and sweet, as she rubbed behind the dog's ears. Too easily he remembered her smile, the way she'd called him Cowboy. He tightened his hands on the steering wheel in an attempt to focus on the essentials.

Just because God had brought her back to his horizon didn't mean he could let his daydreams take hold again. So she had a cute smattering of freckles, beautiful eyes, and an authentic smile. Her last memory of him included his wry admission of guilt.

A guy in his shoes didn't have time to figure out what mysteries prompted her cutting exit from the café. Still, he couldn't deny the desire for a second chance someday when this mission was over, and he could introduce himself simply as Will Masterson, national soldier or just a cowboy from South Dakota and add a lazy Western smile. Maybe she'd smile back, like she had before, and he could take her out for a steak, perhaps spin her a few back-home stories of life on the prairie. . . .

Okay, he was definitely not operating with all synapses firing. Even if they did get past the ugly ending of last night's nondate, Will's lifestyle didn't lend itself to investing in a relationship.

Unless, of course, it was just a friendship. Slow. Comfortable. Nothing that might get him into trouble. Then maybe . . .

It felt like years since this feeling of hope had welled in his chest.

Will watched Dani walk with Missy down to a scenic overlook, where a scattering of picnic tables sat. Will climbed out of his pickup and followed her, thankful he was downwind. She didn't unhook Missy's lead but walked slowly along the perimeter of the picnic area. Missy's snout raised windward, and Dani watched the dog. Will had often wondered about the symbiotic relationship between dog and handler. He'd read that while a dog had over one hundred million olfactory receptor cells versus a human's paltry five million, it couldn't talk. So it took a handler with astute understanding to reason out the clues from her K-9's behavior.

Will stole closer when Dani and Missy disappeared on the northern edge of the rest area. He hid behind a trio of birch trees and peered out, wondering if his thundering heartbeat could be heard by Missy's floppy ears.

Was Dani looking for Amina? Yes, they were technically only a couple of miles from the farm, as the crow flew, but she could be out training Missy or looking for someone else.

Yeah, there was a regular epidemic of lost kids in the woods. No, his gut told him that Dani was on the hunt for his missing package. At least he'd have a jumping-off spot when he returned and resumed his search.

Missy barked and bounded from the forest.

Will felt a rush of fear. He shook his head in self-disgust. He'd been on so many clandestine trails, he should be used to feeling naked and vulnerable, accustomed to the possibility of discovery.

Only, for some reason, he couldn't bear the thought of cementing all Dannette's presuppositions about him: the local predator.

More barks, and suddenly Missy appeared, running full tilt after a soaring Frisbee. She jumped, her body contorted, and caught it.

Will froze, feeling sick.

Missy looked in his direction, her ears pricked. Then, tail wagging, she sprinted over.

Will cringed but dropped to his knees and accepted her welcome. "Hey there, girl. You know, in about ten seconds I'm dead meat."

"Sooner than that."

He closed his eyes, winced. "Hi."

"What are you doing here?" Dani's voice held no warmth.

He looked at her, gave Missy a final pat, then rose.

Dani had her hood pushed back, the wind raking her cropped hair, her gaze dark and hot with suspicion. "Are you still digging for information on your murder suspect?" She narrowed her eyes. "I'm sure Fadden would be more than happy to let you quiz him. I've already been interrogated."

He held his hands up in surrender. "Whoa, okay, so I know I didn't score any points last night, but I'm not the embodiment of evil here."

"Who says?" She patted her leg. Missy trotted over and sat, dropping the Frisbee.

He glanced past her into the fold of forest where Dannette had disappeared. "What's the Frisbee for?"

She picked up the Frisbee, tapped it against her leg. "It's a reward."

"For finding something?"

She shook her head, sighed. "Can't you leave well enough alone?"

He looked at her and saw a flash of pain behind her expression. For a second it swept any response right out of him.

Pain, as if his presence actually dredged up an ancient agony. He felt like a jerk when he forced the next words out. "By any chance are you hunting for a teenage girl?"

He could have knocked her over with a seagull feather. She paled, glanced behind her, back at him. "What?"

"A teenage girl, lost in the woods. That's why you're here, right?"

She took a step back. "How did you know that? Fadden didn't do a call-out—"

"I . . . have my sources." Wow, it hurt to say that. For the first time in about three years, his chest actually spasmed as he dodged her question. He stepped toward her. "Did you find anything?"

She narrowed one eye. "Maybe." Then she turned and strode back toward her pickup.

Missy followed her, looking back twice at Will.

Will opened his mouth. Maybe? "Hey, Dani, wait!"

She shot him a dark look over her shoulder. "It's Dannette, thanks. And I'm not waiting."

He caught up, despite the fact that she'd quickened her pace. "I want to help."

"Yeah, sure you do." She reached her truck, opened a supply box on the bed, and pulled out a Ziploc bag. She didn't look at him as she shoved a piece of light blue fabric into the bag.

"That's a part of her coat, isn't it?"

She glanced at him, her brow furrowed. "Go away. Please. No one needs your kind of help." She tucked the bag into her pocket, opened the kennel for Missy. She hopped in.

"What do you have against reporters?" He shoved his hands into his pockets. "Can't a guy just want to help out?"

She closed Missy's door. "Yeah, right." She gave a burst of disgust. "You'll have her grieving family on the cover of one issue and the next be blaming them for her disappearance." She shook her head as she headed for her driver's door. "Good-bye, Mr. Masterson."

What was *that* about? Only he didn't have time to unlock her meaning. If Hayata didn't already know Amina had escaped, they would soon. He suddenly heard the sounds of screaming, explosions. Saw friends, soldiers . . .

"Listen, I'm on your side here."

Dannette reached for the door, but he braced his hand against it, feeling panicked and not a little angry. Excuse me, but did he have *National Enquirer* tattooed on his forehead? Not every reporter hoped to unearth the dirt that destroyed reputations, soured lives.

And why was he even bothering to defend his nonprofession?

She froze, stared at his hand like it might be a bomb. "Get out of my way."

What was it about her that churned up his desire to see respect in her eyes? In fact, she might be the first woman who didn't respect him. Or at least admire him.

That was probably a good thing.

Still, he could strangle her with his frustration. "Why don't you go ahead and string me up from that white pine over there? I mean, after all, I've committed a couple of capital crimes here— taking you out for dinner and wanting you to think I am a nice guy. In fact, I pretty much deserve to be shot at high noon."

She stared at him, wide-eyed. She had very pretty eyes.

"I don't know what you have against journalists," he said, aware that he'd probably put too much regret into his previous words. "I'm only out to make a living, just like anyone else."

"No, not like anyone else," she snapped.

He opened his mouth to retort, but words clogged in his

throat when he saw her eyes glisten. *Way to go, Will, make her cry.*

"Other people live to help people," she said, voice trembling, "not destroy them. Other people don't dig around in a person's life, hoping to find enough dirt to eviscerate them. Other people think about the consequences of their words."

He felt sick. *Eviscerate?* So much for wanting to make friends. Not only had he offended her but he was smart enough to figure out that he'd somehow treaded over all sorts of buried wounds.

She turned away, as if embarrassed, and for a second he had the urge to wrap an arm around her. To hold her close, run his hand through that unkempt hair, and tell her that he was sorry. He'd make it better.

Yeah, right. He was a pro at making things better.

He backed away from her, feeling brittle and not a little like the town bully. "I'm . . . sorry, Dani. I didn't mean to—"

She turned back and stared at him, wariness in her eyes. "I'm not telling you anything, Will. I'd rather . . . have my tongue nailed to a table with a fork. Just . . . go away." Her hand shook as she reached for her door.

He couldn't help it. Something about the hurt in her voice made him touch her arm.

She jumped, yanking it away as if she'd been burned. She held her arm, eyeing him with fear.

"I'm really sorry," he said quietly, and slightly rattled. "I'm not trying to hurt you here. But I have to know what you found."

Confusion filled her eyes. Then, slowly she edged back, shoved her hands in her coat pockets. She lifted her chin. "I might look like easy prey, but believe me, I know how to defend myself." But fear had pinched her voice high and thin, and she looked about two seconds from snapping.

Defend herself? What kind of scumbag did she think he was? How exactly did this morph from a little look-see at her morning fun into an encounter that she might term as an assault? He backed away and purposely added kindness to his voice. "That's not what I meant."

She glared at him.

He shook his head. "I promise, hurting you is the furthest—I just . . . need to know—"

She lunged at him, swinging a Maglite she'd hauled out of the pocket of her oversized jacket. It clipped him across the temple. Okay, she wasn't kidding about being able to defend herself. His head rung. He fell to one knee, reached out to her. "Don't—"

But she dived for the door. "Stay. Away. From. Me!" She slammed the door, locked it before turning the engine on, and popped the truck into drive. As he blinked back little black splotches, she floored it.

Ten feet away she stopped, cracked her window. "If you come near me again, Mr. Masterson, I'll introduce you to the German shepherd side of my dog."

Her tires squealed as she peeled out of the rest area.

Will rubbed his head, feeling a bump. So much for trying to get on her short list of friends. He returned to his truck, picking up Missy's Frisbee along the way. At least he knew where to start looking for Amina.

He glanced at the sky, remembered the pain prowling Dani's—Dannette's—eyes. *Okay, God, I know I'm not so good at being Your man, but I really, really blew it this time.* He shook his head, hardly believing he'd somehow turned into a terrorist in Dannette's eyes. *Please forgive me for scaring her, even though You know that wasn't my intent.* He could probably forget starting over with her.

He turned, stared into the woods. *And if Amina is out there, I'd sure appreciate Your help in finding her.*

✦ ✦ ✦

Dannette eased off the gas, pretty sure that she had broken a few speed records barreling down the road. A gal who made her living as a search-and-rescue operative might do well to remember she had a very valuable K-9 in the back of the pickup. She slowed the truck and even pulled over to the curb, feeling as if her heart were already back in Moose Bend, packing her things and heading south.

Putting miles between herself and Will Masterson's questions.

Jerk.

She held the steering wheel and touched her forehead to it. It felt cool against her sweaty brow. *"I don't know what you have against journalists—"*

She didn't even know where to begin in responding to that statement. Emotions, more than memories, flashed through her mind as she stared at him. Dismay, betrayal. How about raw fury? or grief?

Will Masterson might think he was out to make a living, but he did it at the expense of others' lives. Happy lives.

Dannette forced back the taste of sorrow and eased out onto the road. Focus. And not on Will's hand on her arm or the color of concern in his eyes. Yes, unfortunately, she'd noticed his eyes. Brown flecks ringed with dark blue, and boy, did they pack a punch up close and sorry. She had nearly fallen for the apology in them, nearly wanted to risk trusting him. Thankfully memory broke through the fog like a bullhorn and shook free her common sense.

If he came near her again, she'd wallop him with more than her Maglite. Her threat echoed in the back of her head, and the barest smile touched her mouth. Yeah, Missy was about as vicious as a lop-eared rabbit. Still, she hoped her warning resonated. Never would be too soon to see Will Masterson again.

Even if he did look like a modern-day Joe Cartwright off the set of *Bonanza*, wanting to help her solve her problems.

Which, at the moment, included one very lost girl. At least, the hunch that the girl was still out there felt right as it sat in the pit of her stomach. She'd found a scrap of fabric tangled in the brush, and Missy had alerted to the scent. Tired and hungry, the girl couldn't have gone far, even if she was on the run.

Dannette hoped to talk Sheriff Fadden into at least using Kelly's dog and doing a semi-call-out. Besides, Kirby needed the practice.

Pulling up to the sheriff's office, Dannette got out and noted that the RV and company hadn't stuck around. She appreciated the fact that they'd taken the time to even stop in and report the girl, however.

Of all the rotten luck, Fadden stood in the reception area, as if waiting her return. He looked up from where he was reading over Mary's shoulder and took a long sip of coffee before addressing Dannette. "Well?"

Dannette gathered her composure as she pulled out the bag of fabric. This didn't have to be ugly. She'd been around enough SAR skeptics to understand that change didn't happen with one success. Or ten. K-9 SAR wasn't a science. It involved animals who could be cranky, tired, or even hungry and afraid. It involved people who could read signals incorrectly and misjudge terrain and behavior. But if this girl had been gulped by the endless north woods, Dannette and Missy might be her only decent chance of finding a warm bed and grub in the near future.

"I found a piece of fabric." Dannette laid the scrap on the counter. She felt Mary's gaze on her, as if waving her away. She ignored it. "And Missy alerted to human scent. I think the girl's out there."

Fadden pursed his lips, looked at his coffee, then back at Dannette. "Well, as it so happens, we found her."

Dannette stared, wide-eyed, her heart thumping. "Really?"

He nodded, strolled toward her, victory on his face. "Yeah. Someone called in shortly after you left, said they'd lost a young girl, but that they'd found her." He set the coffee cup down on the counter. "Case closed."

"Yeah." Dannette fingered the bag of fabric. "Did you get their name and number? I'd just like to follow up."

Fadden rolled his eyes. "Just can't leave well enough alone, can you?"

She wanted to wince at his jaded comment. But she'd been in SAR long enough to know that it was *not* letting well enough alone that saved lives. She forced an innocent smile. "I guess not. Do you have the number?"

Fadden turned, picked up a report on Mary's desk, read the number off.

Dannette pulled a pen out of her jacket and wrote it on her hand. "Thanks. Can you buzz me in?"

He didn't even try to hide his scowl as he let her into the offices.

She strode down the hall to the coffee room and dialed out.

Fadden was probably right. She was letting her SAR sixth sense push her into people's lives.

Except a disconnect tone played in her ear, along with a computerized voice that informed her that the number was out of service. She checked the number, dialed again.

"I think she was afraid," said the old woman again in her head.

Dannette hung up the phone, feeling shaky. She returned to the reception area. "Mary, what was that number again?"

Mary handed Dannette the report, and as she read it her chest tightened. "I think this girl is in trouble," she said softly.

When Mary raised her gaze, Dannette saw concern in her expression. Whether for Dannette or the lost girl, Dannette didn't know. "I'll bet that if Sheriff Fadden sends a cruiser to this address, they'll find an empty field," Dannette said as she handed Mary the report. "And the phone number is a dead end."

Mary studied the report as Dannette beelined to Fadden's office. He was on the phone, leaning back in his chair, laughing. His smile dimmed when she knocked on the open door. He covered the phone receiver with his hand. "What?"

Dannette hesitated only a moment. "It's a decoy. This girl is out there, and she's in trouble. The phone number is bogus, and I'll lay odds the address is also. Was it a man or a woman on the telephone who filed the report?"

One dark eyebrow angled down. "I'll call you back," Fadden said into the telephone and hung up. He buzzed Mary. "Do you remember the gender of the person who filed the missing person's report?"

"Male."

"Two men pulled up and she ran." "I'm not feeling good about this, Sheriff," Dannette said.

Fadden wore his default exasperated expression. "When do you feel good about anything, Miss Lundeen? Isn't that your modus operandi—jump to conclusions?"

He left the other half of his accusation dangling . . . conclusions that could cost the sheriff's department hard-earned cash.

She tried to ignore his jab. "I just think that we should take this seriously."

"Listen, they gave her description. It matches the description from the couple who filed the report. And they said they found her." He held out his hands as if in surrender. "She's not missing."

"Doesn't it bother you in the least that we can't confirm this?"

He shook his head, dismissal in his eyes. "I think we're done here."

"No!" Dannette winced at the panic in her voice. "Just let me call in Kelly."

Fadden's dark eyes fired, and for a moment she thought she actually saw his skin ripple. She stiffened as he angled his head slightly and drilled her with a look that she could have felt in Kentucky.

"You might want to keep in mind, Miss Lundeen," he said, keeping his voice low, "that you are here by invitation. *My* invitation. And since you've arrived, you've managed to dig a tidy hole in my SAR budget—"

"But we needed the scents, the dummies—"

He held up his hand. "Drop this before we drop you. You are not to go digging around and igniting panic. This is a small town, with small-town resources." He stood and his rolling chair slammed against the wall.

Dannette tried not to flinch.

"We not only have no proof. *On the contrary*, she's been found. You go out there, Lundeen, and I guarantee you that I'll be on the telephone to ARDA, making sure you never work again."

She felt her lips move, but no sound came out. Not a snort. Not a nod. Nothing. She felt as if he'd taken her insides and reeled them out, inch by inch.

Mary didn't even look up from her computer as Dannette shuffled out into the sunshine, but Dannette saw her shake her head.

She didn't care. Dannette hadn't been in SAR for ten years to ignore the niggling in her gut. That girl *was* in danger.

But so were hundreds of children every summer, and if she dumped her credentials for this . . . ghost victim, well, maybe real victims would die.

Real victims like Ashley.

And this *was* about Ashley. Dannette's entire life, for that matter, had been about Ashley.

Only . . . what would she do if that girl was out there . . . and she did nothing . . . and she died?

Dannette strode out to her truck and paused. Decades-old emotions churned in her chest as she sighed, looked skyward. *God, You know where this girl is. Please, please give me wisdom.*

The sun was high and had dried the puddles from yesterday morning's storm. Dannette blinked as tears filled her eyes. It was times like this, when life felt fragile, that fear seemed to engulf her. It took on breath, filled her soul, and it was only by gazing heavenward that she disentangled herself from its grasp. God was out there, watching, and as long as she told herself that, memories stayed in their dark corners.

But if this girl showed up in a month as ghastly headline news, those memories might start creeping out into the light of day.

Don't forget this girl, Lord. Keep her safe until I find her.

Chapter 7

DANNETTE SPREAD THE topographical map over the hood of her pickup, trying to delete Sheriff Fadden's words from her mind. She seemed to be making friends all over town today, what with her right hook to the resident gossipmonger and her outright in-your-face disobedience to the local law. Good thing Missy still liked her.

The dog scampered around the rest area, playing with a tennis ball. Dannette knew Missy needed playtime before a search, something to separate her from the tension. Even during a search, Dannette brought along a toy, plenty of water, some treats. A dog, like a human, had to decompress from the stress and needed to feel rewarded, despite successes and failures.

A slight wind ruffled Dannette's hair, carrying with it the hint of river water, the fresh scent of pine. The sun had begun to slide toward the west end of the day, and shadows reached across the parking lot for her pickup. Even in her layered clothing, Dannette shivered, and she made a mental note to add her down vest to her pack, along with her space blanket, radio, and water supply. Starting a search this late in the day might be the worst possible time, but she didn't expect to go far and would hike out before darkness trapped her in the bramble of the northern forest.

She wished Kelly were here. A thousand voices of reason resonated in her skull, the loudest telling her that going into the woods alone broke every SAR rule she tried to uphold. She could get lost, hurt, disoriented; and if she found the girl, and the victim was wounded, Dannette would have to carry her out herself . . . or return for help and pray she found her again.

No, a smart K-9 handler, one with years of SAR experience under her belt, would call in reinforcements . . . like . . . whom? She scanned through her list of available resources. Nil. Kelly was out of town, working her EMT shift in Duluth and wasn't due back for three days. And, well . . . beyond that she had no one left on her list of rescuers aching to face Fadden's firing squad.

Dannette smoothed out the map, drew a line to box in the search territory. She'd work in quadrants for now, charting Missy's responses, and tomorrow when the sun came out, she'd know how to proceed for a free search.

Unless, of course, there was no one out there, and she was on a wild-goose chase.

Probably better not to let that thought sink too deep.

She whistled for Missy, who bounded over. Dannette crouched, rubbed Missy's muzzle. The dog sniffed her chin as Dannette scratched behind her ears. Her golden brown eyes seemed to search Dannette's, as if asking if this was wise.

"What should I do here, Miss? I can't just leave her out there." She wrapped her arms around the animal and held her close, smelling the forest in her fur. She felt Missy's heartbeat in her ears as she contemplated her actions. If she did nothing, the girl could die. At worst, the girl was safe and Dannette would spend hours beating the forest for nothing.

Fadden didn't have to know how she spent her time off, right?

At any rate, bushwhacking through a shadowy forest, underneath towering pines and paperwhite birches, was better than sitting in her dark motel room, channel surfing and wondering if Will Masterson was slurping down hot coffee or eating chili at Nancy's.

Now where did that thought come from? She stood up and shook away Will's amazingly stunned, even hurt, expression when she'd broadsided him with the flashlight. Folding the map, she pocketed it. Just because she'd met a man who had gotten under her skin with his intriguingly pretty eyes didn't mean she was spending the next five hours parting bushes and ducking tree branches in an effort to exorcise him from her mind.

No, this was about a lost girl.

About a pledge made years ago.

This was about Ashley.

Dannette pulled on her orange SAR vest, grabbed her water bottle, her compass, a flashlight, and her supply pack. As she was clipping on Missy's vest and tracking collar, her cell phone trilled. She answered it, turning to catch a decent signal.

"Dannette?" Sarah's voice came through crackly. "Where are you?"

"Where are you?" Dannette heard the immediate cheer in her voice.

"I'm at your motel. But you're not."

"You're here? When did you get in?"

"About an hour ago. Where are *you*?"

Dannette poured water for Missy. "I'm sniffing around for a lost girl at a rest area out of town." Even to her ears, it sounded stupid. She should listen to reason, pack up, and head into town for a pizza.

"A lost girl?" Sarah's voice sounded pinched. "How old?"

Dannette kicked herself. Sarah's scars had nothing to do with this lost girl, but the mere mention of a woman in trouble was enough to ignite Sarah's protective impulses.

"I don't know. Teenager maybe."

"Was there a call-out?"

Dannette cringed. "No. Just a hunch."

Sarah was silent, and Dannette heard a car door slam. "Okay, tell me how to get there."

"What? No, I'll only be a little while. You've had a long drive. I got you a room—check in at the front desk and I'll see you in the morning." Dannette heard the car engine rev.

"Sorry, Dan, but I'm coming your way. I didn't drive eighteen hours to hang out in my motel room. Besides, we were going to go camping anyway; this will jump-start our trip."

"Really, Sarah, I'm just taking a look around."

"Tell me this—are you alone?"

"I . . . ah . . ."

"Then you wouldn't even be out there if you didn't believe she was in trouble."

Dannette couldn't help but smile.

"Brief me when I get there."

"And I want to hear all about Hank Billings." As if she were sitting beside Sarah, Dannette could see her redden, her blush a sharp contrast to her blonde hair, which was probably tied back in a ponytail. Maybe she wore a baseball cap, for sure little makeup, and probably a blue NYU sweatshirt and jeans. She'd have her jaw clenched and be staring at the road as if she hadn't heard Dannette's comment.

Dannette laughed. "Listen, I already talked to Andee. I know you saw him . . . or rather he saw you. All I'm saying is, I want details from your perspective."

"There isn't anything from *my perspective*. He was there. He hung out with Conner and Micah."

"He gave you flowers? and a CD?"

Sarah groaned. "What didn't Andee tell you?"

"She didn't tell me if you smiled when you got them. If you think he's at all a remote possibility. She didn't tell me if you like him back."

"I don't. He's . . . infuriating."

Okay, that description hit a little too close to home. *Will Masterson* was infuriating. He knew how to tangle a girl's mind and make her wish she had turned around and run for the hills. The way he hooked his thumbs into his belt loops and stood there roping her thoughts, screaming arrogance with his cowboy swagger and lazy smile, made her wish she'd given him another good wallop with her flashlight. Hank Billings, however, was . . . sweet. With a slow smile and a Texas drawl and tease in his voice. Sarah just didn't have eyes to see it.

Or maybe she did. Which attested to the way she had, in fact, run.

"Okay," Dannette said, "I'll drop it. But I'm looking for details tonight over a medium pepperoni pizza with black olives."

She heard the smile in Sarah's voice. "How far out of town is the rest area?"

"About thirty miles."

"I'll be there within the hour. Wait for me."

Dannette clicked off and shot a look toward heaven, feeling for the first time in a long while the gaze of the Almighty upon her.

✦ ✦ ✦

"Yeah, Jeff, I'm going in after her." Will held the telephone to his ear while he threw his night-vision goggles, a sleeping bag, a couple of MREs he had stored in the back of his truck, his Beretta, a knife, a rope, a tarp, a compass and flashlight, a canteen, and two pairs of extra socks into his rucksack. He was already dressed for stealth—black ski hat, BDUs, black sweater, and hiking boots. He'd gone without the camouflage paint for now but tucked the compact into one of his many pockets.

He had no doubt that right now Hayata was combing the woods for their little lost rabbit.

"How about search and rescue? Are they in on this?" Jeff asked, his voice grim.

"If you mean, am I teaming with them, the answer is no." Or maybe no wasn't strong enough. How about, not in a billion years, not if they strapped him to a piece of C-4, not if they stuck toothpicks under his fingernails and tied his tongue to a hornet's nest. N-O, no. He wasn't going to trail along in Dannette's shadow. Aside from the obvious fact that she'd probably shoot him on sight, with this getup he was bound to obliterate his cover.

And wouldn't that be fun? He, disclosing his true identity; she, overjoyed to discover that he'd lied to her . . . again. She'd probably have to wrestle her dog for who got to tear him limb from limb.

"I've heard extraordinary things about K-9s. If you follow her—"

"I'm not exactly an amateur here."

Jeff stayed silent.

Will rubbed his forehead, staring at the man in the rearview mirror, and noticed the bruise on his temple. He looked like the terrorists he was hoping to thwart. If Dannette caught sight of him, he wouldn't have to endure her disgust—she'd run for the border.

"I'm sorry. It's just . . . I don't need her. I'll find the girl. Trust me."

Jeff's voice was sober. "We have to trust you. We have no choice. There is an agent on his way to help you look, so don't forget to check in. But find her—and soon. Before they figure out that she's deliberately gone AWOL and give our man Nazar an early morning bullet to the head along with his goat milk and *plov.*"

Will wasn't sure if that was a vote of confidence or not, but he nodded and clicked off. He tucked the phone into his pants pocket and shouldered the pack before pulling onto the road.

He had no intention of running into SAR queen Dannette Lundeen. And if he did, maybe *he'd* run for the border.

He parked on a dirt road, a quarter mile from the rest area. The late-afternoon sun ran fingers of light through the trees, dappling the shadowed ground with pools of fire as he tromped through the woods toward the area where he'd seen Dannette tag the scent. He noticed her truck in the parking lot. A Jeep Cherokee was parked beside it.

So Dannette had returned with reinforcements. He felt his pulse jump and wasn't at all pleased by his reaction. Okay, so he could admit she had sparked his admiration. And his curiosity, with her jaded comments about newspapermen.

But he had a mission to accomplish. One that, if successfully completed, would ensure him a quick and painless exit from her horizon.

He hiked into the forest, looking for broken limbs, crushed grass, and quickly found where Dannette and her dog had entered. In fact, as he wound deeper into the forest, it was easy to follow the footprints. The dog's path seemed erratic, straying from the deer trails, the clear brush, and diving through tangled forest where it seemed illogical for a human to pass.

Unless that human was trying to hide.

The sun continued to disappear, and twilight hued the

forest a dingy gray. He heard voices and the cracking of under-
brush and slowed his pace. It wasn't like he'd find much at
night, but after Dannette gave up and returned to a hot dinner
and a warm bed, he'd pick up the trail. He hoped to find Amina
by morning.

He tracked the depressed soil and broken forest to a creek
bed. It seemed a spring run, and from the way the water had
been despoiled, he knew the group had crossed not long ago.

He took a drink of water from his canteen, wiped his
mouth, replaced the cap. He should hang back and make sure
Missy didn't pick up his scent. No, he should do better than
that. A dog could smell detergent and fabric softener a mile
away. He crouched by the river, picked up mud, smeared it
over his face, his clothes. *Yum, the fresh scent of worms and
decaying loam.*

He waited, his heartbeat ticking out time, until he heard
only the rustle of wind against blossoms. Then he crossed the
river and prayed that the wind didn't change.

"What's her name?" Sarah walked behind Dannette, who had
her eyes on her dog, analyzing her behavior. Missy still had her
snout in the air, and every once in a while would barrel ahead,
confident of her course. Then she'd double back in confusion,
circle, and rework the area.

It didn't help that the wind seemed to change its mind,
carrying with it a thousand different scents. They'd already
walked half a mile, and again Dannette thanked the Lord for
His opportune provision. Sarah had talked Dannette into packing her rig with the essentials for an overnight bivouac—a
single tent, her sleeping bag, food, and water—just in case they

had to pitch camp. And now, with her dog excited and on the trail, Dannette didn't want to surrender to the night. She had a wide-beam Maglite and an abundance of batteries. Add that to the adrenaline pumping through her veins, and she felt she could hike all night.

The girl was out here and, judging by Missy's movements, was on the run. A normal victim would stay to obvious paths or head toward the sound of a highway. This one ran into bramble and occasionally depressed the ground behind large felled trees as if hiding. Who was she afraid of, and why?

"I don't know her name," she answered Sarah. "An elderly couple reported her missing, and they gave only a cursory description."

Dannette had been pretty accurate about her friend's attire. Sarah had tied up her long, straight, blonde hair with a rubber band, and it stuck out of her baseball cap. She wore no makeup and looked like an ad for L.L. Bean in her faded jeans, hiking boots, and Gore-Tex jacket under a lime green down vest.

"So, you really don't know if she's even out here?" Sarah, the practical one in their group—even more so than Dannette—had an NYC accent that made her sound sardonic even when she was only asking a question. Dannette knew her well enough not to bristle.

"It's worse than that, Sarah. Someone called in and reported her found."

Dannette heard Sarah stop behind her. "What?"

Dannette turned and saw Sarah frown. "Yes," Dannette said. "But the couple also said the girl seemed scared. As if she was in trouble. And in my gut I can feel it. She's out here."

Sarah stared at her, and Dannette knew she was rehashing all the times they'd worked together when Dannette had gone on instinct rather than cold facts. Much of SAR work was accurate guesstimate. The other half was the God factor. Dannette couldn't help but feel she had a pretty good amount of both.

Well, most of the time. She wasn't going to think about the times she'd been wrong.

"Okay, I'm in this with you to the bitter end." Sarah smiled. "What better way to hang out with my best friend than by traipsing through the woods?"

Dannette grinned. "I wish Andee were here."

Sarah nodded. "She misses all the fun."

Missy bounded through the woods. In the darkening twilight, she looked more shepherd than retriever, the dark markings on her haunches and chest turning her wolflike. In the shadows, she could raise the hairs on the back of a burglar's neck. Sadly, that was about all she'd do, even if said bad guy had bathed in A.1. steak sauce.

Missy barked twice.

"Good girl!" Dannette said. "Refind!"

Missy had trained long and hard to find her victim, return to Dannette, and lead her to the find. Now the dog turned and ran out ahead, stopping now and again to confirm Dannette's trail. Dannette's pulse thundered in her ears as she parted the forest, hoping that they might all end the night with a sauna in the motel's exercise room.

Missy stopped suddenly, standing over a bulge in the ground. Dannette's heart lurched as she squinted to make out the form. *Please, Lord, no.*

She edged forward. Relief swilled through her when she recognized the heap as a ratty blanket. Dannette knelt, put on a rubber glove, and picked up the blanket as Missy sat, her eyes bright. "Good girl," Dannette said and reached into her bag for Missy's tennis ball. She threw it a few feet away. Missy ran to retrieve it while Dannette and Sarah stared at the blanket. It had obviously seen better days, but it didn't look like it had endured a few rainstorms.

"It's been recently dropped," Sarah concluded.

"Yeah, that's my take also."

Missy returned with the ball. Sarah took it from her mouth, tossed it back down the trail from where they'd come.

"Well, what do you want to do? Pitch camp, head back, or keep looking?"

Dannette stood up, stared at the forest. It seemed to darken and close in on them with each passing step. And she couldn't ignore the disappointment that hung in her chest. She'd hoped—*seriously* hoped—to find the girl before dinner.

In fact, that hope had been so alive, it kept her from feeling the fatigue that now weighted her legs, her shoulders. "I don't know—"

Missy barked. Short, alarmed. As if in warning or . . . fear?

Sarah glanced at Dannette, then raced down the trail. Dannette ran behind her, her heart blocking her wind supply. It wasn't unheard of for a dog to attract the attention of a wolf or even a bear. They had bears in these parts, right? grizzlies?

"Missy!" Dannette picked up her pace, hearing Missy's growls, and caught up to Sarah.

Sarah skidded to a stop, her arm out, and thwacked Dannette neatly across the throat.

"What?" Dannette choked out. She spied Missy up ahead, and a streak of fear ran through her. Missy's nape hair stood on end, and she had her legs planted, her lips drawn back and showing incisors.

She hadn't seen Missy this angry since she'd gone face-to-face with a skunk on a search in Oklahoma. "Whoa, Missy," Dannette soothed as she crept toward her dog.

Sarah grabbed her arm.

Dannette shot her a look, took in Sarah's whitened expression, and followed her gaze.

A man stood on the side of the trail, slightly concealed in the trees. Dressed in black from head to toe, with mud smearing his face, he held up his hands as if in surrender.

Only he held a knife in one of those surrendering hands. One that could probably carve out the heart of Dannette's dog. Or hers.

"Um . . . we don't mean you any harm, mister." She kept her voice soft as she curled her hand under Missy's collar. "Please don't hurt us. We're just out here looking for someone."

He stared at his knife, then lowered it. "I'm sorry . . ."

Dannette felt her breath gust out, fast and hard, as if she'd been punched in the chest.

No, it couldn't be.

"I'm looking for the same thing you are," he said as he sheathed his knife.

Beneath her hand, Missy relaxed, even began to wag her tail.

Traitor.

"Any luck, Dani?" he asked with that Western drawl that had the power to sizzle the nerve endings under her skin and drive her to fury.

Was she seeing things, or had Will Masterson gone from nosy, annoying reporter to die-hard stalker?

Chapter 8

"WERE YOU PLANNING on using that thing?" Dannette's voice held only a touch of fear. The rest was 100 percent pulsating anger. "Because I don't appreciate your threatening my dog with it."

"Missy, shh, it's just me," Will said, holding out his hand to the dog."

Dannette made a sound of disgust but put a hand on Missy's head. "C'mere, Miss. It's just Mr. Can't-Understand-No."

Missy sat, and her tail swishing in the leaves told Will that perhaps she had a better opinion of him than her mistress did. Will felt a twinge of guilt. He hadn't meant to scare the animal, but when he heard something rushing through the forest toward him, his reflexes kicked in and he'd palmed the knife and headed for the brush.

Of course, Missy had to follow him. He felt sick when Dannette appeared before he could silence the dog—nicely, of course—and hide.

She glared at him. "What are you doing here?"

"Like I said, looking for the same thing you are. A teenage girl. Lost, maybe hiding."

Dannette narrowed her eyes. She glanced back at a tall blonde, who had an equally angry death-ray look zeroed in on him.

"How did you know she was hiding?" Dannette asked, wariness in her tone.

He opened his mouth, trying to dredge up words.

"Forget it. Really, I don't want to know." Dannette shook her head. "You are the most tenacious reporter I've ever met. And that's putting it as politely as I can. Don't even try to find a decent explanation for your getup. I can spot a stalker when I see one." She grabbed her dog's collar, tugged her gently to her side. "Get lost, Masterson, or next time I'll tell Missy to fetch, as in your nose."

He made a face, conjuring up that visual.

Dannette and her friend turned and headed up the trail. He heard the woman ask Dannette, "Who is he?"

"I'm a reporter," he answered, amazed that he was still sticking to that story. Someone who was trained in stealth should obey Dannette's words and turn around—at least far enough back so his scent would blend in with the forest. Then he'd reacquire Amina's trail.

Only following Dannette's and Missy's footsteps the last hour had confirmed a few basics—namely, he'd find Amina faster on Dannette's tail than sniffing out his own lead. And with darkness closing in and Hayata on their own determined manhunt, Dannette and her friend might need a little protection. Especially if Hayata decided on commandeering the K-9 team for their own personal SAR use.

That last thought made him speed up the trail behind her. "I'm also a guy who wants to help."

Dannette whirled, and if he wasn't already wearing mud, the look she gave him would make him feel like pond scum. "We don't need your help. We're just fine."

Her friend wore a frown. "Dannette, maybe he can help us." She shot Will a look. "If he takes a bath somewhere and doesn't stand too close." She wrinkled her nose, waved a hand over her face. "You've got the sneaky thing down to a science."

"Obviously not, or Missy wouldn't have found me." Will touched Missy's head. "You're too smart; you know that?"

Dannette moved between him and her dog. "What is it with you? Do you not understand the meaning of the word *no*? I don't want your help." She held up a finger to stop her friend's protest. "We've been down this road. This girl's trail is erratic, so my guess is you're right on the idea she might be in trouble. I do think she's hiding. If you do the math, you can probably guess that any news articles about her aren't going to make her life better. In fact, you're liable to decimate it. So turn your smelly self around and head south, Cowboy, before I unleash Missy on you."

Will crouched before the dog, who was pushing her snout around Dannette's hand, looking for his affection. "Missy loves me." He rubbed her jowls. "And what if I promise not to write a word?"

Dannette frowned at him as he looked up. "I'm not sure you're physically able to make that kind of promise."

More able than she realized. Writing wasn't his forte, and in fact, he'd sent more than one article off to HQ for them to hone and edit before turning it into the paper. He grinned. "No articles. Scout's honor." He held up two fingers.

She rolled her eyes. "I don't know. Do you even know how to survive in the woods? The last thing Sarah and I need is deadweight. You gotta keep up."

He stood. "Yeah. I've been on a couple of camping trips. I'll be all right."

"This isn't camping. This is make do and keep warm and don't get hurt so we can find a young girl before she dies of exposure."

O . . . *kay*. She'd be a good addition to Special Forces if

they took women. Will nearly saluted. "I'll try not to be a
burden," he said instead, keeping his voice small and warm.

"Just . . . don't get hurt." Dannette turned, headed back up
the trail.

Yeah, right. Don't get hurt. This mission had the makings
of a world of hurt, starting with the Hayata terrorists then on to
the cold draft from the local K-9 handler. Only he had a feeling
the deep freeze from Dani—no, *Dannette*—might hurt more
than anything Hayata could dish out.

He caught up to Dannette's friend. "Are you her partner?"

She gave him a half glance, with a matching smile.
"Missy's her partner. I'm a friend. We planned to go canoeing
this weekend."

"Ah, right, the girls'-night-out canoe trip."

The woman frowned at him.

He gave her his nicest I'm-not-a-bad-guy smile. "Before
I turned into the reporter-slash-stalker, Dannette and I had
a nice dinner date."

"Did not!" Dannette yelled, but she didn't slow.

"Will Masterson," he said, holding out his hand. "And I
promise, I'm not out to stir up trouble." *Well, sorta.* At least he
was out to make sure that if the pot got stirred, they'd all make
it through alive.

"Sarah Nation. From New York. And if you're a reporter,
I'm a cyborg." She gave him an icy look, from the feet up. "You
look like a creature from the *Swamp Monster Returns.*"

He gave her a mock-offended look.

She smiled. "Listen, I know that Dannette wears her skin
scratchy side out during searches, but she's really warm and
cuddly when you get to know her. Sorta like Missy."

"Sarah, don't talk to him." Dannette glanced over her
shoulder. "You'll end up as quote of the week."

Sarah laughed, but Will couldn't help but feel as if Dannette had kicked him low and hard in the stomach. What was it with her and reporters? So he hadn't scored any trust points with his sneak-up-and-scare move, but really, it wasn't like he was a terrorist, intent on wreaking havoc on her life, was it?

Okay, maybe he looked like it just a little.

He clicked on his flashlight as the darkness invaded the forest. Twilight still hued the sky, but the clasp of forest turned the light tenebrous and gloomy. The feeling mixed with the soggy smells of spring and the spongy crack of twigs breaking beneath the thump of hiking boots. A fine layer of sweat simmered between his sweater and his skin, and he tasted his worry in the pool of saliva in his mouth.

Somewhere, lost in the tangle of pine, poplar, and bramble, Amina hid, hoping for her deliverer. *Please, Lord, let us find her soon.*

Fadima dragged the coil of brush against the overhang of rock, climbed inside, and pulled more brush in to close off the entrance. She'd built a bed of pine boughs, berating herself for dropping her blanket. Although it had had more holes than cotton, it had staved off the sharpest bites of the cold air, and she dearly longed for it as she pulled her flimsy, torn jacket around her. How she longed for the arid heat of her home, the smell of steppe grass in the wind, even the feel of perspiration that lined the robes she wore to protect her body and face from the sun.

She was lost. And hungry. And very, very alone. No Hafiz would come to her rescue. Her contact was dead, and if she didn't find help soon, she and her family would follow him.

Sorry, Father. Defeat filled her throat. What had her father been thinking to label her their rescuer? Couldn't he see that she didn't possess even an ounce of her mother's courage? She curled into a ball, propped her backpack under her head, pulled her arms out of her sleeves, and wrapped them around her body.

She'd filled her water bottle in the stream she'd crossed early this morning and eaten the rest of the scone she'd purchased in the London airport before changing planes. Her stomach clenched with hunger, but she ignored it. People could go weeks without eating if only they had water. She'd learned that while watching her father interrogate prisoners over the years.

She had to focus on finding help. She'd nearly escaped this morning—she'd seen safety and compassion on the faces of the elderly couple. But she'd hesitated too long, trying to gauge their intent. She didn't know if it had been Hayata operatives who screeched up to the rest area, but she hadn't lingered to find out.

They would have shot the old couple on the spot and left their bodies for the crows. And who knew what they would do to her? *See, Father? I'm not brave.*

She had to put kilometers between herself and Hayata and then find help. Only . . . where was the nearest road? She felt as if she'd been walking in circles or perhaps just trekking farther into this immense tangle of woods. Blood dappled her skin where branches had snagged her jacket, scraped her wrists. She never felt so dirty, her fingernails embedded with mud, her hair inhabited with foreign forest creatures.

She clenched her teeth and tried not to cry.

Father, help me. She imagined his face and the face of her brother, Kutsi, and tried to soothe herself with their smiles, their warm assurances that they would soon all be safe.

Yes, just like her mother had been safe. Her father had

tried, three years ago, to send his wife and Fadima's younger sister to safety, hoping they wouldn't be detected inside a refugee camp. Yet Hayata had found them and made examples of them as traitors. Her father hadn't allowed her to see inside their wooden coffins.

But Fadima imagined enough images to wail and sob herself to sleep for months afterward. In fact, it wouldn't be too hard to let the old grief consume her now. She took a deep breath, trying to clear the images out of her head. No. No, she wouldn't be caught, wouldn't allow them to do to her what they'd done to her mother and little sister.

She would be Amina. Bearer of truth.

If only in her father's dreams. She closed her eyes, trying to relax in her cubbyhole, and let exhaustion wash over her.

✦ ✦ ✦

Dannette watched her dog's movements, the circling, whining, lifting her nose to the wind. "C'mere, Missy," she said. Missy trotted over, put her snout into Dannette's cupped hand. "You need a rest." Dannette rubbed her hands over her dog, debating her options.

Darkness had closed in without absolution, and Dannette could barely make out her hand in front of her face. The wind rushed against the trees, and her stomach had begun to rub against her spine. More than that, Missy was getting frustrated. She needed a break, some playtime.

"Let's find a place to make camp," Dannette suggested to the two other searchers. Sarah was out ahead, scanning the forest with her Maglite for tracks, while Will hunched over his topo map. Dannette found it more than suspect that he'd brought along not only a map but a few extras, like water, food, a sleeping bag, and a tarp. As if he might be serious about help-ing Dannette find this lost girl.

She wished it didn't dent the icy anger she felt at finding him. She wanted to knock herself upside the head. Pay atten-tion to the facts, *Dani*. He wasn't invested in the search; he just wanted a good story. A story he wouldn't get, if she had her druthers.

Still, he had kept up and had been relatively quiet about it. Most of all, he had the brains to keep his distance from Dan-nette, which also increased her respect for him.

Or maybe it hurt. She wanted to flog her rebellious heart for jumping in traitorous glee when they'd found him treed by Missy. His all-black getup fed her soldier-in-hiding suspicions, not to mention accentuating the muscles that accompanied those mental images. As if he didn't have enough in his arsenal, the dirt still caught in his five-o'clock shadow upped his stun power by a trillion.

Just what she needed: Rambo in hiking boots shadowing her through the forest, tugging at her concentration. Thank-fully, he didn't smell good.

If she let her musings loose, she'd even begin doubting his profession. He didn't seem . . . ruthless enough for a jour-nalist. Except he had dogged her into the forest, intent on spying on her. That behavior had the makings of paparazzi written all over it.

Sarah walked over to Will, studied his map. "Looks like we're not far from the Superior hiking trail. There are marked campsites."

"Okay, let's head there." Dannette unhooked Missy's vest and snapped on her lead. "All done, girl." Reaching into her pocket, Dannette found a treat and gave it to her.

Will scanned his flashlight through the forest and checked

his compass. "We need to go this way." He let his light linger on a towering pine some fifty feet away. "We'll take another marking there."

Dannette followed him, amazed at his confidence. So maybe he'd spent time in the woods. In fact, letting him lead felt like a balm on her razed, tight nerves.

In ten minutes they emerged onto the hiking trail. He turned west and found a pocket of campsites within an eighth of a mile of each other.

Dannette watered and fed Missy while Sarah shook out her single tent.

"You ladies surprise me," said Will, nearly invisible in the night, save for the dim light he held over Sarah's movements. "I thought for sure you'd head back to your motel room."

Dannette glanced at him. "Not when we can pick up the trail tomorrow. But you're free to go if you'd like."

He quirked a half smile. "And leave you here as bear bait?"

Dannette shook her head, unsmiling. "Sarah and I both have single tents, so we don't have one to loan you."

Will shrugged. "Don't need one. I'm camping across the way." He pointed to the campsite across the trail. "You ladies give me a holler if you need anything." He swung his own pack off his shoulders and headed to another campsite.

Dannette pulled her tent out of her bag and had it up in less than five minutes. She flung her sleeping bag inside, then began scouting around the site for firewood. Missy chewed on a rawhide treat.

"He's kinda cute," Sarah said as she sought firewood behind her tent. "I don't see why you don't like him."

"He's a reporter." Dannette stepped on a large branch, breaking it in half. "Enough said."

"Yeah, but he's a nice reporter. And I think he cares about you."

Dannette gave a derisive laugh. "He cares about a hot story. So he has incredible eyes; I'm not melting into a pile of mush. I know my priorities—and my history. I need a guy who is stable, honest, safe. And I want a man who is sold out for God. The dead last thing I need in my life is a nosy reporter digging around in my nightmares."

Sarah stood, a bundle of twigs in her arms. "He doesn't have to know. Besides, that chapter of your life is over. Not every reporter is like Steve Oullette."

"I'm not taking any chances, thanks." Dannette strode over to the fire pit and dumped her bundle. "I don't see you taking any big leaps in the love area either. Hank likes you, but you won't give him a second glance."

"Hank is a redneck from the hills. He'll sit up and bark at anything that crosses his territory."

Dannette laughed at the solemn look on Sarah's face. "Oh, give me a break. Hank helped us find Micah, helped us save Lacey. He's a nice guy, and just because he talks with a Southern drawl and looks good in a pair of faded, holey jeans doesn't make him a redneck. And he's from Texas, not Tennessee, which puts him in a whole different category."

Sarah shrugged, dropped her pile of wood, knelt, and began propping her twigs into a teepee.

Dannette stilled, staring at her movements. "You *do* like him."

"No, I don't. He's just . . . persuasive."

Dannette shook her head. "Yeah, well, after what you've been through, perhaps you need persuading. Even romance."

Sarah glanced up. Her eyes glistened. "Maybe it's not Hank. Maybe it's me. Maybe I'll never be ready."

Dannette wanted to weep. She touched Sarah's arm, then pulled her into a quick embrace. "Hang in there. Give Hank a little room to woo you. Let yourself see what the rest of us do. I promise, we won't let anything happen to you." She pulled away from Sarah, her throat thick. Sarah deserved to meet a guy who respected her, who cherished her. "Maybe God put Hank in your life to remind you that His compassions never fail."

Sarah nodded. But her attention fell back to the fire she was assembling.

Dannette's own words rang in her mind: *"His compassions never fail."*

Please, Lord, don't let them fail tonight with Your lost child. Keep her warm and safe. And help us find her.

Dannette helped Sarah build the fire, and in a few moments, flames flickered from the kindling wood. Sarah banked it while Dannette pulled out a dehydrated packet of goulash.

"Yum," said Sarah. "Fine dining."

"Only the best." Dannette filled her coffeepot with water. Missy rose from her treat, sauntered over to her, and settled at her feet.

"What do you think? I saw Missy alert a couple of times today for scent. Are we on the right track?" Sarah asked.

"I don't know . . . I hope so." Dannette watched the fire chew at the wood. Somewhere out there a young woman might be trying to keep warm. The thought made her hollow, and she felt frustration pool in her throat. "Or . . . maybe I hope I'm wrong. That she's somewhere else safe and warm."

Sarah gave her a soft smile, as if reading her torn thoughts. "You know I'm on your side, so I'm just going to ask it. You're not overreacting to this report of a missing girl after the incident with Emily, are you?"

Dannette closed her eyes. Ouch. Yes, the search for Lacey's daughter, Emily, had dredged up her demons enough for them to play havoc with her emotions, but she wasn't dreaming the blue fabric, the filthy blanket, or Missy's reactions.

Was she?

Sarah knocked down the fire, added the fire grate, and set the pot on to boil. "Like I said, I'm on your side. If you want to talk about . . . well, out here it's no one but you, me, and Missy."

"And our local Boy Scout." Dannette forced a smile, listening to the breath of night in the trees and enjoying the smell of spring as it stirred up the damp loam. She touched Sarah's arm. "I know you're on my side. And I appreciate you trusting me and my gut feelings."

Sarah met her smile. "Yeah, if I were lost, I'd be thankful for your stubbornness."

"I'd better see how Will is doing," Dannette said, suddenly feeling a flint of compassion for him despite his intrusion on their lives. He probably hadn't brought any dinner, especially if he figured on their returning home for the night. Dannette and Sarah, already stocked up for the canoe trip, had packed provisions for three days. If they didn't find the girl by then, they'd head back to Moose Bend. And then Dannette would decide whether or not she should throw herself over Sheriff Fadden's desk and demand a call-out.

Dannette ignored Sarah's teasing smile and trekked across the trail to Will's camp. Missy followed and Dannette dug out her ball, throwing it down the shadowed trail. Missy shot off after it.

Will the Eagle Scout had a small fire going and had constructed a simple A-frame tent using a large poplar tree, a couple of ropes, and a tarp. He crouched beside the fire, spooning out his dinner from a brown packet.

"Is that an MRE?" she asked, sitting on a log across from him.

"Yep." He glanced at her, held out the dinner. "Want some?"

She made a face. "Sorry, but I had my share of those during a training exercise we did with the Iowa National Guard. How did you get them?"

He shrugged. "Army surplus."

"Same with your getup too, I guess, huh?" Although, in his black fatigues and boots, he looked close enough to the real thing. Something about him—perhaps the sly smile, the casual confidence in his demeanor—made him look like a man who handled life with a shrug, not letting it get under his skin. No wonder he was difficult to shake—her pleas hadn't done more than glance off him.

Still, the fact that he was camped here, close enough to hear a scream in the night, felt . . . safe. Sorta . . . sweet. She crossed her arms over her chest. "So, tell me, isn't this a little over the top for a story? A lost girl . . . it'll maybe make page B of the *Minneapolis Star Tribune*. Not exactly a Pulitzer-prize contender."

He finished his meal and sealed his trash into a Ziploc. "Nope. But like I said, I want to help." He sat on the ground, leaned back onto his hands. "Your friend Sarah is nice."

Missy returned with her ball, dropped it at Dannette's feet, then collapsed into a pile of fur. "Yeah. She'll be an asset when we find the girl. She knows how to handle trauma victims."

He raised his dark eyebrows.

"She's seen some pretty bad stuff." Not to mention, been a victim herself. Dannette shook her head, trying to escape the memory as she ran her hand through Missy's fur. "So, how does a cowboy become a reporter?"

Will picked up a stick and jabbed it into the campfire. Sparks shot skyward. "Just kind of ended up that way."

Dannette leaned forward, watching his lean, strong hands. "Okay, I gotta know. You have military written all over you. Did you do time in the National Guard or something?"

She watched his face, and didn't Mr. Cool swallow, as if caught. She even saw his Adam's apple bob in the dim light. A muscle pulled in his face. Perhaps she could dig for a few secrets too.

"Something like that," he answered. He rubbed his whiskers, dislodging some dirt.

The wind stirred the branches in the darkness beyond the ring of firelight. Her disappointment felt sharp as she realized that was his full, annotated answer. "C'mon, Will. Play fair. You invaded my life, so I get to know something more about you than you like to dress in black and make a pretty decent bivouac."

He glanced at his tent. "You like that, huh?"

"I'm moderately impressed." She clamped her hands on her knees. "Something like that?" she repeated.

Will exhaled, and it seemed more from relief than stress. "Okay, yes, I did time in the military." He didn't look at her. "My pa was a cop. And when I graduated from high school, it felt like the only way out."

Those words scraped another layer off her defenses. *The only way out.* Boy, did she feel those words. "I'm sorry."

"Yeah, well, my best friend joined up too, so it felt like a club. I found that I was pretty good at PT and handled a weapon well, and it gave me the confidence to believe that I was more than just my father's punching bag."

Unexpected tears filled her eyes, and her voice turned soft before she could stop it. "Oh, Will, I'm sorry." She had the sudden urge to reach out to him.

But then he grinned and even . . . *chuckled?*

She stared at him. And he met her gaze. Hard, unflinching, but with the slightest upturned mouth. In the horrible second that followed, she realized he was playing her. Playing to her sympathies. Or worse, making her feel like a fool.

And for a second, it had actually worked.

"Good try, Cowboy." She rose, startling Missy, who jumped up beside her. Dannette stalked a few feet away, then turned, fury gathering in her throat. "We'll be up at dawn. Try not to be late."

Jerk.

✦ ✦ ✦

Will blew out his breath, his heart thundering. He'd hurt her. But what was he supposed to do when he realized he'd accidentally let her into a private sector of his heart? What was he thinking? He hadn't let someone—anyone, especially a woman—inside that dark pocket of his life—*ever*. Laughter was the only thing he could do to mask the vulnerability that radiated from him like an odor.

Good grief. No wonder he couldn't cultivate an authentic, honest relationship with a woman of substance. Every time she got close enough for a good look, he put on camouflage.

Except that was a lot safer, wasn't it? For both of them.

He threw the stick into the fire, watched the sparks spiral upward, aching that he'd somehow stomped out the tendrils of friendship that she'd so gently tended.

Apparently, he hadn't reformed quite as much from the jerk he'd once been.

Five years ago, he would have read her visit to his campsite as some sort of invitation. He would have turned the Masterson charm into overdrive and delivered some heartrending lie that would eventually entice her into his arms.

But he wasn't that man anymore, right?

Oh, how he longed to be that new person God promised to make him. But watching Dannette's stiff and angry retreating form, he knew he hadn't a clue how to be that kind of man.

His past knew how to gnaw at him, to whisper defeat and tempt him with sweet rewards that he knew would turn his heart to ash. But his new desires included discovery and loss and grief. They made him lock up his heart and sent him running.

So, why had he told her the truth about his father? That question rattled around his mind as he unrolled his sleeping bag and climbed inside his shelter. He listened to the forest sounds, the crackle of the campfire, and prayed that God would help him complete his mission before someone got seriously hurt . . . namely, him.

Chapter 9

"WE HAVE COMPLICATIONS." Bakym paced the compound, trying to find the strongest signal for his satellite phone. "Fadima has escaped."

He held the telephone away from his ear, deciding that this was a strong enough signal to hear his ataman's displeasure. Thankfully the guy lived ten thousand miles away and wasn't likely to actually do any of the things he threatened to Bakym. At least not personally.

No, Bakym would be doing those things to Fadima when he found her. Fadima was practically his property now. Technically he had to wait for Nazar to arrive for the wedding, but by that time . . . well, Nazar would be attending her funeral. A martyr's funeral.

The ataman finished his discharge. "What are you doing to find her?"

"I sent Gazim and Daniel. They'll track her down. She couldn't have gone far. I told them not to return without her."

"She could be useful to the wrong people if she succeeds in escaping."

Bakym nodded into the telephone. In the late twilight, the air felt crisp, damp with the breath of spring. He saw his two other women—Karli and Mara—fetching firewood for the fireplace. Karli wore her new American low-rise jeans and her long black hair loose. He didn't want to sacrifice her—the rules of their *sotnya* on this side of the ocean gave him liberties not embraced back home. Yes, he'd miss Karli, especially now that she'd learned how to please him.

But there were higher goals. Sacrifices to be made by all. Unless he could find Fadima.

"You have three days. Don't disappoint me, Bakym. And when you find her, shoot her."

"*Konyeshna.*" Of course. Except that shooting Fadima was lower on his list of priorities.

He had greater plans for Nazar's little girl.

Dannette stared at the sky through the screen in her tent, a thousand voices taunting in her head. *See?* they said. *You start to care, and you'll get hurt.*

She rolled over in her bag, thumped the wad of clothing she used as a pillow, and ignored the voices. She wasn't going to let that cowboy under her skin, even if his childhood trauma—probably *false*—dug at her. Okay, it was more than that. It was the flint of pain in his eyes that accompanied his words. It was the fact that, despite his laughter, she wondered if he might be telling the truth.

She thumped her wad of clothing again. Beside her, Missy raised her head, roused from slumber. She stared at Dannette.

"Well, he's not exactly Mr. I-Cannot-Tell-a-Lie, is he?"

Missy wagged her tail.

"At least I can count on you, Missy. Loyal, honest, and warm." She rubbed Missy behind her ears and smiled.

Stars punctuated the canopy of darkness with bursts of brilliant light. Dannette closed her eyes. *Lord, You know my history with men. You also know that I don't have time or room in my heart for a man. So please help me not to be drawn in by that lazy smile or those chocolate eyes. Please, Lord, protect me.*

She felt the smallest breath of peace filter through her soul and drifted off into a dreamless sleep.

Sunlight had only begun to dapple the ground and skim off the dew as Dannette awoke. She let Missy out, then climbed out of her sleeping bag and, while in the cover of her tent, pulled her Gore-Tex pants, wool socks, and sweatshirt over her cotton undershirt. She opened the flap and pulled her shoes out of the waterproof bag. Lacing them up quickly, she pulled on her jacket, noting movement in Sarah's tent. Birds chirruped in the early morning, and the breeze had died to a mere whimper.

"Howdy."

She froze, searched for the voice, and found Will on the trail petting Missy, who had obviously forgiven him and had rolled over, letting him scratch her belly. So much for Missy's loyalty.

"Good morning. Can I come onto your site?" Will asked.

Will was already packed for the day, and he looked like a cover model for L.L. Bean/Mercenaries R Us in his hiking boots, black soldier's uniform, and tousled dark brown hair. Oh, she so didn't want to give in to the tug to like him. Even though he was petting her dog and, like a good little Boy Scout, respecting the unspoken camping rule to right of privacy. And he'd risen early, ready to scout, just like she'd asked. As if he truly cared about this mission. But what could she do when he added that cute little smile under his goatee? Scoundrel.

"Sure," she said, trying to sound rough and angry. "Wipe your feet at the door."

He let Missy up, then pretended to wipe his feet and open a door. Okay, that was kind of funny.

He set down his pack near their fire ring. "How about I get this going again?"

"Have at it, Eagle Scout. I'll reward you with some dehydrated eggs."

He smiled.

Will worked the fire while she and Sarah packed up their tents. By the time Dannette had everything tucked into her rucksack and Missy watered and fed, the water had come to a boil.

She crouched beside Will as he prepared the eggs, aware that he must have bathed or something, because his face was clean, his whiskers around his goatee shaved, and he even smelled good, a blend of masculinity and power.

Uh-oh.

"It's going to be a hot one today," Will said, looking at the sky. "No clouds and only a whisper of breeze."

Sarah joined them, holding a sierra cup filled with instant coffee crystals. Will filled her cup, and she stirred it. "Beauty of a morning. Better than shopping, don't you think, Dannette?" Sarah asked.

Will glanced up, and Dannette smiled coyly.

"I was reading Lamentations 3 in my Bible this morning." Sarah blew on her coffee. "'Great is his faithfulness; his mercies begin afresh each morning. I say to myself, "The LORD is my inheritance; therefore, I will hope in him!"

"'The LORD is good to those who depend on him, to those who search for him. So it is good to wait quietly for salvation from the LORD,'" Will added quietly.

Dannette shot him a look. The guy knew obscure Scripture?

He shrugged. "Vacation Bible school. We learned it in a song. My best friend dragged me every year."

Was that the morning sun, or had Will actually turned a shade of red? As if, like last night, he'd given out more of himself than he planned? If, in fact, he was telling them the truth . . . now *or* then.

Dannette spooned eggs into her cup. "My grandmother used to quote that passage. She was a King James woman, and her version said, 'The LORD is my portion, saith my soul; therefore will I hope in him.'"

"I did a word study on that once," Sarah said, holding out her now empty cup for her helping of eggs. "The word *portion* is used in a lot of different contexts." She set her cup down, pulled her pack over, and wiggled out a slim-line pocket Bible.

Will helped himself to eggs, but Dannette noticed how he watched Sarah. As if interested in her . . . or in her Bible study? Dannette shook out the thought. Did she not pray last night and ask God to protect her heart? Perhaps Will *should* be turning his attention to Sarah.

Then again, a gal with Sarah's past needed a guy who didn't play games with her heart. A guy she could *trust*.

Sarah flipped to the back of her Bible. "I keep a list of all the words I study and the allegory references." She ran a finger down the list. "*Portion* means 'reward,' 'influence,' 'abundance,' 'sustenance,' and 'all your worldly possessions.' In other versions, the word also refers to God being our redeemer, our reputation, and our rescuer."

Will scooted back onto a rock as he poured himself a cup of coffee. "That's a fairly large scope. I just thought it meant God was enough."

"Or 'all,'" Dannette said. She took a bite of eggs. "Ooh, needs salt."

Will reached into his sweater pocket, handed her a salt packet from his MRE.

"Thanks," Dannette said and seasoned her meal. "My grand-mother quoted that verse a lot, especially when she was over-whelmed by life. I remember her saying it over my grandpa's grave." And other graves. She swallowed back a lump that had nothing to do with dry eggs. "I always thought it meant that God filled up all those dark and empty places."

Her own words rubbed on her heart. She hadn't exactly let God fill up any dark places, had she? She'd basically let them scar over. But letting God inside to heal would mean scraping open scars, exposing her wounds.

No, thanks.

God was enough . . . for what she needed Him for. A friend. A companion who watched over her from above. She didn't want to have to need Him too much.

"Well, I like the first part of the verse," Sarah said. "'His mercies begin afresh each morning.' And that's what we have today, a fresh chance." Her voice fell. "I hope."

Silence settled among them. Dannette thought of the wind that raked the forest, the frosting of dew on the ground. *Please let Will be right about it being a warm day, Lord.* The warmer the day, the heavier the scent, the easier for Missy to find the girl.

They finished with few words. Will cleaned up quickly by rinsing their cups with water. Dannette tied hers onto her pack to let it dry.

Will doused the fire, then kicked dirt over it. "Ready?" he asked, hoisting his pack.

Sarah stopped him with a hand to his arm. "Dannette and I have this tradition . . . we always pray before we head out."

He didn't seem surprised or offended, instead nodded and bowed his head.

That did it. The sight of Reporter/Cowboy/Rambo/Boy Scout Will standing there, his hands clasped, his head bowed, praying . . . well, Dannette felt every barrier take a swift tumble to dust. How could she not like the guy?

C'mon, surely she could think of a few reasons.

She listened to Sarah's prayer, deciding that okay, maybe she'd give him provisional friend status. Only.

✛ ✛ ✛

The woman was merciless. Forget making her a Ranger—she could rocket straight up the chain of command to five-star general.

Which made Will like her way more than he should.

With the exception of watering her dog about every half hour, Dani set a relentless pace. Yes, *Dani*—sorry, he couldn't get the formal Dannette version to stick in his brain, even if he did force out the name through his lips. *Dannette* sounded so . . . stuffy. This woman was, well, gritty. In a painfully attractive sort of way. She marched through the forest like the best of his Ranger cohorts. She read a topo map as if she'd been born with magnetic north embedded into her, and she analyzed their victim as if she had a PhD in psychology.

Only Amina wasn't a victim but a fugitive. A very, *very* desperate young lady carrying dangerous secrets.

Although Dani had the tenacity of a special-ops soldier, Will wanted to drop to his knees and kiss her feet for her dedication.

They stopped for a ten-minute lunch near a stream, where Will filled his canteen and added some purification drops. He saw Dannette shake her head, but a little gleam of admiration tweaked her expression. As if she were still amazed that a journalist might know a bit about camping.

He tried not to think about how he was lying through his teeth. He needed her to trust him. Wanted her to like him.

Because he liked her, oh so very much. Especially the way she was with Missy, knowing when to call her close, rub her ears, let her settle down with a toy. And the fact that Dani wasn't about impressing him . . . impressed him. He'd fallen into conversation with her as the morning dragged on, and it played again in his mind.

"You seem like a guy who's spent a lot of time in the forest," she'd said as she munched on an energy bar.

He'd debated for only a moment. After last night and the sick feeling he'd had after he'd hurt her, he decided that there were parts of himself he could give away for free.

In fact, letting her inside, knowing she had no agendas felt . . . safe. Easy.

Or maybe it was because he'd never see her again.

In a strange, unexpected way, maybe he could let her inside a little.

"We didn't have a lot of forest in South Dakota, but I did grow up outside, I guess," Will had said. "In between his bottles of whiskey, my dad took me hunting, so I got pretty good with a rifle. Brought home my share of deer and pheasants. Went out on my own when I was only twelve and pegged a six-point buck." He held a branch back for her to pass through without getting swatted. "My mom wasn't around much. At least not like most other moms I knew, so I got used to pulling a steak out of the freezer, slapping it on the grill for supper."

"Did your mom work?"

Her innocent question had brought up a bevy of ugly answers. "No, not really. She was a free spirit. She joined a commune for a while, then an artist colony. She came home in between adventures. My dad never had eyes for anyone else, so for a while, when she came home, life felt pretty good. She baked cookies, and at night we'd make shadow animals on the walls. I'd tell her stories and she'd listen, tracing letters on my hands. And then one day I'd come home from school, and she'd be gone." He swallowed hard, amazed at how his chest seized up with those words.

Or maybe because of Dani's quick intake of breath. "That had to hurt."

Yeah. Like a knife to the heart. He had shrugged away her words, suddenly realizing how small his voice felt. "I got used to it." *Sorta.* If Lew hadn't invited Will inside the Strong family, he might have ended up like his old man—broken, buried in a bottle, angry at life. Holding out feeble and bitter hope that the woman he loved would return home. Thankfully, the Strongs had poured unconditional love into Will's empty places, especially during his teenage years, and later taught him that sometimes love means letting go.

"I know she loved me. She just couldn't make a commitment that long." But he had never gotten a fix on what triggered her leaving. As if somehow he'd gotten too close. Loved her too much. Scared her away.

And here, all this time, he thought he was more like his father. Rough around the edges and hard all the way to his heart.

Perhaps he was like both of his parents. Hard *and* gun-shy.

Most likely, just confused.

No wonder he wore identities like thermal layers.

Dani had said nothing as she stepped over bramble and tree limbs. The forest was alive with sound—birds, the breeze rusting in the leaves, the gurgle of a nearby stream. Her silence felt . . . perfect. Gentle. She listened like she cared, and as he feared, it seemed way too easy to let her inside, at least for the moment.

"As I grew older, I spent more and more time out on the

prairie, under the stars dreaming of being a cowboy when I grew up. When I was about thirteen, I got a part-time job punching cows."

"Punching cows?" She gave him a half smile.

"Cowboy talk for herding cattle."

Her lips had formed a silent *O*.

Lips he had wanted to kiss.

He nearly shook his head in disgust at the thought. Could he not make one female friend without his past tainting his thoughts? He had turned away from her, kept his gaze on her dog.

"So, why aren't you out there now—punching cows?"

"I don't know. I guess I thought it was a good idea to leave town." Leave memories. Leave the dead end of his bad-boy reputation. "I suppose someday I wouldn't mind going back. Starting a family." Now where had that come from? As if a guy like him could ever have a wife, children. Soldiers shouldn't marry. Ever. He had switched gears before she could respond. "When I got out of high school, I joined the service and stayed in over ten years."

"That's a long time. You said something about joining up with a friend?"

He had glanced at her, surprised she remembered. "Yeah. Lew Strong. He and I were together all the way to the end."

"The end? You mean you were both discharged?" She angled a frown at him.

He had suddenly been aware that his voice had tightened, and a light sweat ran down his back. "No. Lew was killed a few years ago."

She stopped and turned. The compassion on her face made his insides coil, his throat scratchy. He had the sudden urge to laugh or crack a joke, anything to escape the feeling that she'd treaded into uncharted, vulnerable territory of his heart again.

"I'm sorry," she'd said softly. Her luminous eyes searched his face.

He could barely breathe, but he had managed to nod and brush past her. So maybe giving away all that information hadn't been free after all.

They'd stopped an hour later and bent over their maps. Sarah had obviously been on more than a few SAR expeditions, because she also read maps like a pro. They pinpointed their location, atop Mount Maude, and scanned the horizon for the forest-service tower. Sarah pointed to the south, right where it should be, and Will wondered if these two ladies really didn't need his protection, just as Dani had insisted.

They ate in silence. Dani and Sarah both shed their jackets, then their sweatshirts. He kept his shirt on, preferring the protection it gave from the tree limbs. He slipped away once, checked his cell phone, and couldn't get a signal. Oh, joy. Jeff would be so fun to talk to now that Will had disobeyed . . . twice.

They started out again, Missy in a free search, Dani after her, Sarah marking their movements on the map. Will hiked behind them, watching the sky. It had turned from wispy blue to indigo to an eerie bruised green and purple. He felt the wind kick up now and again, despite the oppressive, odd, May heat.

He strode up to Dani. "So, I think all's fair in love and war. I told you my secrets; now you owe me yours."

She gave him a wide-eyed look.

O-kay, he'd meant that as a joke. "I don't mean *all* your secrets, Dannette. Just the public-knowledge ones will be fine. Background, schooling, favorite movie. Favorite flavor of ice cream." *If I can someday kiss you.*

Oops. What was wrong with him? He took a deep breath, erased that thought from his mind. *Sorry, Lord. I'm trying. I really am. Help me be Your man here.*

As if she'd read his thoughts, she narrowed her eyes. "Promise you won't print my answers?"

What? He frowned, gave a snort of disbelief, and then remembered. Oh yeah, he was a *reporter*. Something akin, in her book, to the sludge at the bottom of a septic tank. He nodded slowly.

She kept one eye on her dog. "I grew up in southern Iowa on a farm." She gave him a half grin. "Yes, I know, big surprise, but actually a farm can be a great place to grow up. Animals. Hard work. Lots of open sky."

"Sounds nice. Do you have any siblings?"

Her smile dimmed. "I had a little sister. She died when we were young. But my dad remarried about ten years ago, and I have two half brothers and a half sister."

"Are your parents divorced?"

Another shadow across her face and this time her mouth tipped with a shade of melancholy. "No, she died not long after my sister."

Ouch. Despite the battering his parents had given him emotionally and verbally, he'd never had to deal with the finality of death. He'd always been able to cling to the hope of tomorrow and second chances. "I'm sorry."

She smiled, and her eyes were warm on his. "Thanks. Actually, God was very gentle. I had doting grandparents, and they pretty much took over and raised me. Granny was a solid Christian, and I grew up with a sound belief that Mom and Ashley were in heaven, maybe looking down at me." She reddened slightly. "I know, sorta childish, but it worked for me growing up."

He had the nearly overpowering urge to reach out and draw her to his chest and tell her that it didn't seem childish at all. It seemed more like survival. He gave a slight smile. "Your granny sounds like she did a good job of filling in."

"She did. She made sure I never felt alone. I remember too many nights when I'd lie awake, letting the darkness find my nooks and crannies, and suddenly, as if she knew, Granny would appear at the door. She'd take me on her lap, wrap her afghan around me, and sing hymns to me until I fell asleep. She loved the classics—'Great Is Thy Faithfulness,' 'Amazing Grace.' The smell of mentholated rub still reminds me of her. That and chocolate-chip cookies and homemade cinnamon bread and snowball candles."

"Snowball candles?"

"Oh yeah. Granny and I made homemade candles every Christmas out of the crayons I'd rubbed to a nub over the year. She also knit me a new pair of sippies every year."

"Should I ask?"

Dani laughed. "Slippers. It's the only thing I know how to knit. They're really warm." Her smile turned wry. "Actually, I haven't touched a knitting needle in years. Not much time at home. I do miss sippies."

Something in her voice made his chest thick. "Is Granny still around?"

Dani didn't look at him when she shook her head. "She died a few years back. It's just me and Missy and Sherlock."

"Who's Sherlock?"

"My other SAR dog, a bloodhound. I'm training him to be a cadaver dog for police searches. When I was young I wanted to be a veterinarian and went to Iowa State for a couple of years, but I got into SAR when I adopted Missy and heard about the need for SAR K-9 handlers. It consumes my life.

We've been all over the country, and I try to do a lot of on-site training."

"Nice. You have a way with animals. It's like you can understand them."

She shot a look at her dog, now circling to acquire the scent pool. "Well, if you get to know them, sometimes you can. You don't have to talk. You kind of sense it."

Somehow he wondered if he'd just been handed some sort of cosmic answer to a question he hadn't yet voiced.

"Besides, Missy and Sherlock aren't only pets. They're my partners. Without them, I couldn't do my job. We rely on each other. Not to mention that they're quite valuable. Thousands of man-hours and dollars go into training a good K-9. But even more importantly . . . Missy and Sherlock are like family. It's just been me and them for . . . years."

He glanced at her—something in her tone made him wonder if she, too, had given away more than she'd planned. And, wow, that felt way too good. "So, your favorite movie?" he asked.

She smiled, as if thankful for his rescue. *"Turner and Hooch."*

"I should have guessed." He laughed. "Favorite ice cream?"

"Oh, I'm a homemade vanilla girl. Granny used to make homemade ice cream, and I've never found its equal."

"I don't know. I think you should try the local Moose Tracks."

She made a face.

"No, seriously. Chocolate swirls, peanut butter." He licked his lips noisily. "Tell you what, when we get back, I'll buy you a cone."

She smirked, and he wanted to whoop when he saw the slightest press of a blush on her skin. It kindled his courage.

"I'd really like to be your friend, Dani," he said softly, trying out her nickname. He wasn't sure where the sudden rush of tender feelings came from, but he hung on to them and pressed ahead. "I know you don't like the fact that I'm a reporter, and I don't know why, but I'd really like to get past that if we can—"

The sudden prickling of the hair on the back of Will's neck made him pause.

She stared at him, her eyes wide, and he didn't know if it was from shock or from the hand he raised to cut off any response.

Yes, he had a definite we-are-being-watched feeling. He wanted to bang his head against a tree. He'd been marching along the woods as if they were in a parade, completely forgetting that he might have a couple of Hayata terrorists on his six.

"Keep moving, but keep quiet. I'll catch up with you." He turned and, passing Sarah with a finger to his lips, charged back through the forest. Veering off their trail, he kept it in his sight as he stole back the way they'd come, probably a quarter mile.

There, in the mud right after the river, he saw boot tracks. Two men, probably armed. Less than an hour behind them. Did they even know Dani and her little search party were breaking the trail?

Of course they did.

A chill climbed up Will's spine as he whirled and headed back in their direction. *Oh, God, please, no.*

If the terrorists were behind him before, they were ahead of him now. . . .

He raced through the forest at full speed, knowing his path. He ducked tree limbs, dived through thickets, not caring that he sounded like a herd of rhinoceros. He caught up quickly, breathing hard.

Dani sat on a tree trunk, wresting with Missy's tug toy. Her expression turned toward concern when she saw him. "Will, your mouth is bleeding."

He stopped, bent over, and propped his hands on his knees. "C'mon, we need to keep moving." To where, exactly? He'd have to hang way behind, flank the women, see if he could outsmart their trackers. But sitting here, they were practically waving red flags.

How could he have been so stupid? His only hope was that the Hayata thugs would want to keep Dani alive as badly as he did, for at least one similar reason: to find Amina.

"Will, what's the matter?" Dani was on her feet. "You look . . . worried."

"No . . ." Oh, he so didn't want to lie to her. What was he going to say? *I think there are a couple of terrorists on our tail, and I know that because I'm really not a reporter.* She might actually like that part. But the next sentence would crush any hope of a future to a fine dust. *I'm really an undercover federal agent, and I've been lying to you since I met you.* Only he hadn't completely lied. At least not about his family or Lew. Or even about wanting to be her friend.

"We need to find a place to hole up," he said. "Look at the sky. I think a storm's coming."

Dani stared at the sky, and if he didn't know better, he thought he saw her pale. In fact, she reached out, braced herself on a tree. "Sarah, we gotta move."

He liked a gal who embraced his causes, but he couldn't deny that Dani looked downright panicked. She hauled out her topo map. "There's a lake about half a mile from here. I think we should head there. We can ride out the storm and then come back here after it passes."

"Good. Go," Will said.

Dani didn't even bother to put the training harness back on Missy; she just got a compass heading and took off. Sarah was two steps behind her.

Will hung back, his heart thundering, scanning the forest, wishing he'd brought his Heckler & Koch MP5 submachine gun instead of a flimsy Beretta pistol.

No, he wished he'd sent Dani home instead of strolling through the woods as if they were on some sort of date.

"The LORD is my portion," Dannette had said this morning at breakfast.

He hoped God was also their protector, because at the moment Will could use all the divine help he could get.

Chapter 10

"WILL, WHAT IS going on?" Dannette stood on the lakeshore as Will combed the boulders that had fallen from a nearby cliff. The wind had begun to whip up, and it brushed her short hair and sent a shiver up her spine.

Or maybe the feeling of creeps came from Will's off-the-charts odd behavior. Yes, the storm had her willies on high, churning up memories that she needed to keep buried. But Boy Scout Masterson was spooking her. He was hunting through the rocks like a bloodhound. They simply needed to find a secure area and pitch their tents. She and Sarah both had survival gear made to tough out storms, and she had no problem bunking in with Sarah and giving Will her tent under these special circumstances.

"Will, come back here and tell me what is going on, please!" Dannette heard the pleading in her voice and tried to quell it. So what if his voice, his actions bellowed protection; and he actually looked like a hero, his hair scuffed up by the wind, his eyes intense and driven as he sought their shelter. So what if he'd actually dug a tiny place in her heart with those soft words: *"I'd really like to be your friend."* It didn't mean that she was going to hand over this SAR mission to a die-hard reporter with an Eagle Scout badge. "Will!"

He turned, and something inside her lost its footing. The wind scraped back his hair, and in his solider getup he looked dark and dangerous. His gaze caught hers but he didn't yell. Just held up his hand. Like an Old Testament prophet stilling the crowd.

Okay, that was too weird of a comparison.

Despite his knowledge of obscure OT Scriptures, Will Masterson certainly didn't have white-collared-pastor look written on his demeanor. Nor did his profession lend itself to anything holy. But he had been chivalrous more than once over the past day, from making them breakfast to holding back tree branches. His dedication to her mission felt altruistic. He hadn't hauled out a tape recorder or notepad once. And his request to be her friend . . . well, most fellas she had known in college would have bypassed the request and gone right into assumptions.

So, maybe she'd reserve judgment and allow that man-of-God analogy to linger a little longer.

She turned away and called to Missy, who had her nose to the air, sniffing. Missy came near, sat on her haunches, and whined. Dannette knelt and curled her arms around the dog's neck. "I agree."

"What is he doing?" Sarah asked as she came up beside her, sat, and petted Missy.

"I think he's trying to find us a place to camp."

"How about here? We have a grassy beach and a nice forested backdrop. We'll camp right inside the forest. It'll buffet the wind and rain."

"I dunno. He's . . . something isn't right here, Sarah. Do you feel it?"

"If you mean do I smell a storm in the air, yes."

"No, there's something else. Is it my imagination or did our reporter friend just turn into some sort of special-ops soldier? He's got definite hints of Jim Micah that go way beyond his stint in the army."

"Maybe he's just concerned."

"Yeah, and my middle name is Relaxed."

Sarah laughed.

The sky had turned a deep, angry green, and the wind had churned up the waves. Missy laid her ears back when lightning flashed over the far horizon and a low rumble rippled through the sky.

"We're in for a doozy."

"Dani!" Will came bounding over the rocks.

"You're letting him call you that?" Sarah asked.

Dannette ignored her, not wanting to confront that omission . . . or acceptance at the moment. "What?"

"I found a spot. C'mon." He jumped down to the grassy area and nearly hauled Dannette and Sarah to their feet. "Hurry."

Dannette cast a look over her shoulder. "I don't think it'll get here for another hour."

Will nodded, but his movements didn't slow. He leaped across the rocks, from one boulder to the next, reaching out to help Dannette and Sarah, who jumped past him easily. He led them into a cleft in the rock face. Around the overhang, boulders the size of Volkswagens had fallen to form a small enclave. Grass pooled at the bottom, just large enough for two tents.

"Set up camp here. I'm going to be gone for a little while. Put up your tents and stake them down hard. And tie up Missy."

Dannette gave him a hard look. "I'll bring her inside with me."

"No. Tie her up. If she gets scared, she's liable to hurt you."

"Hardly. Give me some credit for knowing my dog, okay?"

Silence pulsed between them. Finally, he said, "Fine. But make sure you're inside when that storm hits."

He turned, but Dannette grabbed his arm. "What about you? Where will you stay? That flimsy A-frame isn't going to last two seconds."

"Don't worry about me." He reached out, cupped her hand on his arm, and gave it a slight squeeze. The softness in his eyes didn't match the storm brewing around them. "But thanks, anyway." Then he tore out of her grip and rushed away.

She couldn't help feeling that somehow he wasn't at all the man he claimed to be.

✦ ✦ ✦

Will glanced back over his shoulder, feeling the wind against his neck, raising the tiny hairs of fear. He'd found a place where anyone attacking them would have to approach from the front. And he'd be watching that approach from a healthy, sharp-shooter's distance. If only he didn't have just his pistol. He'd much prefer a Barrett .50 cal sniper rifle. Still, he felt the odds were in his favor.

Thank You, Lord, for letting me spot the Hayata tracks. There was a lot, perhaps, that he'd missed in the way of God's protection and intervention over the years, but he planned on spending more time paying attention. Or maybe he'd begun to care about his SAR mates and needed God's help more than he realized. Not that he deserved God's attention, but he shot a smile toward heaven anyway.

He ducked into the forest and hiked up along the cliff where it rose and hovered above the ladies. The sky was begin-ning to crackle and rumble, and he searched the ledge for the best perch to see Dani and Sarah and still watch his back. He circled around to stand over their position, peered down, and was happy to see that they weren't visible from this view.

Which also meant that the Hayata thugs couldn't stand above them and drill them with bullets.

Only it wasn't bullets that he worried about at the moment. If he were a terrorist, he'd go straight for the K-9, grab Dani, and use her friend as leverage to make the handler find Amina.

It sometimes scared him how easily he thought like a bad guy.

He kept walking and climbed down until he found an enclave not far from Dannette and Sarah's position. The natural fortress both bulwarked him from the storm and gave him a full view of the landscape around the ladies. If anyone walked into their territory, at least while they were camped, he'd know.

But what did he do after the storm passed? Without a doubt, divine protection had gotten them all to this beach-head. Once the storm passed, Dani would want to resume the search.

And then what? No, I can't let you keep hiking through the woods, although that is your job, because there are a couple of blood-hungry terrorists out to snatch you and your dog. Yeah, that would be a fun conversation. Even if he had clearance to break cover—which he didn't—he'd be demolishing their feeble friendship and Dani's trust. More than that, even if she let him tag along, he wasn't so sure he could keep them safe and let her do her job. SAR didn't exactly work in a controlled environment. Especially if there were more than two terrorists hunting them down.

Maybe, instead of sitting in his protective pocket, he needed to find their tails and take them out first.

He glanced at the horizon and saw the sky had turned an ugly fungus green. The wind began to bend the trees. Will heard snapping, felt the chill of a northern storm. He peeked one last time toward Dani and her camp, then climbed out of his shelter and stole toward the woods.

Rain began to pelt him as he ran to the trees. His sweater dampened; a shiver ran down his spine. He crouched, watching the forest as he moved along the perimeter of the cliff. They were here—he could feel it.

The rain barraged the forest, and with the gale wind, sticks and leaves blew across his horizon. Water trickled down his cheek. He fought a chill and crept behind trees, squinting in the gathering darkness.

Please, God, protect—

Movement in his peripheral vision turned him. He stilled, scanned the forest.

A twig snapped behind him. He whirled, gun drawn.

Line drive, right to his chin with the butt of an AK-47. Pain exploded in his brain. He caught a glimpse of his attacker—dark hair, darker eyes, and enough anger to make him very, very dangerous.

Yeah, well, me too.

Will sent his shoulder into his attacker's gut. The man fell backward, kicked out, caught Will on his knee. Will's eyes crossed in a second of white pain. He lunged just as the man rolled to his knees. They went down in the wet, spongy loam.

Will drove his arm against the man's neck. The man looked painfully like himself—black BDUs, a face full of mud. Only this version came equipped with a terrorist-identifying Russian-issue submachine gun. Yep, Hayata.

The man drilled his elbow into Will's ribs.

Will gritted his teeth, pushed the man's face farther into the dirt. Around them, rain sliced the trees and the wind howled. Will felt nothing but the heat of fury in the center of his chest.

A shot pinged just past Will's face. He even felt the burn

as it whizzed by him. He launched back off his attacker and dived for a trio of birch trees.

He studied the forest, saw nothing as the wind picked up and swirled the leaves and blurred his vision with rain.

Another shot.

Will ducked behind a tree and searched for his Beretta. He'd dropped it in the tussle, and there it sat, an inconvenient five feet away, on the other side of the tree. He was pinned down, and the terrorist in the mud had vanished.

A thousand fitting words filled his mind, but a roar, loud and full of fury, rumbled through the sky. What—?

A storm wave rolled in, blackening the sky. As Will debated his options, the sky cracked open and heaved. Water, no—*bullets*—of rain shot out of the darkness, followed by a rush of wind that bowed the trees. They broke near the top, toppling over. Around him the sky rained branches, a barrage of litter. Old trees, already dead, exploded and launched themselves across the forest, shredding other trees.

Will clamped his hands over his head, tightening into a ball as a dead birch landed five feet away, spraying broken branches like the debris from a grenade.

The roaring swelled. Deafening, it swept over Will, lashing him with horizontal rain, heaving sticks and trees from its path. Another tree cracked, landed on the old birch.

In all his years in the Green Berets, in the sandstorms of Desert Storm, in the hurricanes on the southern shores of America, in the earthquakes of the Middle East, he'd never seen such violence. Will protected his head as a tree branch arrowed toward him. He closed his eyes, waiting to be speared, and felt his breath rush out fast when the branch landed just above him, lodged in the vee of his now very favorite three trees.

The howling wind diminished slightly, as if it were passing

to its next victim. Still, the wind bent the trees sideways, stripping away buds, feeble branches. Will heard nothing above the lash of rain, felt nothing but his heartbeat in his mouth, the clamp of ice needling his skin, tasted only panic. *Please, God, protect Dani!*

✦ ✦ ✦

Dannette tucked Missy in beside her, nearly lying on top of the dog as the animal whined and pressed her wet nose into Dannette's chest. "Shh," she said, but she too wanted to whine. She saw the frenzied waves of her tortured tent, heard the roaring, felt the *thwump* of trees and branches. She'd lashed her tent down but now felt as if the only thing holding her to the ground was her own body.

That thought sent a chill right to her toes. She buried her face in Missy's head. Closed her eyes.

It felt too real. Too close to *then*.

The noise, the violence, the chaos rushed her back to the past. Missy continued to whine, to wriggle in her arms, as her mind flashed back to the past.

Shh, Ashley, don't cry.

Why, oh why, hadn't they listened to Mama not to go far? not to venture out into the cornfield? Dannette buried her face in her sister's hair, enduring her questions, pleading with God to see them down here, to send an angel to find them, protect them. But how could someone find them when Dannette, set on adventure, had packed a knapsack and set out through the tall furrowed corn, dragging her timid little sister in her wake? It had been a bright, sunny day. And she'd planned to go as far as the road, then hike home. After all, she was six years old. She took the bus to kindergarten. She knew how to get home.

Only the road didn't appear where she'd left it. Not even after the fun died and heat settled into their skin, driving the Iowa dirt into her pores, her eyes. "I'm thirsty," Ashley had complained, and Dannette snapped at her. She felt bad about that now as she held Ashley and listened to the wind howl, felt the cold rain pelt them.

"We'll be okay," she whispered, but even she could hear the tremor in her own voice.

The growl started across the field, like a freight train, but they didn't have a train near their property. The corn began to bend, to twist as the train came closer. Ashley started to scream. Over and over. And Dannette shook with white-hot fear.

"Please, God." She looked up in time to see the cornstalks shredding around her. "Get down!" She pulled at Ashley and dived into the furrow, her hands over her head. But Ashley pushed away from Dannette and stood up, screaming.

She was gone.

Ashley? Dannette's breath swiped out of her chest for an eternal second. *Ashley?*

And then she screamed.

Dannette wound her fingers into her dog's fur, shaking, tears burning her cheeks, fighting that same scream. *Please, God!*

She heard it now, as she had then, the freight train, the rush of wind, the past hurtling toward her. The world spun as her tent writhed. She held Missy, but the dog pushed against her, clawed her way out of Dannette's grip. She felt a toenail slice her chin, but the world had turned orange, her tent cocooning her as it collapsed.

She flailed, fighting it.

Heard her voice screaming.

Felt herself falling, as if the earth had dropped out from beneath her.

Then something hit her, blinding her with a spear of pain. She tasted blood and fell into darkness.

✦ ✦ ✦

Twenty minutes passed before the rain subsided enough for Will to edge out toward the last known position of his Beretta. No sign of the terrorists who had pinned him down.

Maybe the finger of God's storm had taken out the terrorists as well. Will crept toward his weapon and found it buried under leaves and some heavy branches. His heart still lodged in his chest, disbelief waging war with reality.

The forest looked as if it had been hit by an atomic bomb. Leveled, except for the trees that had been cut off at the top by the first attack. Will was counted among the living because his three-pronged birch grouping had withstood the assault. Still, he had to extricate himself from the labyrinth of debris. Ears perked for gunshots, he climbed over broken, once towering birch trees, contorted pine, and stripped balsam.

What was that—a tornado in the middle of the forested north woods?

More than that, what had happened to the man he'd tackled and his cohort who had fired the shots?

Had they found Dani and Sarah?

"Dani!" Will wrenched himself through the tangle and raced down the cliff line to the shore.

His heart stopped dead in his chest.

Forest debris had pummeled the rocky enclave he'd so carefully chosen for its protection. He climbed over the rocks, adrenaline thundering in his veins. He could make out their tents. One orange, one purple. Both had been pinned by trees, yet the orange one lay scrunched up against the rock wall.

His throat dried and he couldn't make out movement. "Dani?"

As if to mock him, the sun peeked between two clouds.

"Sarah?" He holstered his gun, ran over to the purple tent, relief shaking out his muscles. It wasn't pinned after all—a boulder had protected it from being flattened. Sarah unzipped the flap, stuck her head out. "You okay?" he asked as he helped her out.

She nodded, but her face turned ashen when she saw Dani's tent. "Oh no."

Will surveyed the scene, trying to keep his thoughts crisp, tight. A tree had landed right above the tent, propped up by the wall of rock. Still the tent looked as if it had been thrown by angry hands. Will rolled the log away and stood for a moment, his hands shaking.

Sarah moved in front of him. "I'm an EMT." She reached for the zipper, and he swallowed for the first time in minutes. He recognized combat mode in Sarah's movements. Mechanical. Determined. She pulled down the zipper of the one-man tent.

Dani lay huddled inside, sobbing. She had her arms around her dog, her face buried in Missy's fur.

"Dani?" he said and heard how panicked he sounded.

She looked up, pain in those hazel eyes, a trickle of blood down her chin, her lip fattened.

Will felt something inside him rip from its moorings. "You're hurt."

"I'm fine," she whispered. Her face crumpled as she fought for words. "It's Missy. I think she's . . . dead."

Chapter 11

DANNETTE STOOD OVER Sarah, rubbing her hands on her arms, feeling hollow and weak.

Please, Lord, no.

Missy lay still as Sarah checked her eyes, felt for her pulse. Will had extricated Dannette from her K-9 and helped her out of the tent before going back for Missy. The fact that he crouched next to Sarah, concern knotting his brow, somehow kept the scream contained deep inside Dannette's chest.

Please, Lord, no.

Sarah leaned back, her steady, calm eyes on Dannette. "She's not dead. I found a thready pulse. She may have internal bleeding or just be in shock. Whatever the case, we need to get her to help soon."

Dannette felt her world sway, reached out, and felt strong hands supporting her as she crumbled to the ground. Will had appeared out of nowhere, and suddenly she was in his embrace, tight against his wet sweater.

She gulped a shaky breath, trying to sort through Sarah's words. "We're miles from the nearest vet hospital," she whispered.

Will nodded. His arms tightened around her, and for the first time since she met him, she felt profoundly grateful for his never-say-no presence. She closed her eyes, nearly giving in to the temptation to grab onto his sweater and hide in his arms.

He was just a friend. A very nice friend.

"We have a couple of options as I see it," Sarah said as she knelt before Dannette. Sarah herself looked pale and scared. "We can carry Missy out on a litter." She glanced at Will. "Or one of us can hike out and send back help."

"No." The tone of Will's voice, curt and without room for debate, brought Dannette's head up.

"No," he repeated, looking into Dannette's eyes. "I'm not leaving you ladies here alone, and I'm not letting you or Sarah hike out by yourself."

"I'm a big girl," Sarah said, her eyes darkening. "I don't need your permission or your protection. Besides, what about the girl we're tracking? She's . . . she might be hurt."

He gave Sarah a look that he must have learned at boot camp. The guy could be a drill instructor with no practice whatsoever. "No. We can't find her without the dog."

Dannette glanced at him, then back at Sarah. Sarah was right—what about the girl? Dannette remained on her knees, feeling weak. "We have to keep looking. . . ."

Will's eyes widened.

"But what if I'm wrong?" Dannette said. "Oh, Sarah, what if you're right? What if . . . maybe she's not even out there . . . and now Missy's hurt—"

"Stop." Will rounded on her, wrapped his hands around her arms. "Stop. You're not to blame for this. Breathe. Slowly. We'll take Missy out. And then I'll come back and keep looking." His eyes locked on hers, held them.

Breathe. Slowly. She felt his words more than heard them, saw the compassion, even strength, in his eyes. "Will, she's probably not even out here. I've probably made up the entire thing."

He stayed silent, but something like pain crossed his expression. Yeah, well, she felt the same way. Sick at heart.

"Okay, then what?" Sarah said. "We carry Missy out?"

"Yes. That's exactly what we're going to do," said Will.

Dannette frowned at him, noticing up close that his whiskers had hints of gray amidst the deep brown. She disentangled herself from his arms, common sense faintly kicking in. "Wait, Will. All that jostling might injure Missy even more." She crouched next to her dog, ran her hand down her fur. *Missy, oh, Missy.* How could she have let this happen? What had ever possessed her to drag them out on a wild-goose chase?

Old voices, accusations rose like specters, and she fought to close her ears.

"Yeah, and hiking out to bring back help will take double the time." Will hauled out his topo map and studied it. She saw his concentration in the rise and fall of his chest, the way he ran a strong finger over possible trails. For a moment she wondered where he'd ridden out the storm. He had a welt on his jaw, as if he'd been nicked by a branch, and he winced once when he repositioned his legs. Yet she had a feeling that he could have all his teeth knocked out and he'd still grin and deny any pain.

"We're on Tom Lake. I'm not sure how we got here, but if we follow the shoreline, we can cut off at the forest-service road. And from there, we'll find Tom Lake Road. We can flag down a ride, or if the road is clear, I'll run up to my truck and get it."

Sarah peered over his shoulder. "Your route will bring us out a good ten miles from the rest area. And you'll just *run up* and get your truck?"

He gave her a lopsided, shy grin. "I'm in pretty good shape."

Sarah lifted her hands in surrender. "Whatever."

Dannette recognized her friend's frustration. She never reacted well to a guy telling her no.

Maybe it *would* be faster if Sarah went alone. She had the experience and knowledge to navigate the woods quickly. Then again, Will did seem to know his way around the woods. Dannette had to give him credit—he'd kept up like a trooper. No, more than that . . . he'd tried to get them to safety before the storm hit.

And right now, he was proving to be just that friend he'd asked to be.

Will rose, strode over to Dannette's mangled tent. "Help me fashion this into a stretcher. We'll carry Missy between us." He laid the fabric out and produced his knife. She'd forgotten he'd had it and tried to ignore the cold slide of shock down her spine.

In five minutes he'd made a makeshift bed, using downed tree lengths, the tent, and Dannette's sleeping bag.

"Sarah, cover Missy with a blanket, and if you can, Dani, put on a muzzle. Disoriented and in pain, Missy might react with fear. But make sure she can still breathe."

What, now he was Dr. Doolittle? Dannette, however, dug through her pack and unearthed Missy's muzzle. She and Sarah transferred Missy to the stretcher, tucked her in the sleeping bag, then strapped it down to keep her immobile.

Missy appeared so frail, so dwarfed by the swaddling and the sleeping bag, Dannette wanted to cry.

As Will shouldered his pack, his jacket opened.

Dannette stared hard at a small black piece of hardware in a shoulder holster. "Is that a gun?" she asked, her voice high and tight.

Will turned, and any last shred of belief that he was some

backwoods reporter vanished when she saw his granite expression. "Let's get moving. We're running out of time," he said.

Was he talking about Missy . . . or something else? An image of Will Masterson looking dark and dangerous burned into her mind as she followed him down the shore.

"Two men got out of the pickup, and when they came down to the picnic area, they asked if we'd seen a young girl. I think she was afraid of someone."

Dannette hid a gasp as she followed Will. What kind of journalist was he? If at all?

Suddenly she wondered if her unnamed, perhaps even phantom victim, might be safer if she was never found.

Will didn't want to push Dani, and he knew that she'd feel better helping carry the animal, but they would make twice the time if he took the dog in his arms and ran. What was left of the day disintegrated slowly as they traversed the shore, cut south at his determination, and finally found the forest-service road. It looked like it had been hit with the same ammo used on the shoreline. Trees down, branches littering the road. At one point he suggested Sarah take one handle, Dani the other so they could move faster through the debris.

Dani walked in silence. Whether from agony or from horror, he didn't know. What he did know was that she had questions. And he didn't want to have any part of the answers.

He felt nearly ill thinking about the possibilities. If it weren't for the fact that Dani and Sarah could be ambushed, he might have talked them into letting him pack Missy out alone. He couldn't escape the rather ugly picture of Amina weathering the storm only to be killed by the two Hayata thugs who had jumped him in the forest.

His Special Forces training in the Green Berets had taught him to deal with one task at a time. To plan ahead but not borrow trouble. He'd get these ladies out safely, hopefully pick up his new partner in town, even up the teams a bit, then head back to Tom Lake and complete his mission.

But when he looked at Dani's tear-soaked face, he had a hard time remembering exactly what that mission was. A huge part of him wanted to haul her into his arms and tell her it would be okay.

Which it wouldn't be if her dog died. He was smart enough to know that much. Missy might be a canine, but Will knew that she occupied a special place in Dani's heart.

Will wasn't going to let the dog die on his watch.

He heard about a billion ticking clocks even as he upped his pace. Hayata terrorists were still searching the woods and if they hadn't found the girl yet, they would. Nazar was waiting to be extracted from the game he played, and Hayata poised to take out another target . . . possibly like the one that had killed Lew and a hundred other soldiers.

And Missy lay as still as death.

Will lifted his end of the stretcher over another log. "How are you doing?" He directed the question at both women but glanced at Dani. She looked strung out, her hair wild from the storm, her eyes reddened. She didn't smile at him, and he saw suspicion in her eyes.

He forced an encouraging smile. "Not much farther."

They hiked the rest of the road in silence. By the time they emerged to Tom Lake Road, the moon had risen. Stars twinkled, as if a reminder that, while their corner of the world had been ravaged, the universe was still intact.

Or at least some of it. Dani looked unraveled as she sat by the road, stroking a motionless Missy.

"I'm going for my truck," he said.

"No, please get mine," Dani said suddenly. She pulled out her keys, tossed them. "It's got a first-aid kit in it."

Sadly, his was closer. Much closer. But he wasn't thrilled to tell her that. He shook her keys in his hand, wanting to meet her eyes, to tell her it would be okay. "I'll be right back," he said quietly, then took off in a run.

He reached his truck nearly an hour later. Sweat dripped off his temples, drenched his sweater, and his feet felt on fire. He climbed in behind the wheel and floored it to the rest area, where he switched vehicles. As he drove away in Dani's pickup, in the gleam of the headlights he noted a Jeep Cherokee and beside that a beat-up Chevy with a bed topper and sticks littered over the windshield. As if it had been sitting there as long as their vehicles had.

Will punched the gas.

Dani and Sarah had made a shelter just off the road. Good. Even with the moon, they were difficult to spot. He pulled up, and silently they loaded Missy into the built-in shelter in the back of the truck. Dani climbed in with her K-9, her eyes on Will as he shut the door. He climbed into the driver's seat, Sarah into the passenger side.

Sarah was already on the cell phone, waking up the local vet.

✦ ✦ ✦

Fadima shook, the chill finding her bones, her every molecule. Hunger had her by the throat, and she felt as if she might be better off simply surrendering.

The storm had scared her. Like an ancient god, its hand

covered the sky, its breath flattened the forest, its anger spewed out tears and sweat. She'd huddled in a pocket of forest, just beyond what looked like a lake, and prayed for forgiveness to whatever being was controlling the elements.

She should have never run away. Maybe she could have bargained. Maybe she could have waited. Maybe she was going to cost her family their lives.

Maybe she wasn't truth at all but a pitiful, giant lie.

She gulped a deep, shuddering breath. *"Fadima, you are my light."* Her father's face flashed through her mind, picking at her fears. *"You will free us all. It is your destiny."*

Freedom. She was so *free* it was going to kill her. She knew there was a lake not far off. If she could reach it, get a drink, and maybe find food . . . She forced herself to her feet and stumbled forward, the press of night nearly suffocating into its completeness. If it weren't for the occasional fractured beams of moonlight, she'd be without hope. But she saw the gray dent of shoreline through the knot of forest and kept her eyes riveted.

Night sounds pecked at her courage—a hooting owl, the rush of wind, trees cracking.

Voices?

She stilled.

A flashlight beam scraped the night, and she crouched into a ball, her heartbeat filling her throat.

"This is stupid. She couldn't have lived through this."

Men. Their feet broke branches, the cracks resounding in Fadima's soul.

"We have to find her. We can't return without her body."

Her body?

She made herself very, very small, tucking herself under a tree, breathing in shallow breaths like her brother had taught her.

The thought of Kutsi nearly brought tears to her eyes. She

conjured up his face, trying to find his calm as her searchers scanned the forest. Kutsi had never seen her like the other men did—as her father's princess. Of course not. He was only one year older, and they'd spent their youth fighting, studying the way of their people, handling weapons, learning strategy and even evasion skills. Her father's idea of fun meant dropping them off in the far hills with instructions to return before dinner.

As if he knew that someday her life would be about hiding. About fighting.

"The key to a good defense is surprise," Kutsi said once as they'd watched their father scope the hills for his children. Just knowing he was looking for them, despite his words, had sent warmth to her chest. He may have been the esteemed ataman of a hundred warriors, but he was still her papa.

A papa who believed in her.

She would die before she let him be executed or discovered as a traitor.

Instead of running through the forest looking for help, she should have been fashioning a weapon, concocting a surprise for the men trailing her.

A branch snapped a few feet away, and she ducked her head as the flashlight beam skimmed slightly beyond her.

If she got out of this alive, next time she would be prepared.

She may be only a woman where she came from, but in this country she was a priceless asset. And despite her gender, her father had taught her well. The eldest daughter of Ataman Erkan Nazar would die as a warrior.

Chapter 12

WILL HAD GONE back to his cabin, changed clothes, and looked every inch like a swaggering South Dakotan cowboy when he strolled into the vet's office. And from the pleasant smell of soap emanating off him, Dannette guessed he'd showered.

He changed his appearance like a politician changed platforms. Where had the guy with the look and equipment of a special-ops soldier disappeared to?

Dani didn't know what to believe about Will Masterson, and the worry around his dark eyes did nothing to sort things out in her heart.

"You okay?" he greeted Dannette, who was sitting in the vet's waiting room, her knees up, her hands locked around them. Next to her, Sarah slumped in a chair sleeping, her hair tumbling out of her ponytail and wisping around her dirt-streaked face. They both looked wrung out and rumpled.

Dannette answered with a shrug. No fair that Will looked like he'd had a complete eight hours of sleep, even though he'd left only an hour ago. The Boy Scout side of him had waited until Missy had emerged from surgery with a positive prognosis before he went to clean up.

"Any news?"

"They don't know. They bound her broken ribs and stopped the internal bleeding. She's sedated for now." Dannette pressed her fingertips to her eyes, feeling weak, fighting another wave of tears.

Will knelt before her and touched her knee. He'd not only bathed but added some really nice-smelling cologne. Devastatingly nice. Or maybe it was the contrast to her oh-so-yummy forest-and-sweat scent. She felt as if she'd crawled through cobwebs and had twigs and moss and crawly things tangled in her greasy hair. A real beauty queen.

"You need some sleep," he said.

She sighed, nodded. "I wish Missy were human. I'd go in there, lie down beside her, hold her hand, tell her how much I love her." She hadn't quite meant to unload all that, but the kindness in his eyes drew it out of her.

"She knows, Dani." Will took her hand, rubbed it. She stared at her hand in his, startled by the gesture, especially when he trailed his thumb over the back of her hand. He had strong, capable hands and arms, and she couldn't deny that a large part of her simply wanted to sink inside them and hang on.

She must be very, very tired.

She pulled her hand away. In addition to feeling like walking toxic waste, she felt as if her emotions had been mauled by a couple of large rottweilers. And she was hungry; she was pretty sure she hadn't eaten in about forty days.

As if he could read her thoughts, Will stood and picked up her backpack. "C'mon. I'm taking you back to your motel. You should shower and climb into bed." He nudged Sarah with his foot. "You too, sunshine."

Sarah groaned, came half awake.

"In the meantime, I'll drive up to the rest area and retrieve the trucks."

"Who? You and your clone?" Sarah sat up and pulled her hair back into a ponytail. "Or are you going to simply jog out there and pick them up? I mean, it's a mere thirty miles. You'll be back in a jiffy."

He gave a sardonic grin. "I called a friend from the paper."

Dannette let him pull her to her feet, his words carving into her sleep-fuddled brain. Oh yeah, he was a *reporter,* not a member of a north woods SWAT team.

Obviously, she'd left rational thought back there on the shore and returned with only her suspicions. She should pay attention to the fact that he had helped her carry Missy to the vet, abandoning any sort of diabolical agenda he might have had for sneaking around in the woods. And that included even his reporter's agenda, right?

Confused, she swallowed hard and trudged over to the reception desk. "Can I inquire about Missy?"

The vet tech gave her a sympathetic look. "She's still in recovery. Why don't you leave your number and we'll call you?"

Dannette scratched out her number, then followed Will and Sarah out into the parking lot. The sun simmered over the eastern horizon, warming the puddles left by the storm. Even here in Moose Bend carnage littered the parking lot.

Dannette suddenly felt frail, remembering the way the tempest had simply picked them up and tossed them against the rocks, buried them under debris.

Just like Ashley.

She often wondered how her sister had felt, gulped by the twister. Now she knew.

She wished she didn't.

Dannette decided to let Will drive and slid into the middle seat of her truck. Sarah climbed in beside her.

"Where are you staying?" he asked.

Dannette gave him directions, then asked, "Was anyone else hurt in the storm last night?"

Will started the truck and backed out. "I stopped by the office. Evidently the storm started in northwest Minnesota, and by the time it hit the BWCAW they clocked winds at 120 mph. The wind can toss a semi at 70 mph, so we're lucky to be alive."

"Hopefully we'll all live," Dannette said softly.

Will glanced at her as he turned onto the street. "She'll make it."

Dannette nodded.

"There are people missing and lost up and down the shore," Will continued after a moment. "If you weren't already searching for that little girl, you'd be answering a call-out."

"I'm not going anywhere without Missy." The very thought of facing the woods alone sent a shudder through her. She knew all about being alone with her fears, and somehow Missy or Sherlock, her bloodhound, had always been enough to keep those fears outside her perimeter.

Without Missy, the nightmares would close in.

"Will, how about if you wait around while I change; then I'll drive with you to get your truck and Sarah's Jeep," Dannette said.

Will frowned, one eyebrow down in disagreement.

Dannette shook her head. "I can't sleep. Not with Missy in danger. I gotta keep moving. Please?"

He searched her eyes, and for a second she thought he might be able to read right through to her fears of being alone right now. He even reached out and squeezed her hand. Reassuringly. Friendly.

When he let go, she hated how much she missed his touch. Yes, she'd definitely left a huge part of her common sense back in the woods. Perhaps he *was* a stalker—he certainly knew how to blindside her heart.

No, *no* she would not fall for a guy who spilled secrets and destroyed lives for a living. Even if he did have a way of making her feel oddly safe, even protected.

"Okay. I'll wait in the truck while you get changed," he said.

She managed a slight smile.

"I'm going to call Micah and update him," Sarah said, looking out the window.

Dannette leaned her head on Sarah's shoulder. "Thanks for everything."

Sarah took her hand. "God's mercies are new every morning. Remember that, okay? His grace is sufficient for this moment."

Yeah, and what about the moment when Missy died? Dannette closed her eyes, forcing herself beyond that thought.

Will nearly argued with her. Dani was tired and needed some rest. But the fact that she'd leaned into his hand, squeezing back a little and looking at him with some sort of silent request . . . well, the feeling of longing that he'd been fighting went to full boil in his chest.

Friends. Full stop. *Just* friends.

Dani had looked pretty good in the duds she had on—even if they were grimy. Yet, when she emerged from her motel room less than thirty minutes later, her hair still wet, wearing jeans, a clean sweatshirt, and a down vest, he had to admit that it was worth the wait.

Just friends.

She slid into the truck, smelling of shampoo. Fresh. Sweet. "Thanks for waiting."

"Thanks for your help." *Just friends.*

He hadn't quite figured out whom he would get to help him haul the vehicles home. Sarah's suggestion that he jog out there didn't feel so far from the truth. Maybe hitchhike. It wasn't like he really had any friends at the paper to ask. Not the kind who would do him a favor at least. He thought of Sally Appleton at border control. He wouldn't count her in his circle of friends.

Okay, he'd admit that his circle looked pretty meager. Dani, however, had managed to stick one foot in, as if testing the water. It was all he could do not to lunge at it like a largemouth bass, despite the warnings screaming in his head. He didn't have time to make friends or anything else. He had a mission—find one very lost girl and intercept one terrorist attack.

Hopefully, however, his only mission for today was to keep Dani's mind off trekking back into the woods and to sit tight while HQ checked out a report of a trucker who'd picked up a teenage girl thirty miles south of Moose Bend. But if said report panned out, he'd be heading south by tomorrow.

So much for being Dani's friend.

He tried not to let that thought dampen the fact that he had about eight clear hours to spend with Dani before he turned in his reporter's badge and became yet another person.

"Are you hungry?" he asked as he pulled out of the lot.

"I think I could eat a moose."

He glanced at her, and she wore a soft smile. It did dangerous things to his pulse, especially when she added a hint of warmth in those hazel eyes. "Great. Okay. Let me buy you a venison sausage omelette from Nancy's. I promise it'll be better than our last meal together."

She buckled her seat belt. "Promise no digging for information? No hint of sniffing out a headline or tunneling for SAR facts?"

"Yeah, I promise." His job as a reporter was the last thing on his mind at the moment, but her hatred of journalists still bothered him, like an itch longing to be scratched. What was that about, and how could they get past it?

The one logical answer—honesty—made him flinch, and he put it out of his mind as they drove to Nancy's.

"This town has really been razed," Dani said as they passed downed tree limbs, two electrical trucks, and a tow truck.

"I guess the power went out for a while too. The hospital ran on generators for three hours."

"Those winds were scary."

"Yeah. I've been in lots of storms, but nothing like that."

"Life's like that, I think. We never know what forces are out there until they affect our lives."

"Like the attachment to an animal?"

She gave him a sad smile. "Or maybe an unexpected friend."

Oh. His mouth dried and breath fully left his chest. He swallowed twice before words came out of his mouth. "I appreciate your faith in me."

"Well, perhaps I recognize God's provision in my life. You were really a lifesaver out there last night. I'm really sorry that I was so hard on you."

He shrugged, but her words felt like gentle rain on all his dry and achy places. Probably too much. He smiled, covering the emotions that roughened his voice. "So, how is Sarah doing?"

"She crashed. She told me not to wake her until I had news on Missy."

He resisted the urge to touch Dani's hand, give her reassurances. Suddenly that gesture seemed way too . . . friendly. Just having her admit that they were friends had put images into his head. Images that he was pretty sure weren't included in her definition of *friend*.

Like her in his arms, running his hands through her soft hair, maybe getting closer to that smell on her skin.

Kissing her.

Okay, see, Lord? I'm totally weak. You've given me a chance to be the guy You want me to be. A friend. Someone she can trust. Help me to learn what it means to do things Your way. To be just friends.

He pulled into Nancy's.

"Think she'll remember us?" Dani asked.

Us. He liked the sound of that pronoun. "Yeah. I think she will." He noticed she'd turned slightly pink and couldn't stop himself from touching her shoulder. "But it'll be okay."

She got out of the truck. "As long as you don't have any more deep hidden secrets, I think I'm safe."

His smile dimmed as he got out of the truck, slammed the door. *Oh yeah, real safe.* He felt like a dog as he followed her in. So much for friendship, for doing things God's way. What about honesty? A real friendship was based on truth.

And truth was the one commodity he didn't have to trade.

He held the door open. Nancy was behind the counter, loading a fresh batch of cinnamon rolls into her counter display. "Ah, the happy couple," she said.

Dani reddened.

Will shook his head. "We had a misunderstanding, that's all. I'm trying to buy her friendship back with one of your venison-sausage omelettes."

Nancy grinned. "That'll work. Two?"

He nodded and led Dani over to a table. She let him pull

out a chair for her. In the morning light, she looked clean and fresh, despite the hue of fatigue in her eyes and her rebellious blonde hair. She clasped her hands together and leaned her chin on them, resting her elbows on the table. "Thanks for this."

"Thanks for a second chance." He signaled to Nancy as she emerged with a coffeepot.

Dannette put a hand over her cup and asked for tea.

"Just curious, but you got a little red when she mentioned *couple*. Am I interfering with someone else's time with you?"

If it were possible, Dani reddened further. *Whoops*. Or *yeah!* Not like it mattered . . . oh, brother, what exactly was he thinking? He wanted to dive under the table.

However, she elaborated. "It's just me and my dogs. God hasn't brought His man for me into my life yet."

Oh. She was waiting for God's choice. Okay, another good "just friends" reminder from the heavens. Words barely made it out of his dry throat. "So, you mentioned something about Sarah being on an SAR team with you?"

Nancy emerged with the tea. Dani unwrapped her tea bag and dipped it into the hot water, unfazed—or maybe relieved— at his change in topics. "Yeah. A few years ago Sarah; her cousin Conner Young, a former Green Beret; my former room-mate, Andee; Conner's captain, Jim Micah; and I formed this loose travel group."

She knew Jim Micah? And Conner Young? What kind of cruel small world was this? The one woman he wanted to start a friendship with as a born-again God's man was friends with two former Green Beret teammates who know the old Will. Wild Will. He kept his smile pasted on but couldn't ignore the feeling that God had just sliced him through with a sickle.

"We all like to cave and climb and canoe, so we'd get together when they were stateside for some outdoor R & R. But of course type A alpha male Jim Micah can't breathe without some sort of life purpose, so he decided that we should use our skills to become a freelance SAR team. Since Sarah and I are rescue personnel by career choice, it seemed a natural fit. He's thinking of turning professional. We haven't done much so far, but I like the idea." She ran her fingers over her cup rim. She had pretty fingers, with blunt, clean nails that fit with her no-nonsense, what-you-see-is-what-you-get personality. They nearly hypnotized him out of the panic that had coiled in his stomach.

So much for keeping his little secret. Or for her thinking he might be the kind of guy she could trust. True, Micah and Conner didn't know him now—not since Lew died and Will had asked God to change him from the inside out. In fact, he'd seen little of Iceman and Sparks since the first Gulf War. Still, the reputation he'd seared into their minds would compel them to warn Dani to run—and fast.

God certainly used creative ways to answer Will's prayers to help him keep this thing *just friends.* He felt like putting his hands over his head and moaning.

Thankfully, Dani didn't seem to notice the guy having an emotional meltdown across the table from her as she continued. "In little towns like Moose Bend, the SAR team tends to be part of the sheriff's department. They don't have much in the way of equipment or even advanced training. When someone is lost, like this girl, we have to move quickly, without a lot of time for detailed instruction. That's where Team Hope comes in. All of us are trained, in one form or another, in wilderness rescues, map reading, victim psychology, and EMT skills. We can assess a situation and move in a flash.

"And Conner, our tech expert, has us hooked up with the latest in gear and resources. He just purchased a computer program that allows us to input the pertinent information—

terrain, size and weight and age of the victim, weather conditions, and even psychological factors—and receive a relatively accurate SAR plan."

Yeah, that sounded like Conner. Mr. Gadget. "We could have used some of that equipment looking for this girl," Will said.

Except what if the victim didn't want to be found?

Sorrow washed across Dani's pretty face. "Think she's still out there?"

He looked down at his fork. "Not sure. I stopped by the sheriff's office. Evidently they have a report of a teenage girl getting picked up south of here." He gave a nonchalant shrug, thankful that at least, in this, he told the truth.

"What?" For a second, Dani actually looked like she might jump from her chair, race over to the sheriff's office to confirm his story.

"Whoa, calm down, speedy. You need some grub, and then we'll head over to the sheriff's office."

"How'd you know I was thinking that?"

He tapped his head. "Good reporters can read minds."

"Ah. Right." She shook her head, folding her napkin into squares. "I hope it's her."

Yeah, he did too. But if Jeff called with bad news, Will planned to go back out with gear, including a flak jacket, his Colt Commando rifle, plenty of food, first aid, and a sat radio.

But definitely *without* Dani and company. Especially if that company included her army pals to detonate his cover. At least the one he'd constructed over his past.

Besides, the last thing he needed was an audience—or liability—if he also had to hunt down a couple of terrorists.

He'd miss Dani though. The sound of her rain suit swishing as she trailed her dog. The way the sun touched her smile. Those beautiful eyes as she tried to assess his real motives.

Either way, however, this meal would be the last moments they'd spend together. He'd take off, and when he returned, hopefully with the package in hand, he'd head back to Washington. To begin a new alias. And hopefully before she found out the kind of guy she'd let into her life.

Melancholy filled his throat.

"What if it's not her? Will you go back out after her?" Dani asked, her eyes on his, unflinching and difficult to lie to.

"I don't know," he said. Yes! *Yes!* Wow, the woman should work for the CIA the way he longed to give her the truth. "She's more than a story now. I feel . . . responsible, in a way."

She nodded, and a small smile touched her lips. "That's what I thought. You're very different from any reporter I've ever met, Will."

"I am?" Oh, that sounded pitiful. Desperate. Hopeful. He tried not to wince as he tucked his heart, kicking and screaming, back into his chest. The old Will would be shaking his head in disgust.

Somehow that made him feel better.

Dani shrugged but gave a self-deprecating laugh. "Well, it's not like I've met many journalists, but the one that sticks in my mind left a horrible taste."

"Ouch. What happened?"

Her smiled faded, and for a horrible second he thought he saw tears edge her eyes.

"You don't have to tell me," he said softly. Now where did those words come from? He'd only been aching to hear this story since she'd let the door slam on their dinner date three days ago.

"No, I . . . want to." She took a deep breath but didn't look at him. "I told you my sister was killed, right?"

He nodded slowly.

"She was killed in a tornado." She shook her head. "It was my fault. I wanted to pretend we were running away from home—"

"All kids do that—"

She held up her hand. "Thanks, Will. But let me get through this."

No. He didn't know why it hurt like a vise crushing his chest, but he feared the rest. Could actually taste the fear well up in his throat.

"I mentioned we lived on a farm. Well, we had acres and acres of corn, and I dragged Ashley through the fields, thinking we'd run into the road that edged our property. But I got lost. The field seemed endless. Hours later, there we were, completely turned around. And that's when it started to rain."

"How old were you?" He noticed how tight his voice sounded and didn't care. He could see her as a little girl, cute blonde pigtails, her face pudgy and dirty, fear in her pretty eyes as cornstalks hovered over her. The image had the power to make his eyes burn.

"I was six."

Six. He blew out a breath.

She reached across the table, touching his hand with two fingers. "You're awfully sweet, you know that?"

He wasn't quite sure how to respond, especially when everything inside him wasn't about sweet. Had never been about sweet. He'd been about power, about pleasures about living life for the moment. None of that felt sweet. But then again, he'd never taken the time to really get to know a woman. To hear her deepest fears, her darkest nightmares. He'd bypassed the rewards of friendship for the here-today, gone-tomorrow pleasures. No, he wasn't sweet. He was a scoundrel. A *redeemed* scoundrel, yes, but the old desires didn't die without a daily to-the-death grapple. But maybe . . . maybe this was God's way?

He suddenly longed for God's way more than breath.

"Thanks." He captured her hand with his and focused on the feeling of warmth as she continued.

"Anyway, I knew that something was wrong. The rain was so strong. And sideways. Ashley was crying, and I was so scared. I held her, shaking, wishing my mommy would find us. Then the storm swept over us. I let go of Ashley, dug a hole in the dirt, and covered my head. But she was frozen. Just *frozen*."

For a split second Will could see the past in her eyes, the moment of sheer terror, hear the roar of the tornado, taste the rain and wind in his mouth.

"The tornado just swept her away. One second there; the next, gone."

He went completely still. *Gone?* He wondered, perhaps, if his heart had stopped beating.

She brushed her thumb over his, and his pulse restarted.

"I sorta blacked out, probably from crying, and when I woke up, the field was torn up. Most of the corn was flattened, but some of it was still standing, broken or shredded. The earth had been furrowed up as if a giant had taken a finger and dragged it along the middle of the field." She closed her eyes.

He wanted to do the same.

"I found Ashley about thirty feet away. She was still alive. I don't think the tornado passed right over us, just the peripheral winds, but they were enough to throw her. She was badly hurt and in lots of pain. I stayed with her all night, praying that God wouldn't forget us, that He'd send an angel to keep us safe. We were found the next morning."

"But your sister had died," he supplied, dreading that conclusion.

She nodded. "The thing is, I couldn't help but feel that if there had been SAR dogs out there, they would have found us. Even with the tornado, there was so much field left; it had been a hot day, and our scent would have been left in the soil. And if they had found her sooner—"

"She might have lived." He felt moisture in his eyes and gritted his teeth. Dani met his gaze, and in it he saw trust. Precious, sweet trust. It swept through him like a fragrance, lifted him past the image of Dani holding her broken sister— or even the rather powerful impression of Dani in his arms— to a place of peace.

It had been ages since a woman trusted him like that.

Okay, maybe never.

Nancy appeared, holding their omelettes. She ranged a curious look between them, then quirked a smile.

Dani leaned back, letting Nancy place her order in front of her. Will used the moment to reel in his composure.

"Should I pray for our meal?" Dani said, a slight blush on her face, as if she had seen the emotions in his eyes.

He heard himself say, "No, I will." Perhaps it was emotion, but for the first time in his life, he didn't have to fight to conjure up words to talk to God. It felt almost natural to say, "Lord, thank You for this time with Dani. Please bless this meal." *Please bless this . . . friendship?* "And, Lord, watch over this missing girl wheverever she is . . . please bring her to safety." He peeked at Dani, saw her nod, noticed her still puffy, red-streaked eyes. "Finally, please take care of Missy. Heal her, Lord, and comfort Dani."

"Amen," Dani said after his pause, and he saw her run a finger under her eyes. "Thanks, Will."

"Yeah, amen," Will said, feeling warm right to the center of his being. He dug into his omelette.

Dani took a few bites, then resumed her story. "After the storm, people started asking questions as to why two little girls were out in a field so far from home. And why my mother hadn't found us before the storm hit. A reporter in town started nosing around my family and accusing my mother of things in the category of irresponsible and reckless. It started a maelstrom of public opinion, waged mostly in the letters-to-the-editor column. But the battles behind the lines—in my world—were the worst. My father began to believe the letters, or . . . maybe not. Maybe he was so emotionally undone after losing Ashley that he had to blame someone. Grief had already hollowed my mom, and my dad's betrayal crushed her." Dani poked her omelette but made no move to cut any more.

Will's food grew tasteless in his mouth. He put down his fork, pushed the plate away, all appetite obliterated. This was . . . well, not what he'd expected today. But it felt oddly endearing. Surrendering to the emotions inside him, he reached out and touched her arm. "What happened to your mom?"

Dani's eyes filled, and crystalline tears rushed over the edge. She wiped them away, gave him a tremulous smile. "You know, I thought I was over this."

He said nothing.

"One day when I was at school, she closed the garage door and turned on the car."

He closed his eyes, feeling pain wash through him. *Please, God, no. Don't let her say—*

"I came home and found her."

He groaned and took a deep breath, pushing past this sudden, crushing pain.

He opened his eyes and saw her staring down at her plate. He leaned forward, cupped her cheek with his hand. "I'm so, *so* sorry, Dani." Sorry didn't even begin to describe his feelings, but he didn't know what else to say.

She glanced up, her eyes glistening. "Thanks, Will. I guess I haven't told too many people that story. But now you know why I'm so close to my dogs. And why I'm not fond of reporters."

"I have this sudden urge to destroy my computer, maybe set the local paper on fire." No, actually, if he were honest, his feelings ran more toward flooring it to Iowa and reinstituting the Old West tradition of public lynching. He swallowed a hot ball of fury. "No wonder you smacked me with your Maglite."

She gave a one-sided, apologetic grin. "Misplaced anger."

"If it would make you feel better, you can have a go at the other cheek."

She giggled.

Oh, did that feel good. Like a soft blanket on his ravaged heart.

"Thanks, Will. You're a good friend."

He opened his mouth. Closed it. Smiled. *A good friend?*

But looking at the smile on her face, the warmth in her eyes, even the way she dived into her cold omelette . . . yeah, maybe in all the important ways he was.

Chapter 13

SARAH WAS SITTING on Dannette's deck, feet up and staring at the Lake Superior surf, when Dannette opened her motel-room door. Sarah waved, and Dannette shed her jacket, laid it on the bed, and peeked out the sliding-glass door. "Who let you in?"

"Kelly's mom, of course." Sarah raised a bottle of old-fashioned root beer. "I haven't had one of these since college. Want one? I stocked your fridge."

"Thanks, but I'm full. Will fed me—twice." She let those words linger as she kicked off her shoes, relishing the look Sarah was giving her.

She *was* full—full of food, full of friendship. She tiptoed out to the deck and sat in a lounge chair. The sun hovered over the horizon, sending a swath of orange and gold across the lake. Waves lapped the shoreline, gentle after yesterday's storm. Farther out, the outline of a freighter shadowed the horizon. Seagulls cried, a few riding the swells. The air smelled fresh and pine-laced.

"Before we get into that comment," said Sarah, "let's cut to the chase. How's Missy?"

Dannette felt relief, like a hand embracing her heart.

"She's out of recovery and doing okay. The vet says that if she stays quiet, she should be out of the hospital within the week. She wagged her tail when she saw me."

"You stopped in?"

Dannette felt herself blush. "I spent most of the afternoon in her kennel. With . . . Will."

Sarah took her feet off the deck rail, leaned forward on her knees. "Tell me everything."

Dannette shrugged, not sure where to start. "I was wrong about him."

That felt good to say. She smiled, letting his image run through her mind. Yeah, he made a charming package with that slightly Western drawl, those worn cowboy boots and jeans, the way he filled out his suede shirt and jacket. He should probably have a warning label attached to him. And he had the most beautiful, devastatingly powerful eyes. They did crazy things to her—like make her reveal her secrets for humiliating scrutiny.

Only he'd treated those secrets like a gift. And that's when she knew he was more than a package. He was the genuine article. He might have *reporter* written on his forehead, but she felt sure she wouldn't see any of her skeletons unmasked on the front page of the *Moose Bend Journal*.

"Will took me out for breakfast, and then we walked along the shore and he fed the seagulls scraps that Nancy had given him." She rubbed her arms, remembering how the seagulls had swooped out of the sky and argued for the meat and bread. And mainly how the wind had raked Will's dark hair, how his smile had nearly turned her to a puddle right there on the rocky shore. Especially after he'd listened to her story, not only with his glistening eyes and posture but with his heart. "Then we took his truck and made two trips to retrieve the vehicles. Your Jeep is out in the lot."

"I saw that, thanks." Sarah motioned with her root beer for Dannette to continue.

Dannette grinned. "We spent the rest of the afternoon at the vet. He climbed right inside the cage with me and didn't make me feel strange or weird as I petted Missy. He even listened to a few SAR stories. In fact, he's a Christian. At least I think so. He prayed for our meal and for Missy. In a restaurant. In *public*. I should have guessed. He seems so honest, even for a reporter. Amend my first statement—for *sure* I was wrong about him."

"I think you like him."

Dannette felt heat rise to her face. "Nah. He's only a friend. But it feels pretty good."

Sarah shook her head, smiling. "I have to admit, he's cute. And capable. To be honest, I'm not sure we would have made it out without him last night."

Dannette lowered her voice into I've-got-a-secret mode. "He held my hand. Twice. Once at breakfast and then when we walked on the beach."

"That doesn't sound like 'just friends' to me. When is the last time Conner held your hand?"

Dannette stared at the lake, knowing she wore a silly grin. "It just . . . I don't feel like it was a date or anything. He didn't try and kiss me—"

"I hope not!"

Dannette rolled her eyes. "Seriously. He acted like the perfect gentleman, and even the hand holding was either because I was going to fall or because I . . . ah . . . told him . . ." A hard lump suddenly lodged in her throat.

Sarah's smile vanished. "You told him about Ashley, didn't you?"

Dannette nodded, staring at her hands. "I wanted to

explain why I didn't like reporters . . . and well, one thing sorta led to the next."

Sarah turned the bottle in her hands, staring at the label. "I knew you needed to talk to someone after the incident with Emily. I didn't expect it to be him." She looked up at Dannette. "Just be careful, okay? I don't want you getting too close to this guy until we know more about him."

"What's to know? He's a small-town reporter."

"With a predisposition to stalk—"

"He was looking for the girl."

"And, why? I mean, he's not exactly an SAR type, is he?"

Dannette frowned. "Actually, I think he's very search and rescue. He's dedicated, he doesn't stop for trees in his way, and he believes in hope. He prays out loud."

"Or maybe he wanted to impress you."

Dannette didn't like the feelings roiling through her chest. She fought her rising voice. "You're just jealous because you can't let yourself enjoy Hank. You have to suspect every man who walks into your life."

Oh, man she *so* didn't mean to say that, but the words hung there between them, stinging.

Sarah's eyes filled, and her voice was tight, quiet. "You're right. So right. But I guess I don't feel any shame about wanting to know a guy pretty well before I let him into my life. Or spend any time alone with him." A tear crested down her cheek.

"I'm sorry, Sarah." Dannette reached out and touched Sarah's knee.

Sarah stared at Dannette's hand only a moment before she covered it with hers. "I forgive you."

Dannette closed her eyes and squeezed Sarah's hand. "Don't worry. I'm not going to get in over my head with Will.

It's just that he was a good friend today, and he seems trust-worthy to me."

Sarah swiped away the tear. "He is nice. And I hope, for your sake, he turns out to be everything you hope."

Dannette frowned. "I don't have any hopes. I don't have room in my life for hopes."

Sarah tipped the root beer at her. "Yeah. Me neither."

Silence descended between them as waves lapped the shore.

A knock sounded at the door. Sarah turned, but Dannette rose and went inside to answer it.

Kelly stood in the doorway. "Hey there." The petite EMT with the long brown braids, intense brown eyes, and a slow smile looked like a woman in a hurry, her jacket open and swinging her car keys. "I called the vet to check on Missy. I'm so relieved."

Dannette gave her a hug. "Are you coming or going?"

Kelly made a wry face. "I just pulled into town, and I'm headed up the trail to dig out some campers from their crushed RV."

"Sounds messy."

Kelly braced her hand on the wall. "I'll be there for a while. But I talked to Sarah earlier, and she said that you might be heading back out, looking for that girl?"

She was?

Scary how well Sarah knew her. Better, sometimes, than she knew herself.

"Well, I would be, but they found her."

"Um . . . well, maybe not, Dannette."

Dannette turned to look at Sarah.

"Well, there's a bit of a hum at the sheriff's office about your little field trip. The dispatcher—I think her name is Mary—told me that the sheriff himself went out to check out the address, and according to her, he came back swearing."

"I knew it." Dannette shook her head. "That girl is still out there."

"Yeah, well, there's more. Evidently, another call came in. This time it was local and reported seeing the girl about thirty miles south of town. Said she must have gotten picked up, possibly by a trucker."

Dannette frowned. "That's what Will said. I've been thinking about that all afternoon, but it doesn't make sense. We found a blanket in the forest, and Missy alerted to scent right before the storm."

Kelly shrugged.

"Did Fadden get a number on that report?"

"No. They hung up when Mary started pressing for details."

Dannette leaned against the doorjamb. "I don't feel good about this."

"Me neither." Kelly took a deep breath. "You can take Kirby."

Surprise must have shown on Dannette's face because Kelly smiled reassuringly and nodded. "You know him. And we've trained long enough together for him to know you also. I trust you." She glanced toward Kirby's kennel, out near the driveway. The shepherd lay curled in the corner of his pen, a pool of fur. "Besides, I'm sure he's itching to get out. And he could use more practice before our certification trial."

"You sure?"

"Yeah. You'll find his trailing harness and vest in the little shed by the kennel."

Dannette sighed, looked back at Sarah, then at the darkening sky. *If there had been SAR dogs out there, they would have found us.* "Okay. Thank you, Kelly. I'll keep you posted."

"Be careful."

Dannette nodded, then stood for a moment watching Kelly

descend the steps and climb into her SUV. Dannette waved as she pulled out.

Sarah came up behind Dannette, touched her shoulder. "I figured that if you wanted to go back out, I could stay here and watch Missy. I'll call you if something should happen."

Dannette shook her head. "I shouldn't go out alone."

"What about Will?"

"Now that would be a *really* bad idea. Alone in the woods? I thought you said I needed to know him better."

Sarah made a face. "Sorry, you're right. Listen, why don't you go out during the day tomorrow? You can start from the forest-service road we hiked out on."

"I dunno. Let's look at the maps."

They unrolled them on the bed, leaned over them. "Okay, we were on Tom Lake, right?" Sarah said.

Dannette nodded, traced her finger to where she thought they'd camped.

"Look at this. Tom Lake has cabins on the southern end. If she made it to the lake, it's feasible she'd see the cabins. And maybe hike to one of them and hole up. I doubt they have telephones or electricity, but at least it would be warm."

Dannette saw the girl in her mind's eye, trekking toward the cabins, breaking in, maybe wrapping herself in a blanket. "That's a good idea. Worth checking, I suppose."

"Not with Will." Sarah made it sound more like reassurance than a question.

"Of course not." But Dannette smiled, her heart warming probably a little too much at the memory of him in the woods, looking like an over-the-top Boy Scout, keeping her company with stories and, most of all, helping carry her dog to safety.

"I'll leave first thing in the morning," Dannette said. "But

I'm taking my cell phone. And if anything happens to Missy, you call me."

"Of course." Sarah sat down on the bed. "You'll find her, I promise. *Dani*."

Dannette gave her a good swat with her pillow.

✦ ✦ ✦

"What idiots!" Bakym exploded in anger and slammed his fist into Daniel's face. The skinny one—a weak American with earrings and a nose stud—grunted in pain. Then Bakym rounded on Gazim. "Why didn't you follow them?"

Gazim flinched but didn't move. "We did. They hiked out. Their dog was injured."

"Are you sure they were looking for Fadima?"

Daniel held his mouth where blood trickled out. His eyes flashed. "There's a bodyguard with them. Someone with 'special ops' written all over him—he's carrying a gun and knew to hide the women before the storm. But they're heading into town."

Gazim cut his glance to Daniel, then back to Bakym.

"And if he goes back out?" Bakym asked.

"We'll kill him."

"We need fresh maps and radio batteries," Gazim said. "Fadima's out there, and we just have to know where to look."

"We're running out of time." Bakym walked over to the window. The storm had shredded trees around the compound, littered it like bomb debris. He smiled at the comparison. "Her father has disappeared."

Silence behind Bakym made him wonder if they understood the ramifications of his statement. Ataman Erkan Nazar, a key player in Hayata, had gone AWOL three days before what would be their greatest victory on American soil. It didn't bode well for confidence among the Hayata terror masterminds.

What if Nazar was betraying them? He'd always been the weak one. Philosophical. A purist, he'd voiced dissent on occasion—such as their liaison with North Korea and the bombing in Macedonia.

Then again, he was probably trying to spare his wife from the justice of Hayata. Thankfully, they found the traitorous woman and her daughter. And Bakym had been among the privileged who made Nazar's wife suffer for her betrayals. Nazar should remember that.

"We have to find Fadima. Find out what she knows. Draw her father out of hiding." Then Nazar would be reminded what it meant to turn on his Hayata brothers.

Bakym turned, zeroed in on Daniel, stepping an inch away from his face. "Get back out there. Find her. Or I'll do to you what I plan to do to her."

Daniel nodded, a cold glint in his eye, probably meant for Bakym but useful for the task. "We'll find her. I promise."

✦ ✦ ✦

"So, she's still out there." Will tucked his night-vision goggles into his rucksack and readjusted the cell phone in his ear. "I can't wait for your guy, Jeff. I gotta go. Tell—"

"Phil Branden."

"Right—Phil—that I'll contact him when I get back, and to check the progress of the ME's investigation on Simon."

"You going back out with the dog team?" Jeff asked.

Will had already dismissed the idea of bringing Dani and Sarah along. They'd been good company and had even led him to his current lead. But this time he was going alone. Just in case the terrorists still scoured the woods.

"Nope. I studied the map, and I think I have a pretty good idea of where she might be hiding out. We tracked her to an inland lake, semiprivate with rustic cabins on the southern end. I'm going to hike in just before first light tomorrow and start a systematic search. My gut is telling me that she's hiding out in one of the cabins."

"What about those Hayata operatives you saw?"

"I don't know. They were in the same stretch of forest I was, and the storm nearly sliced and diced me. I wonder if they're even alive."

"You better hope not."

Will sighed, grabbed another ammunition clip, and shoved it into one of his vest pockets. "Any news on General Nazar?"

"Yeah, and it's not good. He's disappeared, along with his son. We think he went into hiding."

"Or Hayata figured him out."

"Maybe. But you gotta find that girl. Our hunch is that only she knows where he is. And if we don't find her soon, Hayata is going to find them both—and accomplish their mission."

"Right," Will said, smelling the smoke, hearing the screams of his own Hayata nightmares in Kazakhstan. He checked his watch and grimaced. The new agent, Phil, had sacrificed hours tracking down a phantom caller while he'd spent the day with Dani.

Well, he wouldn't really call *that* a sacrifice.

"Will, when you find her, don't stop. Get on a plane and bring her back here."

"Roger that." Will clicked off the phone, tucked it into his pocket, and surveyed the mess he'd made of his room. He'd packed little for this undercover mission, and it had taken him less than an hour to assemble most of it into two duffel bags. The rest he'd stuff into the rucksack he planned to carry on his back as he hiked into Tom Lake.

It hadn't escaped him that he wouldn't be able to say good-bye to Dani. Or Sarah for that matter, although somehow that didn't feel quite so painful.

"Thanks, Will, for being my friend," Dani had said today as she got out of the truck. Those words felt like fingerprints on his heart, marking him as a different man. He'd smiled, and something akin to peace filled his heart. It felt really heart-sweepingly good to be called a friend. So good that he'd even managed to keep in check all the desires to run his hand into her short, silky hair, pull her close, and kiss her.

Friends didn't do that.

Right?

Will picked up a pile of books off his nightstand. Bonnie's wedding invitation lay on top. He'd retrieved it from the floor of his truck, and now he smoothed it against his leg, opened it again.

It was dated for this weekend. He was going to be a real slouch and not show up. Even if he wanted to go, he couldn't. But it wasn't too late to do the right thing. To check in and be the friend he should have been to her . . . to Lew. Especially since he seemed to be batting one thousand in the friends department.

He sank to the floor, his head back, eyes closed as Lew strolled into his mind.

"Hey, pal, great hit!" Lew, hanging out of the dugout, baseball cap shadowing his lazy brown eyes, a shank of blond hair peeking out the back. He slapped Will on the back as he jogged in after clinching the game with a homer. "Let's get out of here."

Will threw his hard hat into the bag and joined the team for the endgame congrats. The Cotter Bulls raking in another victory. The sun blazed, still powerful despite the late hour, even in its downward slide. The smell of barbeque simmered in the warm air.

Baseball fans dispersed as Lew gathered his stuff. "Mom's got lasagna waiting. Wanna join us?"

Will's mind tracked to his own house. His mother had left a couple of weeks ago, and things in the Masterson household had deteriorated like Jell-O on a hot day. Currently, food wasn't high on his father's list of priorities. Will had breakfasted on a bag of microwavable burritos and washed them down with a cold beer, hoping his dad wouldn't notice his dwindling supply. Dinner at the Strongs' would fill the nooks and crannies of latent hunger.

However, hanging out with the Strongs felt like salt in open wounds lately. Probably because Will's mother had stayed longest this time. Nearly a year. Long enough for it to really rip his heart from his chest when she left. Long enough for Will to see his father cry.

Still, the Strongs offered an escape from his dark house. And if he was especially unlucky, his dad would be there, already drinking hooch, and he'd have to duck a few good swings. In the end, he'd wind up sleeping on the Strongs' front-porch swing anyway.

When Lew came out of the showers an hour later and repeated the dinner invitation, Will gave a slight nod. They exited the locker room of the high school, and Lew waved to Bonnie and a friend, sitting like ornaments on her father's Mustang. Will tried to ignore the stab of envy. Bonnie so adored Lew it felt like they were already married. Even so, Will knew that Lew and Bonnie had some sort of religious agreement—one that said they were only close friends until Lew put a ring on her finger in a church.

Will had earned a shiner once, challenging that agreement, calling Lew a fool.

"Hey ya, Will," Bonnie said. "I want you to meet my cousin Katie."

He could like Katie, with her long brown hair, slightly mischievous eyes, the look of danger in her smile. She hooked her thumbs into the waistband of her Levi's 501 jeans, drawing them low, revealing skin. "Hi, ya," she said softly.

But he heard the invitation in her voice loud and clear. She was Bonnie's cousin?

"She's in for the weekend," Bonnie said, not seeing or perhaps ignoring the sudden shift in temperature. "She's a freshman at Brookings College."

An older woman. "Glad to meet you," Will said and ignored the warning on Lew's face.

Katie turned out to be just the girl he'd expected. In town for the weekend meant in town for fun. And he'd lived up to her expectations.

He never did get that lasagna, though, and years later, as he watched Lew toss his daughters in the air and share a kiss with Bonnie, he knew that there was only one wise man between them.

Until, of course, a bomb had destroyed the perfect life.

And now, Bonnie was starting over. With some other guy who wasn't Lew. Well, at least she'd kept going with her life despite her grief.

Will sat down on the bed, fished out his cell phone, and scrolled down to her number. His chest tightened as he pressed Send.

The phone rang once. Will glanced at the clock. It was still early, and he could imagine Bonnie outside with her girls, pushing them on the backyard swings, her dusty blonde hair caught in a sweeping wind.

The phone rang again. The black-eyed Susans would be blooming in her backyard, and the smell of prairie grass coming alive after winter would lace Cotter with a nice, husky scent. Neighbors would be banging their front doors as they wandered out to the street to call in their children. He could nearly taste nostalgia, bittersweet in his mouth.

Maybe Cotter wasn't such a bad place to grow up.

Three rings.

"Hello?"

Will opened his mouth, but nothing came out as panic gripped him by the throat. What was he supposed to say? That he was sorry he'd never so much as called to check on them in three years? That he didn't know how to be a friend to the wife of his best buddy?

"Hello?"

He hung up. Shaking, he dropped the phone. So much for that euphoric feeling he'd had all day, the one in his pretend world where Dani and he lived happily ever after in Moose Bend. No, reality was Cotter, South Dakota, his past, and his new responsibilities. Dani may think he was a good friend, but she knew practically nothing about him. Well, okay, she knew a few things—things that he'd never told other women. Things about his father and his childhood. But it didn't mean she knew him. She didn't know the places he'd been, the things he'd done.

Not like Bonnie did.

Dani had no idea that darkness had once lurked in his soul. How for years he'd felt half dead or numb, like one of those lepers in the Bible. In his brain, he knew that God had made him new. He wanted so much to believe God when He said, "This means that anyone who belongs to Christ has become a new person," to truly be a new person, someone who could be everything he saw reflected in Dani's beautiful eyes.

Trustworthy.

Honest.

Honorable.

It reminded him of the way Bonnie had looked at Lew.

That thought spasmed his chest, and he put a hand to it as if to loosen it. He had seen himself as honorable in Dani's eyes today. He had thought he'd never, ever feel that way. And it nearly made him weak with longing. Like she was looking past his layers, his duplicity, to the real Will.

Or at least the Will he wanted to be.

He took a deep breath and reached for the nearest book to shove the invitation into. His hand closed on Lew's Bible. Bonnie had sent it to him shortly after the funeral. He carried it with him like a . . . good-luck charm, he supposed. It felt as if Lew might be there, whispering wisdom into his ears.

He heard Sarah's words from yesterday morning—Lamentations 3—and he flipped it open to the verses: "The LORD is good to those who depend on him, to those who search for him. So it is good to wait quietly for salvation from the LORD. And it is good for people to submit at an early age to the yoke of his discipline."

Maybe if he'd submitted to God's discipline, done things God's way, he'd have a lady like Bonnie—or Dani—waiting for him to come home to.

God's way. He tracked to an earlier verse, to where Sarah had begun quoting. "I say to myself, 'The LORD is my inheritance; therefore, I will hope in him!'"

His inheritance.

Will stared out his window to the twilight. The urge to start over had never felt so strong, so real. Since Lew's death three years ago he'd thought long and hard about eternity, wondering why God had chosen to take Lew instead of him. Will knew that he'd been given a second chance, a reprieve, so to speak. That if he'd been killed beside Lew there would have been a different eternity for him. And he'd felt guilty over his relief.

He missed Lew's smile, his honesty, his wisdom. There were long nights when he'd wanted to surrender to the lonely ache in his heart, find a short-term friend, or turn to his father's method of pain control. But Lew's life had made an impression on him, and somehow surrendering felt like dishonoring his memory. As if Lew might look down from heaven and frown.

Will related to Dani's childhood coping mechanisms more than she realized. He'd even found himself on his knees in a church on the day of Lew's funeral, weeping, asking God for another chance.

Only he wasn't quite sure what that meant. How to go from there. He read the words again. "The LORD is my inheritance." *"Portion,"* Sarah had said. He remembered the other words: *reward, influence, abundance, sustenance, reputation.* Dani had said, *"All."*

Will closed the Bible, held its cool cover to his forehead. *Help me, Lord. Help me know what secret Lew had. What did he mean when he said You were his deliverer? his sustainer? his reward? Help me to understand, because most of the time I'm confused and getting it wrong.*

His prayer sounded painfully desperate. Well, he'd been feeling desperate for about three years now. *I really want to be Your man, Lord. Please teach me what that means.* He rubbed the cover of the Bible. *Thank You for letting me meet Dani. For letting her show me what it feels like to just . . . be the right kind of guy.*

His throat thickened. It would have been nice to know her longer, to see where their friendship led. . . .

Or maybe it was better this way. He didn't have any room to disappoint her. He could hang on to that sweet smile, that trust in her eyes.

He'd never have to tell her that their friendship was based on a lie.

Chapter 14

DANNETTE FOLLOWED KIRBY through the forest, trying to read the dog and become more sensitive to Kelly's SAR dog. She missed Missy's sweet brown eyes and fought to trust Kirby's responses. Missy's absence felt sharp and raw the farther they progressed with the search.

Dannette used Kelly's clicker to encourage Kirby as the dog sniffed the shoreline. She'd left at 4 a.m., as sunrise pierced the night, turning it silver, and by the time she'd worked her way up the forest-service road into Tom Lake, the sky was mottled with glorious shades of pink, lavender, and cinnamon.

The breeze lifted the collar of her jacket and wove the smells of pine and lake water through the morning air. Birds called to her and water lapped the shore, disturbed only by an occasional plop of a feeding trout.

She missed Will. But she pushed him out of her mind as she trekked across shore. Sarah's suggestion that she call Will, albeit a rash and unwise one, had tempted Dannette sorely as she had driven into the lonely forest.

She liked him. It didn't take off a slice of her heart to admit that. Yes, he was a reporter, but he was a guy with morals, and she had a sneaky suspicion he was also a Christian, although yesterday she hadn't had a chance to really dig. She couldn't seriously consider him anything more than a friend until she got a fix on his beliefs.

She smiled as she hopped another boulder. *Okay, Dani, you're getting past yourself.* Will probably wasn't interested in her. Yes, he'd held her hand and even sat in a stinky kennel with her, but he'd been just as kind to Sarah. He'd been a good reporter, the way he'd listened with his eyes, his hand on hers. She simply wasn't used to having a man's full attention.

Except he called her Dani, which made her feel . . . cute. Attractive. Maybe she'd start thinking of herself that way . . . once in a while.

Even though she hadn't liked the way Will had barged into her life, once he was past the outer perimeter, it felt slightly appealing to have him hovering inside the borders, calling her a pet name, and smiling in her general direction.

Kirby's ears suddenly flicked back. Dani's pulse lurched. "Good boy, Kirb! Find!"

A smart dog for being only three years old, Kirby had picked up the trail and now threaded through the rocks. Kirby and Kelly would have no problem with certification.

And right after that, Dani would be leaving Moose Bend. For good. Which meant she shouldn't linger too long on the image of Will's beautiful eyes or the feel of his hand on hers.

Then again, Moose Bend wasn't so far from Kentville, Iowa, right? Twelve hours?

She wanted to smack herself upside the head. She had known Will for only three days, and most of that time had been spent not liking him—or trying not to like him. She shouldn't be calculating mileage and gas costs.

It would help if she didn't trust Will so much. It felt like an eternity since she'd ever let a man this close . . . mostly because she'd seen what loss did to a family, to a marriage.

She refused to let herself become her father.

Besides that, risks and long hours comprised the SAR lifestyle. Hence the reason she hadn't even considered the outdoor adventure jockeys she'd met as fair and eligible game. She wanted a nice, safe man, who came home at five o'clock and stayed all weekend. Who considered mowing the grass or painting the house his version of adventure, volunteering in the church nursery his contribution to saving the world. A guy who would be there for her to return home to, perhaps with a couple of steaks on the grill and a tossed salad on the counter. Yes, it felt like a double standard, but since trauma and catastrophe were the fabric of her life, she needed normalcy behind the scenes.

Maybe she needed a guy like Will. A guy who enjoyed small-town coffee shops, who made friends with the café owner, who fished with the local sheriff. Of course, that didn't totally define Will, but he seemed down to earth. Perhaps a little zealous and over the top when it came to SAR, but then again, what guy didn't have dreams to be a Rambo type and save the world?

Dani stopped, a soft smile on her lips. Will *had* been Rambo in real life. Maybe not like Micah, but Will had done enough time in the army to be proficient with a weapon. In fact, he still carried one, if she'd seen that correctly. Only . . . how did a guy go from being a soldier to writing the police beat in a backwoods smudge on the map?

Kirby disappeared behind a wall of rock. Dannette moved quickly, wanting to keep him in her sights. Even though Missy and Kirby were trained to never stray farther than twenty-five to thirty feet from their handler, Dani didn't know Kirby that well. She climbed over the rock and dropped down.

Kirby had found a long trail leading to a cabin overlooking the lake. Deeply shadowed by towering black pine and ancient birch trees, the cabin had no electricity lines running to it, and the windows still had winter boards over them.

Kirby ran to the door, pawed it.

Dani's pulse rushed in her ears while she ran up the porch steps. She fought her breath and knocked on the door.

Nothing.

She tried the handle. It didn't budge. Crouching before Kirby, she gazed into his honey-colored eyes. "What do you scent, pal? The place is locked up."

Suddenly, Kirby wrenched out of her grip. He growled, his lips pulled back, his ears flattened against his head as he backed away from her.

Dani stiffened. Turned.

Screamed.

Fadima froze, hearing the sounds of footsteps on the porch outside. She slowly lowered her spoon into the open can of pork and beans, listening past her roaring heartbeat for more sounds, signs that she'd been discovered.

Another footstep.

Her heart lodged in her throat as she grabbed the can and scooted behind the hanging curtain in front of the sink. She'd been fortunate to find the small cabin, even more lucky to discover the unlocked back bedroom window and locate canned goods in the pantry. Despite the dust, the peaches, tuna, and cold pork and beans tasted just fine in her empty stomach. She was even beginning to warm, feel her toes, dry her clothes. The sunshine squeezed between the cracks of the boarded-up front windows, and she hoped whoever or whatever crept in the grass outside wouldn't see the stump she'd used to hoist herself up to the window.

She pulled her knees up tight to her chest, kept her breaths low, tight. Hope had felt tangible this morning, especially after surviving the night in her hideout, after the flashlight beams of the Hayata searchers stopped just inches away from her.

She might even believe that she could be the person her father told her she was.

She heard another creak, then a bang. Her heart leaped right out of her chest, and she made a fist to hold back a cry. Were they coming in? She closed her eyes.

Silence. It stretched on painfully, filling every moment with dread.

Nothing. No footsteps, no hand reaching through the curtain to grab her by the throat.

She knew they were out there. She'd heard their heavy stomping through the forest this morning, shivered at the contempt in their voices. Heard their commitment in their sharp words, their hot anger.

Still, she stayed tucked away, holding her knees as hope started a slow bleed.

"Dani, it's okay," Will said, trying to keep his voice low, scanning past the cabin into the dark fold of forest.

"What part of you scaring my skin off is okay?" Her voice shrilled, matching the white panic that hued her face. "And why do you always dress like a mercenary when you're in the woods? Good grief, Will, who do you think you're going to get in a fight with—a great horned owl?"

He couldn't hide the smile or his emotions, it seemed. When he'd seen her sneak up, he totally turned off the common sense screaming in his head. No, he'd been propelled by sheer panic. "I checked this cabin. She's not here. And neither should you be."

Her expression told him exactly how odd his words sounded. "And why is that?" Her eyes widened and she reached for the cabin door, as if to brace herself. "Is that an *assault* rifle?"

He slung it off his shoulder, set it away from him, from her. Why couldn't he have let her simply knock on the door, find nothing, and leave? He could have stayed hidden.

And then he'd have two women to protect—Dani and Amina, if he ever found her. "I'm just being prepared."

"To what, shoot and skin your own deer? With a . . . what's that, an M16?"

"A Colt Commando rifle, sort of an American version of an AK-47."

"Oh, right, my mistake. I have one of those in my truck, because, you know, every good woodsman *should have one*." She had real fire in those eyes, and she didn't look in the least amused by her own joke. "I think you've taken this search-and-rescue thing too far. This is not a top-secret, special-ops mission." She turned and held her hand out to the scenery. "What part of this says bad guys?"

Whoa, she was cute when she was sarcastic. But at the moment he couldn't give in to the desire to laugh, because she was so utterly wrong it hurt him right in the middle of his chest.

"Dani, please trust me. You need to go home and let me find this girl."

She frowned at him, pointed to her orange jacket, then the shabrack vest on her dog.

Now where had she found a new K-9 so quickly?

"See these little white crosses? They mean we belong out here. Our job is to *search* and rescue. Do you, by any chance, see a difference between, say, my outfit . . . and yours?"

He smirked but reached for his weapon and took her by the arm. "Okay, just yell at me when we get off the porch and back into the woods."

This day had started out dark and was only worsening as he moved into daylight. He'd driven to the rest area and to his dismay had seen that the Hayata truck had moved. That feeling turned to sickened dread when he found the vehicle parked on the forest-service road he used to wind in to Tom Lake.

Not good. Not good at all. *Please let it be some tenacious hikers*, he'd thought. Sadly, he'd seen no sign of Dani, which meant she'd taken the long way in, and he'd surprised her.

She was too smart and determined for her own good.

"What's going on, Will?" Dani said as she yanked her arm out of his grip. "What are you doing out here, anyway?"

What was he . . . ? "Well, I'm not rabbit hunting."

"Ha-ha. See, the thing is, you look like you might be hunting very *big* rabbits . . . and how did you know the girl was still missing?"

He was doing some fast math and came up with the obvious—she too had found out the report was bogus. "The sheriff told me."

She shook her head. "I thought so."

He hid a grimace. His last chance to send her packing, blown.

"Oh no." Dani dug into her pocket and fed Kirby some kibble. "Don't tell me you were the scent Kirby found?"

"I don't know. But I do think that this girl is somewhere in one of these cabins, and I can find her by myself."

She gave a harsh laugh. "Somehow deep in my heart I truly

believe that. But just for kicks, why don't we use the K-9 that we've spent a year training?"

He shook his head, turned, and headed for the tree cover, with a bittersweet hope that she'd follow. Because he didn't really want to throw her over his shoulder and haul her out of danger, like a *real* Boy Scout.

Okay, maybe a little.

But the fact that Little Miss SAR was back—and obviously fully charged—meant trouble.

And even more dangerous were the little feelings of happiness that were exploding all over his heart.

Bad Will. Bad, *bad* Will.

As she followed him into the forest and stood there with her hands on her hips, he wanted to reach over and hug her. "Dani, please, for the last time, you need to leave."

"Give me one good reason." She held up one elegant finger. "One."

He made a face, opened his mouth. She had a point . . . without knowing it. He couldn't rightly explain without blowing his cover. And without blowing his cover, he couldn't get her to leave.

Besides, what if she was caught hiking out?

Maybe it would be better if he just . . . hung around or vice versa.

"Promise to listen to me? And to obey me if I tell you to do something?"

She looked at him as if he had turned purple and spoken Russian.

"I know the words *you're not the boss of me* sound childish . . . but *you're not the boss of me.*" She turned to her new K-9, sitting beside her and eyeing Will like a moldy sirloin. "C'mon, Kirby."

This time he really did stop her. He put all two hundred pounds between her and her exit and wore a face he hadn't used for quite some time. "You're not going anywhere without me, Dani," he said slowly and dangerously. "And I *am* the boss of you, starting right now."

She backed away, tilted her head. "Now you're freaking me out."

"Good. Please take me very seriously. I know things you don't, and suffice it to say that they are part of my job. So when I say things like, 'go home,' which I realize you won't, trust that they are for your own good. Because I am your friend."

She swallowed, and suddenly he realized that he didn't want to be her friend. Not at all. In fact, he'd spent the entire morning lying to himself when he said it felt great to be trusted, that the feelings of honor she dredged up were enough.

He wanted more. Now that he'd gotten a taste of what it meant to be around her smile, her laughter, even her confused anger, he wanted more.

Lord, help me be Your man. He closed his eyes against the image of reaching out and crushing her to his chest, of silencing her arguments with a kiss.

Just friends.

"Will, I know you're my friend," Dani said haltingly, as if in sync with his thoughts. "But you're sort of scaring me." He felt her take a step toward him.

Too close. He smelled her soft perfume, the kind that lingers after a shower, and could nearly feel her breath on his cheek. He opened his eyes. She stood only a foot away, so close that if he leaned forward a little . . .

He turned away, blew out a breath. "I'm sorry. I'm not trying to scare you."

She touched his arm, and he nearly jumped right through his BDUs. "Let's just find this girl, okay?"

He nodded. Find the girl, don't stop, fly to Washington. And pick up his next set of lies.

He slung his gun over his shoulder as he followed her and Kirby through the forest, nearly shaking with frustration. How was he ever supposed to figure out how to walk God's way when He kept throwing Dani in his path?

Only what if she was part of the answer?

They walked in silence, trailing Kirby who wound a path over logs and downed timber and branches. Birds chirruped and occasionally startled into the sky. Will's skin raised gooseflesh. This felt worse than being in Iraq, waiting for insurgents to mow him down.

"Where did you get the dog?"

"My friend Kelly," she said and glanced at him. She looked worried. "You going to tell me why you're going off the charts here?"

"No."

She licked her lips, sighed, turned back to watching her dog. "So, you figured the same thing Sarah and I did."

"That anyone who was lost would head toward habitation? Yes. Like I said, I'm going to systematically search the cabins here on the south end of the lake. My gut says she's here."

"Mine too." She gave a faint smile.

He hated how her smile made his heart leap. "How's Missy?"

"She's good. Sarah's watching out for her."

"Sarah's a good friend."

Dani nodded. "Only she doesn't try and tell me what to do."

He cringed. Yeah, well, Sarah didn't have to keep Dani alive, did she? "Sorry. Like I said, I didn't mean to scare you."

"You'd scare Jack the Ripper in that getup."

He scowled, looked at his clothes. Traditional BDUs, boots, and face paint. What was the deal?

"Just don't tell me that this little war thing you have going is a regular event." She shot him a look. "Or are you going to be gone every weekend, playing terrorist in the woods?"

Every weekend? He couldn't help but smile. "Why? Wanna be the lady terrorist? You'd look good in green face paint."

She sent him a mock glare. "No, Rambo, I'm just wondering if a gal wanted to see you, would she have to understand latitude and longitude and know how to read a map?"

He nearly winced at how accurate she was. He swallowed around a lump of guilt and tried to keep his smile. "Maybe a guy could come to your neck of the woods. Iowa?"

"Know how to drive a tractor? milk a cow?"

He grinned. "I could learn."

She laughed, nodded. "I'll bet."

They were coming up on another cabin, and Will grabbed her shoulder, pulling her back into the cover of the trees. "Call Kirby."

She frowned at him but obeyed. Kirby bounded back and sat next to Dani.

"Stay here," Will ordered.

He knew it looked way too suspicious for him to sneak away and peek into the cabin, but he wasn't going to let her walk into the open, as if waving her arms and yelling, "Shoot me!" He ignored the burn of her curious gaze on the back of his neck and quickly scouted the perimeter of the lot before approaching the building.

This cabin, much like the last one, had been boarded up for winter. He saw nothing but a couple of mice holes in the foundation. Which a seventeen-year-old girl wasn't going to squeeze through.

Please don't let me be wrong about this hunch. He ran back to Dani, who was shaking her head. "All clear, tough guy?"

He ignored her. "She's not here. Let's keep going."

They crossed the lot, worked their way down to the beach, and headed for the next cabin.

"I was only half kidding about the visiting thing," Dani said, casting him a look.

He saw the vulnerability on her face, and like a punch, it hit him that she might . . . like him too? Wow. He scrambled to find words. "Me too."

A slow, sweet smile appeared on Dani's face. Like sunshine after a long, chilly day. "When you can get away from Moose Bend and your job, that is."

His smile faded. "Yeah, right." When he got away from Moose Bend, he'd have a new job in a new little town. Far, far away from Dani and Kentville, Iowa.

The sun hovered in the east, and sweat trickled down between Will's shoulder blades. The shoreline looked as if Bigfoot had tossed the forest in his wrath, and Will and Dani picked their way to the next cabin. "Be careful, Dani," Will said as she climbed over a large broken birch. He saw it rock, and in his mind she'd already fallen and lay in a crumpled mess.

"Were you this bossy when you and Lew were hunting bad guys?"

Her question stopped him cold. "Who told you about Lew?"

She looked at him. "You did. A couple of days ago. You said he joined up with you."

His heartbeat restarted slowly. Oh yeah. But this time it didn't have to hurt, if he was careful. "Yeah, Lew was my best friend. He and his wife, Bonnie, and I all hung out together in high school. He joined Ranger school when I did, and we served together."

"You were a Ranger? I thought when you said you were a solider you meant regular army. I didn't expect Special Forces . . . well, I mean, not really."

It wasn't a question, and her voice held that little bit of awe he'd come to expect, but from her it felt like respect. Honest, friendly, no-strings-attached respect. He smiled into the warm feelings gathering in his heart.

Even though, no, he'd been more than a Ranger. A Green Beret. *But please don't ask, Dani, and I won't tell.*

"How did he die?" she asked softly. Thankfully, she didn't look at him.

"Lew died in a bombing of a refugee camp in Macedonia three years ago."

She stopped, turned, and her face paled. "I'm sorry, Will. Were you there?"

He followed her as she resumed walking across the rocks, amazed that yes, this came easier. Except for the next part. "Yes." What he didn't add was that sometimes he still awoke in the night, bathed in a cold sweat, breathing hard. "Lew died right in front of my eyes."

Dani stopped again. "Poor Bonnie. Did they have kids?"

"Three little girls. The youngest was only eight months old."

Grief flashed across her face. "That's horrible." She stood there for a moment, the wind catching her hair, empathy in her eyes. "Good thing they have you."

Right, he was a real comfort. He said nothing as she called to her K-9, pulled out a water bowl. "I need to water Kirby. Do you mind?"

Did he mind that she made a great target out here on the beach? He hooked her elbow, moved her closer to the rock. "Nope."

He scanned the shoreline as Kirby drank. No movement,

not a glint of light off a gun barrel. Still, his reflexes were on full alert.

The Hayatas were out there; he felt it in the tiny raised hairs on his neck.

"I could never marry a military man." Dani braced a hand on a huge boulder, ran a handkerchief around her neck. "So much to lose. I hate good-byes. I was never good at them. I couldn't imagine telling my man good-bye, thinking it might be for the last time."

He kept his expression stoic, scanning the rocky shoreline for any hint of disturbance, but he felt as if she'd just taken out a machete and chopped him off at the knees. *"I could never marry a military man."* Well, he wasn't exactly in the military, but his job wasn't much better—in fact, maybe worse. It wasn't like he came home for leave.

"So, has Lew's wife gotten remarried?"

Dani could earn master markswoman with the accuracy of her questions today. He swallowed. "Is the dog nearly finished?"

"Yeah." She leaned down, picked up the bowl, shook it out. "Ready?"

She just stared at him as he moved away. Fine, let her be mad. Some things were personal. Hadn't he told her enough?

Only she'd told him her most private nightmares.

And he'd let her believe he was a reporter.

Somehow it didn't feel quite equal.

"Bonnie's getting married this weekend," he said softly as he climbed a large boulder.

Dani ran to catch up to him. "That's great, right?"

He said nothing.

She caught his arm, tugged. "Isn't that great?"

He couldn't look at her, studied his boots instead. "Yeah. Maybe. I don't know. I haven't met the guy."

Silence.

He closed his eyes, seeing the disappointment in hers. Yes, his best friend's widow and he didn't even know if the guy she was marrying was a scumbag or a saint.

Paul Whoever had better be a saint.

But what was Will going to do about it when he'd walked out of her life without so much as a forwarding address?

"It hurts that bad, huh?" Dani whispered.

He opened his eyes, feeling her words hit him square in the chest. Something about the softness in her eyes, the concern in her expression . . . for a second he thought he might . . . well, it hurt more than she could ever know.

Although, maybe she *did* know. Maybe she knew better than anyone. She'd watched her sister die in her arms, just like Lew had died in his. Slowly, Will nodded, realizing that he stood out in the open, not only a sitting target for Hayata but with his heart now on the outside of his body.

Dani stepped closer, put her arms around him, and brought his head down to her shoulder. "I'm so, so sorry, Will."

She was . . . hugging him? He heard his breath catch, felt himself weaken. For probably the first time ever in his life, he didn't take it as an invitation. In fact, as he put his arm around her—awkwardly because he still held his gun—he only wanted to hold her close. To let her gentleness, her friendship balm those still-ragged wounds. He could almost hear her kindness chipping at his walls when he buried his face into her neck. He squeezed his eyes shut, clearing them from a sudden rush of heat. Good grief, he felt like an idiot.

Or, perhaps, just a man who hurt right down to his soul.

Danger sirens blared in his mind as he took a deep breath and pulled away. How had he let Dani this far into his life? into his heart? They were past being just friends, hurtling in a direction he'd never been before, never even scouted. This relationship had blindsided him, and he hadn't a clue at the mission objective, the tactics. Nor any words whatsoever. Nothing but slightly moist eyes and a dazed half smile.

And Dani staring up at him, gentleness in her eyes, his green greasepaint on her face. She touched his cheek. "You know, you should just call Bonnie and tell her that you miss him too. I promise, it'll be okay. I'm sure that if Lew was such a great friend, his wife was a champ too."

Will nodded and turned away before she could see the shame on his face.

Chapter 15

DANI CROUCHED IN the trees outside the clearing, checking her cell-phone signal while Will did his little Rambo routine. She had been only half kidding about his playing war games every weekend. She'd heard stories of men who played soldier in the woods with paint guns and other high-tech devices. Thanks, but that felt too close to the real thing.

She raised her cell phone, turned it. No signal. She sighed and scratched Kirby's fur to encourage him to stay. They'd stopped for lunch a few hours ago, after sneaking up on another cabin as if it might jump them. She figured they had one more hour before she had to go back to the motel.

Alone, if she read Will right. He hadn't hinted at slowing down. Not that she felt overly eager to leave the girl out in the cold another night, but her doubts had begun to shred her confidence. Maybe the girl really hadn't run into the forest. Maybe Dani and Will were on a useless hunt, propelled by Dani's nightmares from the past and fear of leaving a child in the woods to perish. Maybe the girl had been picked up by a trucker and only wanted to be left alone.

A huge part of Dani wanted to head home, curl up with

her dog, and start apologizing to everyone for being gung ho
without anything more than a hunch.

She could even accentuate her apology with a dinner invitation to one overcommitted reporter. . . .

Will appeared, nearly out of nowhere.

Dani startled. "How did you do that?"

When he grinned through all that green and black paint,
she saw mischief in his eyes. It had taken him a long while to
ease out of the melancholy she'd inadvertently sent him into.
She hadn't intended to scrape open his private grief, but
despite his hurt, his brooding, a very large place inside her
felt glad she had.

Because he'd held her so tight, so long, that it made her
weak. Like she might be giving back to him a little of what
he'd given to her yesterday. A great big dose of unconditional
friendship.

And when he'd turned away, his eyes wet, thinking she
might not see it, it dried her mouth. Inside all that grit-and-
macho exterior lay a tender heart.

She heard Sarah's words in the back of her head: *"Just
don't let him too close until we know more about him."*

Oops. Too late. Good thing Sarah wasn't here, because his
war paint and cloak-and-dagger thing would have her New York
friend freaked out.

Dani thought it made him cute. In an I'm-here-to-protect-
you kind of way. If he wanted to play cowboy/soldier/defender
of the woods, she'd let him. Within reason. As long as he didn't
point his gun in her direction.

"So, is it safe to cross the clearing, O Keeper of the Gate?"
she asked.

He rolled his eyes. "Listen, I know this feels funny to you,
but we're strolling onto private property for a look-see. You have

no idea what kind of hermits live out here who aren't going to take kindly to us interfering in their lives."

"Oh, and they're going to welcome a shotgun-toting, special-ops solider with a fresh-baked blueberry pie and a song?"

He grinned, then let out a long sigh. "Whatever. C'mon. I don't think she's here, but let's look around. The door's unlocked."

Okay, that bit of information piqued her curiosity. "Any sign of life?"

"I gave it a cursory once-over. Nada. But maybe you and your trusty bloodhound can pick up a trail."

"German shepherd/retriever mix." She followed Will to the cabin, and when she found herself crouching just a little, she felt like an idiot. Apparently he'd tugged her too far into his game.

While she stood sentry, he knocked, then creaked open the door. As he stepped forward, he looked back at her.

"What?"

"Just . . . shh."

Yes, Sarah would be off-the-scale jumpy, and, truthfully, Dani wasn't far behind. He eased into the cabin, using his body as a shield between her and the cobwebs.

"I thought you'd already checked this out," Dani said.

"Shh."

Oh, brother. Still, the cabin did feel creepy—or was it guilt over breaking and entering? The cabin smelled of dust and old wool and was swathed in shadows, fractured only by slivers of late-afternoon sunlight through the boarded-up windows. A door led off the main room, probably to the bedroom.

"There's nothing—"

"Shh!" He held up his hand, soldier style, closed fist, as if they were on some tactical-ops mission. It reminded her of Micah or maybe Conner, and she stifled a giggle.

A mouse hiding under a worn green sofa scurried across

the floor into the kitchen area and disappeared under the curtain of a sink.

"There's your bad guy," Dani said and stepped out from behind him. She scanned the room, letting Kirby in past her.

The dog sat on the floor, laid his ears back.

Dani stared at him. "She was here."

Will frowned at her. "What?"

"Well, someone was here recently. Look at Kirby. And look at the floor."

He crouched, studied the floor.

"The dust has been kicked up," she said in explanation.

"I see that." He stood, peered into the sink. "And a couple of empty cans of pork and beans, freshly opened."

"Maybe it was the people who owned the cabin."

"Maybe," he said slowly. "But I have to wonder if it was her, and your dog just confirmed it."

Dani advanced into the room, turned in a full circle. "Where would she go?"

He put a finger to his lips, pointed to the closed door. "That was open when I came in the first time," he whispered.

She couldn't deny the streak of fear that skidded up her spine. She swallowed, then moved away.

Will crept toward the bedroom door, put his hand on the knob. He flung the door open and swept the room with the muzzle of his gun as if the girl might run out and tackle him.

Dani tried to tuck her heart back into her chest. "Oh, good grief, Will. She's a young girl, most likely hurt and very scared. You're going to give her a stroke. Besides, the wind probably blew the door shut when we opened the front door." She walked past him into the room.

Sunlight poured into a back window. The boards swung free, probably loosened from the storm. The bedspread was off the double bed, leaving only rumpled sheets. She stared out the window, heart thumping, disappointment lining her throat. "She was here—"

A thump. *Outside*, on the porch. Will met her eyes, and suddenly she got it. He wasn't playing at Rambo; he *was* Rambo. And right now Rambo Will had the little hairs on her neck standing on end. "Get down!"

What?

Only she did, more from reflex than obedience. Then he turned and disappeared, taking her heart with him. *Will!*

"Drop it!"

"You drop it!"

She fought to untangle the voices.

A shot, splitting the fear.

No! "Will!"

"Dani, stay down!"

Not on her life.

They'd found her. And she'd been careful, just as Kutsi had taught her. Fadima had cleared the log from the window, and she circumvented the regular path down to the waterfront so she hadn't left a trail. Of course, Kutsi had taught her on the steppe, but she'd applied the principles of stealth. Maybe they'd used the dog.

Fadima stood outside the clearing. In her hands she held a bottle she'd dug out of the cabin owner's recycle bin, and as she trembled, it spilled lake water onto her shirt. She swallowed a pool of dread and edged back. She'd been looking forward to sleep, to warmth. To another can of beans. Thankfully, she had taken the blanket off the bed.

But if the weapon the man held and the two men who followed him in were any indication of the kind of trouble stalking her, she'd better run.

Now.

✦ ✦ ✦

"Jim Micah, the next time you decide to bushwhack me, I'd appreciate advance warning," Dani said. "Are you okay, Will?"

Will sat on the cabin floor, a towel to his nose where Dani's so-called friend had drop-kicked him while some other high-energy soldier he recognized as Conner Young had shoved a Beretta M9 that looked sickeningly like his own into his face.

If she hadn't run out and jumped on her friend's back, Will had no doubt that someone would be seriously injured and in need of a medevac. Maybe even him.

Sadly, he knew these friends—too well—and if he didn't do some fast thinking, they'd know him too in about five seconds. Wouldn't that be a great way to tell Dani that he'd been lying to her since he'd known her?

Please, please don't let Jim Micah remember him. Thankfully, the first time he'd met Micah face-to-face had been in the dead of night during a rescue raid on a terrorist camp on the wrong side of the Iraqi border. The 10th Special Forces was big enough for them not to bump heads or operations too often. If Lew hadn't been assigned to Micah's team the day they'd gone out on patrol and been snatched by Kurdish rebels, Will probably wouldn't be in this mess now.

At least Will was wearing war paint, and had the advantage of this being the last place in the world Micah would expect to see him, right?

Think fast, Will. The only thing that balmed his wounds

was that Dani sat next to *him*, nursing *him*, while Conner dealt with his own blood and a huge swelling lip.

She glanced at Micah, who looked like he wanted another go at Will if only Dani would get out of the way. He wondered if Micah would have hit him if he'd known he was jumping a fellow Beret. Well, if he'd known it was Will, probably . . . yes.

Wasn't this fun?

Micah leaned against the doorframe, scraping Will with a gaze that looked downright poisonous. "One of you over-the-edge jokers want to tell me what's going on?"

Dani's gaze snapped to Micah, and Will hid a smile. "Joker? Is that what you call hanging out in the bush for days, nearly getting myself and my dog killed?"

"I'd call it breaking and entering," Conner said quietly, still every inch the stealthy, deadly type. He didn't look at Dani when he spoke.

"We're searching for a teenage girl. She was reported lost a few days ago." Dani turned to Will, checked his nose. "It's better."

He didn't look at her as he wiped his hands off. "Who are these guys? Your friends?"

"Yes, these are my *good* friends. Remember that search-and-rescue team I was telling you about?" She gave a grim nod. Then she rose and gave the tall blond a hug. "How are you, Conner?"

Okay, that warm and friendly gesture felt like a sucker punch right to Will's sternum. He even blinked, as if in pain.

"Jim Micah." He held out his hand to Will in greeting. However, his gray eyes, hard as flint, held no welcome.

Will met his grasp, feeling like a jerk. Most likely, Micah would be on his side if he knew the full scenario. Except, perhaps, for the part about Will lying to Dani—over and over and over. "Will, local reporter."

Conner gave a harrumph of disbelief.

Will shot him a look.

"No, he really is," Dani said and gave Micah a kiss on the cheek. Will felt instantly jealous. "I met him a few days ago. He's been helping Sarah and me with the search."

"Really?" Micah said, but it didn't sound like a question.

"Yeah, *really*," Will snarled, surprised at his tone. "I'm just a guy trying to do the right thing."

Dani stared at him.

He sighed. So much for staying calm, not blowing his cover.

Dani got up and leaned against the table. "Okay, so what are you guys doing here? I thought you were supposed to be planning a wedding, Micah?"

He smiled slowly, his gaze still pinned like a rattler's on Will. "Lacey's got that covered. I'm just in the way. Besides, when we got the call about Missy last night, well, we decided to gets a hands-on look at what was going on up here." He finally loosed his glare on Will and gave Dani a soft look. "She's doing okay, by the way. Andee flew us up. We arrived after you left this morning and hung out with Sarah. She got nervous when she couldn't raise you on your cell phone."

"Yeah, I lost the signal around lunchtime."

"Hence, our timely arrival," Conner finished. "I tracked you through the GPS equipment I installed on your cell phone." He took his own scrutiny of Will. "I still don't get the interesting SAR getup. You look like—"

"A terrorist," Micah finished.

Will sighed in relief. "Thanks," he said, climbing to his feet. "I really like your friends, Dani."

Micah raised one dark eyebrow. "Dani?"

Was she blushing? She tried to glare at Will, but it didn't quite work. "They grow on you," Dani told him.

"Sorta like a wart?"

"Okay, that's good, soldier. Who are you, really?" Micah took two steps toward him.

Suddenly Will recognized Micah as Iceman, a guy whose reputation preceded him. Jim Micah had been his hero in more ways than Will could count—mostly because of his legendary battle tactics and his ability to think without his emotions and get the job done.

Will tensed, fishing for some sort of truth. "I'm a reporter. But I used to be in the Rangers."

Micah frowned as if digesting this information. "So why the getup?"

Will sighed, growing very, very quiet. Even Dani cast him a frown. "I'm not at liberty to say."

Pain flashed through Dani's eyes. "What? Will, are you . . . hiding something from me?"

Will turned away, picked his weapon off the floor. "I'm going for a little walk. Don't go anywhere 'til I get back."

Her silence in his wake spoke volumes. He might have preferred a slap across his face.

Conner stepped out beside him, keeping pace as Will left the cabin.

"Go away," Will said.

"In your dreams. It's obvious to both myself and Micah, the two former *Green Berets* in the room, that you are on a mission op here. And we don't much appreciate your dragging our friend Dannette into it."

"She followed me." Okay, that wasn't quite true. "I didn't have a choice."

"There're always choices."

Will stopped, turned. Conner stood eye to eye with him. "Not always. Not this time. Dani was determined to tag along.

I couldn't leave the lost girl out there, and I was afraid if I sent Dani home alone she'd get hurt."

"Define *hurt*."

Will's jaw tightened. "Snatched."

Conner didn't blink. Didn't flinch. "And the girl? What's she about?"

Will shook his head. "That's the part I can't tell you. But feel free to throw Dani over your shoulder and haul her out of here. You're armed. Just . . . be careful. And good luck. She knows how to deliver a wallop."

He got a hint of a smile from Conner. "She hit you?"

Will moved his jaw. "I probably deserved it."

Conner's eyes darkened, and suddenly Will saw his own reflection in the man's gaze—haunted eyes, smeared grease-paint in his goatee, training in his stance, and power in his arms. More than that, he saw his past. Wild Will.

Conner probably saw it too. "You want to elaborate on that?" he said quietly, warning in his tone. "In what way did you deserve it?"

Will held up his hand, took a step back. "Don't get your dander up. I was the perfect gentleman. She just . . . doesn't like reporters."

Conner frowned. Then finally he said, "That's right; Dannette doesn't like reporters. Which means that—" he stared hard at Will—"if she's defending you, you must have won her trust."

Will gave a curt nod. "Thank you. *Finally*. I promise, I have only Dani's best interests at heart here." He turned.

Conner's hand clamped his shoulder, stopping him. "Dannette's heart is a precious thing, pal. I'm using a friendly tone, but take me very, very seriously. Don't break it. Or your nose is only the first thing Micah will break."

Oh, Will had no illusions about how Micah would react. And rightly so. In fact, he was living on borrowed time, and he knew it.

Maybe getting Conner and Micah on his team was the only way to protect Dani from the terrorists.

From himself. From Wild Will.

They'd crossed to the far edge of the yard, out of earshot. Will sighed, looked away from Conner, his chest knotting. "Conner, it's me, Wild Will Masterson. From the 10th."

Conner stared at him. Stepped back. Mouth open.

"The girl I'm tracking is part of a top-secret, deep-cover op that went south. I gotta find her. And Dani's been helping me. I swear to you that I'm only trying to protect her."

"By making her a target?" Conner kept his voice low, but Will heard the danger in it.

"She's . . . so . . . *stubborn*." Will's frustration spilled out, and he fought to reel it in. "She went out ahead of me, and I couldn't talk her or Sarah into quitting, so I tagged along."

"You used them for your own gain."

Will clenched his jaw. "I didn't expect her to follow me here today. And when I saw her, I was stuck. I couldn't send her back, or they'd find her—"

"Who'd find her?"

Will glanced past Conner, toward the cabin. "There are a couple of guys looking for this girl. They tried to take me out during a storm yesterday, and I have this gut feeling they're still around."

Conner glanced at the cabin. "We need to get Dannette out of here. But not tonight. We'll camp here and head out at first light."

Will nodded, feeling relief loosen his chest. "Thank you."

"Don't thank me, Wild. I just don't want Dannette to be

around when Micah finds out who you are—and I'm not talking about your lying about being a reporter." He shook his head. "Of all the ladies to charm, Wild, you sure picked the wrong one."

Chapter 16

"SERIOUSLY, MICAH, WHAT are you doing here?" Dani walked onto the porch of the cabin, aware of a chill lacing the air as the sun slunk behind the horizon. They were surrounded by the smell of pine and the sounds of twilight—chirruping crickets and the rush of wind. Micah's and Conner's sudden arrival had begun to chip away at her confidence, add credence to the very real possibility that she had helmed a wild-goose chase.

Not to mention Will's cryptic *"I'm not at liberty to say."*

What did that mean? She had the eerie feeling that Will might know more about this missing girl than she did. A smart woman would pack up Kirby and head back to Moose Bend before Sheriff Fadden found out she'd defied him. Again. And, oh, again.

Maybe Will was just protecting his source. And while that stung, that supposition only confirmed the reason for his weird behavior. Will wasn't an unscrupulous reporter. He did have integrity.

Dani poured out water for her dog and set the bowl down before taking a chair next to Micah's. The words *breaking and entering* throbbed in her brain like a second-degree burn.

Micah sat forward in his chair, his arms dangling over his

knees. His low, powerful voice hummed under her skin when he spoke, and she couldn't deny she felt glad to see him. Even if he had tackled Will.

For a second there, she hadn't known whom she should protect. And that confusion in itself had her heart in a painful tangle. Since when did she side with a guy she hardly knew over one of her best friends?

"Sarah was really worried about you. She thought you might be feeling strung out after the last couple of days, and she dropped a few hints," Micah said.

"Which you were all too happy to take?" But Dani couldn't help smiling. The fact that Micah and Conner had tromped through the forest to find her felt nearly like family.

"Lacey came with me to Moose Bend to talk wedding stuff with Sarah and Andee, and . . . well, a guy can only take so much pink. Who knew that Lacey would turn into a Southern belle, complete with frills and froufrou?"

Dani laughed. She had a hard time wrapping her mind around that image also. Especially since Lacey had made a living as a hard-living CIA agent for most of the past fifteen years. "C'mon, it can't be that bad."

He shrugged but smiled, and his expression radiated such joy it felt nearly palpable. The guy turned into a mess of goo around his fiancée, a woman he'd waited twenty years to marry. Dani knew that Lacey could march down the aisle wearing combat gear and a full-metal jacket and Micah would think she was the most beautiful woman on four planets.

She sorta wished she knew what that felt like.

"I am glad to see you, Micah. But only if you're going to join in the search. I know she's out here—I can feel it—and the very fact that Will is still here, beating the bushes with me, tells me he believes it too."

"That's what you call what he's doing? Beating the bushes?" Micah asked. "Excuse me for stating the obvious here, but he's a wee bit strange."

Dani gave him a mock glare. "He's nice. And harmless. I don't know why he's got makeup on. But he is a nice guy. I think he's even a Christian. He's trustworthy and kind and loyal and dedicated. And under normal circumstances when you're not holding a gun on him, he's patient. You'd probably like him if you got to know him."

"Really." A small smile played at the corners of Micah's mouth.

"Yeah, *really*," she said. "He's honest—he even told me about his best friend who got killed."

Micah's smile dimmed. "How did he die?" Too late Dani remembered that Micah, too, had lost his best friend. Only his friend John had been a CIA agent, and the lady Micah was about to marry had been his accused killer.

"A bombing in Macedonia, I think he said."

Micah frowned, and she saw his gaze rove the forest beyond her, as if searching his mental files. "Not the Red Cross bombing?"

"I don't know; he didn't say. It happened three years ago."

Micah's expression turned grim, and something about it made her heart seize. Micah had been a Green Beret for much of his adult life and knew the gruesome details of some of the most brutal terrorist attacks across the world, especially in the eastern European theater. "The Red Cross incident redefined the land-scape of the war on terror, at least for those behind the scenes. Until that point, we thought we were dealing with many tiny blazes around the world that had to be stomped out. This bomb-ing woke us up, made us realize we needed to refocus our efforts."

Dani shook her head. "I don't follow."

Micah rubbed his large hands together and sighed deeply. "In an effort to help the Macedonians deal with the crush of refugees from Albania and Yugoslavia that had fled after Milošević's reign of terror, the US and most of the NATO countries banded together and funded a huge Red Cross effort. We set up housing, opened hospitals and schools. And staffed them with military from all these nations: Australian, American, English, even Polish and Turkish personnel. The United Nations at work in a very experimental capacity. Obviously also the perfect opportunity to shake all of us up."

"How?"

"We were attacked, the entire camp—buildings, ware-houses, vehicles were triggered to blow simultaneously. The devastation was . . ." Micah shook his head, and in his eyes Dani saw the horror of being faced with the ugly realities of the war on terror. "Before the attack, they caught one of the terror-ists—actually a refugee who knew that the bombs had been planted. She and her daughter had escaped from the terrorist cell behind it and had gone into hiding at the camp. Their intel gave the soldiers who were on peacekeeping detail enough evidence to start a search. As some of the teams evac'd the camp, another unit did a systematic search."

He closed his eyes. "I specifically remember at least one Green Beret unit." The look he gave her when he opened his eyes made her want to cry. His voice dropped. "They didn't find all the explosives before they blew. There were hundreds killed, most of them military personnel." He shook his head. "They brought in my team to help clean up. It wasn't pretty. And of course the countries blamed each other for lack of surveillance or supplies. Most importantly, no one took the blame. Not al Qaeda, not Hezbollah. Not any of the splinter groups tucked away in Europe. No one. Which felt pretty odd to us, but it played right into the information our informant told us."

"Who was responsible?"

"Until this time, we'd only heard whispers of this group, and I hadn't given them any thought. They weren't linked to religious zealots or a political agenda. They were a phantom group called Hayata."

She'd heard that name before. Somewhere. "Wait, isn't that the group that tried to steal Lacey's Ex-6 program?"

Micah smiled. "Roger that. And Lacey nabbed one of their key players. Hayata's agenda isn't religious or political. It's about purity. Purity in power. According to this woman—who disappeared right after the attack—they believe they are descended from one ruler and that they are decimating the world powers, systematically maneuvering to take out their communications or economic base to prepare for this ruler."

"Okay, that's very freaky, Micah. So Left Behind series. I'm not buying it."

"Yeah, well, like I said, they're a phantom organization in many ways. They don't get their hands dirty, but they supply resources to many other groups in trade for allegiance. They're extremely wealthy, and their endgame is one-world government."

She gave a fake shiver. "The Third Reich, take two."

"A few Nazi groups are linked to Hayata." His face betrayed his feelings. "But the right hand doesn't know what the left is doing. Only the mother ship has control. Think bees. They have a queen bee, which feeds the rest of the bees until she sends them out to make new hives. Hayata is the queen. We think the Red Cross bombing had a twofold purpose—to keep our attention focused on eastern Europe while they did their business in Asia and to introduce them to the world. To make the UN nations fight amongst themselves and stumble around in confusion."

Dani petted Kirby, then dug a ball out of her backpack and threw it. Kirby sprang after it, diving off the porch. "So, Will's buddy was in this bombing."

Micah stared out into the gathering darkness. His profile spoke louder than his words. "They found only pieces of some of the guys."

Dani closed her eyes against a spasm of pain in her chest. "His friend left behind a wife and three daughters."

"Wow. That's hard." Micah had recently resigned from service, but Dani knew he understood what it meant to leave loved ones behind.

"Yeah. What's worse, I think he sorta blames himself. He didn't tell me why, but I have a feeling he's still grieving." She couldn't tell him that Will had nearly cried in her arms, but the image pressed against her eyes.

Micah gave her a strange look, something that made her wonder if she might be so transparent that he could see right past her words to the feeling lurking in her heart. Feelings she wasn't quite sure she felt ready to voice. "He always will, Dannette. The question is, has he moved on?"

"I don't know. I think so. But—" she gave a half grin—"he does seem to be firmly planted in the glory days, doesn't he?"

Micah didn't smile. "Make no mistake. Guys like Will don't just walk away from the Rangers. It becomes a part of them. My gut tells me that there's something else going on here."

Kirby ran up to Dani with the ball and dropped it. She threw it again and he charged after it. "I believe him, Micah. He's here to find that girl. And so am I. So, as long as Missy's okay, I'd like to keep looking."

Micah glanced out toward the lake, where the departing sun threw it into shadow. "Don't want to leave her alone as long as there's a chance, huh?"

Dani smiled and met his eyes with a soft nod.

He gave her a sad smile. "You know you couldn't save her, right?"

Dani looked away, rubbed her hands on her pants as his words sank in. He wasn't talking about this mystery girl, and she knew it. "Yeah. I know."

"You were six, honey. Let it go."

She winced. "Yeah, well, you know how easy it is to escape your regrets, don't you?"

Micah had spent nearly twenty years regretting letting the woman he loved marry another. It drove him to risks, hot spots in the world, and most of all to eventually believe that woman could be a murderer. "Okay, that was fair, but still, it wasn't your fault. You know that."

She sighed, examined the dirt in the lines of her hands. It felt like ages since she'd had a shower and a decent meal. "I have let go of that grief. It was so long ago. But the thought of someone out there—hungry, hypothermic, hoping someone cares enough to rescue them . . ." Alone. Afraid. The sudden empathy she felt made a shudder sweep through her. She knew all too well how it felt to look out across a deserted, destroyed landscape and feel utterly alone. Abandoned. "No, I can't give up."

Micah nodded, then reached out and took her hand. "Dannette, I know you have a huge heart and that you want to help. But you have nearly nothing to go on. You've been out here for three days—unauthorized, I might add. You've nearly gotten killed, your dog's been injured, and now you're running around in the woods with a dog that is not your property. Your contract—and maybe your reputation—is teetering on a quickly eroding edge, and you're in the company of someone who looks like he's just as likely to take a twelve-inch Peace Keeper blade to your throat. Can I be the voice of reason in your life and say it's time to throw in the towel? Come back to Moose Bend. We'll straighten out this mess with Sheriff Fadden—"

"What did he say to you?" She yanked her hand away. "Wait, this isn't about Sarah or Missy. Fadden sent you out, didn't he?" She suddenly felt as if he'd taken said dagger and plunged it into her chest.

Micah's face turned grim. "No. I didn't talk to Fadden. I only talked to Sarah. But I can see the writing on the wall here, and I know you're in over your head."

"I'm following my gut. This girl is out here. I know it. In fact, I think she's been in this cabin." She looked at him, knowing she wore frustration on her face. "How many times have you had to trust my instincts?" Her voice rose, and for some reason she wanted to cry. She knew her Team Hope cronies considered her the unemotional one, the one who looked at life with steel-edged realism, and the concern on Micah's face told her that he definitely thought she was losing it.

She took a deep breath before she said something that really sounded crazy. Like *Will trusts me; why can't you?*

"Is this about Will?" Micah said softly, as if reading her mind.

"Oh, please. You know me better than that. I'm not going to discard my common sense for the first man who smiles at me. I'm not that desperate—" Only that was *exactly* what it looked like. She wanted to climb under the porch and hide.

Micah touched her arm. "Of course you're not. But Sarah told me you like him. That you'd spent the day with him yesterday."

"Sarah's very informative," she snapped. Her throat thickened, especially when Micah scooted closer to her. She felt his sturdy presence close in and braced herself. She didn't need a father, thank you. Still, Micah hadn't been the captain of his Green Beret squad for his blind spots. Sometimes she thought he could look through her as if she were made of gauze.

"I'm sorry. I didn't mean to hurt you."

She sighed, leaned against his shoulder. He did have wide, safe shoulders. "I don't know. Maybe I do like him. Will makes me feel safe, and I haven't felt that way for a really, really long time." She drew away and pulled her knees up as Kirby ran back, dropped the ball at her feet, hunkered down, and began to chew on it. "He sat with me all day yesterday in Missy's kennel, just listening. Really listening, with his eyes and smile, without trying to flirt or make a move on me. Just being a friend." She gave a rueful chuckle. "He looks a lot different without the Hulk paint."

Micah grabbed the ball, wrestled with Kirby. "We all do."

Yeah, without Micah's BDUs or the battle demeanor he usually showed at SAR incidents, he could be a giant teddy bear.

"Just remember," he said, finally wrenching the ball from Kirby's mouth, chucking it out in the forest. "A heart is a precious thing. When you give it away, you do it 100 percent, and you never get it back whole. So make sure you know what you're getting into."

Did she have any idea what she was getting into? Not a chance. Still, Will's dedication to this mission, his concern for her protection . . . that felt like a good prescription for hero in her mind. And the fact that he might be a Christian had seeded all sorts of scenarios. Maybe for once she could stop suspecting him of hidden agendas and simply reach out in trust.

After all, wasn't that what Will did for her? Kept pushing until he shook her defenses? Proving himself despite her restraining-order demeanor?

He deserved her trust.

"Have you asked God about it?" Micah asked softly.

She winced. How had she gone so far into this relationship without consulting the One who knew Will better than anyone?

Only, for the first time since that day in the field when she'd asked for an angel to protect her, she wondered if God was finally answering her prayers.

"You know, this doesn't have to be a one-man show. Micah and I are both trained in search and rescue. Fill us in."

Will glanced at the sky, at the shadows that stretched across the grass, pooling darkness in the woods. Will felt as if he had a pit bull attached to his leg. How was he supposed to do a perimeter search with this guy tagging along?

With Conner not far behind, Will stalked back to the house, mulling over his options. Options that didn't include Dani or this overzealous duo. "I don't need help," he said sharply. But doubts tugged at his words. He'd seen Dani's new dog indicate a passive alert, meaning he'd picked up someone's scent. And the pork-and-beans cans evidenced someone's recent presence.

Time ticked down. If he didn't find the girl soon, General Nazar would be discovered, neutralized, and they'd be back to square one, digging through the rubble of their failed mission. Not only that, but somewhere out there Hayata was planning another attack. And soon, if Will read his instincts correctly. No, too much was at stake to disregard Kirby's abilities.

But he couldn't drag Dani along. Not if he didn't want to repeat history. Lew climbed into his mind, along with his words: *"We should wait for the rest of the team."*

Yeah, hindsight was twenty-twenty. And every single time Will relived Lew's death, he heard and obeyed Lew's words. Unfortunately, reality had played out differently. He'd charged ahead, Lew ten loyal steps behind him.

Only ten steps earlier or later, and Lew would have lived. Only ten seconds earlier or later, Lew wouldn't have been trapped under the roof joists while the building collapsed around him.

Only ten steps earlier or later, it would have been Lew who awoke fifteen feet from the rubble. Will still fought the screams embedded in his brain—Lew's screams—as Will dragged him out of the flames only to watch him die in his arms.

He couldn't be the guy who dragged Dani to her death. He stopped, turned, and gave Conner a hard look. "Just keep your word. Pack up Dani first thing in the morning and take her home. Please."

Conner frowned but said nothing as he started to move past Will.

Will clamped a hand on Conner's shoulder. "Please." Only his tone didn't plead.

Conner shook out of his grip and stared at him. Then, finally, "Someday we're going to know what is going on, right?"

Will looked past him, to the enclosure of forest, listening to the frogs serenade the approaching twilight. "Not if I'm successful."

Conner didn't blink, didn't move. "Okay, we'll leave first thing in the morning. We'll bed down here tonight. Dannette will sleep in the cabin. You and Micah and I will take turns at patrol."

Will managed a crisp nod. He'd take the last watch, and then, before dawn crested the sky, he'd sneak out with Kirby.

He crossed to the front of the cabin. Something twisted inside him when he spied Dani sitting on the porch, hands clasped around her drawn-up legs, sitting closer than necessary to her large and overzealous friend Micah. And the soft smile on her face made Will's jealous heart ride to his throat and lodge there.

She welcomed Kirby as he bounded onto the porch, then ran one of her strong hands into his fur as she picked up the slimy ball he'd dropped and pitched it back into the forest. She belonged here in the woods, amid the trees, fighting the elements, courage in her step. But she had a softness with her animals that dug up all his longings.

Today it had nearly made him confess. He'd almost told her that he wasn't a reporter. He was just a guy trying to do a job—one that included lying to her. He even saw himself dropping to his knees, heard himself pleading for forgiveness.

And then, oh joy, in his imagination he'd seen her face crumple and heard the resounding whack across his cheek.

He took a deep breath. Obviously, he'd let her creep in under his defenses, something that the arrival of her friends/thugs only made painfully clear.

Where was the guy who said he'd never let a woman in his life for longer than twelve hours? He cringed even as he thought it. He wasn't that guy anymore.

Conner strolled up behind him as they reached the cabin. "I think we should tuck in here tonight, head back to town in the morning," he said to Micah.

Dani gazed at Will. "Are you serious?"

He didn't look at her; instead he trudged up the steps, into the cabin. Behind him, he heard Conner fill Micah in on the details. Why did he feel slightly sick? This was best for Dani. To go home and now. But her friends would have to hog-tie her and throw her over their shoulders when she discovered he'd taken her dog.

He felt like a jerk.

Putting down his weapon, he walked into the back bedroom, closed the window, and surveyed the room for anything out of place . . . like a terrorist?

He wasn't hiding from Dani—he *wasn't*.

Dani stood in the kitchen when he came out. Her hands were folded over her chest. "You're giving up?"

"I want you to go home, Dani," he said, opening the pantry. Three cans of corn, a jar of pickles, and a box of saltines in a Tupperware container. No mice droppings. He was aware that they were trespassing, so he made a mental note to find out who owned this cabin and write them a healthy check, along with his apologies.

"So the search is over. You're going to believe Fadden?"

"Yes." For her, the search was over.

She sighed, said nothing as she opened the cupboard, found a stack of paper plates. "I'm just surprised, that's all."

Get in line. She wasn't the only one surprised. He couldn't believe, for example, that he hadn't tried to kiss her, not even once. Or that he'd let his guard down and let her inside his grief. Or even that now he planned on breaking her heart and stealing her dog. No, actually he shouldn't be surprised about that—sometimes things had to be sacrificed for the nation.

Like, perhaps, his heart.

They all sat at the small table and shared a meager dinner—two MREs from Will's pack, plus the pickles, cold corn, and saltines. Conner had gone to the lake for water and filled up their canteens.

Dani retired early into the back bedroom, closing the door without a word while something inside Will died a little. No, a little *more*.

Perhaps he'd been wishing for another campfire chat like they'd had three nights ago. One that might end with some star-gazing, maybe with her getting chilly and needing a strong, warm arm—

There he went again, thinking like a guy who hadn't lied to her, who didn't have plans to stomp what little trust he'd been granted to splinters.

He sat on the porch, his weapon across his knees, watching the night bathe the lake. The sky, cleansed by the storm, gave an unadulterated view of the Milky Way. How many times had he lain out under the stars with Lew, listening to him read a letter from Bonnie, hearing the longing in his voice.

He suddenly knew how Lew had felt, despite the fact that the woman Will was falling in love with was only fifteen feet away.

Falling in love? Okay, all this greasepaint had gone straight to his brain and turned it soft. He had no room to love her. Ever.

Only the thought settled into his heart and produced a smile. If there was ever a woman he might love, maybe forever, spend his life trying to please, trying to coax a smile from, laugh with and tease, it might be Dannette Lundeen.

Because Dani made him feel like the guy he wanted to be. Trustworthy. Honorable. She made him want to be more, to do anything to see respect—even love—in her eyes.

"I'm taking the first watch." Micah sat down on the other end of the porch. "You going to let me have that weapon?"

"No."

Micah smiled, cast him a look. "You *were* a Ranger, weren't you?"

Will frowned at him. Nodded. Oh no, he was going to have to tell him.

"Dannette told me about your buddy who was killed."

Well, that hurt like a right hook. Will could even feel his chops ringing.

"Sorry about your pal." Micah said. "That can be hard to live with. I saw my best buddy die about eight years ago. I even saw the person I thought did it. I spent my life trying to track her down and send her to prison."

Wasn't that interesting? "Did you find her?"

Micah chuckled, and it sounded like regret. "Yeah. I found her and I'm going to marry her in about a month."

Will went still. His mouth opened long before words emerged. "Excuse me . . . did you say *marry*?"

"I did. Because what I'd seen wasn't the truth. It only felt like the truth. And when I realized that, I was able to see what really happened—she had only taken the blame for the crime. The real killer stalked her for years. It wasn't until she confronted him and won that we both escaped our pasts."

Will nodded, staring out into the dark forest, dodging the accuracy of Micah's words. "Congratulations."

"Thanks." Micah stretched out his legs. "It feels pretty good, knowing that we finally found the truth. Sorta like we made it through a dark night to morning. She has a little girl. I'm going to adopt her."

Will managed a smile. "My buddy Lew had three girls. His wife is getting remarried this weekend."

"Lew?"

"Yeah, Lew Strong." Will dredged up his courage. "I'm sorry I didn't tell you earlier, Micah. It's me, Wild Masterson." *Only not me. Not really.*

Micah stayed silent. Crossed his arms over his chest. "I'm getting old. I can't believe I didn't recognize you."

Will shrugged. "That's my specialty. Hiding from people."

Micah nodded. Will couldn't read his silence. Then, "Sorry to hear about Lew. He was a good soldier. A good man. You came after him in Iraq with Lacey, didn't you?"

"Yeah. Lacey and John Montgomery. They got married after that."

"I know." Micah gave a wry smile. "She's the one I'm marrying next month."

Will had no words for that. He just stared at Micah, who smiled, a lot more warmly than Will had expected.

"Things have changed a little for both of us." Micah glanced toward the cabin. "You like Dannette."

Will didn't answer.

"Dannette told me you're a Christian. That's not part of your cover, is it?"

"Listen, I know you want to protect Dani from the Wild Will you used to know. But the fact is, he's gone. I'm just trying to keep her alive and do my job. And I don't need to confess any sins, so you can take off the priest's collar. I promise, I've been a good boy."

Micah raised his eyebrows, and the look he gave Will told him that his defenses had shifted to alert status. Still, Will wasn't under his command, and he didn't need a chaperone. All he needed was Micah doing his job and making a successful skedaddle back to Moose Bend with Dani, maybe kicking mad, but alive.

He'd deal with the fallout later—or never. Because he'd be on a plane to DC.

Suddenly, Micah's tone changed, became commando captain. Of course he wasn't going to stop at the raised eyebrows. "Listen and listen good, Wild. Dannette's been through a lot and she likes you, so don't mess up. I don't want her heart dragged through some minefield by a guy who knows how to turn on the charm. Maybe you don't need a priest. Maybe you need a friend. But make no mistake; I will be neither if you break her heart."

So now he'd been warned in stereo. Good grief, he should be counting his blessings that he'd gotten two days with Dani without getting pummeled.

"I'm not going to break her heart. In fact, as soon as I track down my target, I'll be double-timing out of Dani's life. Have no fears." Will clenched his jaw, trying to stem his flow of words, but he was tired, frustrated, and sorry, and he wasn't going to let a blast from the past turn the very gentlemanly way Will had been conducting himself into something tawdry. "For your information, Dani's not easy to shake, which I've been trying to do for two days. Yes, I am out here for a reason, and you'll just have to trust me on that. If you care about her, you'll head home at first light. And for your information, yes, I do miss Lew. I do feel like I blew it. So what? That's life, and I know it."

"But you don't know where to go from here."

Will blinked, frowned. Micah's soft, calm voice dazed him more than if he'd punched him. "What do you mean?"

Micah blew out a breath. "My friend John and I were inseparable. We grew up together, played football together, got in trouble together. When he was killed, I thought someone had scooped out my insides and stomped on them. I poured myself into being the best Green Beret out there. I lived and breathed dangerous missions, and if it had a zero factor of success, I was your man. Problem was, I didn't realize I was only digging myself deeper into grief. I didn't know that God had bigger plans for me until I let Him have His way. He pulled me out of that grief, gave me another chance. I don't know what's eating you, Will. But God is all about second chances. He's about making all things new."

Will sighed, anger dissipating from his knotted chest. He lowered his voice. "Okay, here's the deal. I was pretty torn up when Lew bought it. I sorta figured that I would get to heaven by association. Lew was one of those sold-out Christians, a guy who had that Galations 2:20 Jesus-in-me concept nailed. He was always preaching to me, and despite my mistakes, he never made me feel like a loser. It's because of him I didn't die of a drug overdose or drive my car into a wall during high school."

Will breathed out, a hot breath of sorrow, before he continued. "He never gave up on me. So when he died, I hit bottom. I realized that I'd held out all my life because I thought Lew was the only salvation I needed. But without him . . . well, I went back to the church and had it out with God. I said, 'Fine, I'll do it Your way.' I asked Him to forgive me and start over."

He glanced at Micah, who was watching him without a blink. So, that hadn't hurt as much as he figured. Maybe . . .

"The thing is . . . I'm *not* really sure where to go from there. That was three years ago, and yes, I still feel a lot like I did at that moment—dazed, confused, aware that something is different but unable to get my hands around it. I want to be God's man, like Lew was, but frankly, I don't know how.

"My friendship with Dani is the first time I haven't let my desires get in the way of what I know is right. I mean, I've dodged the opposite gender since Lew was killed, so it isn't like I played with fire, but Dani, she snuck in under my skin and now . . . just take her home, okay?"

Micah nodded, looked out into the darkness, unfazed, thankfully, by the emotion in Will's voice.

Will swallowed hard, not sure why he'd unloaded all that but feeling lighter somehow. Maybe now Micah would take him seriously, not pry, and haul Dani away.

Silence threaded between them, woven with the sounds of the night and the soft breeze that picked at Will's hair.

"You know," Micah said finally, "I guess I never thought how hard it might be for someone to learn how to walk in faith, especially if he never did it. I was raised in the church. It felt like second nature." He angled a look at Will. "Are you familiar with the story of the ten lepers?"

Will shook his head.

"So, Jesus is on His way to Jerusalem, and He passes this colony of lepers. They have to live outside the city because the disease is contagious, smells bad, and is disgusting. Not only that, but the lepers are required to cover their mouths and shout, 'Unclean, unclean' as people pass by."

Will winced. Sometimes he still felt like yelling, "Unclean!"

"Here comes Jesus, and the lepers yell out to Him, 'Have mercy on us!' They want Him to cleanse them. Of course, Jesus *does* have compassion for them, and He says, 'Go show yourselves to the priest.' In those days, in order to be declared clean you had to wait for a priest to check you over. Except it took a miracle to make a person clean, because leprosy was incurable, so it wasn't like the priests made regular visits to the leper colonies. At Jesus' command, the men break all the rules, go into the city, and show themselves."

Will nodded. "I can relate to that leper thing."

Micah gave a soft chuckle. "We all can. But here's the great part. When they left to show the priest, they still had leprosy. They were cleansed *on the way*. Their lives were restored as they obeyed God. And you know, that is the Christian life. They were healed as soon as Jesus spoke the words, but it didn't show in their lives until they'd begun to obey Him. We don't break free from our pasts until we start walking with Him, abiding with Him. One day at a time. That is how you become a guy like Lew. Or like Jesus."

"It is good for people to submit at an early age to the yoke of discipline." The words from Lew's Bible blazed in Will's mind. Yes, this is what Lew had done, and it had turned him into a man who'd lived for God.

"I believe you when you say you've changed, Will. You're not Wild anymore, at least the Wild we knew. When Dannette described you, well . . . suffice it to say it wasn't a description I'd ever pegged for you. God has been about changing that guy you were, one day at a time. Maybe that's why I didn't recognize you." Micah smiled when he said it.

Will let those words resonate in his soul. Just what had Dani said? He felt a painful mix of euphoria and shame. "Lew also said that God was his portion. I never got that."

Micah nodded. "It means God was his all. It means that when he went to meet Him, Lew was rejoicing."

Rejoicing. Yeah, Will could see that.

So, why was it so hard for those left behind?

"How did he do it?"

Micah frowned at him.

"Made God his portion."

"Oh. Well, I think the answer is in Acts 17:28: 'In him we live and move and exist.'"

Will didn't want to sound like an idiot, but *huh?* "And that means . . . ?"

"Just trust God one day at a time, Will. That's a good place to start." Micah reached for the Colt Commando. "I promise not to shoot you in your sleep."

"That's very thoughtful of you." But Will released the rifle and watched as Micah strolled out into the night.

One day at a time. If they made it to morning, he just might try that.

Chapter 17

FADIMA PULLED UP her knees and locked the blanket around her shoulders, clenching it tightly in her fist. Fatigue lapped at her like the soft waves of the Aral Sea, rushing at her, leaving its fingerprints on her hungry, tired resolve. Dawn ran golden threads across the sky, as if parting the dark cloth of night. She needed to get up, to push ahead . . . but to where?

She should crawl back to the cabin, throw herself on the mercy of the searchers. Yes, one *had* looked like he might cuff her and send her back to her homeland gift wrapped for Hayata, but the others—especially the blonde woman with the dog—looked compassionate.

Fadima felt she might sell her soul for compassion right about now. Or maybe a pile of *plov* or even a campfire, flickering into the velvet expanse of sky over the Kolsai Lakes back home in Kazakhstan, warming her hands, her face. She imagined her mother's voice, humming a folk tune, and Kutsi playing with their baby sister. She remembered other campfires, other voices humming in the night—some gruff, others soothing. Faces weathered by cold and a rough way of life filled her mind—Baki's, her crippled cousin who had taught her how to read their tribal language, and Mama Emine's, who knew herbs and medicines that made a person healthy . . . or sick. Did they miss her?

A twig snapped. She bolted upright, jerked to the brutal present, the cold breath of early morning pressing into her pores. Sucking her breath into her chest, she strained to hear above the blood pounding in her ears.

Nothing.

Her stomach growled and she pressed against it. She thought of the cans of food back at the cabin. She should have grabbed them, tucked them in her backpack. She'd been foolish, *so* foolish to leave her hideout without supplies. Kutsi would have yelled at her, called her *doraka*.

In her stupidity, she would die out here; the dogs would find her bones and the birds would pick them clean. And her father would never know what had happened to. Amina. His instructions had been simple: Wait for Hafiz.

Instead, she'd run. Based on what? The word of a terrorist? Panic had deceived her, and now it would drive her to her death. Her father's death. Kutsi's death.

For sure, it had killed her mother, Saiba. Saiba had been sent to hide. Only she'd known about the planned massacre and betrayed Hayata, saving thousands of lives but costing her own. The one event that her father had intended to use to enable his wife and daughter to make their escape, and Saiba hadn't been able to stifle the panic or the pain of watching unknowns perish. In the end, she'd fled right back into the unforgiving grasp of Hayata. As if they'd been waiting for her all along.

Papa, I'm sorry.

She would return to the cabin. Wait until they left, find food.

Despair crashed over Fadima. Then what? She pulled the

blanket closer, starting to shake. She wrapped her arms around her waist, hunched over, and tried to quiet the betraying sobs that rushed over her.

Soggy to her bones and hungry enough to eat a sacred white leopard, her options felt as frail as the pale dawn filtering through the forest.

Better to die, however, than to let Hayata find her.

Shivering, she curled again into a ball in the grass. Later. She'd figure out what to do later, after the warm waves of sleep had found her, had run up her legs, covered her with soft swells.

Her eyelids dipped into the sweet abyss.

Another snap.

She froze. Then a hand clamped roughly over her mouth, crushing her lips to her teeth.

She jerked her head, flailed.

The smell of unwashed breath choked her, a body pressed her into the earth, soaking her blanket through.

"Fadima," said a low voice, "you've been a bad girl."

Dani startled awake, her heart racing in her ears. Something . . . she dangled her arm over the bed, felt Kirby on the floor curled in slumber. Early morning pressed through the windows, pouring gold across the wood floor. She felt punky, and sleep tugged at her, like a friend calling her. But she couldn't deny the lurch in her heart, something . . . amiss.

She pushed herself up. She hadn't slept under the covers—that felt way too invasive and she already felt like a burglar here. Instead, she'd piled her coat over her and tried to stay warm.

She'd obviously slept hard from the way the lines drove across her face. She felt them as she rubbed her cheek, then combed her fingers through her hair. Okay, that was useless. She stood, and Kirby raised his head, searched her actions with his molasses eyes. "Shh," she said and stepped over him, walked to the window.

She couldn't see the sunrise, but from this angle, she saw the dent of morning against the dome of night in streaks of pale yellow and gray. The trees, which last night seemed to close in and knit together like praying hands, opened their gnarled white fingers in the wan daylight. Dani wondered where the girl was and if she'd found shelter somewhere in their grip.

Micah's warnings and hesitations about her search undulated in the back of her mind. She shook them off, picked up her day pack, and cracked open the door.

A stopover in the bathroom to brush her teeth told her just how terrific she looked. Probably it was time to drag out her bandanna and tuck her hair into a scarf. Oh, well. SAR work wasn't a fashion show, but it would have been nice to look good for Will.

Then again, he'd already seen her at her worst—dragging out Missy, red-eyed, tired. And that hadn't stopped him from . . . what? Being kind? Perhaps she was reading too much into his friendship.

He hadn't said much to her last night as they'd put together a paltry supper. In fact, if she were to scrutinize his actions, she might have labeled him aloof.

Or . . . secretive? He had hinted at another agenda. Still, when Conner returned from his stroll around the yard, he'd told her that Will was only trying to do his job. Maybe she should have asked exactly what job that was. Because she didn't know any reporters who dressed like special-ops guys to get a story.

Okay, what about war correspondents?

See, she was letting her curiosity get her into trouble. Just like it had when she was six. Again, she should simply trust him.

Micah had bedded down on the floor, Conner on the ratty sofa. Both men were fully dressed and rolled onto their sides, blanketless. They too had felt more than uneasy about taking up residence in this cabin. The owner was likely to find a large windfall and a thank-you/apology note in his or her mailbox before the week's end.

She patted her leg. Kirby jumped to his feet and eyed her. When she put a finger to her lips, the dog walked obediently to the front door and waited for her.

Conner opened one eye while she tiptoed across the room. She made a walking motion with her fingers. He hesitated, looked around the room, then seemed satisfied, nodded, and closed his eyes again as she cracked open the door.

The morning wind gusted through her coat. She didn't feel quite so grimy when the air smelled like fresh pine and lake water. To the east, over the lake, a brilliant orange sun barely peeked over the horizon, simmering as it consumed the night. She walked down the porch steps, vaguely aware that she hadn't seen Will yet, and trekked down to the beach. Crouching at water's edge, she splashed water over her face, and it dripped off her chin. The cold snap of lake water opened her pores and made her feel as if today might bring mercies.

"Great is his faithfulness; his mercies begin afresh each morning." Sarah's words from Scripture sang in her mind, and she let them settle in her heart as she turned to return to the cabin and maybe some grub.

A figure caught her eye. She looked down the shore and saw Will sitting on a large boulder, watching the dawn. He'd washed off his funny face paint and held his gun across his lap. Sitting there like that—quiet, pensive, hidden—he appeared lonely. Even . . . sad. She saw him as he'd been yesterday on the beach, broken and for a second desperate.

As if he had wanted to sink into her arms. Just like she wanted to dive into his.

"Will makes me feel safe." Her own words to Micah had startled her. How long had it been since she'd felt safe, all the way to her soul?

Probably never. At least not that she could remember.

Will had listened to her secrets without rushing past them, bearing them as his own. He'd carried her dog to safety, sat with her while she acted like a worried mother. He'd laughed with her, listened to her, held her hand, and been her friend. He'd even revealed his own dark places. Despite his rather iffy exterior—first as a pseudo policeman, then as a sly reporter, and now as a special-ops commando—she felt as if she knew him, at least the man under the masks.

A man of honor. God's man, maybe.

Her heart thumped against her ribs as she climbed over the boulders toward him. He looked up at her with red, cracked eyes, as if startled. As if he hadn't slept in about three weeks. Whiskers dotted his face, blending with his goatee.

The wind had learned Dani's weaknesses and wafted his scent toward her. He must have taken a swim because he smelled devastatingly fresh and woodsy. So utterly Will. At least the Rambo Will. The cowboy, dinner-date Will had smelled of cologne and shaving cream. She liked them both.

"Good morning." He gave her a small, one-sided smile. "You're up early."

She rubbed her hands on her jacket arms as she came closer and stood in front of him. "I heard something. It was probably a bird. I'm a weird sleeper—when I wake up, that's it."

He nodded, turned back to the sunrise. "Me too. I have too much whirring around in my brain to sleep a full night. I can't shut off that long." He gave a self-deprecating laugh. "Whoops, I guess that might have been too much information."

She ran a finger through the paint still remaining behind his jaw. "You didn't get all your makeup off." She showed him her green finger.

To her surprise, he reached up, caught her hand. His smile had vanished, and his eyes were on hers. "I'm sorry, Dani," he said softly.

She frowned at him, not sure if he was serious or what he might be apologizing for. "That's okay. It's not a big deal. It'll come off—"

"No, I mean for . . . well, for everything. For nearly hitting your dog when we first met, for scaring you twice in the woods, and even for—" he closed his eyes, let go of her hand—"for being a reporter."

She laughed and put a hand on his shoulder. His muscles twitched beneath her touch. "Oh, that. Well, I've already forgiven you."

He didn't smile, didn't even look at her. Something felt wrong. She touched his cheek, turned him to face her. From where he was perched, he could look her straight in the eyes. Instead, he looked away . . . down . . . anywhere but at her.

"Will, is there something you're not telling me?"

He sighed. "There's so much I wish I could tell you, Dani." He met her gaze. The pain roaming in his eyes made her heart lurch. He brushed the backs of his fingers across her cheek. "You're so beautiful." When he said it, however, it sounded more like a groan.

She took his hand, threaded her fingers through his. Then she surprised them both by kissing the back of his hand.

His eyes widened. He opened his mouth slightly, blew out a breath, his gaze still holding hers.

A loon called, a haunting melody across the silent lake.

She saw desire pool in Will's eyes right before he closed them and pulled his hand away. Like the loon, a haunting cry lingered, something so deep it reached out and tugged at her.

Could it be that he was just as afraid as she was? that he needed safety too? Her fingers traced his neck, touching the hair at the nape. Her heart thumped hard, as if just catching up to her intentions, but she ignored the warnings.

Will opened his eyes as she leaned close and touched her lips—gently, sweetly—to his.

He went very, very still.

She closed her eyes, kissed him again.

Then his hands went around her waist, and he pulled her to himself. His lips moved, and he slowly kissed her back. Tenderly, as if he were afraid she might break, or worse, run away.

He tasted like fresh toothpaste, with a hint of coffee, and inside his embrace, she felt his heart beating against hers. She wound her arms around his neck, deepened her kiss, letting herself fall into the moment. Will, her Boy Scout reporter, in her arms . . . the notion couldn't find footing, so she released her clutch on reality and slid into the dream.

Will, the man who'd been her friend when life seemed to shatter. Will, the one who believed in her hunches. Will, the one who listened to her nightmares and cared. Will, strong Will, holding her as the sunrise crept toward them, as she escaped the nightmares that embedded the night and clung to this moment, this new morning.

Will released her suddenly, taking one deep breath, then another. He kept his eyes averted as he held her upper arms and put her slightly away from him.

Panic spurted into all the warm places in her heart. "Will?"

"I'm sorry." He shook his head. "I'm sorry, Dani. I shouldn't have—"

"*I* kissed *you*."

He stared at her, searched her face, and then, while her heartbeat thundered, the barest smile broke through his whiskers. "Yeah, you did, didn't you?"

Yeah. She grinned, waggled her eyebrows. "You looked like you needed a little help to . . . get something started."

He reached up, and with something like boyish wonder in his eyes, he touched her hair. "It *is* soft."

She gave him a teasing frown. "Are you okay?"

He sighed, nodded. Then, with his hands cupping her face, he pulled her close and kissed her again. Devastatingly sweet. Lingering. When he let her go, he seemed to shine. "Are we starting something?" The words had the power to hurt her if it weren't for the hope palpable in his voice.

She ran her hands down his powerful arms—way too powerful for the average reporter—and smiled. "I don't know. But . . . well, I was thinking about our conversation about Iowa yesterday. You said you'd learn to drive a tractor?"

"I'll learn to drive anything you want, Dani." But he exhaled as if the idea had him around the throat. He shook his head. "Only you don't want to start anything with a guy like me. I'm just—"

"A nosy reporter? I got that part."

But he didn't laugh. "Are you sure? I mean, well . . . I don't know if I'll be any good at—"

She took a step away, feeling sick. Any dummy could see

that she'd been stupid. How had she thought that he'd want her in his life? She'd already treated him like the town dog, over and over. No wonder he felt skittish. She wanted to call back to that loon her own cry of defeat. Or maybe just slink back up to the cabin—

He grabbed her hand. "Dani, please don't get me wrong here." His face wore panic. "I *do* want to start something with you. I can't get you out of my mind—your smile, the way you are with your dogs, even your determination to find this girl. You're *amazing*, and it takes my breath away most of the time. I'm still reeling that God brought you into my life, and more than anything, I want to be that guy who makes you feel safe, who protects you." His expression twisted, and he wore a pained look. "I'm just afraid that . . . I just don't want you to get hurt."

He didn't want *her* to get hurt? *Please, please don't let that be a line.* "You've already proven to be a true friend. And you *have* kept me safe." She chuckled at her words. "More safe than I think is necessary at the moment, but it's very nice. I think God's used you in my life for today, and . . . I'm willing to take my chances on tomorrow." Had she really said that? It felt very much like scooping her heart out and handing it to him, but the slow, honeyed smile that curved on his face felt like a sweet reward.

"Yeah, me too," he whispered.

Kirby bounded up, a piece of driftwood in his mouth. He sat, dropped it.

Dani was reaching for the wood when she heard a screech like the one that had wakened her. It ricocheted through the woods and sounded like an owl or even a mountain lion.

Kirby perked his ears, the ruff around his shoulders standing on end.

Dani froze, glanced at Will.

He was looking past her, toward the cabin or beyond, a dangerous look on his face. "Stay here," he said as he slid off the boulder.

She frowned, made to argue.

Will gave her a dark look, held up a finger. "For once, Dani, let me be the boss, okay?"

Then he stalked away from her. Rambo, off to save the world.

Will stole up the beach, aware of Dani's gaze burning the nape of his neck. But that scream had sounded human. And young. Because the morning was still and the air light, the sounds may have traveled across the water . . . or maybe they had come from somewhere nearby.

His heart shoved into his ribs, and he picked up his pace, ran into the forest. For a second he wished he'd taken Kirby, just like he'd planned earlier. But for the same reason he hadn't left with the dog at first light, he knew he couldn't take him now.

He simply couldn't do that to Dani. Especially after she said she'd take her chances on him. Oh, wow, he couldn't believe the feelings that had exploded in his chest when she said that—joy and fear and more than a little panic.

It made him thankful that he'd lingered on the shore after his patrol, watching the dawn crest over the water.

He stopped and listened above his racing heartbeat. He heard far-off footsteps crushing the forest floor.

He moved quickly toward them, berating himself for not spending the last eight hours combing the forest. If he'd done his job better, rather than tossing away the night chewing on

Micah's words and fighting the memories of Dani's smile, maybe his mission wouldn't be hanging by a fingernail hold.

The forest was still bathed in the swath of night, deep shadows eclipsing the ground. It made for loud passage for someone in a hurry. Will stepped carefully, picturing the two goons he'd met before the storm muscling a struggling teenager out of the woods, perhaps even subduing her with their fists.

Or otherwise.

No, please, Lord. I know I've been distracted here, but I need Your help. Help me trust You, like Lew did.

Lew would have enjoyed Dani. Enjoyed her honesty, her courage. Warmth churned in his chest. She'd kissed him. Not because she was after something tawdry, but because she was after something . . . better?

"You don't even think about kissing a girl until you love her." Will nearly stopped short as Lew's words burned in his brain. He climbed over a downed tree, fighting the claw of memory that grabbed him:

"What are you doin', man?" Lew had been waiting for him, holding the reins of his two workhorses as Will drove up to the Strong ranch that Monday morning, fresh from a hot weekend with Bonnie's cousin.

Will had smiled, feeling at the top of his game. What had he been doing? Wouldn't Lew like to know? "What do you think?" He gave Lew a cocky grin as he got out of the car.

Lew didn't smile. He tossed Will the reins to one of the horses. "Are you ready to marry this girl? Because you don't even think about kissing a girl until you love her. And you don't say you love her until you're ready to marry her."

Will laughed. "You're letting the preaching go to your head, Lew. Loosen up. Life is short. Sorry, but marriage is so not in the cards for me. Hello, I see my parents and thanks, but no thanks."

Lew shook his head. "Don't you get it?"

Will frowned, and his defenses burned. "Yeah, I get it. Pretty well. And so did Bonnie's cousin."

Lew made a noise of disgust and turned away. "There are times I don't know why we're friends."

Will froze, just stood there while Lew climbed on his horse. He felt as if the guy had taken a dagger to his gut. Lew was more than a friend. Without Lew and his family, Will might be sitting in juvie hall right now or six feet under in the local Eternal Rest Cemetery. Will swallowed a lump of fear and mounted the horse. "Sorry, Lew. I didn't know my personal life was so important to you."

Lew turned, fury in his eyes. "I guess if you want to screw up your life, I can't stop you, even if I try."

Will stared at him, feeling punched. "Screw up my life?"

Lew rode out into a nearby field, then reined his horse. "Listen, here're the cold facts. You can fool around with love, indulging in the desserts without getting the nourishment. But like any sweet, too much will burn you out. You'll lose the taste for it. And then you'll have nothing but a fat gut and a wasted life."

"I doubt that." Only, despite his weekend with Katie, if he were to pull out his feelings and take a good look, he might admit he felt sorta empty, even sickened.

"But if you do it right," Lew continued, "you'll have the full-course meal. The nourishment and the desserts. And in balance you'll never go hungry."

"And what you and Bonnie have is nourishment?" Will laughed harshly and spurred his horse into a run.

Even now, Lew's silence dug into Will's soul. Yes, Lew and Bonnie had created a friendship that had nourished Lew while he served his tours, that gave him reason to return. It had probably even made their desserts better.

"You don't even think about kissing a girl until you love her. And you don't say you love her until you're ready to marry her."

Whoa. Will swallowed a rise of remorse as he ran through the forest. He wasn't ready to go there. Except, well, the thought of waking up every day to Dani's smile . . . he pictured her playing with their children, tenderly, patiently, the way she was with Missy and Kirby. He saw her listening to him with her eyes, praying for him in that calm voice that seemed to soothe all his ragged edges.

He heard her calling him Rambo or Cowboy, and it arrowed directly to the soft places of his heart and dug deep. Dani wasn't glitz and shimmer; she wasn't false agendas and a quick fix. She was substance. Nourishment.

The real deal. That feeling exploded again within him as he stopped, braced his arm against a tree, and climbed out of his emotions to assess his direction.

Only reality had him by the throat.

He was falling for Dani. Hard, fast, and with no escape. For the first time in his life, he wanted to be a man who wouldn't kiss a woman until he loved her. Until he was ready to marry her.

He closed his eyes, trying to shake himself out of her grip, and heard the sound of branches snapping.

Will whirled and his heart sank when Kirby ran up, tail wagging, as if to say, "isn't this fun?"

He knelt. "Shh. Go back."

But dread had already fisted his heart. Through the woods, he could already make her out, like blue neon. Dani, her hood pushed back, charging toward her dog.

Just like she'd charged into his heart.

Chapter 18

"DANI, PLEASE GO back." Will watched her with a wide-eyed—even horrified—expression as she approached. It made all those happy feelings she'd had on the beach take a dive for her toes. What was his problem? Weren't they in this together?

Once again she realized that no, they weren't. Her chest tightened just like in the cabin yesterday when he'd dodged her question about his hiding something from her. Why had she ignored it? Something felt painfully *not right* here.

She sat on a downed log next to Kirby and ran her hand over his back, not looking at Will. "Look, if there's someone out here and you heard her, then let me help you. Kirby knows what he's doing. He found you, didn't he?"

Will shook his head. "Hardly. He followed me." He knelt before her. "Please trust me. Go back with Kirby. I'll find the girl."

She searched his face, saw worry in his expression. "What is it, Will?"

He touched her jaw. "Go back to Micah and Conner. Let them take you home. I'll be there soon." He looked away when he said it, and even she could see his smile was forced.

"I can't abandon some girl out in the woods," she said quietly. "Not unless you tell me—" Words left her as she saw a man emerge from a clasp of trees. Dressed in head-to-toe terror black, he looked like something out of the news.

In fact, he sorta matched Will.

She grabbed Kirby's collar, feeling cold seep into her bones when the man aimed an assault weapon at Will.

Will read her face and turned. Tensed.

"Put your weapon down," the man said in a slightly accented voice.

What is going on here?

She stared at Will, horror radiating through her veins, her muscles. Who was Will Masterson? And why did everything he said about being sorry on the beach suddenly make painful, clarifying sense?

She stood up, held Kirby, her gaze locked on Will as he dropped his weapon.

"Let the lady go," Will said. "She has nothing to do with this." His tone felt distant, removed.

She tried not to let that dig into her soul.

The man's eyebrows lowered in disapproval. "Move." He motioned with his gun.

Will made to obey, but he glanced back at Dani, dark eyes intense. "Run," he whispered.

Run? How? She felt frozen. Kirby, however, lurched away from her and lunged toward the assailant.

It happened in warp-time speed.

The man cuffed Kirby.

Will pushed Dani hard as he dived for his gun. She hit the forest floor before she could blink.

A shot frayed the leaves above her.

Dani screamed.

Another shot.

Wood sprayed Dani.

"Get down, Dani!" Will yelled, returning fire.

She was down, for pete's sake. Only maybe she should be inching away too.

Except where was Kirby?

A barrage of shots, wood chips, branches, and leaves rained down on her. Dani screamed again, and the echo filled the forest.

"Go! Run!" Will's voice caught somewhere in her brain.

Run?

Another shot, and Will roared in fury. She looked over at him, saw blood gushing down his arm. He shot her a look, and in it she recognized agony.

A hand fisted her hair. Someone hauled her to her feet.

"Drop it." Whoever had her also pointed a gun at Will.

Will laid the gun back down.

Dani struggled against the shooting pain in her scalp. She twisted, aiming for his shin, something—anything—and earned a fresh batch of anguish.

"Stop," the dark voice ordered with a sharp edge of menace. She stilled and let him lead her awkwardly over to Will's weapon. The man picked it up, slung it over his arm, then shoved her away from him.

She landed in the dirt next to Will. He was clutching his upper arm, as blood rushed through his fingers. His face had turned white despite the grim set of his mouth.

"Tie his hands."

She turned, scowling at the guy with the gun. "With what?"

He narrowed his eyes at her, then scanned the forest. "Call your dog."

She froze.

He took a step closer and pointed his gun at Will's head. "Call him."

Yes, okay. Calm down. She somehow managed a whistle.

Kirby emerged out of the woods, slunk toward her, the hair up on his back.

"Take off his collar."

With trembling hands, she undid Kirby's collar, then ran a hand under his chin. "Good dog." *Go find Conner. Find Micah.* She pushed the dog away, hoping he could read her thoughts.

"Tie him up."

"He's bleeding," she snapped.

The man fired, aiming not far from Will's head. She jumped, screamed. The shot chipped up dirt and loam from the forest floor and left a ringing in her ears.

"Next time it'll be the dog. Or your boyfriend."

She nodded, words stifled in her throat.

Will glared at the man as he turned to let Dani tie his hands. The blood ran freely down his arm, and she noticed his jaw tighten. Why hadn't she listened to him? trusted him? But no, she'd had to be the boss, had to have her way.

Just like she'd had to drag Ashley along on her misadventures. It seemed she still hadn't figured out how to keep the people she loved out of trouble.

Loved? The thought dug a trench through her heart as she tightened Kirby's collar around Will's wrists. He didn't look at her, but she glimpsed the fury on his handsome face. Dirt embedded his whiskers, and blood smeared his face, probably from diving for his gun.

While she lay in the dirt and screamed, he'd been trying to protect her. Regardless of who he was, he still played the hero.

Yeah, she might be falling in love with Will Masterson. She knew she loved his smile, his teasing. Loved the way he tried to keep her safe, even bossed her around. Loved the gentle way he played with her dog and even the tender place inside him that let her see his pain.

She finished cinching the collar, hating the way one of Will's eyes crinkled, as if absorbing his pain. She ached for him clear through to her bones.

"Get on your feet."

She stood, then helped Will up. He still didn't look at her. She didn't blame him. She couldn't look at herself.

"Move." The man motioned with his weapon.

"Let me at least bind his wound, please."

"Dani—"

"Will, please. You're bleeding. You could lose your arm."

He met her eyes, and the grief in them felt like a rake over her soul. He clenched his jaw. "I should have never dragged you into this."

Into *what*? "Let me do this," she said, ignoring his comment and the way it speared her through. She pulled off her pack, dropped it, and fished out a bandanna. She put a wool sock over the wound. He tried to hide a wince when she tightened the bandanna around his arm to hold the sock in place and staunch the bleeding, but she saw it. Tears burned her eyes. She reached for her pack.

"Leave it," the man said. "Move."

Will glared at him again, then turned and began to hike through the forest.

Dani followed, wondering what she'd gotten them all into.

✦ ✦ ✦

If things could get worse, Will knew he'd hit bottom when he saw the waif of a girl crumpled on the forest floor. Something inside him seized up and burned when he realized she'd been roughed up. Outside and in. Blood trailed from a slightly puffy lip, a bruise on her face, and she held her arm, as if it had been sprained.

When she lifted her gaze to his, he wanted to moan. Her dark, almost black, eyes were lined with sorrow.

He'd failed her. And Dani.

He could barely look at Dani. Every time he did, pain wrapped bitter tentacles around his heart. Why hadn't he forced her to go back? ditched her in the night?

Never let her into his life.

That thought closed his throat. No, he didn't want her out of his life. But he didn't have any other choice now, did he? He had to figure out how to get Amina out of Hayata's clutches and to DC. And then he'd have to disappear again.

So much for learning to drive tractors in Iowa.

His guard motioned for him to sit against a tree, across from Amina. They ordered Dani against another tree, far enough away to discourage clandestine conversation. She pulled her knees up to her chest and stared at Will. Tears had etched grimy trails down her cheeks.

He leaned his head against the tree, listening to the two Hayata terrorists discuss their fate. The big one—large and dark and looking exactly how Will had expected—thought they should simply dispatch them here, where their corpses could decay into the soil.

The other one—with light brown hair, Asian features, and wearing earrings—seemed to want to bring them back to the compound, perhaps for questioning, maybe a little torture fun.

Yes, things could get much—much worse.

Will cast another glance at Dani. *I know I screwed up here, God, but please let Dani live.*

He gritted his teeth as he twisted his wrists inside Kirby's collar. The dog had taken off shortly after Dark and Armed had thrown a stick at him. He prayed the animal had returned to Conner and Micah, who, hopefully, would read the signs and alert the cavalry. But what would they think? Kidnapped by terrorists certainly wouldn't be the first assumption that popped into their minds.

Thankfully, however, he'd told Conner enough to make him wonder.

With some time, Will could work himself free. But he'd have to gauge the moment. And now that he had two victims to look out for . . . it wasn't impossible, but it certainly made things more interesting.

Especially with one wing damaged. His wound burned, one continuous searing as if someone had jammed a poker through his arm. He'd actually moaned when he'd been jostled into a tree.

When Dani had carefully tended it, he'd felt that moan clear to his heart as her gentle hands ministered to his wound. He couldn't believe that he'd dragged her into this, hadn't been strong enough to push her away.

Oh, he was really doing things God's way, wasn't he? He should earn medals, get a prize for letting his heart lead the woman he wanted to love to her death. And, if he was really lucky, he'd watch her being tortured. He yanked himself away from that image before it consumed him.

The light-haired man won the argument. "Get up," he said, kicking Will. Will doubled over, his empty stomach roiling. Blondie patted him down and withdrew his knife, extra ammo, and his cell phone, crushing it into the dirt with a sneer.

Will watched as they walked over to Dani. If they so much as touched—

She stood, gave Will a pale look, then walked over to the girl. And, oh, bless her, she helped the girl to her feet.

Dani, the compassionate one. He wanted to hobble over and kiss her.

The terrorists made Will lead the procession, the ladies behind him. The sun climbed overhead, eating off the mist trapped in the forest, digging regrets into his chest with every step.

"God is my portion." The words lined his brain, one footstep after another. *Redeemer . . . reputation . . . rescuer?*

Please, God, be my portion and Dani's portion in every way.

The day wore on as they trekked back to the forest-service road, confirming—as if he needed it—that these were the same thugs he'd tussled with before the storm.

By midafternoon, they'd broken free of the forest. Dani said nothing as she held the girl's hand. He had to give Amina credit. She hadn't whined, hadn't even spoken a word. She had to be tired and hungry after days on the run. And wearing nothing but a pair of jeans, a T-shirt, a torn jacket, and a blanket, she must be near hypothermia.

No wonder Dani hadn't left her side.

The Hayatas shoved him toward a filthy pickup truck with a bed topper. He recognized it as the one he'd seen in the compound during his sneak and peek. Up close, it was dirtier and smelled of smoke and oil. The blond thug checked Will's bonds, and for a second, as he loosened them, Will's adrenaline surged into his veins. He turned, yanked his hand free, and sent it into Blondie's chin.

Blondie flinched; Will ducked for a tackle.

Dark and Armed clocked him with the butt of his weapon.

Will hit the ground, head spinning. A knee to his back and he ate dirt as they trussed him back up. The collar dug into his wrists, cutting off blood, as they cinched it tight.

He heard Dani stifle a sob when they kicked him again in

the kidneys. He fought a black wave that threatened to suck him away from the noise and pain. *Awake*, he had to stay awake. Because if the terrorists got them to the Hayata compound, it was over.

Will staggered to his knees, then to his feet. They dumped him into the bed of the truck, which reeked with the cloying scent of gasoline and wood chips. He crawled to the back, hunkered down in the corner.

Dani moved to follow him, but Blondie grabbed her.

Will started toward her. "Let her go."

"Shut up." Blondie pushed Dani's face into the pickup bed, seized her arms, and wrapped them with duct tape.

She said nothing when she climbed in beside Will.

Will wanted to howl. He felt her nestle close to him, felt her frailty, her courage. "It'll be okay, Dani," he said quietly.

Still, she said nothing. But when she looked at him with a broken expression on her face, he knew that it wasn't going to be okay.

Not ever.

The men closed the tailgate, bathing Will and Dani in filmy grayness.

"Where are they taking us?" Dani asked. Obviously she thought he knew the answer.

He swallowed slowly, not sure what to say. What a jerk. She'd been kidnapped and now was probably going to be killed, and still he wanted to live a lie? She deserved better. She deserved the truth.

Will knew this moment would come. But it didn't make the words any easier to claw out of his throat, nor did it kill the moan in his voice. "They're terrorists. And they're probably taking us to Azmi, their camp."

Dani sighed. "Oh."

But that simple word was a direct hit right in his heart.

✦ ✦ ✦

Fadima climbed in between the two men, a repeat from several days ago when they'd picked her up from the airport. Why hadn't she trusted her instincts and returned to the cabin? Obviously the soldier wasn't out to capture her, and if it weren't for the tall blonde woman, she might have let despair overtake her.

As it were, her jaw ached and she felt numb.

They would torture her, then kill her.

Papa, I'm sorry. After years of patient training and months of plotting, she could hardly believe that everything they worked for would sink into the soil with her blood.

If she was going to die, she'd do it taking out the Hayata operatives who had killed her mother. Fadima's death would be a victory. She only regretted costing the lives of the two innocents in back.

While the darker one called in their position on his radio, the other turned the truck around, muscled the gears into drive, then headed down the dirt road, kicking up stones and mud. Forest flanked the road, ageless trees that hovered with bushy arms, gullies that descended into spring-fed creeks.

Fadima rubbed her sweaty palms on her muddy jeans, her heartbeat wild. They hadn't tied her up like the other two— probably because they didn't suspect that the princess of Tazar might have the courage of the warriors she grew up with.

She hid a smile. She would die the hero her father had trained her to be.

Chapter 19

THEY RODE ALONG in bumpy agony, jostled by the ruts in the road. The acrid redolence of the pickup raked her nose, but Dani succumbed to her emotions.

Terrorists? Her mind had stopped working at that word. If Will had said anything else, it had been lost in the churning of her panic.

Terrorists?

She felt her world slowly skidding from her grasp. Oh, who was she kidding? Her world had taken a right-handed, two-wheeled screech to frightening the moment she'd seen Terrorist A emerge from behind a tree and shoot the guy she thought was a reporter. The same guy who was now trying to keep her calm by saying, "It'll be okay."

Yeah, right. Which part?

She gulped a breath. Time to replay the events so she could catch up. Starting with the day Will had nearly run over her dog. "Who are you?" Dani asked Will.

Sitting tightly against him probably didn't do her breaking heart any good. But despite feeling like he might be a stranger—and a scary one at that—she needed his warmth.

Needed that reminder that she wasn't the only one with her world in shambles.

Certainly this wasn't in his game plan, right?

"My name is Will Masterson."

"But you're not a reporter, right?" She closed her eyes. Please, *please* . . .

"No."

She wasn't sure if that was relief or regret whooshing out of her in a sigh. But she felt cold trickle down her spine. "You're some sort of cop, aren't you?"

He sighed too, and she wondered what that meant. "Yeah. I'm with Homeland Security. We've been tracking these guys for a while, and this girl you and I were looking for—her name is Amina—she's a really important asset. If they get back to camp with her, they'll kill her. But not before they torture information out of her. And they aren't afraid to go for the gusto, do what they—"

"Yeah, that's good, Will. You don't need to paint a picture for me."

"I think I do, Dani. Because the thing is, you're in this, and if you know what might be waiting, maybe you'll be prepared."

For? She froze. "You don't mean that they'll . . ." She glanced at him.

He nodded, and his bleak expression dried her mouth. But the wretched pain in his eyes was even worse. "Dani, I'm so, so sorry. I should have dodged you from the beginning. There's no excuse for my getting you into this."

She took a calming breath. "What are you talking about? I kept following you, if you remember."

He looked sick. "Yeah, but I knew you had Missy, and in my brain, I thought, well, maybe I could follow you. Then when I realized we were in danger, it was too late, and all I could think about was keeping you safe—"

"So that was the secure-hideout bit before the storm?"

"Yeah. I knew they were on our tail, and—" he shook his head—"I shouldn't have let you follow me yesterday. I should have sent you home—"

She gave a huff of laughter. "I don't suppose you remember my 'you're not the boss of me'? I was there, and I wasn't going anywhere."

"You might have if I had told you the truth."

His solemn tone, the look in his eyes—he was *serious*. He blamed himself. She wanted to reach out and touch his face, to tell him that it wasn't his fault. . . .

Wake up, Dani—Dannette—*he lied to you.* Lied.

She backed away, feeling pain, sharp and bristly. Lied. More than once. And she'd even given him a measure of trust—saying that she could accept his job as a journalist. She wanted to wail. He must have been laughing, chortling—oh, *ha ha ha*—at her stupidity. *To think she'd actually called him honest. Trustworthy.*

Not only that, but he was a soldier. A danger guy. The Rambo act wasn't a short-term gig. It was permanent.

She eyed him, feeling her heart twist. "Who *are* you?" Her voice shook. She hated it for betraying her—again. Where were Jim Micah and Conner when she needed them?

"I'm just a guy trying to do the right thing," he said softly. "Please believe that."

"I don't know what to believe," she snapped. "Are you even from South Dakota? Or was the cowboy swagger just a put-on to get me to . . . to . . ." Her voiced seized as she remembered how she'd *kissed* him. "I'll take my chances," she'd said. Ha! What had she been thinking? Her grandmother would have taken her out to the barn with a switch if she knew how easily *Dannette* had given away her heart. She felt repugnant.

"I never meant to hurt you," Will said, and she hardened her heart to the agony in his voice. "I purposely didn't . . . well, you kissed *me*."

She closed her eyes. Thanks for digging that knife in farther, Will.

Silence. Except for the pinging of stone against the truck's bed, the grind of the wheels against the dirt. "I can't believe I ever trusted you. I'll never make that mistake again."

"Dani, you have to believe that with the exception of my profession everything I told you was the truth."

She couldn't bear to look at him. "Lew was the truth? Or just a way to sucker my feelings?"

He drew in a shaky breath, and despite her fury, it sounded like he'd been punched in the chest. *Oh, please, Lord, don't let me love this man. Don't let me buy his story.* He *lied*!

"Lew was the truth. But here's the bigger truth." His gaze burned into her until she turned away. His eyes were dark, and she felt them on her—no, *inside* her, touching her soul. "I know I'm not the guy you thought I was. But in every important way, I want to be. I want to be your friend and . . . more. I want to be the guy who makes you feel safe, who you turn to when your dog is hurt or when you just need a hug. I want to be the guy who makes you homemade ice cream and buys you every dog movie on the planet." He swallowed. "I want to be God's man for you—today and every day. Please believe that about me."

She recognized the wounds she'd inflicted on his expression. But could he see the way his words had touched her, found the cracks in her anger? *"I want to be God's man."* What was she supposed to do with his betrayal? *Help me, Lord.* She could hardly believe she'd thought she knew the real Will. Just who was this man really? "Will, I—"

All at once the pickup squealed, spun.

Dannette slammed against the side of the truck. "Will!"

Gravel pinged against metal. The engine shrilled as they went airborne. Dannette screamed, slammed her head up against the topper.

They rolled over and over. Dannette was thrown from the topper and spun through the air.

They crashed hard—metal screaming, wood cracking, tires spinning.

Pain exploded through Dannette's body.

Darkness sucked her under.

✦ ✦ ✦

Will knew he'd dislocated his shoulder the second he blinked to consciousness. Pain radiated down his arm, crunched the breath from him. The good news was that the dog collar, which he'd been slowly fraying since they got in the truck, had ripped free.

What happened? He wrestled himself to a sitting position, cringed against the fractured pane of light.

Dani. She lay crumpled on the ground near the truck. Her forehead was bleeding. As he pulled himself toward her, he saw that her leg was broken, the tibia protruding from her shin. For a second, he felt light-headed, and he had to gulp in calm. He found a pulse in her neck and went weak with relief.

Scared to move her, he climbed over her.

Blondie lay in the road in a bloody heap. Will stumbled around to the front of the pickup. It lay on its back in a gully, its nose angled down into a creek, the cab half submerged.

Please, Lord, no! "Amina!" He scrambled down the edge, peered inside the cab.

Empty.

"Amina!" He crossed to the other side of the pickup, where

he found Dark and Armed. His throat had been dissected by a shard of glass.

"Amina!"

"I'm here." She stood in the road, holding her arm, blood running down her forehead.

Will raced toward her. "Are you okay? What happened?"

She stepped away from him, fear on her pretty face. Okay, so he didn't blame her. He wasn't exactly dressed like one of the good guys.

"Don't go anywhere. I have to move Dani in case there's a fire." The smell of gasoline fumed the air.

To his profound relief, Amina waited while he gripped Dani by her coat and dragged her away from the seeping truck. She moaned slightly. He knelt beside her. "Dani, I'm sorry."

"Is she your wife?" Amina crouched next to him.

He could hardly breathe around the lump in his throat. "I wish," he said softly. He turned to the girl. She didn't look more than fifteen, but she had courage in her eyes. "Amina?"

"Hafiz?"

He gave a slight painful smile as he nodded. Finally, Simon's mission, almost completed.

"I thought you were dead," she said, wariness in her eyes. "Bakym said he killed you." She inched away, jumped to her feet, suddenly wary.

"Okay, wait. Yes, Hafiz was killed. I'm his partner. I've been looking for you."

She narrowed her eyes.

He made no move to corral her. How he wished Dani was awake. She'd tell her the truth—

Oh yeah, right. What truth? Dani was just as likely to run as Amina. And he didn't blame her. After the lies he'd told, he wanted to run too.

"Listen to me—" Will kept his voice calm—"I know you are the daughter of General Nazar. I know he sent you out with information that will tell us where he's hiding."

"Is he okay?"

"Yes, I think so. I don't know. But the sooner we get you to safety, the sooner we can help him."

She studied him as if gauging his trustworthiness. Oh, sure, he had trustworthy written all over him, with his bloody arm, his dislocated shoulder, the bruises and cuts on his face, and the woman he was falling in love with—yes, those were feelings of love, evidenced by the fact that he'd never felt anything so terrifying yet so exhilarating and complete in his life—crumpled at his feet. He couldn't manage a reassuring smile to save his life.

"Okay, listen." Amina angled her head, as if testing out his response. "My father said I wasn't to tell you one word until you have me safe." She looked around. "I'm not seeing safe."

"Yeah, you're right." He glanced at Dani and felt sick. Now what? He'd been stripped of his weapon and his cell phone when Blondie patted him down. But Dani had a cell with a GPS. . . .

He reached into her pockets, discovered a couple of doggy treats. No cell. It must have been in her backpack.

"What are we going to do?" Amina crouched beside him again. "She's hurt, and so are you."

"And you." He reached over and brushed a piece of glass from her hair. "How's your arm?"

"I think my shoulder's broken. It really hurts, and I can't move my arm." She held her wrist, slightly in, and if he had to guess, he'd say it could be her clavicle.

He stood up, walked over to Blondie, checked his pulse, then stripped the jacket off the dead body. Cushioning Amina's arm with the body of the coat, he tied the sleeves around her neck, forming a sling. "Anything else hurt?"

She stared at Dani. "How bad is she?"

The answer felt too close to the surface of his battered emotions. Besides receiving a head wound and a broken leg, her trust in him had been shattered. "I don't know. But she could go into shock." He took off his coat, working it gently down his mangled arm, and put it over Dani. "We need to keep her feet elevated."

Amina found a stump, dragged it over. "Now what? We have to go for help."

He brushed Dani's hair back. It was matted with dried blood; he saw that the blood came from a vicious gash on her forehead. She'd need a couple of stitches. But with her eyes closed, so gently . . . she could still take his breath away. "I can't leave her."

"What?" Amina stared at him in horror. "My father is out there hiding, risking his life for America. We have to go."

"I can't! I'm not going to leave her here alone. But I can't carry her into town. And I can't leave you alone." He sat back hard, next to the dirt road.

"Trust God one day at a time." Micah's words whispered in the back of his mind.

Will covered his eyes with his hand. *Lord, I'm in trouble here. Please, please help us.*

"Are you okay?"

He looked at Amina. Then, slowly, he shook his head. "I'm not leaving her."

"Then my father and thousands of others are going to die very soon." Amina got up and stalked down the road.

Chapter 20

DANI COULD HEAR voices as she clawed through the layers of darkness to light. She moaned and felt the darkness ease its grip, replacing it with pain. For a moment, she jerked back into the sweet embrace of oblivion.

Then came Will's soft voice and his touch on her hand.

She forced her eyes open. He sat overlooking her, worry on his bloody, bearded face. His eyes were red, and she saw lines where tears had etched down his dirty cheeks. His left arm was in a makeshift sling made from a tattered black shirt.

"What happened?" She started to push herself up on her elbows, but pain shot through her leg and exploded in her brain. She lay back with a gasp. The sky had gathered the twilight, and darkness edged in. Cold laced the air, and she fought a shiver.

"Hold up there, speedy. You're not going anywhere." But she heard relief in Will's teasing voice. He touched her cheek, his gentleness comforting.

"Where are we?" Clearly, they hadn't made it out of the forest, although she had a hard time remembering anything. The last clear memory she had was being on the beach in Will's arms . . . yes, she could smile about that memory.

"One question at a time." Will pulled a jacket up to her chin, tucked it into place. "Amina grabbed the wheel and rolled the truck. You were thrown, and your leg, if not other parts, is broken."

Amina? Truck? "What are you talking about?"

He gave her a wry look. "What is the last thing you remember?"

She felt a blush, looked away. But his hand on her cheek pressed her gaze back to his. My, but he has warm chocolate eyes, and they looked at her with such tenderness. No wonder she remembered only the kiss they'd shared. "Uh, the beach."

"Oh." He sighed. "Well, I'm going to skip a lot of the particulars, but the bottom line is that we were in an accident after finding the girl we were looking for. Now we're somewhere in the woods, about forty miles from civilization, and we need medical help."

"That good, huh?"

He wore the hint of a smile. "You really don't remember what happened before . . . ah, before we crashed?"

She narrowed one eye. "No. Why?" She pictured herself in his strong arms.

"Nothing." He smiled, pushed back her hair. "Someday, when you're feeling better, I'll remind you."

"Is that a promise?" She meant it as a tease, but he made a funny face—

"Is she awake?" A young girl sat beside him. She was thin, and had dark hair, dark eyes, a bruise on her cheek, a swollen lip, and her arm was in a sling. She looked vaguely familiar. "Amina?"

She smiled. "Yes. How are you feeling?"

"I'm . . . I don't know." Dani looked at Will. "I guess I have a broken leg."

Amina nodded. "Sorry. I couldn't think of any other way to get—"

Will touched her arm, shook his head.

Okay, her brain hadn't been that jostled; Dani could still spot a cover-up when she saw one. "What's going on?"

Amina frowned at him. "Tell her."

"Amina, please go wait for me by the truck."

"We had a deal." Her eyes sparked.

"Go, please." The last word sounded more like a groan.

Amina turned to Dani, touched her arm. "Thanks for everything."

Dani opened her mouth, not quite sure what to say. What was she thanking her for?

Amina got up and disappeared into the gathering darkness.

"What's going on?" Dani asked again.

"Dani, I know you don't remember what happened, but I gotta fill you in on a few essentials." He held her hand but didn't look at her, which hurt, probably more than her leg or her head or even the strange bruising in her chest.

"I'm not a reporter. I work for the government. And that girl over there is an important government asset. She's running from a terrorist organization named Hayata—"

Dani blinked as images raced into the broken, empty spaces of her mind. A man with a gun. Will covered in blood. As he finished his explanation, memory hurtled back to her.

"She has secrets, and I have to get them to HQ—"

"Homeland Security," she filled in, and her voice sounded like she felt—cold and distant.

He noticed and looked at her. When she pulled her hand away from his, he said, "I guess your memory is coming back."

"Yeah," she said, knowing that word spoke volumes. "She has information that can take down this Hayata group?"

"Her father does. And she knows where he is. But the deal is, we don't find him until she's safe. And he's gone into hiding. But he's the only one who knows when and where the next attack will be. And we're running out of time."

"So, getting her to safety is a matter of national security." Will flinched. "But . . . I'm not leaving you, Dani. I can't."

Dani looked away, felt tears burn her eyes. "We can't be that far from civilization. You can go, send help back."

She closed her eyes when he touched her cheek. Still, he turned her face toward his and waited until she opened her eyes. One tear ran down his cheek, and he let it sit there, obviously not caring that she saw his emotions glistening on his face.

Oh, Will.

Her throat thickened. Suddenly, their heated argument in the back of the pickup rushed back to her. He'd lied to her. And she'd said she'd never make the mistake of trusting him again. Only that was a lie. She did trust him. She trusted him to her soul. He might not have told her his real profession, but he'd told her about himself. About the man he was and wanted to be. She probably knew him better than she knew Micah or Conner. She knew the real Will, the man behind the aliases. The man who wanted to keep her safe, be her friend—maybe more. And now he was crying. For her.

Gulp.

"Will, go. I understand. And I'll be okay." She fought the panic that came with those words. Go? And leave her here by herself, unable to move? What part of that was okay?

But if he didn't leave, it might take days for them to be rescued, and by then, maybe Amina's father would be killed. Or worse, Homeland Security would never intercept whatever terror event this group had planned, and all chance of destroying these terrorists would slip through their fingers.

All the sacrifices paid by people on the front lines—people like Micah and Conner and Wendy, her deputy-sheriff friend turned MP soldier from back home in Iowa—would be undermined. America was fighting wars on both sides of the ocean.

"Go," she repeated, hearing how her voice came out as a squeak. "I want you to go."

"I can't leave you—"

"Please. Before I beg you to stay."

"I'll send help back as soon as I can," he said softly.

She tried to smile, tried to summon her courage, but all she heard was the wail of fear inside. Alone. He was leaving her alone.

Abandoning her.

So much for feeling safe with Will. She'd never felt more deserted in her life. Even if it was her choice.

"I'll be all right," she said again.

He leaned down, and she felt moisture on his cheek as he kissed her. "I'm sorry, Dani. I wanted this to turn out differently."

"Just go," she said and turned away before he saw her break into tears.

She heard his footsteps thump against the forest floor, scuff out onto gravel, then finally disappear into the curtain of the night.

✦ ✦ ✦

"Just go."

Those two words fueled every step but pinged louder in Will's heart as he trudged away with Amina. He felt nearly nauseous as he struggled for breath.

"Just go."

How could he leave her? He forced his breath out and

stared at the stars. The moon hung like a fingernail in the sky, pointing north. *Please, oh, God, be our portion tonight.* Never did he long for those words to be true. Never did he need God more than at this moment, when he'd left the best of all he wanted lying cocooned in his jacket under a pine tree.

"The LORD is my inheritance; therefore, I will hope in him! The LORD is good to those who depend on him, to those who search for him." The words from Lamentations in Lew's Bible imprinted on Will's mind as he escorted Amina along the black ribbon of gravel road. How ironic that he'd sat on the shore this very morning, watching the earth escaping darkness to morning, pondering those words.

He'd attended more than a few of Lew's Bible studies, Lew's unveiled attempts to pull Will toward salvation. But for some reason, the Lamentations study had been slightly intriguing. The Israelites were a people struggling with pain, with understanding the reasons behind God's heavy hand, and yet in the middle of the book sat a testament to grace and trusting in God in the darkest hour. He remembered their conversation:

"You know what the word *good* means in that verse, Willy?" Lew said, sitting on a jeep, his feet swinging as he took a sip of warm water from his canteen.

The desert had rippled out for miles. Heat embedded their dirty pores, sizzled the skin under their filthy uniforms. Will recalled the first tour of Desert Storm and the way Lew patiently counseled his fellow Green Berets toward eternity.

"*Good* means 'precious,'" Lew continued as he wiped dirt from his face with his sleeve. "And *waiting* means more than just drumming our fingers on the table. It means longing for and *expecting* God to show up. It means trusting God fully, especially for victory. The verse, as I understand it, means that if you trust God with your entire heart, especially in the darkest hour, you will see God faithful, and His salvation will be sweeter because of the waiting. Like Bonnie said about our daughter. Having Anna in her arms made her birth and the waiting that much sweeter. I can't wait to see her."

He'd grinned, swung down from the jeep, screwed the top on his canteen. "But you will only experience that sweetness if you seek God. Long for Him."

Will remembered how Lew had clapped him on the shoulder and even now felt it, despite the burn in his injured arm. "God wants to be enough for you in every area of your life. But you have to pursue Him to find Him. Walking with God means getting to know Him and His Word a little more every day."

One day at a time.

Micah had said the same thing. One day at a time.

Sorta like how Will had gotten to know Dani. And she'd wound into his heart and become precious. God could become that.

Will had thought that once he fell to his knees and admitted his failures, God would swoop in and turn him into Lew. Only how many times had he seen Lew in the early morning, his Bible open, saturating himself in God's Word? pursuing God.

If Will stopped looking at his everyday failures, lifted his eyes toward heaven, and began walking toward God, one step at a time, he might become that man along the way.

Somewhat like those lepers being healed.

He gritted his teeth, and for the first time he realized why he hadn't known how to walk the path of a Christian.

Because he'd been afraid.

Although Lew had blazed the trail, Will had been afraid to take the first steps toward knowing God. Toward trusting Him. Because, frankly, although he knew God had saved him, cerebrally, he hadn't *felt* it. Not really. His scars seemed too impenetrable.

Until he'd met Dani.

Until she'd looked him in the eye and said, "I'm willing to take my chances." She'd reached past his iffy exterior and been his friend. Trusted him. Believed in him.

With a realization that should have sent the stars leaping across the sky, Will looked heavenward, a strange, wild feeling springing into his heart.

Lord, You've been trying to teach me this entire time about knowing You, and I haven't been paying attention. I've expected You to change me, to heal me, but I haven't taken more than baby steps in Your direction. Mostly because I've been afraid that You'll take a good look and revoke all that forgiveness. But I'm going to believe You when You say Your compassions never fail. Help me remember that as I walk every day in Your direction.

Please be with Dani tonight. Great is Your faithfulness, and I ask You to make that known to her. And please keep her alive. Thank You for bringing Dani into my life, but even if I never see her again, You've taught me about friendship. About taking a chance on someone even if you don't understand them. Teach me to take a chance on You. Teach me to be Your man.

Amina hobbled beside him, holding her injured arm. She looked exhausted and defeated.

"It's going to be okay," Will assured her. "We'll find your father."

She gave him a soft, disbelieving smile.

They rounded a bend, and in the distance, he saw Lake Superior, a shining pool of moon-kissed water. And at the end of the road cutting down to the lake was County Road 63.

"We'll flag down a car."

She nodded, but fear edged her eyes.

He knew what thoughts sparked her worry. She had told him that the Hayata thugs had radioed in their position before the crash. In the time since, someone surely would have gotten suspicious.

As if on cue with his thoughts, lights heralded a vehicle turning off the county road and onto the forest-service road. Will grabbed Amina's arm, pulled her toward the ditch, but not before lights illuminated them like deer caught in midflight.

Amina scrambled into the ditch with him, trembling. "Don't let them take me," she said.

After the lights had passed, Will put his arm around her and ushered her out of the ditch and back into the dark forest.

"The LORD is my portion. . . ."

Don't be afraid. Dani heard the voice in her head—soft, like a song—as she shivered under Will's coat. The wind rustled, hidden in the trees overhead, and night sounds rippled under her skin. She shouldn't sleep; she knew that. She didn't want to slip into shock—more trauma victims suffered from shock than their actual injuries.

Will had left her. "Just go," she'd said, but inside she'd been screaming, *Stay. Oh, please, stay.*

She fought a fearful tremble. He'd left her.

Somehow she wondered if that scared him more than it had her. That thought helped. In fact, it found the still-aching places in her heart and soothed them. She searched her memory for the moment before the crash and found Will's words: *"I know I'm not the guy you thought I was. But in every important way, I want to be. I want to be your friend, and . . . more. I want to be God's man for you—today and every day."*

Lord, I thought I asked You not to let me fall for him. Tears slipped down into her ear, pooled there, turning cold in the night air. Not only had she fallen hard for Will the reporter, but he *wasn't* a reporter. He was some die-hard federal soldier who lived life on the edge. A guy whose life defined the word *danger.* Who could come home any day in a box with a folded flag. If he came home at all.

She could not fall in love with Will. *Could not.* Because even if she could forgive him for lying—and everything inside her yelled yes! to that thought—she couldn't stand on the door-step and wave good-bye to him, maybe forever, every time he went out the door.

Another tear dripped into her ear. The trees swayed overhead, caught by a breeze. She remembered the night after the tornado long ago. She'd sung and held Ashley's hand and told her so-very-quiet-sister stories. As the night wore on and help failed to arrive, she had tucked herself into the furrowed earth next to Ashley and draped an arm over her cold body and slept.

She dreamed that night of a friend. Someone strong who lifted her sister and carried her into the vault of heaven. Some-one who then carried her, held her to His chest, and kept her warm. She remembered His smell, sweet like the corn silk that lay in tangles around her.

When she awoke she was in her bed, covered in her mother's quilts, her mother's arm over her body. They'd waited a day to tell her the truth, but she knew it anyway. She'd seen Ashley go to heaven, after all.

Since then, her adult mind told her that stress had conjured up the dream and that the arms had been her rescu-ers'. Still, in the private, small place where she stored her child-hood, she fell into that smell and embraced it. Believed that, yes, Jesus had visited her that night. That she and Ashley hadn't been abandoned.

God is my portion. My sustenance. Sarah's words felt like a long-awaited embrace. How long had it been since God had been her portion? She'd done a pretty good job of filling up her life with her SAR career, her dogs, even her Team Hope friends. She couldn't even remember the last night she'd spent alone. Another tear slipped down her cheek, bypassed her ear, and fell into her hair.

Missy had been her portion. Missy and Sherlock. And before them, her grandma and grandpa.

In fact, God had provided someone to love her throughout her life, despite her losses. He'd even provided Will to watch over her as she tramped through the woods. What if the Hayata terrorists had found her? They might have forced her and Missy to help them find Amina. And then left them as crow fodder in the woods.

But instead of seeing Will and Missy and even Team Hope as God's provisions, she'd made them her portion. Her lifelines.

Great is Thy faithfulness, O God my Father,
Morning by morning new mercies I see;
All I have needed, Thy hand hath provided—
Great is Thy faithfulness, Lord, unto me!

The hymn filled her mind, and with a gasp that she felt to her toes, she realized that God *had* been faithful. All she had needed, He'd provided. From a grandmother who filled her dark moments with songs of faith to a man who had filled her heart with a new song. And God would not leave her tonight or tomorrow, for that matter. Morning by morning He'd be there.

Even if Will wasn't.

God may have provided Will, but tonight she was on her own. And if she decided to give Will her heart, to love him, she'd have countless nights on her own.

Or with God. Who had truly been her portion since she'd been lost, or rather, alone. Not really lost. Not ever. And not forgotten.

Lord, I know that I asked You not to forget me and to send someone to find me, to save me. And I guess You have. You've provided and protected me in ways I can't even imagine. She smiled as she watched the stars, feeling warmth pervade her muscles, her bones. Maybe she did need God as much as her friend Lacey did. And maybe Dani too could radiate her own salvation.

Lord, You are my portion. And I am satisfied to wait for Your deliverance. Just as You have been faithful to deliver me over and over . . .

She heard the sound of tires crunching gravel up the road. She tensed, tried to hear past her thundering heartbeat. The car stopped, doors slammed; then flashlights scraped over the forest above her.

She closed her eyes.

. . . and over. . . .

Chapter 21

"YOU'RE NOT GOING in there, Wild." Micah stood outside the emergency-room door like the commando captain he'd been, and by the look on his face, Will would have a better chance moving a longhorn steer than Micah.

"I am. Please, Micah. My boss and Amina are waiting for me. I just have to say good-bye."

Conner joined Micah, a look of compassion on his face. "What if it were Lacey, Micah?"

Micah gave Will a hard look. The fluorescent lights of the hospital did nothing to soften his expression of anger.

Well, get in line. Will already felt disgusted with his behavior over the past several days, and Jim Micah's indictment wouldn't do any more damage.

"Listen, I just want to see if she's okay. I . . . probably won't see her again, and I . . ."

"Then it's better if you leave. Now. Without breaking her heart. You've already done enough. I know this isn't totally your fault, but what if she never walks again, Wild? Then what?"

Will turned away from Micah, feeling rotten.

Conner paced in a small circle not far from them, and Will could play a mournful tune from the tension in the hospital hallway. Inside the emergency room, the doctor and Sarah attended to Dani. Her friend Andee and Jim Micah's fiancée, Lacey Montgomery, had gone for coffee. As if Will needed a reminder of the guy he'd been, the guy who had let his emotions finally have sway and suck the woman he cared for into trouble, Lacey had to recognize him as the wild-living Green Beret who'd helped her infiltrate Iraq and rescue the man she loved.

Obviously, he hadn't changed too much.

"Wild!" But she'd hugged him as if he'd been a friend instead of a scoundrel.

Despite the fact that he had to walk out of Dani's life, he still wanted to be the guy who made her feel safe. The guy who did things God's way, one day at a time.

"Micah, I gotta go." Will caught sight of Jeff Anderson—his ride—in the hallway with a look of exasperation on his face. He turned to Micah. "Just . . . tell Dani . . ." Tell her what? That he was falling in love with her?

He felt sick with the hollow feeling he'd become accustomed to years earlier, when *Wild* had been an appropriate moniker for his love-'em-and-leave-'em lifestyle.

Only, he didn't want to leave Dani.

"Tell her . . . thank you for being my friend." He stalked out, past Jeff, straight to the SUV, and slid in beside Amina, hating the man he had to be.

Had every friend she had abandoned her? Dannette lay in a hospital bed with her leg elevated—hungry, bone tired, wanting to rewind time and start over.

But would she have done anything differently? Probably not. Her instincts had told her to find the girl. Mission accomplished.

So maybe her heart was an acceptable casualty.

She could hardly believe, even after a day in the hospital, that Will had left without saying good-bye.

That thought had the ability to sweep her breath out of her chest, leaving only heartache in its wake.

A knock at the door. Conner poked his head in. "Hey."

"I thought visiting hours were over." Dannette smiled, however. "Did you bring me a pizza?"

Conner grinned, slipped into the room, and produced a box containing a Sven and Ole's pizza from behind his back. "Pepperoni, mushrooms, and double cheese. Just hope the nurses can't smell it."

"You're my hero, Sparks," Dannette said as she motored the bed into a sitting position. "When did Homeland Security cut you loose?"

"About an hour ago. Micah's still under the lights, but he'll be over later too."

"Doesn't anyone care about the sleeping needs of the infirm anymore?" Andee said as the door opened and Andee and Sarah swept into the room, followed by Lacey. They each toted a two-liter bottle of soda.

"I could get into so much trouble." Dannette laughed.

"Yeah, well, if it were up to Sheriff Fadden, you'd be sitting in a jail cell right now. Good thing you have a friend at Homeland Security," Sarah remarked.

Yeah. A friend. Who would remain unnamed.

Conner set the pizza down and opened the box while Sarah poured Dannette a glass of Coke.

"I still can't figure out how you found me," Dannette said to Conner as she wiggled a slice of pizza out of the box.

"You dropped your GPS in the forest," Conner answered as he helped himself to pizza. "Micah and I found it and Kirby, collarless. We tracked you for a while, and when we realized you were hiking out a different direction than where we'd parked our vehicles, we took a chance and headed into town for Sarah and Andee. We got out our maps, did some quick home-work, and found Service Road 16. Good thing, um . . . Will and that girl were hiding in the woods, because we might not have found where they hid you after the crash."

"They hid me?"

"Yeah. And Will was really torn up before he left. Wanted to say good-bye, but Micah wasn't having it."

Oh. Well, she couldn't really blame Micah for his over-protective streak. That's what made him Micah.

And she'd certainly been thankful for said protectiveness when he and the rest of Team Hope appeared in the forest to rescue her. She still shuddered when she thought of that moment of panic when the car drove up and flashlights illumi-nated the dome of forest over her.

"Dannette?" Andee MacLeod had shouted into the dark-ness, her petite frame belying her loud, panicked voice.

Dannette had mustered the strength to groan. Loudly.

"Thank You, Lord," Andee said and yelled for Micah.

They had Dannette bundled and in the backseat of Sarah's SUV in record time. Micah held her head in his lap as Andee muscled the Jeep out of the hills and into Moose Bend.

Shortly after they'd checked her into the hospital, a few Homeland Security agents showed up, taking Sarah, Micah, and Conner with them for the better part of yesterday. So much for their girls' weekend canoe trip. By the time the agents debriefed her friends, she'd been out of surgery, was starting to get cranky, and wondering why Will hadn't shown up. She hadn't asked because, well, the answer hurt too much.

Obviously he hadn't cared for her as much as she thought.

Thankfully, Sarah had read her silences. She'd found a quiet moment, sat on Dannette's bed, took her hand, and simply said, "He wasn't much of a reporter, anyway."

No. He was probably the worst reporter in history. But he made a superb undercover operative. Had her completely fooled.

Lacey sat on Dannette's bed. "The doctor says you'll be discharged tomorrow. I want you and Missy and Sherlock to come and stay with us while you recuperate. Emily is dying to see you, and I need wedding advice." She smiled, kindness in her silver eyes.

Dannette nodded, Lacey's words soothing some of her ragged wounds. "How is Missy?"

"Good." Andee pulled up a chair next to the bed. "I've got her bed made in your truck, and the vet said he'd discharge her tomorrow also. Conner will follow you and Sarah in your truck back to Kentucky. And I'll be there in a month for the wedding." She touched Dannette's hand. "I'm sad we didn't get our vacation on the trail. We'll have to have a cookout on the beach or something tomorrow, a sort of Memorial Day consolation prize."

"Next year we'll hit the BWCAW for sure."

"What's going on in here?"

Dannette froze, and the look on Conner's face said *busted*.

Dannette recognized the night nurse, the one with gulag-guard warmth.

"Out of here, all of you," Nurse Guard commanded.

"Right. Okay." Conner saluted her but grinned, softening his sarcasm. "We're just tucking our friend in for the night."

Obviously even the night nurse wasn't immune to Conner's charm. She smiled and even blushed.

Dannette saw Andee roll her eyes and laughed.

Maybe in time being around her friends would make Dannette forget the man who'd infected her with his own charm.

The group left, and she was alone with her pizza, her heartbeat, and the night pressing against the windows.

Will, wherever you are, I pray that you find the man God wants you to be.

✦ ✦ ✦

"That's him." Fadima pointed to a man on one of the four video monitors.

From his position in a room in the dome of the U.S. Capitol Building, Will used his binoculars to scan the crowd of ten thousand strong gathered on the Washington Mall, looking for the man she indentified.

The holiday had warranted roping off the mall, posting added security, and requiring a security screening to enter. Homeland Security had capitalized by setting up cameras at the four entrances so Fadima could eye each visitor entering the mall.

Will couldn't contain his fury that Hayata had picked Memorial Day to bring their brand of terror to American soil. Balloons, parades, hot-dog carts, and war protesters clogged the mall from this end, past the Washington Monument, down to the Lincoln Memorial. Music from the U.S. Drum and Bugle Corp set a festive beat, and right below the steps of the Capitol, the U.S. Marine Corps Chamber Orchestra warmed up in anticipation of the president's speech. The aura of honor, of America, of freedom hung in the air, and a brilliant sun gave the illusion that all was well.

Hardly. Will tried to slow his heartbeat, focus on each face. His partner, Simon, had talked about Bakym more times than Will could count, but mostly his description was couched in adjectives like *dedicated, focused, ruthless,* and *evil.*

"Which one is he?" Will asked.

Behind him, Jeff and other Homeland Security agents sat at a bank of computers, running profiles and communicating with agents positioned throughout the crowd.

Please, Lord, help us find him.

"Black hair, silver teeth. Wearing the red sweatshirt."

Will spotted him. Figures the scumbag would wear a University of Minnesota sweatshirt. Just an average college student. But looks could be deceiving. Will knew that better than anyone.

Only not today. Today Bakym was going to find out that Will lived up to every inch of his past reputation. Because God might have changed Wild Will on the inside, but on the outside he'd be exactly who he appeared to be. Dangerous. Wild for justice. A man who got the job done, despite the shoulder sling.

"Got him." He keyed his radio. "Target is wearing a University of Minnesota sweatshirt, dark hair, about six feet tall. Approach with caution." Especially since Bakym had parked himself next to a family with a double stroller. This could get ugly, fast. "I'm coming down there."

"Wait!" Fadima grabbed his good arm. After her flight to DC and a day of debriefing, which included a supersize order of French fries, a shake, and a couple of cheeseburgers, Amina—or Fadima as she had introduced herself—had become one of his best informants. Her brother, Kutsi, and father, Nazar, were in a safe house in Turkey, awaiting their transport to America after being found at Nazar's "hideout" at a resort on the Black Sea. No doubt a location he'd use as a cover for his return to Hataya if the CIA hadn't rescued him. Nazar easily gave up the when and where of Hayata's next attack in exchange for asylum.

Fadima's voice rose in pitch. "I think I see one of the girls from Azmi—the Hayata camp in Minnesota. Black hair, wearing a pink poncho."

Fadima even knew American fashions? Will searched the crowd, found the target. It took him only three seconds to see that the bump under her poncho wasn't her lunch. In fact, if Nazar's specs were correct, tucked inside that poncho was a dirty bomb—a conventional Semtex bomb laced with radioactive materials.

Talk about impact—thousands of families, children, and soldiers remembering the sacrifices made for American freedom would walk away from Memorial Day with a death sentence.

Not on Will's watch.

"I found our delivery girl." He relayed the information to the teams on the ground and fought a wave of hatred for a man who packed explosives on a girl no more than eighteen. Will then turned his attention back to Bakym.

Gone.

Will studied the crowd, panic filling his throat. "Find that girl!" he yelled into the radio. "Anyone on Bakym?"

"He shook us, Agent Masterson."

He wanted to slam his fist into the wall. *Please, Lord, help us . . .* He focused on the edges of the crowd, on the ones leaving. . . .

Yes! Bakym was climbing into a pickup parked right off Maryland Avenue. In fact, Will knew that pickup . . . Simon's pickup—a silver birch Chevy Silverado, his pride and joy, next to his wife and ten-year-old son.

Will updated his men on the ground as he slammed out of the control room, descended the stairs two at a time. He shrugged out of his sling, leaving it on the stairwell, and thanked the Lord for DC traffic. Bakym wouldn't get far. Not today with Independence Avenue blocked off to the west, and SUVs snarled to a standstill on Independence East and Fourth Street.

Will's heartbeat raced. He didn't wait for a cab; he tore across the street, dodging traffic, cut out onto Third Street, and angled down Independence.

Please, God, be on my side today. Because he knew he was right. Bakym had a reason for leaving, and it wasn't so he could get back to his motel and order a large pizza.

Yes, yes! He saw the Silverado with the Minnesota plates ground to a stop only three cars from Fourth Street. Will pumped up his speed.

Nearing the truck, Will noted that Bakym looked frustrated as he tapped his hand on the steering wheel to some unintelligible hard rock on the radio.

Worried you might get blown up, scumbag?

Will dived toward the truck, had the door open and Bakym yanked out and on the ground before Bakym knew what hit him.

A cell phone bounced out of his hand onto the pavement. Will speared Bakym in the spine with his knee, diving for the phone.

He felt Bakym grab him, claw at his leg, but Will's hand closed around the phone. His injured shoulder screamed.

So did Bakym. *"Nyet!"* Bakym's fist clipped his jaw.

Will's head snapped back. He felt nothing but elation as he recovered and launched himself at Bakym. He cuffed him hard—the best pain relief on the market—and Bakym hit the pavement.

Will was about to jump on him, maybe get in a couple of licks for Simon, when Jeff flashed into his peripheral vision and pounced on the thug. "That's enough, Will. We got him."

Will stumbled back, breathing hard. He sank to the street, the pain in his shoulder now searing his brain.

While Jeff slapped cuffs on Bakym, Mirandizing his rights, Will glanced at the cell phone still in his hand. Bakym had logged a number in. It blinked, waiting to be sent. Will blew out a breath, carefully pushed End, and deleted the call. Just about then, he felt himself break into a cold sweat.

Jeff and a host of other Homeland Security agents hoisted Bakym to his feet. Bakym swore, then glared at Will. "You!" He seemed stunned, his black eyes wide. "You're not a reporter?"

Will gave a dark laugh. "Hardly. I'm the guy who's going to make sure you pay for what you did to Simon." He turned to Jeff. "Get him out of here before I do something I probably should regret."

They hauled Bakym off just as the orchestra began the first strains of "Hail to the Chief" on the mall not far away.

Chapter 22

WILL STOOD ON the front porch, rocking from toe to heel, feeling like an idiot in his suit coat and tie. He held a wrapped gift, and right about now it would take very little for him to dump it at the door, turn, and dive for his pickup.

The coward he was.

But he stood his ground. *God is my portion.*

The door creaked opened, and a little blonde head peeked out. "Hello?"

He crouched, held out the present like a peace offering. "Hey there. Is your mommy around?"

The little girl, he guessed about four, eyed him with huge round blue eyes, then turned and slammed the door in his face.

Oh. He frowned, stood up, and searched for a place to leave the gift. Obviously he'd scared her and—

The door reopened. He prepared to give his best cowboy smile. Only it wasn't a four-year-old blonde in a sundress this time. It was the child's very pretty mother, wearing a matching sundress, her hair down to her shoulders, and surprise on her face. She stared at him for a moment before she smiled. Like the sun peeking out from behind dark clouds. His chest loosened.

"Will Masterson," Bonnie said. "I just don't know what to say."

He held out the gift, feeling that, yes, it would have been a much better move to simply leave it and flee. He swallowed past a Mount Rushmore–sized lump in his throat. "Howdy, Bonnie. I'm really sorry I didn't come earlier. I had some stuff to do, and well . . . but that's no excuse and I . . ." He dredged up a shaky smile.

Her gaze went to the gift, then to him. A heartbeat passed before she stepped out onto the porch and hugged him hard around the waist. "You're right on time, Will. Thank you for being a friend."

For a second he simply stood there, feeling foolish; then he settled his arms around her shoulders. Closed his eyes. And somehow in her embrace, he felt a smile, right out of heaven, touch his heart.

Yes, indeed, God was on his side.

Dannette sat with her leg propped on a chair on the grounds of the country club. Red roses fragranced the summer air, and a slight wind frightened away the clouds over the lush Kentucky hills. A country-western band singing love songs, frills, and bows—well, Lacey got her wish. Dannette couldn't help but laugh at Micah, trying to balance a glass of punch in one hand and hug guests with the other arm. He looked resplendent, however, in his black tails, his black hair freshly cut, his gray eyes shining.

Lacey, too, looked radiant. She'd woven lilies into her red-as-a-penny hair and wore a floor-length gown that made her look twenty rather than thirtysomething and on her second marriage. Except for her daughter, Emily—cute in a flouncy white dress and white patent-leather shoes, her blonde hair now grown out to her shoulders—Dannette would have thought Lacey was a brand-new, never-been-kissed bride. She floated when Micah took her in his arms at the altar and blushed to match her hair when he kissed her.

If any two deserved to be together, it was Lacey and Micah, the star-crossed childhood friends who'd waited twenty years for this magical day.

Dannette took a sip of her punch as Conner sat down beside her.

"How are you feeling?" He knocked on her leg cast before sitting down next to her.

Her compound fracture still burned at times, but she hoped to have the cast off in another couple of weeks. After a month or so of physical therapy, she'd be back in the woods again.

Thank You, Lord. The doctors had made her well aware of the fact that had her friends not tracked her down, she might have lost her leg. That thought still left her feeling weak.

"Good." She smiled at Conner. She did feel good. Healing.

Okay, yes, inside, she still hurt, just a little, wondering why Will had simply dropped off the planet. Then again, she had told him to go.

But she hadn't meant completely out of her life.

Homeland Security had told her exactly nil when they finally flew down to Kentucky to interrogate her. Which meant that Will Masterson was on a new assignment.

Never to be seen again.

It was that thought that salted the wounds in her heart. Especially accompanied by memories of his soft smile and the look of pain in his eyes when he'd left her. She'd run over their conversation that night he left her in the woods a hundred times. Around the sixty-seventh time she realized he'd never promised to return. Only promised to send back help. Which accounted for the last words he ever said to her: *"I'm sorry, Dani. I wanted this to turn out differently."*

She sighed, forcing away another wave of pain. Yeah, he wasn't the only one.

Conner reached for her cake. "You going to eat that?"

She grinned at him, pushed her uneaten cake toward him. "Hey, um . . . did you ever . . . you know, hear from him?"

She tried to sound casual, but Conner tipped his head, his long curls rubbing against his collar. "Uh . . . who?"

She threw her napkin at him.

He shook his head and laughed. "Well, yeah, actually."

Her heart stopped. Right there. Her smile vanished. "What?"

Conner just grinned.

"Is he okay?" She leaned forward, touched his arm.

He glanced down at her grip, raised an eyebrow. "I thought he was out of your life. That you didn't care."

She swallowed, unsure of what to say. Out of the corner of her eye, she saw Micah staring at her. "Well, I . . . of course I care. We were friends. And he just dropped out of my life."

"What if he were to drop back in?" Only it wasn't Conner speaking. The voice came from behind her.

She felt weak, as if her heart had stopped. She hiccupped a breath, then turned.

Will. Charming Cowboy Will, filling out a brown sport coat over a pair of jeans, and wearing, of course, cowboy boots. He smiled down at her, his eyes shining, a wide smile on his handsome face. He came around beside her.

"I think it's time for me to go bug Sarah," Conner said and stood up. "Hank's here, and she's trapped in a conversation about acid rain and conservation techniques."

Dannette couldn't respond as he vacated the chair. Will. Here? Had she missed a giant setup?

She glanced at Micah. Oh yeah, he had helmed this; she could tell by the way he grinned wildly at her. And from the looks of it, Sarah was in cahoots also. She raised her punch glass, not looking all that tortured in her conversation with cute, good-old-boy Hank Billings.

Will put a bag on the table, then pulled out the chair she had her leg propped on, sat, and put her leg across his lap. "I brought something for my favorite girl," he said and reached for the bag.

A gift? He'd brought her a gift? She took it, opened it. Laughed. "Dog biscuits?"

He smiled, and it was so devastatingly sweet she couldn't speak. He looked at her cast. Then he raised those beautiful eyes and quietly asked, "How are you?"

How was she? She ached for his friendship. She'd buried herself in the memory of his kiss, dreamed of tomorrows. And now that he was here, she could probably fly.

It was better to take things slow, right? Not leap into his arms?

"Good. Healing." She indicated his injury. "How's your shoulder?"

He shrugged. "We make quite a pair, you and I." His smile dimmed, and he ducked his head.

Silence pulsed between them, and she felt the familiar warmth of just being near him, remembered his strong, gentle hands in her hair. *Please, Will, don't give up on us.* "How's Amina?"

He brightened, as if glad she'd found a topic they could discuss besides the obvious—their shattered friendship. "I had to leave for Washington immediately. They wouldn't let me stick around for your surgery. I'm really sorry. But . . . I called. A lot."

But he'd never talked to her. Why? She tried not to let that hurt. Because he was afraid she'd say, *Just go?*

"Amina delivered the information, and we extracted her father and brother in time to stop Hayata's planned attack. General Nazar is still being debriefed, but he's given us the names and locations and intimate details of over fifteen international terrorist groups that have been on our A list for years. Many of them have cells in the United States. It's a great victory for the war on terror, Dani. You did a great job. . . ."

He looked away, and his voice thickened. "I'm so, so sorry I left you. I've been sick about it. I was going to drop out of your life, because you don't need a guy like me . . . but . . ."

He gave a tentative, almost pained grin. "Your friends Conner and Micah tracked me down in South Dakota. I went back there to talk to Bonnie and meet her new husband."

She felt something like pride take hold. "You did? Will, that's great. I'm so proud of you."

Her words obviously touched him, for he blushed. She'd forgotten how heart-stoppingly adorable that made him look. The tender warrior.

That was probably not a good thought. Especially if he was trying to close the door on their friendship with a final good-bye. "What did Micah and Conner say to you?" She could hardly believe she'd asked, but he was here after all, and that had to mean something, right?

He traced an outline of one of the names on her cast. "They convinced me that I owed you a face-to-face opportunity to kick me out of your life." The tremor in his voice told her he wasn't kidding.

Kick him out of her life?

"I know you told me to go, but I was sorta hoping that was just a temporary thing. That maybe I could change your mind." He was wearing his emotions right there on the outside of his body, and for a second the enormity of it swept the breath out of her.

"Now what kind of search-and-rescue gal would I be if I left you to splutter around in the wilderness without me?"

When he smiled, joy exploded in her heart.

"Really? Because, you know, I was thinking that maybe we could start over." He held out his hand. "Will Masterson. Guy just trying to do the right thing."

She laughed, met his grip. "Dani Lundeen. Girl who doesn't take no for an answer."

"Dani. What a pretty name. Is it a nickname?"

She giggled.

He ran his finger along her cast. After a moment, his face became very, very serious. And, as usual, he couldn't look at her. She could nearly guess at the tenor of his next words. "Dani, you know I'm a soldier of sorts. And I don't think that's going to change anytime soon. I remember you telling me that you could never marry a guy like . . . well, a guy like me. But I was thinking that if someday you felt you could love me—"

She touched his arm, cutting off his words. "Oh, Will." She gathered her courage into a fiery ball of emotion. Sure, she could do this. God was her deliverer and right now her strength. She didn't care if Will was a soldier or a shoe sales-man or even a reporter, because she wanted to be with him so much she ached. "Don't you know that God sent you into my life to be the guy I needed?"

He opened his mouth, swallowed, then found a smile. For a wild second, she saw his emotions in his eyes. And they fueled the last spark of courage in her.

"Besides, it's too late. I'm already falling in love with you. At least, I want to try and love you. Because I already trust you." There, she said it. And it felt good. Like she'd escaped from a dark, lonely place into a gloriously brilliant morning.

"You trust me?" Will whispered. He took her hand. "You're sort of in love with me?"

She shrugged but felt herself blush. "Don't take out an ad or anything."

"That works pretty great for me, because I think I'm falling in love with you too. Pretty much since you stormed out of my life that first night. You make me want to be the guy I see in your eyes, Dani. If you'll let me, I'll try and prove that to you one day at a time for the next, say, eighty or so years."

Her heart leaped. Actually jumped in her chest and did a swing dance. "Only eighty?" she managed to say without singing.

He glanced at her leg. "Well, maybe longer, but you have to let me be the boss of you sometimes."

She laughed. "Okay, but it has to be rare, and you have to tell me why."

His smile faded, and his gaze studied her face. "I promise you, Dani, I'll never lie to you again. Ever. And if I can't tell you something, you'll just have to believe that I want to, but I can't."

She ran her fingertips down his check, rubbed his goatee, her smile also vanishing. She poured her love into her eyes, hoping that he read it as he heard her words. "I do trust you, Will Masterson. You found my buried heart, burrowed in, and rescued it with your friendship. And . . . well, I'd like to let it out . . . let myself love you. And . . . let you love me."

His smile was slow, like honey, and heat gathered in his incredible eyes. He cupped her chin, rubbed his thumb over her cheek, then leaned forward and very, very slowly kissed her.

Not urgently. But a kiss that spoke of friendship and pleasures to come that would make the difficult moments bearable.

He pulled away from her but touched his forehead to hers. Wow, did he smell good. Cologne and shaving cream. It had the power to make a girl's eyes water.

Or maybe that was just emotions. Lots of them. And having their way in her heart.

Will gave her his scoundrel grin, then turned and stared at Micah and Conner and Sarah and Andee, who were all huddled in a not-so-subtle eavesdropping posture. He gave them a thumbs-up.

Words left her.

Which was okay, because the next second he kissed her again. Sweetly. Perfectly. Cutting off any objections she might have felt about his behind-her-back schemes.

She probably should get used to that. After all, she trusted the man who was a master of undercover work. More than that, underneath the lies, the black camouflage, and the cowboy swagger, Will Masterson was a real hero. Her hero.

No, her man of God.

A Note from the Author

SOMETIMES DON'T YOU just want to go to bed early? Climb beneath the warm sheets, pull the flannel blanket over your head, and pray that tomorrow might be . . . brighter?

It's been a long day. The morning started out bleak, the sky a slate gray, the temperature plunging to a breath-stealing twenty below and a nasty wind picking at the cracks around my windows. It should have been a day for hot cocoa, a good book, and the electric blanket on high.

Except, across the hall one child is fighting the flu, while another is downstairs struggling with a homeschool, creative-writing assignment. Laundry calls my name from the basement, and I'm pretty sure someone is going to want dinner in a couple of hours. Another child has a school report due (why do they always wait until the night before?), and the last one needs help cleaning the bunny cage.

Oh, and I think I might have been trying to write a book in there somewhere.

Is 4:00 p.m. too early to retire for the day?

The theme passage for *Escape to Morning* comes from Lamentations 3:22-24: "The faithful love of the LORD never ends! His mercies never cease. Great is his faithfulness; his mercies begin afresh each morning. I say to myself, 'The LORD is my inheritance; therefore, I will hope in him!'"

I need God's mercies to be fresh each morning if I'm going to face my day, because, frankly, life is overwhelming, and if I think too far ahead I won't get out of bed at all.

I love Will and Dani—two people who are just trying to make it through life one day at a time. Dannette is a heroine I understand. Driven to do a job well, she was afraid to trust God too much with her life. Because, well, what if He let her down? What if He wasn't there when life turned dark? when she felt at the end of her herself? And Will—he's just a guy trying to figure out what it means to be a man of God.

As I began to study Lamentations, the word *inheritance* (or *portion* in KJV), stood out to me. It's used in many verses and means not only "reward" but also "sustainer, redeemer, rescuer" . . . basically everything. Or "enough." We hope in God because He is enough. Enough wisdom. Enough strength. Enough forgiveness. Enough grace. Enough.

Flee the Night was about being freed from mistakes and dark pasts into hope. *Escape to Morning* is about walking toward that hope one day at a time in faith, expecting God's mercies anew each morning and trusting Him to be enough for that day.

The Christian life is a journey. One day at a time, sometimes one hour at a time. Some days are successful—healthy kids and word counts reached. But others, well, they're days of slogging through until bedtime. Through each, however, we can expect God to be our portion, our sustainer. And finally, our reward.

Thank you for reading *Escape to Morning*. I pray that Will and Dani's journey encouraged you on your own. And may you find God to be enough.

In His Grace,

Susan May Warren

About the Author

Susan May Warren recently returned home after serving for eight years with her husband and four children as missionaries in Khabarovsk, Far East Russia. Now writing full-time as her husband runs a lodge on Lake Superior in northern Minnesota, she and her family enjoy hiking and canoeing and being involved in their local church.

Susan holds a BA in mass communications from the University of Minnesota and is a multipublished author of novellas and novels with Tyndale, including *Happily Ever After*, the American Christian Romance Writers' 2003 Book of the Year and a 2003 Christy Award finalist. Other books in the series include *Tying the Knot* and *The Perfect Match*, the 2004 American Christian Fiction Writers' Book of the Year. *Escape to Morning* is the sequel to *Flee the Night* and her second book in her new romantic adventure search-and-rescue series with Tyndale.

Susan invites you to visit her Web site at www.susanmaywarren.com. She also welcomes letters by e-mail at susan@susanmaywarren.com.

Turn the page for an
exciting preview of book 3
in Susan May Warren's
Team Hope series

Expect the Sunrise

TEAM

HOPE

AVAILABLE SPRING 2006
AT A BOOKSTORE NEAR YOU

ISBN 1-4143-0088-3

Visit **www.tyndalefiction.com** for more information

Expect the Sunrise

STERLING McRAE SHOULD have known he couldn't escape his duty, even deep inside the forests of northeastern Alaska, a hundred miles from civilization.

No, duty found him in the form of a grimy terrorist in an orange hunting vest and cap. However, said terrorist hadn't a prayer of escaping the McRae brothers. At least that's what Mac told himself as another branch slapped him across the face and he plowed through a bramble of thistle berry.

He heard Brody behind him, thundering like a bulldozer through the forest, occasionally yelling his name, but Mac didn't stop. Couldn't.

He'd been hunting Ari Al-Hasid and members of his cell for nearly three years. Maybe if he caught him, he might be able to breathe a little deeper, sleep more than two or three hours at a stretch. He could rip down one of the many pictures clipped on the bureau's bulletin board.

Sterling could barely make out Hasid's form, a sickly orange blur between a stand of bushy black spruce. He needed to get out into the open and close the distance between them. But Hasid carried a .338 Winchester, a weapon that could blow a nice hole through a bear and lay waste to a man. Mac needed the trees for protection, even if they picked him off like a Lakers forward.

"I'll cut him off!"

Mac glanced behind him, saw Brody heading for the clearing, and his chest tightened. His brother didn't know the first thing about suspect apprehension—i.e., don't announce your intentions to the enemy. For the second time in ten minutes, Mac wondered if he should stop, call the sighting in, and let the on-duty heroes handle Mr. Al-Hasid.

Except Mac's answer to that dilemma lay fifty feet to the west in a swath cut out from the forest, a snake of forty-eight-inch wide, double-steel-walled piping that stretched eight hundred miles from the northern slope of Alaska to Valdez. A river of black gold.

The Alaska Pipeline System. One of the most vulnerable terrorist targets in all of America. The destruction of the pipeline would cause America to seek new alliances with Arab nations, with Russia, and even tuck tail in their relationships with dictator governments that supported terror, like Venezuela's Hugo Chavez. The war on terror would skyrocket in costs and bring the troops home in defeat. Most of all, little villages like the one he'd grown up in would have to return to dogsledding as their means of receiving supplies. If they received them at all.

Keeping the pipeline safe meant keeping the American way of life safe. Soldiers safe. Families fed.

Mac lowered his Ruger .308 and parted the brush with both gloved hands.

A gunshot broke the huffing of his breath, the breaking of branches. He heard a scream and stopped, then whirled and felt his pulse in his throat when crows scattered into the sky.

Not around the pipeline!

Mac dived after Hasid, blood rushing in his ears. Although more than fifty hunters had accidentally hit the pipeline over the years without incident, a shot from a .338 just might—

Another shot. This time it pinged against metal.

Mac ducked, plowing nearly headfirst into a tree. "Stop shooting!"

He crouched behind the larch and peered out, feeling sweat bead under his woolen cap. His feet felt clunky and chapped in his hiking boots; his body trembled under the layers of wool. So much for having some hang time with his brother. Brody would probably clock him next time Mac suggested they go hunting together.

"I didn't do nothin'! Get away from me!" Hasid sounded drunk, his accent slurred. But after living in the country for the past ten years under the assumed name of Clark Bellows, Hasid had probably perfected redneck lingo.

"Throw down your weapon! I'm a federal agent," Mac shouted.

Nothing.

Mac peeked out, saw Hasid searching the forest. Peeling off his vest, Mac crept along a downed log, then angled toward Hasid. He schooled his breath but could hear Hasid's labored breathing.

Hasid scanned the forest where Mac had been, then beyond, toward the pipeline clearing. The sun glinted off the metal pipeline, and rays of heat rippled the air surrounding it.

A branch cracked.

Mac stiffened—only he hadn't made the sound. His stomach dropped when he saw Brody hunkered down yet moving along the pipeline, peering into the forest.

Hasid raised his gun.

"No!" Mac launched himself at Hasid just as the gun

reported. The recoil knocked him in the face even as he tackled Hasid.

Hasid elbowed him, thrashing.

Mac hung on, fighting to clear his head. He tasted blood running from his mouth or maybe his nose.

Hasid took out Mac's breath with a jab to the ribs.

The gun went off again. Gulping for air, Mac grabbed the barrel and ripped it from Hasid's grip.

Hasid rolled to his knees and swung at Mac's face.

Mac dodged and muscled Hasid into a guillotine hold, one arm locked around his neck, squeezing off the blood supply to his brain. He wasn't a fan of UFC wrestling for nothing. In a moment, Hasid would pass out if Mac could continue to hold.

Hasid slapped at Mac's head, rung his ears.

Mac gritted his teeth and held on. He heard Hasid wheezing.

Still the man kicked, spending the last of his energy on flimsy punches. He finally slumped atop Mac, his body heavy.

Mac let him go, checked his breathing, then whipped off his bootlace and tied the terrorist's hands. Above him, he heard rain begin to fall softly, wetting the leaves, the ground.

The sound filled Mac's ears even as he propped Hasid up, slapped at his face. He stood, dread pooling in his stomach as realization rushed him.

No, not rain.

He held out his hand, and the blood of the earth fell from the sky. One drop, two—black, thick, and sticky.

Then the smell. Pungent, it turned his stomach as Mac tasted his worst fears. Running toward the clearing he saw the ground had already turned black and soggy. A geyser of oil plumed into the sky from a gash in the side of the pipeline.

He needed his radio.

He needed his four-wheeler.

He needed to get to the nearest pumping stations, tell them to close the valves.

"Brody!" He turned as he yelled his brother's name. The fact that Brody hadn't appeared to jump Hasid suddenly felt odd. . . . "Brody?" *Oh, Lord, please—*

His gaze caught on a shadow on the ground just inside the rim of forest. Brody.

"No!" Mac nearly fell as he scrambled toward his brother. He hit his knees as he turned him over.

Brody groaned, blood-drenched hands pressed against his gut.

Oh no. Mac's breaths came one over another, panic shutting down every scrap of training. He pressed his hand against Brody's wound. "Why did you follow me?"

Brody closed his eyes. "I'm in a bit of a barnie here, Mac." His voice sounded strangely weak, and it took another swipe at Mac's calm.

"I gotta get you some help." Mac reached out, not sure how he'd carry his younger brother now that the man had surpassed him in size. Like true Scots, they weren't small men, but Brody had taken after the McRae side, warriors down the line. He had the girth and muscle that made him the grappling champ of Deadhorse High.

Mac pulled Brody's body up and put his arm over his shoulder. He fell trying to get Brody into his embrace, while oil rained down around them.

Brody cried out in a burst of agony. "I can't. Go . . . go get the four-wheeler." His face had turned chalky white. "Go." He nearly pushed Mac.

Mac stumbled back, blinking at Brody. "Brody, I'm so—"

"Go!"

Aye. Mac whirled and raced down the pipeline clearing toward their encampment. His breath turned to razors in his chest, but panic pressed him through the pain. He slipped in the oil, falling face-first, and spit out a mouthful of filth as he scrambled back to his feet. Technically, no one, not even a subsistence hunter, had the right to hunt within five miles of the pipeline. But they'd been following elk and hadn't realized how close they were until they motored right into the clearing, stumbling on a startled Al-Hasid as he checked his weapon. Al-Hasid had looked up, guilt on his face, and bolted.

Mac found the four-wheeler right where he'd sprung off it, and in seconds had it turned around and gunned it back toward Brody. He dug out his high-frequency two-way while he drove, now thankful he'd packed it, despite Brody's ribbing.

"Hello, anyone!" He couldn't remember what channel the EMS might be on or even pipeline security, so he scanned down the channels. "Hello? Please!"

"TAPS Security here. Identify please. Over."

"Agent Sterling McRae, FBI. I have an injured hunter just north of the Kanuti River. Need assistance. Out."

Crackle came over the line.

Mac slowed as he reached the oil-slicked area but plowed through, shielding his eyes as the oil continued to rain from the sky. "Hello?"

"Roger that. We'll send assistance. Over."

"No! I'm coming to you." He stopped the ATV, stumbled off, and ran toward Brody. Thank the Lord, he was still breathing.

"Be advised that the nearest station is at Cross Creek, seventeen clicks northwest of the line. Over."

Seventeen miles. Mac crouched beside Brody. Oil slicked his face, and his breathing seemed labored. Blood mingled with oil, and Mac hadn't the first clue how much blood Brody had lost. Seventeen miles.

"Negative. He'll never make it. We need an emergency extraction." He glanced at the plume of oil. "And be advised that there is a leak in the pipeline at my position."

Silence. Mac could imagine the powers spilling their coffee on their jumpsuits. "Say again, over."

"A leak. Terrorist shot the pipeline. But I need medical assistance."

"Give us your exact position. We'll find you. Out."

Mac glared at the two-way, as if he could somehow reach through it to throttle the dobbers on the other end of the line. "Need medical—"

Overhead, he heard a buzz, a low hum that anyone who'd lived in the bush for longer than a week would immediately identify.

A plane. A beautiful white-hulled bird with red stripes floating in the sky like a gift from heaven.

A Cessna, if he read his plane correctly, and such a bird could land on Dalton Highway, just a skip away.

And if God was on his side, that beautiful little bird would already be turned to the Fairbanks airport frequency, the same one he used during his flight-training days. "Hello? I'm talking to the Cessna flying over Cross Creek. Come in, please."

Static.

"Please come in."

"Sir, this is a channel authorized by the FAA for air-traffic control—"

"My brother's been shot!" He could feel himself unraveling. "Please, will the Cessna overhead come in—?"

"This is November-two-three-seven-one-Lima; how can I help you?"

Yes, yes! "I have an injured hunter here. He's in bad shape. I need a life flight to Fairbanks. Please, can you land on the Dalton? I'll meet you." He held the two-way against his forehead, trembling.

Static. Then, "That's a negative. November-two-three-seven-one-Lima is enroute with another life flight. I'm sorry but I—"

"Please!"

The line went to static. The Cessna came into view. He stared at it as it flew over, a long moment when his heart stopped beating and turned to one gripping pain in his chest.

Then it vanished from view.

No. He felt sick, hollow.

"Mac?"

His brother opened his grease-covered eyes, reached out, and curled his fist weakly into Mac's jacket. "Get me outta here."

Mac nodded, grabbed Brody by the collar, and dragged him over the slickened ground to the four-wheeler. He could still hear the sound of hope dying in the distance.

As he draped Brody over the back of the ATV, wincing as Brody groaned, he made a promise.

If his brother died, he'd never forgive that pilot.

✦ ✦ ✦

"Brother of FBI Agent Killed in Freak Accident."

Andee MacLeod read the headline slowly. And again. Then closed her eyes and felt guilt wrap its sticky tentacles around her heart. Choices. Her life felt defined by them, by regret and confusion.

She scanned the article, wincing at the part that

mentioned a possible aborted aerial rescue. She rolled up the newspaper, picked up her cold coffee, and dumped them into the trash as she exited the hospital cafeteria. What that reporter didn't know was that she'd been responsible for two deaths that day . . . indirectly, at least.

The woman she'd been life-flighting had suffered another massive coronary while Andee circled the airport for a third time, waiting for the weather to clear.

Andee stopped in at emergency services, waving to the night nurse. "I'm going home. I've got my pager."

The nurse nodded and Andee stepped out into the cool August night air. The summer high of eternal sun and energy had mellowed into normal days of sunrise and sunset. Soon, however, the sun would refuse to crest into the terra firma over Alaska, and the night would steal into the nooks and crannies of life. In two months, before the deep freeze, Andee would head south, toward sunshine and her mother. No, toward her *real* family— Micah, Dannette, Sarah, Conner, soon Lacey, and maybe some-day Will. Team Hope, her SAR pals felt like family—the kind who loved you despite your weaknesses or your failures.

Brother of FBI agent . . . the man's panicked voice over the radio hovered in Andee's thoughts, slicing through quiet moments to bring her back to that moment when she'd had to choose. She'd set down on Dalton Highway a number of times before. But she had weighed the life of a mother of four with a hunter's—and kept altitude.

But what if it had been Sarah or Conner down there, hurt and dying? What if it had been her on the other end of the squawk, begging for help? That thought left Andee feeling hollow as she walked out to her Jeep, the lights of the parking lot pooling on the hood. How would she ever forgive the pilot who'd turned his back?

The man thought he'd been chasing a terrorist. Instead, he'd taken down a drunk hunter who managed to spill over two hundred thousand gallons of oil on the ground. She opened her door and slid into her car. Yes, doomsdayers said it could happen—sabotage of TAPS. But with the new age of Homeland Security, it felt far-fetched.

Perhaps the FBI agent had concocted a cover story, something to keep him free from an accessory-to-manslaughter charge. People would do just about anything to dodge their own guilt. Look at her, running from one end of the continent to the other.

She turned the engine over, pulled out, and headed to her efficiency apartment in Earthquake Park.

If some terrorist was going to sabotage the pipeline, it wouldn't be a lonely hunter with a magnum rifle.

And it would take a lot more than a desperate FBI agent to stop him.

THE DEEP HAVEN SERIES BY SUSAN MAY WARREN

Happily Ever After

Mona thought her hero was just a fairy tale. . . .

ISBN 0-8423-8117-1

Tying the Knot

Anne was at the end of her rope . . . until her hero came along.

ISBN 0-8423-8118-X

The Perfect Match

Ellie's life was under control . . . until he set her heart on fire.

ISBN 0-8423-8119-8

Visit **www.heartquest.com** today!

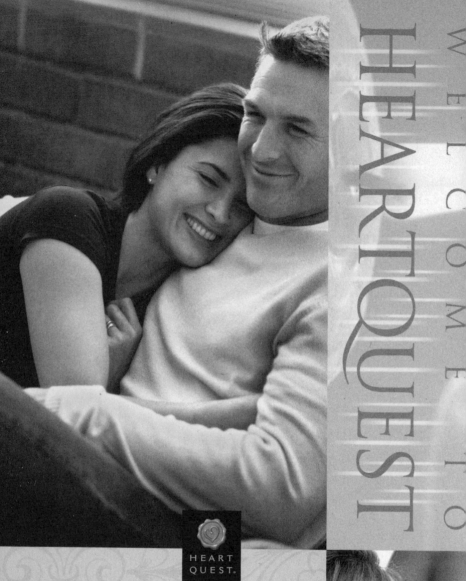

WELCOME TO HEARTQUEST

HEART
QUEST.

Visit

www.heartquest.com

and get the inside scoop.

You'll find first chapters,

newsletters, contests,

author interviews, and more!